Prologue

Of *all* the ways she thought she'd die, of all the scenarios she had pictured, this definitely wasn't one of them.

She watched in horror as he raised his hand to her amid the chaos unfolding around them and without thinking, she threw herself between them. She *had* to stop him.

The full force of his arm slamming into her chest and the back of his hand against her face made her fall back suddenly. The sharp, poker-hot pain in the back of her skull felt like a firework going off inside her head.

Everything went numb. She couldn't feel anything, and yet she could still hear and see the chaos descending into mayhem. A physical fight broke out in front of her. She wanted to shout at them all to stop. She wanted someone to see what was happening. It wouldn't be long before her time ran out. Her clock was ticking faster with every blink of her eye.

Then all eyes were on her as she began to drift out. None of it mattered now. Not the lies, the deceit.

Her eyes closed slowly. The pain began to ease and oddly, a reassuring warmth spread through her until the pain wasn't there anymore.

Until *she* wasn't there anymore.

The Second Wife

Alex Kane is a crime writer from Glasgow. She lives with her husband and three-year-old daughter and in her spare time likes to read as much as possible.

Also by Alex Kane

THE
SECOND
WIFE

ALEX KANE

hera

First published in the United Kingdom in 2025 by

Hera Books, an imprint of
Canelo Digital Publishing Limited,
20 Vauxhall Bridge Road,
London SW1V 2SA
United Kingdom

A Penguin Random House Company
The authorised representative in the EEA is Dorling Kindersley Verlag GmbH. Arnulfstr. 124, 80636
Munich, Germany

A CIP catalogue record for this book is available from the British Library.

Print ISBN 978 1 83598 162 7
Ebook ISBN 978 1 80436 794 0

Printed and bound in Great Britain by Clays Ltd, Elcograf S.p.A.

Look for more great books at
www.herabooks.com | www.dk.com

I

For my Dad, Alex. Cheers.

For my Gran, Margaret.

PART ONE

1997

Chapter One

As Jordan Burns stood by the canal, the only sliver of light other than the moon above him came from the glowing embers at the end of his cigarette.

After receiving a short, handwritten letter from his best friend, Elle, to meet him by the gate at the canal, Jordan knew that it had to be about her husband. Maybe she'd finally decided to get away from him and was going to ask for his help. But she was late and now he was starting to get worried. Maybe she'd changed her mind? Or maybe Ricky had found out and beat her – again.

Sighing, Jordan dropped his cigarette into the murky water and the orange ember died. Turning, he headed along the gravel path, the lights of the bridge twinkling far away in the distance.

'It's rude to turn your back on someone.' A familiar voice floated on the night breeze.

Jordan froze as he realised who was there with him. He turned slowly and their eyes met.

'How did you know I was here?' Jordan asked, thinking back to the handwritten note that had come through his door.

'My wife's handwriting is pretty basic, very easy to copy,' Ricky replied coolly.

Jordan felt his eyes widen at the sheer bluntness of it all. Ricky wasn't even trying to hide what he'd done. He was bloody proud of it.

Frowning, Jordan scolded himself for not questioning the note. Why would Elle put it through the door and not just chap to speak to him?

'Not so fucking cocky now, Burns,' Ricky said, as if seeing the realisation on his face. Ricky's brother, Chris, was stood next to him in silence.

'I've got nothing to be cocky about, Ricky,' Jordan replied. He knew that treating Ricky with respect was the only way to get around his anger and aggression, although it didn't always work.

'You're right about that,' Ricky said. 'You know she'll never let you anywhere near the baby.'

Jordan frowned. 'Eh?' he said, genuinely baffled.

'She's *my* wife and that's *my* daughter. And if you think for one *minute* I'm going to let you walk around after you've been shagging my wife and got her pregnant, then you're wrong.'

Jordan glared at Ricky through narrowed eyes and then turned his attention to Chris Fyfe, who wasn't even looking in Jordan's direction. He was staring out at the canal, as though he'd gone to another place in his head.

'Not this again,' Jordan sighed. 'I've already told you this, Ricky – there has never been an affair with Elle, and there never will. I can't stress that enough.'

'I've seen the way you two are around each other. You don't even try to hide what's going on between you.'

Jordan had to be careful here; he knew how dangerous Ricky was. But he also didn't want to come across as a pushover. Something he most definitely was not. But this accusation had been thrown at him a few times now, and he was getting sick of it.

'Elle is my best friend and has been since we were kids. There's nothing more to it than that and I'm not going to let you tarnish our friendship with your fucked-up ideas of what you *think* you have witnessed between us.'

Jordan felt a fury build inside him. An emotion that Ricky had evoked in him many times before. Today was different. He'd accused Elle of something awful, tarnishing her character. It didn't matter that Jordan was on the receiving end of the accusation, he just couldn't keep his mouth shut even though he knew better of it. 'But I will tell you this; I've been trying to get her to leave you from the minute you first laid your hands on her. She doesn't deserve to be battered every single day just because you're a power-hungry bastard, Ricky.'

The words were out of his mouth and he watched as Ricky processed them. *Shit*, he thought. It was too late to take them back.

No one else in their right mind would cross him. Maybe Jordan wasn't in his right mind? He'd been going crazy trying to get Elle to leave. There was plenty more he could have said but chose not to. Now, he was stood here, with the wildest accusation being thrown at him by a man who was highly unpredictable. Even his brother had a wary look on his face.

'That's exactly what a guilty man would say,' Ricky said, shifting his weight from one foot to the other. He looked relaxed, with one hand in his trouser pocket and the other hanging by his side.

'If you *really* think I'm the type of guy who would cheat on my wife, then you've got several more screws loose than I gave you credit for. I'm not like you, Ricky. Because that's exactly the kind of shitty stunt you'd pull, isn't it? And your wife fucking knows it. But she keeps her mouth shut because you're a fucking nutcase.'

Ricky tipped his head back just a little, clicked his jaw and then pulled a gun from inside his jacket pocket. 'Say that again. Go on. I *dare* you.'

Jordan stared down at the end of the gun, glancing at Chris, who still hadn't met his eye, and then back at Ricky. His stomach rolled so quickly he felt sick. But he couldn't show fear. That was the kind of thing people like Ricky Fyfe craved – fear.

'You're not going to shoot me. You wouldn't get your hands dirty like that. Now, I'm going back to my family. From now on, I'm going to stay the fuck away from you and your family and we can forget this ever happened.'

Jordan turned to walk away and hoped that his abject terror of being killed didn't show. The sound of gravel underfoot made him stop. The little click of the safety catch made him turn to his left and a bright flash was followed by a sharp pain in his abdomen.

'*Fuck!*' he cried out as he clutched at his stomach before collapsing to the ground. Already he could feel the wet warmth of his own blood on his fingertips.

'You won't get away with this,' Jordan said but the words were followed by a splutter of blood and panic set in. He was dying and there was nothing he could do to stop it. He was in the middle of the canal path, in the dead of night. No one was coming to help. No one was coming to save him.

'Oh, don't you worry yourself about that. I have everything under control. Your family won't be subjected to your body being found,' Ricky grinned, and Jordan saw that evil glint in his eye. 'I mean, *I* wouldn't want *my* wife to find me, bled dry and face down in that canal. So, I won't subject *your* wife to that.'

Jordan thought of Georgia. His wife. And his beautiful, newborn baby. They'd have to carry on without him, never knowing what happened to him unless Ricky made a mistake. But he wasn't the type to make mistakes.

Looking up at the dark sky, two sets of eyes stared down at him. Ricky and Chris. It was Chris who was holding the gun. He'd been right. Ricky was never going to get his hands dirty.

He saw Ricky raise his arm. There was something in his hand. Something soft, like a scarf or a t-shirt; he couldn't make it out as his vision began to blur. Ricky let the piece of material fall onto Jordan's body and it landed on his hands where he clutched at his abdomen. Ricky picked it up again, allowing it to fall for a second time.

Jordan raised his head, trying to plead for his life. Whatever Ricky was thinking, Jordan had a small window of time to convince him that he didn't deserve to die because of it. But before he could, he began to choke. The iron-stench of blood in his nostrils and mouth made him feel sick.

Then another shot went off.

Chapter Two

'Congratulations,' the registrar said, handing the birth certificate across the desk. Ricky slid it off the surface and into his pocket before Elle had the chance to move.

'Thank you,' Elle said quietly, smiling, before getting to her feet. Ricky was already towering above her with the biggest grin on his face and gripping Teigan's pram proudly.

'Aye, cheers,' Ricky said, spinning the pram around and heading for the door. Elle followed him out and caught up with him as they walked along Dumbarton Road. He smiled down at their new baby and Elle hoped this would be the beginning of a new chapter for them. Maybe becoming a dad would be the making of him again; that he'd go back to the man she fell in love with at the beginning. The one who said he'd take care of her, love her and make sure she was always okay. Had it been a lie from the start? Or did she do something to him to make him change?

'I know, by the way,' Ricky said, without looking at her.

She frowned, stared at him and said, 'Know what?'

'That she isn't mine,' he replied.

Elle's heart stopped as she watched her husband continue to walk beside her, as though he hadn't just dropped a bombshell. How the *hell* did he know? No one knew. Not even the other guy. In fact, she didn't know for sure that Ricky wasn't the father. Not that she was having an affair. It was one man. One night. But they'd overlapped.

She had to convince him he was wrong, otherwise her life wouldn't be worth living. 'How can you even think that? Of *course* she's yours, Ricky.'

He simply shook his head, leaned into her ear and said very quietly, 'You're a fucking liar.'

'I'm not,' she said. 'Why would I lie?'

'To save your own skin, Elle. I mean, I get it, I'd probably do the same. But I know.' He stopped, looking her dead in the eye.

By the look on his face, she wondered if he really did know the truth? But surely not. The man she'd slept with wouldn't be alive if that was the case.

'What makes you think she's not yours?' Elle said, and she saw his eyes darken and knew she'd pushed her luck.

Ricky turned sharply and gripped her hand so tight she gasped. He pushed his lips to her ear, so close she could hear his teeth grinding together. 'Because I fire fucking blanks, that's why. You happy now? You've fucking embarrassed me; your fucking husband.' He forced his face into the side of her head and then released his grip before he moved away from her.

She felt suddenly sick. This wasn't good. Ricky was an angry man at the best of times. But this? What could she do? Deny it? It was too late for that now. The question was, did Ricky *know* who Teigan's dad was? Because even he didn't know, and she hadn't intended on him finding out. It wouldn't be good for anyone.

'She *is* yours,' Elle said, although even she knew it didn't sound convincing. The revelation that Ricky was in fact infertile left her with nothing to say by way of defending herself.

'Are you deaf? Or maybe you're stupid. Yeah, that must be it. You're thick if you think I'm going to believe that Teigan is mine *after* I told you that my sperm are fucking dead.'

The words pierced through her like a hot spike and she knew that her attempts at trying to convince Ricky were dead; much like his ability to produce a child.

She sighed, closed her eyes briefly and then said, 'If you knew, why did you put your name on her birth certificate?'

He smiled menacingly and raised a brow. 'Because despite the fact that you lied to me and opened your legs for someone else to get you up the fucking duff, I love the bones of that wee lassie and up until a few weeks ago, I genuinely thought she was mine. That feeling doesn't just go away, Elle.'

As much as his words pained her, she was surprised. Any other man would walk away. And then she realised what he was doing. More control. More manipulation. This was his way of keeping her close enough that she couldn't breathe. Same as always.

'What happened?' Elle asked. What she really wanted to ask was what had happened to make him realise he was infertile, but she was too scared to cross that line.

'Had a lump. Went to get it checked. Doc done some tests which came back that I can't reproduce. Bad enough for any man to hear that. But knowing I'd just been told the wee lassie inside my wife wasn't mine made it worse. *Far* worse.'

They walked silently, all the while Elle staring down at her baby girl and wondering how the hell she'd managed to get herself into this mess. She should have walked away from Ricky a long time ago. She should have listened to the one and only friend she had left. But she'd fallen for the idea of someone caring for her for the rest of her life because she'd never had that growing up. Her dad had been absent from birth, and her mother was an alcoholic who only cared about where her next drink was coming from. She did the bare minimum as a mother to Elle, so as soon as she could leave, Elle was out of there. And Ricky was there to scoop her up and he'd been perfect. Loved her kindly and had given her everything she'd never had. A beautiful home. Money. Clothes. All that came soon after she'd first met him in his club. She couldn't believe how lucky she was to meet not only a man who was interested in her, who fancied her, but one who also owned his own nightclub. Ricky Fyfe. He was older, wiser and so handsome she could barely swallow when she caught sight of him.

Then she'd started to see things a little clearer. The home, the money, the clothes, they all came at a cost. He policed everything. How much she spent and what the money was spent on. He chose her clothes for her, chose her food. She was only allowed to eat meals he pre-approved. And when she started to push back, that's when the violence started. Even when Elle started to bite her tongue and do what he said, the violence never stopped. By that point Elle knew she was in too deep.

He'd pushed her into the arms of another man; she'd wanted to escape. But now, she was faced with the fact that he knew she'd been unfaithful and given birth to another man's child. This was going to cause her so much terror and grief for the rest of her life.

'I'm sorry,' she whispered. It was all she could say, but she knew it wasn't going to cut it.

'Is that right?' he replied, drawing his eyes away and glancing up Cleveden Drive. He fixed his eyes on his house; the house that had once belonged to his dad. Ricky had turned that house into a mansion with the money he'd made over the years as one of Glasgow's biggest gangsters, although he'd always referred to himself as a businessman. The house had been left to Ricky and Chris in the will. Chris hadn't wanted it, apparently. Hadn't wanted to live there. The mere mention of their father really stuck in his craw, so Ricky had stopped talking about him. The renovations had been small to start off with. A garden extension. Then an extension at the back of the house. Then, the more it grew, so did Ricky's ideas of living in luxury and he always said he wanted it to be the best house in Glasgow. He wanted a swimming pool. A gym. He wanted it all. It was like the renovation works were a distraction after John had passed away.

He was quiet for a moment. He looked too calm and that was the scariest thing about Ricky Fyfe. His silence meant he was thinking, planning his next move. The Fyfes weren't known for letting things lie. 'Not as sorry as you will be if you ever fucking pull a stunt like this again. And not as sorry as the bastard you shagged behind my back. If you step one foot out of line again, I swear to Christ I'll fucking kill you, Elle.'

The smile that slowly spread across his face did not match the dark glint in his eye. But before Elle could beg for his forgiveness, he took the pram from her and started to push it along the road.

Elle didn't want Ricky's forgiveness. She didn't want anything to do with him. He was the most intense and terrifying man she'd ever met and getting involved with him was the stupidest thing she'd ever done. But maybe now that it was all out in the open, maybe now that he knew the truth, she'd be able to get away from him. Somehow, she knew that was wishful thinking.

'Come on then, your tits are needed to feed *my* daughter,' he called back over his shoulder.

Elle gritted her teeth and stared at the back of his head through narrowed eyes. If only one of his enemies would drive by, stick a gun out the window and fire it at him.

Then her baby's little face came into her mind's eye and she couldn't stop thinking about her escape from the hell that was her marriage. She couldn't allow a man like Ricky to bring up her daughter as his own. How long would it be before he turned his violence on Teigan?

It was time she stood up for herself. She'd been thinking about it for a long time. She'd even had divorce paperwork drawn up by a solicitor. Not that he'd agree to it. She'd have a fight on her hands. But it was what she needed to do for herself and her daughter. It was time to divorce Ricky.

Chapter Three

Elle put Teigan into her cot and sat back on the bed, relieved that Ricky was still downstairs. He'd been in his usual arrogant, prickish mood since they'd got home from the registrar's office, and she didn't have the energy for him. She *never* had the energy for him. She'd never been surer of anything in her life than her decision to get a divorce.

The sound of the front door opening set her on edge.

'Ricky, you in?' a voice called. It was her brother-in-law, Chris.

'Aye, in here,' Ricky replied.

Elle tiptoed her way to the top of the stairs and descended just a few steps so she could hear the conversation more clearly.

'Did you finalise that deal?' Ricky said and his voice filled Elle with a fresh new fear. What new deal? Were they going into yet another business venture that came with more violence?

'They were reluctant on the price you'd set at first but I managed to convince them they wouldn't get better elsewhere. Then they suggested the Marshalls and I laughed,' Chris replied.

There was a short bout of silence and then Ricky said, 'What did they say?'

'They asked what was so funny and then I asked them if they'd heard about the shortage on the streets. That's when it clicked that the Marshalls hadn't been seen or heard from in weeks. From that moment they were utterly compliant. No problems at all.'

'When you say clicked?' Ricky asked and Elle closed her eyes, waiting with bated breath for what she knew was coming.

'Well...' Chris hesitated.

'Did you tell them what we *did*?' Ricky asked, his voice filled with horror. 'Did you tell them the Marshalls are *dead* because of us?'

'Yep,' Chris replied with an overwhelming amount of sarcasm. 'And you know what else, I told them that the Marshalls' remains would never be found because we burned them to a cinder in our very own incinerator. Fucking hell, Ricky, did you really think I was going to say that to some little street dealer. I deserve a bit more credit than that.'

Elle's jaw dropped and her eyes flew open. The Marshall family was the one and only rival family to the Fyfes and Ricky had always claimed he'd get rid of them. And now he had. She hated the fact that the Fyfe name would have such a hold over the city now. There would be no one out there willing to put up a fight against them, given that the Marshalls no longer had any form of power.

'Aye, sorry. You're right. You do deserve more credit than that. My head's just gone with shit going on with Elle.' Ricky stopped talking and cleared his throat. 'Okay, good. People need to know we mean business, Chris. I like that no one will know for sure what happened to that fucking family, but deep down they'll have an idea of the truth. That instils more fear than knowing for sure. Getting rid of that family is the single most important thing we've done since Dad died. We need to show this city that we are Fyfe blood, that we're harder down the line than he ever was.'

Elle had only met John Fyfe once before, when he was in the hospital before he passed away. Ricky had wanted her to meet him before he died. He might have been in his sixties, and a little frailer than he should have been at that age, but he was still a scary, old-style gangster. He'd been polite enough, but she'd immediately seen what Chris had talked about. His misogynistic attitude, which she experienced for all of fifteen minutes, would have been nothing in comparison to what Chris claimed their mother went through. And Elle could believe it. Ricky had always played it down; he seemed more of a daddy's boy. And when John had died, Ricky had been visibly devastated – for one whole day. Not once since then had he shed a tear. She knew why; crying made him look weak. And Ricky would never allow himself to look weak, not to anyone.

'Well, they got the picture. It's all systems go,' Chris replied.

'Good. What about the problem?' Ricky asked. 'All tracks covered?'

'It's done,' Chris said, his voice more hushed than before.

'Good. No issues?'

'None,' Chris replied, his tone a little sour. Elle frowned. Something was up. Not that she'd ever find out. She was never kept in the loop about what went on between them. In business or otherwise.

'Good one bro,' Ricky said, and the sound of an approving back pat made Elle jump. 'Can always count on you.'

'Anyway, I didn't come here to talk business. Where's that niece of mine?'

'Upstairs with her sour-faced cow of a mother.'

Elle closed her eyes and sighed in annoyance.

'Oi, that's the mother of your baby you're talking about.'

'And? She's a slapper, Chris.'

'Watch your mouth,' Chris said sternly.

'What's it to you?' Ricky replied.

'Can you hear yourself? She fucking worships the ground you walk on.'

Silence fell between them and Elle held her breath. She didn't worship Ricky. She never had. Loved him? Once, yes. Not now.

'Does she fuck. She's a fucking liar, Chris. Shagging that bastard behind my back and having his baby will be the last time she ever betrays me.'

Chris was silent.

'I'll tell you one thing, she mucks me about again, I'll choke the life out of her,' Ricky ranted and then his voice trailed off again, although now it was because he was moving out of earshot and into the kitchen. Chris followed and Elle climbed back up to the bedroom. Once inside, she took one look at Teigan in her cot and knew what she had to do.

'Right,' she whispered. 'That's enough now. We're leaving.'

She quietly started packing the essentials. She wasn't going to stay for another minute. Even though he claimed to know he wasn't Teigan's dad, he still wouldn't make it easy on her to leave. She knew that for a fact.

She pulled the envelope of divorce papers out of her bag and held onto them tightly. The moment she handed them to him was going to be one of those moments that could go either way. He could kill her there and then, or simply let her go. The latter was unlikely, but with Chris present, she wondered if she had some protection.

Chapter Four

Ricky cracked open another beer and closed the fridge door to be met with his brother's eyes staring into his.

'What?' Ricky asked, swigging from his fourth bottle of the night.

'If you know Teigan isn't yours, then why don't you just call it quits?'

Ricky shook his head and swallowed back the beer. 'Nah.'

Chris shrugged. '*Nah?*'

'She's not walking away from me.'

Ricky noted how Chris raised a brow and stared ominously at him. 'What's that look for?' he challenged.

'You just said that Elle isn't walking away from you. But if she does, there isn't much you can do to stop her, because the baby isn't yours, Ricky.'

'In the eyes of the law, Teigan is a Fyfe.'

Chris straightened his back, folded his arms across his chest and leaned back against the worktop. 'What do you mean?'

'We registered her birth today. She is *very much* a Fyfe.'

'You registered yourself as Teigan's father even though you *knew* she wasn't yours? What the fuck is wrong with you? I mean, do you even want to be a dad to her? Or is this some weird revenge thing on Elle?'

Ricky glared at his brother in disbelief. Licking his lips, he took another glug from the bottle and stared out of the kitchen window into the garden.

'Well?' Chris asked.

'You know what it's like around here, Chris. There's always someone out there ready and waiting to take down the man at the top. If I bowed down to this, the next fucker would see the weak spot and try to take the throne.'

A laugh escaped Chris's mouth, but his expression wasn't one of humour. 'Are you fucking kidding? You're telling me that you signed a *child's* birth certificate as the legal father so you don't look weak in *business?'*

Ricky narrowed his eyes. 'You and me have always differed, Chris. You were always like Mum. A fucking pushover.'

Chris grabbed Ricky by the collar of his shirt and pulled him in close. 'Mum was a million times the person Dad ever was.'

'Aye.' Ricky shrugged him off. 'A million times weaker.'

His reflexes were a little slower than normal due to the alcohol, but Ricky was still able to anticipate the blow that was coming and managed to duck out of the way. Ricky responded with a blow of his own to the gut and Chris went down like a sack of shit.

'You might be my older brother, but you never could fucking fight,' Ricky said, before kicking his boot into Chris's groin.

'What the hell are you two doing?' Elle's voice came from the kitchen door.

Ricky spun round and stared at Elle. He felt utter hatred towards her now. Before, he just loved the control, to know that he could make her do and say anything. She was like his little puppet. Now, with her lies and her audacity to believe the truth would never get back to him, there was a fire in the pit of his stomach.

'None of your business,' Ricky replied, glancing back at Chris, who was attempting to get back onto his feet.

'Chris, are you alright?' Elle asked.

Ricky shot her a look. 'Oh, is *he* okay? What about the dad of your child? Oh wait, that's not me, is it?'

Elle opened her mouth to speak but with one swift backhander, Ricky stopped the words from snaking off her lips. Because that's what she was – a snake.

'Jesus Christ, Ricky,' Chris said, as Elle steadied herself and raised a hand to her face.

'And that's why,' Elle said, lifting her head and meeting his eye.

'Why what?' Ricky asked.

'I want a divorce,' Elle said and that's when he noticed an envelope in her hand. He stared at it for a few moments and when he met her eye, he saw not just fear, but a determination he'd never noticed in her before. Not even when he'd played Mr Nice Guy.

He gave a guttural laugh and shook his head. 'You want a divorce? On what grounds?'

'We hate each other, Ricky,' Elle replied, sounding deflated even though her eyes told a different story. 'And you're not Teigan's dad. This relationship has been dead for a long time. Please, just sign the papers and I'll be out of your life. I don't want any money from you, I don't expect anything. I just want to be gone.'

Ricky stuck his tongue between his back teeth and narrowed his eyes. Fine, she could have it her fucking way. Turning, he lifted the pen from the kitchen counter and took the envelope from her. He pulled the papers out, signed his name where he was required to and then glanced up at her. 'This is really what you want?'

Elle's eyes were wide, like she was shocked that he'd actually done what she'd asked.

'Yes.'

Ricky slid the papers back into the envelope, tossed them onto the kitchen counter, laughed then shot out a hand, gripping Elle's wrist. She gasped in fright as he said, 'You're not fucking leaving with my daughter.'

'She's *not* your fucking daughter!' Elle screamed.

Ricky slapped her again, this time knocking her off her feet. He watched as she fell into a heap on the floor and leered over her.

'Doesn't fucking matter anymore, does it?' Ricky said. 'You took the piss out of me. You need to pay for that.'

Elle stared up at Ricky and he saw terror etched on her face. He couldn't help but smile. And he couldn't keep it in.

'I've set you up, Elle. Set you up for something that could see you go to prison. One wrong move and I'll execute that plan quicker than you can whip out a tit and feed *my* daughter.'

A look of disgust crossed Elle's face as she got to her feet and it made Ricky smile even more.

'Ricky, mate, enough now. Come on,' Chris said, on his feet now. Ricky turned and shoved Chris away.

'Why would you want her to stay here when she's not yours?' Elle asked, her voice weak and full of terror.

'Because I believed she was mine for most of the time you were pregnant. In my head, she *is* mine. And you are *not* taking her away from me. And you're certainly not getting a fucking divorce. Those papers are staying with me.'

'I hate you, Ricky.'

'Aye? Well, feeling's mutual, hen. And just so you know, Jordan Burns, the real *daddy*, is dead.'

Elle stared at him in shock, her mouth falling open at the revelation.

'Ricky, shut the fuck up,' Chris said.

She stared at him, her eyes filling with tears and her face reddening. 'You're lying. I don't believe you.'

'Believe it, Elle. He's dead. You'll never see him again. End of,' he said, his tone so blunt that she winced.

'He was my best friend,' she said as a sob escaped her throat. 'Why would you kill the only friend I had left because you,' she jabbed a finger at him, 'drove everyone else away.'

'You don't shag your best friend, Elle. You shag your fucking husband and that's it,' Ricky spat the words out, spraying her face with saliva. 'And you never had any friends. That was the whole point of me taking you on. The only friend you had was Burns. And you took that too far, didn't you? I should have made him fuck off years ago too, and I wouldn't have to bring up a baby that belongs to him.'

'He's not...' she sobbed. 'He's *not* Teigan's dad. I didn't sleep with him.'

'You're a fucking *liar*. He's dead and it's because of you.' He jabbed a finger back at her. 'You're responsible, Elle.'

'How the hell do you work that one out?' Elle asked.

'Oh, you don't remember?' Ricky teased. 'You shot him, Elle. His blood is all over your favourite dress.'

Elle's eyes filled with tears, and she sucked air in noisily through her nose.

'Yes, that's right. Your dress. His blood. Let that slowly sink in. Perfect combination of evidence that you killed the man you were worried would reveal your dirty little secret affair.'

Ricky watched as Elle's eyes flickered towards Chris and then back to him. 'We have shit on each other then, don't we? Because I know what you did to the Marshall boys.'

Ricky felt his stomach flip and he stole a glance momentarily at Chris. She'd heard their conversation. She'd been listening like the little bitch she was.

'I'll tell the police everything I know. I'll make sure they know what happened to the Marshalls and you'll be the one in prison, Ricky. Where you *fucking belong*!'

The rage boiled over and Ricky reached for the beer bottle on the worktop before bringing it down on Elle's head. Blood spurted everywhere and Elle's body went limp.

'Ricky, for fuck's sake!' Chris shouted, grabbing the bottle from his hand. 'What the fuck?'

Staring down at Elle, Ricky took a few moments to process what had just happened. He hadn't planned to go that far. He'd only wanted to shut her up.

He bent down and watched her for a few seconds. She wasn't breathing.

'She's dead. You'll need to deal with it. I'm away to check on Teigan,' he said flatly.

'*I'll* need to deal with it?'

Ricky walked out of the kitchen but not before turning back and staring his brother dead in the eye. 'That's what I said. Elle's dead, Chris. You need to get rid because if you've not already noticed, I've a baby to look after now. And it's your fault she found out about the Marshalls. You said too much when she was upstairs. She obviously heard everything, Chris. So, well done. You've just caused the death of a new mother. Excellent work. Now, get rid.'

Chris stared at him, a look of disbelief widening his eyes. Ricky sighed. Chris had never been quite the hardened soul he should have been to thrive in this business. He was more like their mum, Senga, a little quieter during the hardships of their work. Ricky was more like John, not just all bark. He had just as much bite. Maybe now was his time to shine.

'I can't,' Chris replied.

Ricky raised a brow. Normally his brother never talked back. Never tried to defend himself. Which suited Ricky at times like this.

'You can. And you *will*. I'm in charge of this firm and you know that dead bodies aren't good for business.'

Chris's jaw tightened and for a moment, Ricky was convinced that his brother was going to challenge him, or perhaps refuse.

'Look, it's better she's dead. The way I feel about what she's done, I'd have probably killed her anyway and given half the chance, I'd have made sure she suffered a little bit more than she did.'

Seeing a fresh look of shock and disbelief on Chris's face, Ricky rolled his eyes. Jesus, no wonder their dad didn't leave Chris in charge.

'The quicker you do it, the easier it'll be on both of us.'

He thought about the divorce papers he'd just signed. It would be a great way to explain Elle away. They got divorced and she moved out, leaving the baby behind. He never heard from her again. Simple as. Case closed and dismissed.

Chris's shoulder's slumped and he took a breath.

Giving a satisfied nod, Ricky turned his back on the kitchen and his brother and headed upstairs to be with his daughter. And that is what she would always be to him. Elle wasn't going to take that away from him, even in death.

Chapter Five

Opening her eyes, she struggled to adjust her sight to her surroundings. It was dark. She was in pain all over. Then the memory came flooding back along with a searing pain in her skull.

Shit. This is real, she thought.

Elle blinked and blinked again. The darkness wasn't getting any clearer. Fuck, maybe he'd hit her so hard this time that he'd blinded her. With panic beginning to set in, Elle tried to sit up and immediately realised that she couldn't. The space in which she lay was small and cramped. She wasn't in bed in a dark room. She was somewhere else. Initially, she panicked and imagined herself inside a coffin, given that Ricky had access to them without question. But as she raised a hand and tapped on the metal above her, she sighed in relief briefly that she wasn't.

She concentrated on listening out for familiar sounds around her. Teigan's cries. The sound of Ricky in the lounge watching the football. But none of it came. Nothing other than the low hum of a car engine idling.

Shit. No. No. No. She was in a car boot.

The sound of footsteps approaching made her hold her breath and the click of a handle came before light flooded in, causing her to squint. It certainly wasn't bright daylight – more like dusk. But enough to shock her eyes into closing a little more. She opened her mouth to scream but a hand fell over her lips.

'It's me,' came the voice, soft and almost soothing. 'Don't scream. It's okay. You're going to be okay.'

Narrowing her eyes, Elle could make out the familiar yet anxiety-stricken face.

'*Chris?* What are you *doing* to me?'

'I'm getting you away from that fucking psycho I call my brother,' he said, pulling her up to a seated position. 'I'm sorry I had to put you in the boot, but if I'd put you in the front seat and he'd seen me drive away from the house, he'd have known you weren't dead. And from what he said when you were unconscious on the kitchen floor, he'd have made sure he didn't fail the next time.'

Elle's mind whirled in fear and despair. 'He thinks I'm *dead*?'

Chris swallowed so hard Elle noticed his throat move. 'I did too, until I started to move you out to the car.'

'Why were you trying to move me?'

Chris closed his eyes and when he opened them, there was a sadness there that she'd never seen in him before. And that's when it came to her. She was being disposed of.

'He told me to get rid of you. That dead bodies weren't good for business.'

Elle suddenly felt sick. 'Oh my god. Oh Jesus. *Fuck!*' Her body started to quiver and she couldn't control it.

'Hey,' Chris said, crouching down in front of her and taking her face in his hands. 'I'm not going to let that happen. You're not going to end up dead because of him. I'll make sure of it.'

'Teigan,' she said, her throat dry and fresh panic setting in. Her breasts began to ache, and she felt a wet patch growing across her top. She was leaking milk. 'I need to go back for Teigan. She needs me.'

Chris shook his head. 'No, you can't go back there. He'll finish the job, Elle, and probably kill me too. He's dangerous. More unhinged than I ever thought possible. The power has gone to his fucking head and sent him loopy. You need to go without her.'

Tears sprung to her eyes. 'I can't *leave* my baby.'

'You have to. For now, anyway. What's the alternative? You go back and he kills you or sets you up for murder. Neither of those seem like a good option. He's on Teigan's birth certificate, Elle. If you go to prison, he has her. If you die, he has her. And if neither of those happen, he'll probably claim you're depressed after the birth and try to say that you're unfit as a mother. He wants to punish you for lying to him about being Teigan's biological dad.'

Elle's heart thrummed in her chest. Jordan had died because of this. She didn't want anyone else suffering because of Ricky's knee-jerk reactions.

After a long bout of silence, Chris sighed and said, 'Is she mine, Elle?'

Elle knew it wouldn't be long before he worked it out. Their one-night stand had literally been that – just one night. One time. But that's all it took. In some ways, she was so bloody pleased that Ricky *wasn't* Teigan's dad.

Elle nodded. She didn't want to lie anymore. 'I'm *so* sorry. I wanted to tell you, but I knew the harm it would cause. I know it was just a one-night thing after one of his outbursts, but I never planned to get pregnant. I swear to god.'

'Can you be sure she's not his?' Chris asked. 'In fact, how is he so sure? You know, without doing a paternity test?'

Elle glanced down at her feet. 'Ricky can't get me pregnant. He can't get anyone pregnant.'

'Eh?' Chris said, his brow creased. 'How do you know?'

'Because he told me. His exact words were, *I fire fucking blanks.* He said he went to the doctor because he found a lump, they did tests, and it turns out he's infertile. He told me today, when we were walking back from the registrar's office.'

Chris rolled his head back and let out a long breath. 'Fucking hell.'

Elle closed her eyes, hoping that when she opened them, she'd be released from her nightmare.

'I mean, obviously I did think there was a possibility, but why didn't you come to me, Elle? If you'd told me earlier, I could have got us the hell away from him.'

'I was too terrified. But now that you know, you need to do something, Chris. I don't give a shit what he tries to do to me, I can't leave Teigan with him. He won't care for her. He only wants to use her as a weapon, especially if he finds out about you.'

After a few moments, Chris nodded. 'Christ knows what he'll do to me if he finds out she's mine. You need to go away, as far away as you can. I can help get you set up somewhere, a hotel or something. And later, once things have settled down, I'll bring Teigan to you.'

Elle tried to look at him through the wave of tears that kept on coming. Could she really do this? Could she leave her baby? How would she feed? Would Ricky know what to do with a newborn baby? She wanted to push against this so much, but Chris was right. The only way she could help her baby girl was to run, even though every fibre of her being was screaming at her to go back to the house and get her.

'But what if he catches you? He might notice money missing and question it.'

'He won't. Ricky has so much money coming in he won't notice if a couple of grand in cash disappears. Ricky will not become a stand-up, stay-at-home dad. He's going to hire a nanny the first chance he gets. Or even rope me into looking after her. Once his back is turned, I'll take Teigan and bring her to you. I'll make sure it's clear and safe before I do it.'

Elle couldn't stop shaking.

'What about you?' she asked.

'What about me?'

'Don't you want to be a part of her life?'

'Of course I do,' he sighed. 'The idea of her growing up with a dad like my own makes me feel sick. I remember what it was like as a kid. I was always scared of him. My entire childhood was spent walking on eggshells around him. And seeing what he did to Mum…' Chris shook his head. 'No, Teigan deserves much better than him.'

'I can't believe this is happening,' Elle said, wincing as fresh pain reminded her of her head injury.

'You're going to need stitches,' Chris said, placing a hand on the side of her face and gently manoeuvring her head so that he could take a look. She thought about her other stitches after giving birth and the pain of leaving Teigan took over again.

'I need my head checked. How I ever saw anything good in Ricky I'll never know. How can you two be so different?'

Chris's hand fell from Elle's face, and he shook his head. 'Sadly, he got my old man's genes. Sadistic, psychotic fuck that he was.'

Elle sighed. 'Yeah, that sounds just like Ricky.'

Chris stood up and straightened his shoulders. 'I'm going to put you on a train tonight. You're going as far away from here as possible. And you're going to stay away for good. Your life depends on it, Elle. I'll bring Teigan to you in a few weeks. I promise. You can trust me. I'm nothing like him or my old man. Nothing.'

Elle felt her heart surge with pain and fear. 'I can't believe I'm saying this, but yeah, okay. I'll do it.'

—

Elle stood on the platform and glanced around at her surroundings. Train boards above her, announcing departures and arrivals for destinations all over the country. The fear in the very pit of her stomach made her want to throw up. These were her last moments in Glasgow, her home. To her left at the end of the platform, she saw a bin. Running towards it, she hunched over and heaved loudly, emptying only bile, not caring that people could see and hear her. She was already at her lowest, having walked away from her baby, who was still breastfeeding, and leaving her with a psycho. It took every ounce of strength she had left not to turn around and head back home, where death waited for her.

Straightening herself, Elle took a tissue out of her pocket and wiped at her nose and mouth. She clutched the paper tissue in her hand and felt an overwhelming sense of sadness and self-pity. How the *hell* had she managed to get herself into this mess? Marrying Ricky Fyfe was the single biggest mistake of her life. And now, here she was, stood in the middle of Glasgow Central with nothing to call her own other than the clothes on her back and the tissue in her hand. She wrapped her jacket around her, covering her milk-stained top, hoping it didn't smell too much. As soon as she could, she'd buy some new clothes. The thought was ridiculous. New clothes were the very least of her worries. Her thoughts moved briefly to Georgia Burns and her baby. What was going to happen to them? Had Georgia even realised that Jordan was missing yet? Had Ricky harmed her too? She blinked away the thoughts. She couldn't think about anything else other than getting on the train, otherwise she might not go.

Chris had stayed with her until she'd gone to the platform. Watching him go was horrible. She'd sobbed silently as he disappeared out of the station. A cold, unknowing sense of dread washed over her. Something told her she was *never* going to see Chris, or her baby girl, ever again.

Chapter Six

Ricky sniffed the cocaine he'd laid out off the back of his hand and threw his head back. He felt euphoric, not because of the coke but because of the power he possessed over Elle, even in death. He eyed the cremation chamber and watched as Chris pushed the body wrapped in bin liners inside and closed the door. His heart raced so hard he thought he was going to die right there in front of his brother and dead wife.

He looked at his older brother and let out a sigh of relief. Thank the universe he had Chris, otherwise he didn't know what state he'd have ended up in. He'd lost his temper with Elle and before he knew it, she was dead, and it was Chris to the rescue as always.

Chris switched the chamber on, stood back and slipped his hands into his pocket. He stared through the glass into the flames, deep in thought.

'Just so you know, I'm done,' Chris said out of the blue.

Ricky turned to him and frowned. 'Done? What do you mean, *done?*'

He released one hand from his pocket and waved it in front of them. 'All this *pish*, I'm done with it. It was never for me. Drugs. Violence. Murder. Getting rid of bodies at the crematorium because we pay off the owner to keep his mouth shut. I'm over it. You're on your own from now on.'

Ricky's frown deepened. 'You're *walking away* from the business?'

Chris shoved his hands in his pockets and pulled his shoulders up around his ears. 'Naw, Ricky. I'm walking away from you. You can have the business. The money. All of it. It's all yours. I don't want any part in it.'

'Hang on a minute,' Ricky started, but before he could say anything else, Chris spun on his heel and grabbed Ricky by the neck of his shirt.

'Naw, you hang on a minute. I am sick and tired of being dragged into your messes because you can't keep a lid on that fucking temper of yours. First Jordan Burns and now Elle? You're murdering folk for fun and I'm not having it. It's too much, Ricky. Like I said, I'm out.'

Ricky narrowed his eyes and raised a brow. 'I think you'll find *you* murdered Burns. Not me.'

Chris sucked air in through his nostrils noisily and shot Ricky a look but said nothing.

'But that doesn't have to be an issue. What is an issue is that you're trying to tell me you're walking away from the fortune we're making in this city because you've got a fucking conscience about Jordan *fucking* Burns? He was shagging my missus, got her up the duff and then she tried to pass the wean off as mine. The two of them dead is the best thing that could have happened to me.'

'It's not about the money,' Chris said, staring blankly at the chamber in front of them. 'It's exactly what you just said, Ricky. It's the wee things that spiral in your head. You have no fucking control over your temper, or your imagination. You've no fucking proof that Jordan Burns is Teigan's dad, none whatsoever, yet you had me fucking kill him and then made sure it looked like Elle was the one who did it.'

Ricky stared at Chris in disbelief. He had no idea his brother was so fucking sensitive. It was time to do some damage control. 'Chris, mate, I'm sorry I dragged you into this. I am. If I'd known you'd take all this so hard I wouldn't have involved you. But you are involved, because you're my brother. And you're *not* walking away from me.'

Chris glared at Ricky through narrowed eyes. 'You're fucking delusional, mate. I'm not hanging around to watch you go from gangster to serial killer just because you can.'

'Serial killer?' Ricky burst out laughing. 'Jesus, it's only Elle.'

'*Only* Elle? See, that right there is the problem, Ricky.'

Ricky looked at the fire burning in his brother's eyes, almost brighter than the one in the chamber. He was serious.

'What about your niece?' Ricky asked, hoping that the idea of never seeing his baby niece grow up would be enough to make him stay.

'She's *not* my niece. And she's *not* your daughter. You should put that right, Ricky. She doesn't belong with you.'

Ricky's skin prickled as he glared at Chris, who turned his back and headed towards the door.

'Oi,' Ricky shouted, his voice echoing around them. 'Don't you turn your back on me.'

Chris kept walking, his shoulders now slumped and arms swinging gently by his side. He didn't flinch at the sound of Ricky calling him. He hadn't for a long time. Maybe he was telling the truth. Maybe Chris really was finished with it all.

'Chris!'

Suddenly, he turned and walked back towards Ricky, a little faster than before. And then, with a balled fist, he thumped Ricky right between the eyes, knocking him back. His backside hit the concrete floor and his face felt like it had exploded. Chris was on top of him now, raining blows down on Ricky like they were rivals in a pub brawl.

'Maybe the only way to stop you is to take you out, Ricky. Maybe you should be the next one to go into that fucking chamber.'

But Ricky didn't give his brother a chance. He slipped his hand into the back of his jeans and pulled out the gun, pressing it hard into his brother's chest, pulling the trigger without even thinking about it.

The shot rang out so loud it almost deafened him. And then a loud ringing sound descended as Chris rolled off him, his back on the concrete. Ricky stood up, his vision blurred by the punch between the eyes. He stared down at Chris, his mouth agape as air left his lungs.

Chris raised his hands and a sudden rush of guilt took over. Ricky fell to his knees by his brother's side and blinked.

'Fuck. What have I done? Chris, mate…'

Chris was trying to speak but Ricky could barely hear him. He leaned down, put his ear to his brother's mouth and listened.

'She isn't Jordan's. She's mine.'

Ricky sat up, peered into the eyes of his dying brother, unsure if he'd heard him correctly. Then, a very slight smile raised the corner of Chris's mouth, and he whispered, 'Fuck you.'

The rage began to build, with a ferocity he didn't know possible. His brother. His *brother* was Teigan's dad.

The gun poised in his hand, he pointed it at Chris's head, ready to take his vengeance shot, but when he looked down into Chris's face, he was staring blankly up at the ceiling as blood pooled around him. He was already dead.

Ricky turned and glared at the cremation chamber.

Getting to his feet, he pulled his gaze away from his brother, unable to look at him anymore as he bled out on the concrete floor. That kind of betrayal between a husband and wife was one thing, but between brothers? As Ricky thought about it, he came to realise that this was the best outcome. Both Elle and Chris were dead. There was no one left who could take Teigan away from him. He'd raise her his way. She'd never know the full extent of the lies surrounding the beginning of her life.

A thought crossed his mind then. Shouldn't he feel something more after what he'd just done? He'd just killed his brother, his own flesh and blood. And yet, he felt numb. He always said to Chris that bodies were bad for business. It seemed that perhaps, killing off rivals or those who would betray him, was best for business after all. Now, he had no blood relatives left. Parents both gone. Now Chris. Only Teigan was left to share the Fyfe name.

Ricky cleared his throat and straightened out his shirt. He stole one last glance at Chris before he decided that business wasn't going to stop because of what had happened tonight.

'Mr Crawford?' Ricky called as he moved to the bottom of the stairs.

Footsteps descended and Tim Crawford stood on the last step, his face expressionless. He'd perfected that look after years of working with Fyfe senior. 'Yes, Mr Fyfe?'

'I need help with a clear up job.'

Tim's eyes flickered ever so slightly. 'Your wife?' But the look on his face told Ricky that Tim knew it wasn't Elle this time. He'd have heard the shot ring out.

Ricky shook his head. 'No. Not my wife; that's already taken care of. It's my brother.'

Chapter Seven

One month later

This was what life was going to feel like now. A tight, burning knot in the pit of her stomach. Chris hadn't shown up. He hadn't been in touch and Elle had no idea how her baby girl was doing. What if Ricky had found out? What if Chris was dead? It was the most likely scenario. Chris wouldn't have changed his mind, not after everything that had happened.

She missed Teigan so much that it physically hurt, her chest constricting every time her baby girl's face came into her mind.

'I'll take another shot,' she said to the girl behind the bar.

'Sorry,' the barmaid replied. 'But I've been told I can't serve you anymore.'

Elle's face contorted and she raised her chin. 'By who?'

'The boss,' the girl replied, taking a step back.

'Well, I'm a paying fucking customer, and I want another dri—' Gravity took hold of Elle then as she toppled off the bar stool and landed on the floor, her hip smashing into the tiles.

The pain shot through her, but it was nothing compared to the pain of losing everything she'd left behind in Glasgow just one month earlier.

A pair of hands hooked under her arms, and she was raised from the floor.

Shrugging out of their grip, she turned, expecting to see the barmaid but instead, was met by a man old enough to be her dad, with gentle eyes and a sympathetic smile.

'Are you okay?' he asked.

'Service in here's *shite!*' she hissed, turning to glance at the barmaid, who was no longer behind the bar.

'Is that an official review?' the man's smile widened and Elle felt her mood soften a little.

'I just want another shot,' she said.

The man nodded and moved away from her. He slipped round to the bar side and filled a shot glass. 'Vodka, was it?'

Elle frowned. 'I don't think you're allowed round there.'

'It's my club, so I can do what I want,' he replied.

'Awe *shit*,' she slurred.

'Yes, you said that already,' he laughed.

Elle propped herself back up onto the stool and felt her eyes turn heavy. 'Actually, where I'm from in Glasgow, *shite* and *shit* are two very different things.'

The man laughed loudly, handing the shot glass to her. 'Is that right?'

Without hesitation, Elle took the small glass from him and raised it to her mouth before slurring, 'Bon *atepete*.'

Her head slammed onto the bar and she was out cold.

–

She peeled one eye open and although her vision was blurry, Elle knew she wasn't in the hostel she'd been living in for a month. The usual smells around her weren't present, nor were the usual noises of others snoring or talking.

'Ah,' came a loud voice. 'You're alive. I wondered when you'd come round.'

Elle attempted to sit up but as soon as she moved, her head began to pound.

'That was some knock to the head you gave yourself,' the voice came again. She didn't recognise it.

Opening the other eye slowly, a man came into focus.

'Who are you?' Elle asked through a crackled voice.

'It's Frank. I told you last night, although I didn't expect you'd remember.'

Frank? She didn't know anyone by that name. She was lonely living on her own, in a new place, all the while missing her baby so much it physically hurt. She'd kept herself to herself since she'd left Glasgow, living off the money Chris had given her but that was slowly beginning to run out.

'Where am I?'

'You're in my office at the nightclub you told me had, and I quote, "*shite service*".'

Frank started to laugh and picked up a mug from his desk, blew into it and took a long drink.

Elle slowly sat up and rubbed at her eyes. The nausea quickly took over and she took some deep breaths to stem it.

'Did I just *pass out* here?' she asked warily.

'No, you passed out on the bar and when you woke up, you couldn't tell anyone where you were staying, so one of the girls put you in here and you slept on the sofa.'

Elle felt uneasy. She didn't know this man. Had he slept in here too?

As if reading her thoughts, he held his hands up and said, 'Before you ask, you were alone the entire time. I hung out at the bar catching up on some paperwork. There's CCTV to prove you were on your own.'

Elle felt her shoulders relax and she took another deep breath. 'I'm so sorry about this.'

'Ah, we all do it from time to time. A little blow out here and there. That's what my nightclub is for. And just so you know, the offer of a job still stands.'

She frowned, stared at this man she'd met just seconds earlier, from what she could remember, and said, 'A job offer?'

'You said you were looking for work? Last night? You could clean, serve, that kind of thing? You said you hadn't worked in the time you'd been here, and you were running out of money and about to become homeless, so I offered you a job. Then you passed out for a second time, and I just left you to it. You obviously needed to sleep it off and I didn't want to disturb you.'

A slow wave of panic washed over Elle. What had she told this man about her life? Had she told him that she'd fled Scotland because she was supposed to be dead?

'I didn't bore you with my life story, did I?' she asked jokily, hoping that she hadn't potentially blown her cover.

'No. Only that you were struggling to adapt to your new life, but you were willing to try and put the past behind you and move forward,' Frank replied.

Thank fuck, Elle thought. Although she wouldn't exactly put it the way Frank had said. Putting the past behind her would be like admitting that she'd never had a daughter, or a life before her new existence in a different city. Nowadays, she was merely trying to get through each and every hour, coping with the grief and sorrow of not being with her baby.

'Why are you being so kind to me?' Elle asked. She hadn't known kindness from a man in a very long time, other than Jordan and, more recently, Chris. The thought of Jordan created a fresh wave of emotion, and she swallowed it down.

'I didn't have it in my heart to be anything but kind to you. You seem like you need a little bit of that in your life.'

Elle felt her heart swell. It was the single nicest thing anyone had ever said to her. She smiled softly and said, 'Thank you. You'll never know what that means to me.'

She closed her eyes in the hope that it would stop the tears from coming. Again. Crying was all she seemed to do these days. She was still hormonal, still healing after the birth. Still leaking milk, although not as much now. Incurably craving the need to cradle her baby, knowing that it wouldn't happen for a very long time because she had to find a way around her death or going to prison. Because Ricky was a powerful bastard; she knew he'd do everything he could to make sure she never held Teigan in her arms ever again.

Elle opened her eyes and Frank stood up.

'So, this job? You interested?'

PART TWO

2024

Man missing after fire at Glasgow factory. Police appealing for witnesses.

A Glasgow man is missing after a factory fire in Glasgow. Witnesses reported the blaze in the early hours as flames engulfed what was thought to be a disused warehouse.

A tip-off to Police Scotland led cops right to the factory, moments after reports came through that it was engulfed in flames. An eyewitness claims to have seen a man running away from the area just before the emergency services arrived. It is reported that the incident revealed the building was being used to produce the class A drug, cocaine.

If you or anyone you know has information regarding the incident, please contact Police Scotland.

Chapter Eight

Glasgow

Danica Campbell threw her head back and closed her eyes after the powder shot up her nostril for the third time in just ten minutes. It stung like a bastard, but she loved how euphoric it made her feel for all of two minutes. It made life seem that little bit less... she couldn't think of the word. Traumatic? Unbelievable? Mentally exhausting?

The music blared out in the club as she shut herself away in the toilet cubicle, her friends probably still dancing without a care in the world. Nice for them, she thought as she straightened herself and wiped her nose with the back of her hand, sniffing loudly. Not that they were true friends. Not really. Not the kind that she could trust her life with, not the type she'd feel comfortable opening up to about her life and her past.

Right, she thought as she glanced at herself in the mirror on the wall above the toilet. *I look decent.* Decent equated to not looking like a complete cokehead, which was what she was worried she was slowly becoming. Was it any wonder after all the shit life had thrown at her? Growing up in care wasn't something she was proud of and certainly the word *care* didn't ring true in her mind. No one had really cared for her in her life. Most of it, at least.

But now she had Ricky. A strong man, with money behind him. A scary man, if she was honest, given his line of work. In a lot of ways, Ricky did scare her. But *he* did care. He was attentive, gentle and showered her with everything she'd ever needed. Did he make her happy? The word hung over her with a heaviness that she couldn't handle. What was happiness? She'd never known it. But the lifestyle Ricky offered made things a lot easier. He paid for everything for her. *Everything.* They lived together at his mansion, she proudly wore the diamond he'd put on her finger and she knew that once she shared his name, the only way for her was up.

Danica pulled a red lipstick out of her bag, reapplied it as carefully as she could, ruffled her long auburn hair and took a deep breath before opening the door.

'Oh fuck!' she shouted, stepping back into the cubicle. And that was it; the hit had officially worn off.

'Nice to see you too,' her fiancé Ricky laughed and then narrowed his eyes.

'What?' Danica said.

'You missed a bit,' he said, wiping his thumb along the edge of her nose.

'Oh, shit,' she said, turning back to look in the mirror. When she did, she saw Ricky's reflection staring back at her and he was smiling, handsome as ever. In fact, handsome didn't even cover it. For a man who was approaching sixty, he still had it. If Ricky Fyfe was famous, he'd be on Tom Hardy level, if not hotter.

'Make it last,' Ricky said. 'I love you, but I'm not becoming your personal supplier because you can get it for free.'

Danica raised a brow. 'I'm not a cokehead.' She realised the words came out defensively.

'I never said you were,' he replied curiously. Ricky licked his lips, and it almost sent Danica into a spiral. 'I saw you on the camera, Dan,' he said. 'You've been in here three times in the last ten minutes.'

She spun and placed a hand on his belt, just above the zip. 'You've been *watching* me on the camera? You dirty perv.'

Ricky laughed and flashed his bright teeth. Turkey teeth, but he suited them no less. Danica hated them on most others who'd had it done, but Ricky pulled it off. Like he did everything else.

'No. I was keeping an eye on what was going on in *my* club and I just happened to see you disappear off the dancefloor three times in ten minutes,' he said again, as though it was a big deal.

'It's this coke, it's shite. Can't get more than ten minutes out of it.'

Frowning, Ricky took a step back and stared at Danica. 'If it's shite, then it isn't mine. And if it's *not* mine, then someone is being a little snake and selling on my patch.'

'It's not mine either. One of the girls gave it to me. I just assumed it was yours.'

'You assumed the shite coke was mine? Cheers, Dan. Good for business that is, the missus dissing the product. And where did she get it?'

Danica shrugged. She didn't like the look on Ricky's face at all.

'I need to know who sold it to her, Dan. I'm not having some wee scrote selling coke in my club and getting away with it.'

Chapter Nine

Ricky stared at his beautiful, young fiancée and tried to remain calm. It wasn't her fault that she didn't know it wasn't his coke. He couldn't lose his cool with her. Not Danica. She was the one. The one who had changed him. She was the first woman in his life that he didn't want to strangle when she annoyed him, or challenged him. She didn't give him any cause to want to hurt her. The exact opposite in fact. He wanted to protect her, to keep her safe and make sure that he did everything he could to make her stay – and not in the way he'd done before.

He'd grown as a man over the last twenty-seven years. The mistakes he'd made were all in the past now and that's where they would stay. He was a good man these days. Husband material. But right now, he had to find out who the fuck was dealing in his club, or at least in his territory.

'Which girl?'

Danica stared at him blankly. 'Eh?'

'I said which girl? Your mate who gave you the coke, who was it?'

'What does it matter?'

'It matters because I want to know who she got it from.'

Silence, other than the music out in the club, fell between them. Ricky pushed his growing anger down into the pit of his stomach. *Breathe*, he told himself. *Don't let the old Ricky out.*

'What are you going to do?' Danica asked, her voice laced with an accusatory tone.

He smiled softly at her. 'I'm not going to throw her out if that's what you're worried about, Dan. I just need some information from her. Now, *which* girl?'

Sighing like a teenager who was just told they were grounded for the summer, Danica slid out from behind him and into the club. Ricky was at her back and slipped his hand into hers, allowing her to lead him

43

towards the group of girls Danica was at the club with. He didn't know any of her friends, not really. He wasn't particularly interested in getting to know them either. For one, they were all half his age. Too giggly and girly. And secondly, he had a business to run. There was no time for friends. Only the firm and Danica. And of course, his daughter, Teigan.

'Girls,' she said loudly over the music. 'You all know my fiancé, Ricky.'

They all smiled up at him and continued to dance and laugh. Not one of them looked like they were worried. And why should they be? They wouldn't know that they were potentially in the middle of what could turn into a turf war. Not that Ricky was going to let things get that far. He'd put a stop to this little bastard immediately, once he knew who they were. The same way he'd put a stop to the Marshall family all those years ago.

Danica leaned into one of the girls and spoke into her ear, to which the girl promptly raised her eyes and met Ricky's. Danica pulled her to the side and Ricky led them back to his office.

Once inside, he closed the door behind them and turned. 'Sorry to interrupt your night, ladies.'

'Emma,' Danica started. 'Ricky just has something he wants to ask you.'

Emma stared at him, her eyes wide. Full of it, clearly; and on shite gear that wasn't his.

'Where'd you get your coke from?' Ricky asked.

Emma shrugged. 'Some guy.'

'Does this guy have a *name*?'

Emma shook her head. 'Well, I'm sure he does, but I don't know it.'

'How'd you get in contact with him?' Ricky pushed, wishing she'd sense his tone and just fucking spit it out.

'Och, you know what it's like. Friend of a friend of a friend. Why? You want some? I can text him if you want.'

Ricky took a steadying breath. This girl was clearly oblivious to what was going on here and who Ricky was. Not a bad thing, he thought.

'Can you tell me what he looks like?'

Emma pulled a face, which crinkled the already leathery skin at the side of her eyes. Too many sunbeds, he thought.

'I don't know, just a regular dealer. He was wearing a black hoodie.'

Ricky stared blankly at her. 'So, black, white?'

'Aw, white.'

'Accent?' Ricky pushed.

'Definitely Glasgow. Sounded like a right wee ned.'

Ricky let out a slow breath to curb his frustration. 'Thank you. You can go back to your night now.'

Emma didn't hesitate. She spun around and practically skipped out of the office.

'I'll be out in a minute,' Danica said, smiling at her friend.

Once the door was closed, Danica perched herself on the end of Ricky's desk and looked down at him with concern.

'Are you worried about this?' she asked.

'Not worried. Angry. Someone has dealt coke in or near my club. And if you're able to get hold of gear to deal it, then you're in the game one way or another. Which means they'll know who I am and that this is Fyfe firm territory. They're playing a dangerous game, and I want to know who it is. After the factory fire and Doyle doing a fucking runner, I wonder if someone knows I'm low on supply and has decided to muscle their way in.'

Danica frowned. 'It doesn't sound like the guy Emma got the coke from would be clever enough for that, especially as she said he sounded like a ned.'

Ricky shook his head and ran his hand over his short beard. 'Nah, he's just the dealer. It's who he's working for that I'm concerned about. The fact there's another dealer here that I don't know about makes me wonder how long they've been around and if they were the reason the factory went up in smoke.'

Danica slipped off the table and crouched down in front of him. 'You're a Fyfe. You'll find them quicker than they can sell their next gram of shite.'

Something occurred to Ricky in that moment. If the Fyfe firm was being challenged by another organised crime gang, then he'd have knowledge of their operations getting closer to his turf, wouldn't he?

'You think it's one of your own?' Danica queried with narrowed eyes, as if she'd heard his thoughts. 'Surely no one on your payroll would do that?'

'Could be cutting the stuff?'

'But why would he do that?'

'Cutting, mixing with household shit and selling the rest in secret to make himself a little more money,' Ricky said. 'Resourceful, but just bloody stupid if that is the case.'

Danica pursed her lips. 'Want me to get Emma to call him back, get more gear?'

Ricky smiled at her. 'Aye. But not tonight. If it's one of my guys, he might slip up and Emma doesn't need to be involved at all.'

Danica nodded. 'Okay. Well, if you're sure? I'm going to head back out.'

Ricky slipped his hands around her waist and pulled her onto his lap. 'You looking for a high? I'll give you one.'

He nuzzled into her neck and drank in her scent. Ricky was the luckiest man alive right now.

Chapter Ten

She drank the last of the bottle of wine, making sure that her tongue licked every last drop before she opened the next. She filled her glass, staring greedily at the liquid. Alcohol. The one and only thing that could numb her pain and make her ache all at once.

Elle stumbled across the room, half sitting, half falling onto the sofa without spilling a drop from her glass. She opened up her free Spotify account and pulled up the playlist that would fill her head with enough noise that she could just about drown out the memories and images in her head. Artemesia's 'Bits and Pieces' was the first song that came on. Perfect, she thought. The beat took her immediately, relaxing her limbs and she attempted to get back up, stumbling as she did so. Closing her eyes and, out of sync with the music, she swayed in the middle of her small living room. Then her shoulders bounced along to the dance tune and she began to smile. Not out of happiness. That wasn't an emotion she possessed. Hadn't for a very long time. No, this was from relief that the music was able to numb her, yet at the same time give her a weird sense of empty euphoria.

She shouldn't listen to this one. She knew it wasn't a good idea. It was the song of her early teens. The song she used to dance to with her friends as they drank from two-litre bottles of cheap cider in one of their houses when their parents were out. Empties, she remembered fondly. One of the very few happy memories she had. Once Elle had met *him*, it all changed, but she hadn't realised it right away. Maybe if she had, things would be different now. Maybe now she wouldn't be alone in life, trying to get through each day without screaming at how weak she'd been back then. It couldn't be changed now. Now, she just had to get on with things.

Elle took a large mouthful of wine and as it rushed down her throat, she suppressed the urge to gag. This would have to be the last glass. The last bottle. If she was sick, she wouldn't get the full effect the alcohol could offer.

The song stopped and she halted in the middle of the room, opening her eyes and glancing down at her phone. The familiar drum beat from the film *Trainspotting* came on and she closed her eyes once more.

How had life come to this? Living alone, working two jobs for minimum wage and drinking every second she could. Why hadn't she been stronger? Why hadn't she tried to get back to her baby? Why hadn't she just fucking stuck up for herself? Of course, all the answers hadn't changed since she'd first asked herself these questions all those years ago. Ricky would have killed her. But perhaps death would have been better than merely surviving every day and living in sheer misery.

Chris had promised he'd bring Teigan to her. But he never did. And the longer she waited, the deeper the fear became until she could only accept that she was never going to see her daughter ever again. She'd questioned why Chris had failed to keep his promise and she could only ever come up with one answer. He was dead. That Ricky had discovered their secret. But she'd heard nothing and she didn't dare create any social media pages in case Ricky came across them. It was the same reason she'd never searched for Teigan on social media either. There was too much risk involved. Knowing her luck, that would be the way he found her. Not just for that reason though, but because she was ashamed of the person she'd become. An alcoholic who suffered from terrible anxiety, perhaps even depression. Ricky was successful in business, had money and the ability to provide Teigan with a good life. What would Elle have had to offer her without Ricky? Nothing.

Living off-grid had been difficult. Technology had moved on. The most Elle had was a basic mobile phone. It did have the ability to act as a smart phone, but she didn't use it for any other reason than calls and texts and listening to her music on Spotify. And the only person who had her number was Frank, her boss. The only person she had in her life was Frank. The world had moved on and she was stuck. Never moving forward. Always looking back at what life had dealt her.

A single tear fell from a closed eye and she tried hard not to let a second follow. She wouldn't cry. Not tonight. Not again. Every day for the last… what was it? Almost thirty years. She stopped, opened her eyes and jabbed her finger at the pause button on the screen. The music came to an abrupt halt, and the only sound she could hear was the rush of blood in her ears before the inevitable voices crept back in. The shame. The loathing she felt for herself, and the hate she felt for the world. But mostly for him.

Chapter Eleven

Teigan Fyfe stared down at the message on her phone.

> Do not be late for that meeting tomorrow. It's scheduled for 11:30 a.m. I'll forward the address again just to make sure you have it. If you're still out, wrap the night up now. I don't want you stinking of booze when you meet up. This guy is a very important associate and I want it to go well.

Teigan rolled her eyes at the message. He really didn't know her that well if he thought she was out getting drunk the night before a big meeting. That wasn't her way at all. It might be the norm for the men in this world, but certainly not when Teigan was involved.

She simply sent back a thumbs-up emoji and tucked her phone into her bag before heading back into the Indian takeaway to collect her order. Thankfully, it was only round the corner from the hotel she and her fiancé Darren were staying in. She might be treating herself and Darren to a five-star hotel, but there was nothing better than cosying up together on the super-king-sized bed, in fluffy white robes, eating Indian takeaway food. She'd paid close to fifteen hundred pounds for two nights; she was going to make sure she got her money's worth.

'That smells amazing, I'm starving,' Teigan said as Darren handed her the bag.

'Me too,' he replied. 'A takeaway, a few beers and a five-star hotel room. What more can you ask for?'

She couldn't help but smile. She loved how much he enjoyed the simple things and that he wasn't from her world. To Teigan, a fancy hotel room that cost the same as some people's monthly rent for just one night, was becoming the norm. To Darren, it was a luxury. The look on his face when he'd stepped into the suite had made her laugh.

They walked through the front door of The Grand Luxe Retreat hotel and walked along the corridor to the lift. Above them hung elegant chandeliers, and the walls were adorned with contemporary art pieces. To Teigan, they just looked like canvases with black and grey paint splattered across them, but what did she know about art?

Once the lift doors opened onto the sixth floor, which housed just two suites, Darren tapped the key card onto the digital plate and the door clicked open. Teigan switched on the light and noticed that rose petals had been sprinkled on the bed.

She turned, smiled and said, 'You know I hate romantic shit.'

'Yep, that's why I requested it,' Darren replied. 'I love to get you all angry and riled up. The make-up sex is always really good. There's also a bottle of champagne in the bathroom with two glasses. The bath could easily fit six people so I thought we could have a little fun in there too.'

She narrowed her eyes and couldn't stop the smile lifting the corners of her mouth. She nudged him with her elbow and carried the takeaway over to the six-seater dining table. She'd never understood why big tables were needed – who hosted dinner parties in grand hotel rooms?

Even though they'd been together for just under three years, Darren still gave Teigan that fluttery feeling in her stomach every time he gave her a cheeky smile. He'd fully accepted her for what and who she was. A gangster's daughter who would one day rise up the ranks and take over. Whether or not Ricky would ever let go of the business reins was another thing altogether. As much as Darren very rarely commented on the type of business that Teigan was involved in, he did often voice his concern about the potential dangers she could be faced with. As sweet as it was that he cared about her in that way, it also irked her a little that men seemed to think that women weren't strong enough to hold their own when it came to the criminal underworld. She'd grown up in this world, she knew the ins and outs better than most, given her dad was one of Glasgow's biggest crime bosses. Criminal activity is all she'd ever known. And for Darren to comment that he thought it was dangerous for her to be involved irked her even more, because he really had no understanding of what went on, not really.

They plated up their food, slipped into their fluffy white robes courtesy of the hotel and sat down to eat as the television talked to itself quietly in the lounge area of their suite.

'So,' Darren started, and she knew what was coming. He had already mentioned that he wanted to accompany her at the meeting with Ricky's business associate the next day, so she had a fair idea of what he was about to say next.

'Don't go there, Darren,' she said quietly before taking a mouthful of korma.

'Go where? I haven't even said anything yet.'

'But I know you,' she replied while still chewing. 'I know what you're thinking, and I get it, but I'm a big girl, Darren. Men in our line of business don't scare me. I'm practically running my dad's businesses for him while he's living his fantasy life with that stupid bint, Danica. I'm more than capable of taking care of things myself.'

Darren fell quiet and Teigan continued eating.

'I only want to come because I want to be there to support you.'

'We've been together going on three years, Darren. Have I ever needed support in my work before now? No. And why? Because of who I am and my name. I'm a Fyfe, Darren. The daughter of Ricky Fyfe, but that doesn't even need to be mentioned. I don't *need* support during a business meeting, not by you or my dad. How weak would I look if I turned up with my fiancé? The guy wouldn't take me seriously. Also, as gently as I can put this, you're not part of any of the Fyfe enterprises, so he'd question why you're there. He might not even let you in. That would be embarrassing for both of us.'

Darren glanced at her and before he took a bite from his naan bread, he said humorously, 'Okay, fine. I get it. You're this big, independent girl who doesn't need a man to protect her.'

'Correct.' She smiled, feeling a little guilty that she'd put him so firmly in his place. Something she'd always had to do while rising up the ranks over the years. Her dad's associates had never fully respected her, never fully accepted that she was in charge when Ricky wasn't around. 'I never have and never will. Look, I love you. It's not that I don't *want* you there. But I definitely don't *need* you there. And you don't have to worry about me. I can handle anything that comes my way.'

They finished their food in silence before Teigan got up and moved to the sofa. Darren joined her.

'So, what's the meeting about then?' Darren asked.

Teigan turned slowly and glanced at him. 'A potential new supply and distribution deal.'

'If it goes ahead, would you have to deal with cargo yourself?'

Laughter burst out of her and then she composed herself when she saw that Darren's expression was deadly serious. 'Definitely not. My dad will sort that. These types of businessmen have transport and distributors. I only do the organising and deal with the transactions.'

Darren nodded slowly as though trying to understand. It was abundantly obvious that this was all so alien to him. She liked it that way.

'If you want to marry me, you have to be okay with all this. I wouldn't expect you to give up your job. If I'm honest, I like that you're not in this world. It's kind of refreshing. Actually, the less you know about things, the better.'

Darren didn't say anything. She knew he liked his job in car sales. The firm he worked for paid him well, unlike most others.

'I get it, I do. And I wouldn't give up my own job. It's security for me. And I like the idea that my job won't land me in a jail cell.'

Teigan laughed again. 'Are you kidding? The prices you sell some of those cars for should come with a life sentence.'

Darren pulled a face and then smiled. 'Have you ever thought about going legit? I mean, the life you lead is great but one day the police might come knocking. What then? What happens to us?'

Teigan considered that for a moment. And it wasn't the first time she'd thought about it. The business side of things wasn't an issue for her. It was all just admin, really. But often she thought about what her dad's business was doing to people on the streets. Their customers and families. She'd been fortunate enough not to have had experience of that side of things. Teigan knew the effects drugs had on people. Addiction. Violence. She was at the heart of all that alongside her dad, wasn't she? Was that something she'd want her future children to go through? Would she want her own kids doing drugs on the streets? The stark answer to that was no, definitely not. She knew Darren wouldn't want that either.

But she was bloody good at her job. So good that she'd been sent to another part of the country by herself to agree and finalise a brand-new deal with a very well-respected businessman. Those kinds of merits helped get you to the top, didn't they? Running the company on her own one day was something she'd always thought about.

'In all honesty, Darren, I love the idea of living free and not constantly worrying about the authorities coming for me. But I don't *have* anything else. I was born into this. I'm very good at my job, Darren. You don't have anything to worry about. I'm stealthy,' she said and smiled widely. He smiled back but she knew it was forced. 'I'm where I am in this business because of how discreet I am. You've honestly no need to worry about police or anyone else coming for me.'

Chapter Twelve

Elle sat on the tiny balcony of her pokey, one bedroom flat in Chigwell, and took a long draw on her second cigarette that morning. Staring out at the houses in front of her, seeing the occupants getting into their cars and ready to start their day, Elle once again sighed that her life had come to this. Merely existing in a city that wasn't her home. She missed Glasgow more than she'd thought she ever would. As time had passed, her desire to go home had grown. The reality was she could never go back. Not until she knew Ricky was out of the picture. He'd have to be dead. And Elle wasn't that lucky.

The sun was still low in the sky that late winter morning, but she could just about feel its heat on her face. Pulling her dressing gown tighter around herself, she closed her eyes, rested her head back on the concrete wall behind her and drowned out the sound of the Chigwell traffic as well as the chill in the air. She could almost imagine being abroad. Her favourite island of Lanzarote would be doused in sunshine right now, the haze of morning cloud lifting to reveal the ocean views. She'd only ever been once. In fact, she'd only ever been abroad once and that had been with Ricky after they'd got married. Two weeks of wedded bliss in the sunshine. She'd been lulled into a false sense of security that their marriage would continue to be blissful. He'd fooled her on that holiday. He'd fooled her completely.

She opened her eyes, pushing the memories out of her head and glancing down at her phone. The home screen told her the temperature was currently eight degrees and could rise to a high of ten by noon.

Tapping the ash onto the small dish on the round iron table in front of her, Elle decided she'd strung it out long enough and it was time to go for a shower.

Stubbing out her cigarette, Elle stood up, stretched her arms over her head and took a long, deep breath. She really needed to stop smoking, but it was a habit she just couldn't break. She rolled her eyes; she couldn't break out of anything. Not the smoking, not the drinking, not her dark mind.

–

Once she was dried and dressed after her shower, Elle headed out of the flat and along Manford Way towards her place of work, where she was employed for two different roles. In the evening, she was a barmaid, a job that she had come to enjoy. She was good at it, had good banter with the punters and she knew the regulars. They'd chat to her as if she was a true friend and not just the woman who served them drinks. Listening to other people talk about their lives and their struggles was a good distraction from her own thoughts.

In the daytime, she was the cleaner. Her boss, Frank Cranwell, paid her handsomely for doing both because he knew how difficult it would be for her to work until three in the morning and then go in early afternoon to clean, before being back behind the bar by nine at night. Not only did he pay her well, but he also paid her for the bar work in cash, including tips, to avoid the employment law issue of her not getting enough rest time between shifts. Elle liked it that way and she wasn't going to allow something as small as the law stop her from doing what she needed. Those wages combined left her with a decent amount of money every month.

The fifteen-minute walk to the Ace Lounge Casino left Elle's mind feeling a little less foggy from the unwanted memories that always seemed to claw their way back into her mind when she wasn't busy. Walking, trying to sleep, showering – all those minor daily rituals allowed her mind to wander to Teigan. Her baby. Not a baby now, of course. Twenty-seven years old she'd be now. Elle was closing in on fifty with her birthday just weeks away and she wondered what life would have been like if things had turned out differently – if Ricky had never found out he wasn't Teigan's real dad. Would things have got better? She could have grandchildren by now. Teigan could be raising her own family and Elle would never know; would never be part of that.

Reaching the casino, Elle pulled the keys from her bag, let herself in and closed the door behind her before tapping in the alarm code. The place was always so different in the daytime. Quiet, stale. She much preferred her evening shifts, which came with lots of people and lots of noise.

Switching on the lights, Elle took in the sight in front of her. Empty glasses and bottles lay everywhere, the floor was filthy, and she didn't even want to think about the toilets. The evening staff on shift always offered to help her clean up at the end of the night so she didn't have too much to do the next day. But Elle liked having too much to do. Keeping herself busy was the only way to keep the voices at bay. They were never fully silent, but at least the act of being busy drowned them out.

She went over to the sound system and connected her Spotify account. She needed something loud. Something upbeat. Scrolling through the playlists she'd created, she settled on Primal Scream, 'Country Girl'. As the music started, she turned the volume up as loud as she could take it and got to work cleaning the casino. She wanted to make sure it was spotless for when Frank came in later to do the takings from the night before. Not only that, but she always wanted to do a good job because she was so grateful for everything he'd done for her. He'd taken her under his wing, looked after her and given her purpose in life at a time she was close to giving up.

As she scrubbed the bar top and the tables, Elle felt the music take her away to a place where she was able to forget. She felt herself start to dance a little as she wiped surfaces and swept the floors; she even sang along, allowing her voice to match the volume of the song.

Suddenly, the music came to a stop and Elle's voice bounced off the walls. She spun around to see Frank standing by the sound system with the biggest smile on his face.

'Jesus *Christ*, you scared the shit out of me,' Elle said, placing a hand on her chest.

'You should try out for *The X Factor*,' he laughed.

'Ha. Ha,' Elle said, sarcastically. 'But that shit isn't even on the TV anymore. And I'm too good for Mr Cowell anyway.'

Frank let out a loud laugh. 'I wouldn't normally insist on switching it off, but I've got a meeting this morning. In fact, they'll be here in about twenty minutes.'

Elle nodded. 'Okay. Do you want me to do anything? Stick the kettle on?'

Frank nodded. 'That would be great, yeah. Thanks. I've got the whisky in there in case they need something a bit stronger.'

They'd never discussed her past, but there seemed to be an under-standing between them. Like he knew there was something dark lurking in the depths of her soul that she was scared to talk about. He looked after her, was almost like a dad to her. She had no one else. No friends, other than her work colleagues and they were barely friends. She didn't let anyone in that way.

Elle headed back to the kitchen and filled the kettle, switched it on and prepared a tray of mugs, tea, coffee, sugar and a small jug of milk. She carried it through and tapped on the office door with her elbow before entering.

'Cheers, Elle,' Frank said as he sat behind his desk with his mobile in his hand. He was tapping on the screen.

'No bother,' she replied with a smile.

'You seem chipper for someone who worked a late shift onto an early.'

'I'm just used to it,' Elle replied, setting the tray down on the desk. 'You know me, Frank. I like to keep busy.'

'Something bothering you?' Frank asked, as if reading her thoughts.

Elle pursed her lips and shook her head. 'No. Why do you ask?'

Frank shrugged. 'Even with that smile, you just look like you have the weight of the world on your shoulders.'

He'd read her perfectly.

'Not the world, just the weight of the cleaning still needing to be done. And if you've got a meeting, I want the place to smell more like Zoflora than stale beer.'

Frank let out a hearty laugh and it made Elle smile. 'You'd better get on then. But do me a favour, don't use the one you used yesterday. I nearly choked to death on the smell when I walked in.'

'You didn't like the Rhubarb and Cassis? It's my favourite.'

'It was like the place had been scrubbed with a bucket of piss,' Frank replied, sticking out his tongue as if to gag. 'No offence.'

Elle held her hands up and smiled. 'Fine. No more piss. I'll stick to Linen Fresh.'

She went back out to the main area of the club and continued cleaning, trying to push thoughts of her past out of her head.

Chapter Thirteen

As she looked up at the Ace Lounge Casino's sign, Teigan noticed that one of the tiles on the wall beside the entrance was chipped. It was the smallest, most minuscule chip that possibly existed, but she noticed it. That was part of who she was, noticing the little details. It was why her dad relied on her so much in the business. She could pinpoint small issues, sniff out the slightest scent of a rat. It was something she was proud of.

Dealing with her dad's associate, Frank Cranwell, was a first for Teigan, although she'd heard a lot about him through her dad and the business. Ricky and Frank had done small deals before. This one was the biggest yet. Frank could potentially be the new supplier for Glasgow after the factory fire. She knew what she was walking into and the stakes were high.

Glancing down at the cigarette between her fingers, she took the last draw and dropped it on the ground before standing on it. She bent down, retrieved the butt and tossed it into the bin on the street. Exhaling loudly, a plume of smoke billowed into the air above her as she stepped inside.

The first thing Teigan noticed was how clean the place smelled. It made for a nice change, considering every other establishment in the business she'd ever been in smelled like a mixture of sweat and stale beer. She noticed a woman at the far side of the club mopping the floor. Music played quietly, but enough to stop the woman from hearing Teigan come in. Just as she was about to call out to her to tell Frank she'd arrived, Frank Cranwell appeared from behind a door at the far end of the bar. He was on his own, something that Teigan hadn't expected. Usually at these kinds of meetings, there was always a second man in the vicinity. A heavy, who would be there in case things flared up.

But not today, it seemed. Was that because of who Teigan was? A woman? Did Frank see her as just a little secretary who was no threat at all? The idea annoyed her but knowing she had her very own gun in her handbag was enough to stem the frustration. Frank didn't need to know it was there, although he could probably guess.

'Ms Fyfe,' Frank said loudly, his London accent strong.

Teigan pulled her mouth into a thin line; something else to add to the annoyance. She hated being referred to as Ms. When she got married, she vowed never to be called Mrs either.

'Please, just call me Teigan,' she said, holding out her hand in a formal gesture.

Frank smiled widely at her and took her hand. 'Teigan,' he repeated. 'It's good to finally meet the boss's daughter.'

'And second in command,' Teigan pointed out.

Frank's brow raised and his jaw clicked. 'Ah, like a deputy manager.'

'Something like that,' Teigan said, biting her tongue. *These men*, she thought. Now she was even more pleased she hadn't allowed Darren to come along. Frank clearly already had a weak view of Teigan; Darren being present would have solidified that entirely.

Frank let go of Teigan's hand and stared at her for a long time, his eyes searching hers.

'Everything okay?' Teigan asked, the words coming out long and slow.

'You look a *lot* like him,' Frank said. 'Your old man, I mean.'

'I've never thought so,' Teigan replied, inwardly smiling at the thought of Ricky's face if he'd heard someone referring to him as an *old man*. 'So, the meeting?'

Frank's brow furrowed slightly and then, as if he just snapped out of a trance, he said, 'Ah, yes. Come through to the office.'

Teigan followed him through the club and into a decent-sized office. She looked around and took in the décor. Classic club office décor. A white leather couch along one wall. A large chandelier hung above the desk. And on the wall behind the desk, a huge picture of a lion baring its teeth. The lion's teeth were covered in small diamonds and the picture was encased in a white leather frame.

'Don't mind that hideous thing,' Frank said, as though he knew how much Teigan immediately hated the picture. 'It was a present from my brother before he died. He was a bit of a Del Boy. Loved his tat. I hate it, but just can't bring myself to bin it now that he's dead, you know?'

Teigan nodded and gave a sympathetic smile.

'Anyway, have a seat,' Frank said, gesturing to the chair on the opposite side of the desk. Teigan sat down and the sparkly lion glared down at her.

'Can I ask,' Teigan started. 'How long have you known my dad?'

'Oh, now there's a question,' Frank said, pouring coffee into a mug. 'Close to about fifteen years.'

Teigan nodded. 'And how did you come to know each other?'

'Through business. I owned a club up in Glasgow, sold it to your old man and we kept in touch. Done some business here and there since – some club promotions, that kind of thing. He never told you any of this?'

Teigan shook her head. 'To be fair, I've never asked. When you say club promotions?'

'Mainly in-house stuff. DJs will work with us both for an agreed fee, which Ricky has mainly dealt with, but it's mostly the Z-list celebrity appearances.'

Teigan nodded. 'By Z-listers, you mean reality TV personalities?'

Frank gave a wry smile and Teigan found it odd.

'You're not a fan of them?'

'I think it's tacky, but it brings in the cash,' Frank replied, holding up an empty mug. 'Coffee? Something stronger?'

Teigan held in a laugh that threatened to burst out of her when he said that. Tacky was the only way to describe the diamond-studded lion hanging on the wall.

She noticed the various whisky and gin bottles on the shelf behind Frank. Most of which were more than half full. 'I'll have a coffee, thanks. Black. No sugar. Always need a clear head in this game, eh?' Teigan said.

'Good girl, keep that head clear,' Frank said, pouring coffee into a mug and handing it to her.

There was a brief silence and Teigan felt Frank's eyes on her. She glanced at him and queried, 'What?'

'You're not offended.'

Teigan frowned. 'By what?'

'The *good girl* comment.'

Raising a brow, Teigan said, 'The only thing that offends me is when punters don't pay up. And trust me, that offended feeling doesn't last long when I go after debt.'

Frank let out a loud, guttural laugh and said, 'Now, *that* is a reason to get offended. And you're proactive in putting that shit to bed. I'm glad to hear it. I've not come across many women in the business with that attitude.'

'That's because there aren't many who can handle this world,' Teigan said.

'So, Ricky has filled you in on the details?' Frank asked, sitting down behind his desk.

Teigan nodded. 'Yes. He said that you two had a brief chat over the phone about you supplying us for three months as a trial?'

Frank nodded. 'That's right. We just need to go over the details.'

'Okay,' Teigan said, placing her mug down on a coaster that matched the lion on the wall.

'How much do you earn from your sales in a month?' Frank asked, his question so direct that Teigan knew she needed to give as clear and concise an answer as possible.

'Off the top of my head, based on sales in our clubs every weekend, I'd say about thirty grand based on our punters each purchasing a gram across Friday and Saturday nights. That's just in our clubs. That's not based on our street dealers, or our private customers.'

Frank frowned. 'Private customers?'

'You know, folk who come into Glasgow for work regularly.'

Frank nodded. 'And with your street dealers, how many do you have?'

'We've just employed a further ten to cover a new area. Including them, we have sixty in total.'

Frank's eyebrows raised and he nodded again in approval. 'And what are they bringing in each week?'

'They can bring in anything from five to eight grand. Depending on the time of year, it can vary. Give or take a few quid, but that's rare.'

'So, you've got sixty dealers, each bringing in a minimum of five grand per week,' Frank said quietly. 'That's three hundred thousand.'

Teigan nodded. 'Our customers are very loyal.'

'You're changing suppliers because there was an issue?'

She stared at Frank through narrowed eyes. He knew why. He was just testing her to see if she could hold her own.

'He was never our supplier. We were the manufacturer as well as distributor. But our head of operations is on the run along with some of the dealers, hence why we've employed more. There was a fire at the factory after a tip-off to the police. Thankfully, our tracks are always well and truly covered, so there was no comeback to us directly.'

Frank's eyebrows remained raised. 'What was his name again?'

'Aidan Doyle. I'm sure he's long gone. He'll be fearing for his life after what happened on his watch. Likely not even in the country. If I'm honest, I was never a fan of his. I didn't trust him. He was a bit of a cowboy. Never reliable and he always seemed a little too big for his boots. I think he liked the idea of being a gangster, up there with the big boys, but in truth, I never believed he had it in him. Suppose I can't say I'm surprised at what happened to the factory. My dad didn't fill you in on any of this?'

Frank sipped his coffee and met her eye. It seemed apparent that Frank was testing her, perhaps to see if she'd tell the truth and whether she was trustworthy.

'He did. But to be fair, we were both well-oiled during our brief chat on the phone.'

Teigan suppressed an eye roll. Why get pissed *before* discussing a potential business investment, especially after what had gone down at the factory – and then send in the deputy, as Frank had referred to her, to tidy things up?

'Well, the only thing I'm on is the coffee. So, I can assure you that my numbers are as close to fact as they can be without the books in front of me.'

Frank nodded. 'I don't doubt it. You're a Fyfe. I have every faith that you're as bright, if not brighter, than your old man. And you don't get bogged down with the bullshit, from what I can see. You just get on with it.'

'Correct,' Teigan replied.

Frank balled his fist and banged it on the desk twice. The action almost made Teigan jump. 'Okay,' he said cheerfully. 'I'd say that if you lot up there in Glasgow have the ability to bring in that kind of money on a weekly basis, then we have a deal.'

Teigan tried to keep the smile off her face. 'Ricky will be pleased to hear that.'

'Now, of course we need to agree on a percentage of takings.'

'Of course.'

'But with that kind of weekly income, I'd say your cut is going to be substantial.'

Teigan watched as Frank refilled his coffee mug, before turning to retrieve a bottle of whisky. He poured a shot into the mug without measuring and leaned back on the white, leather seat.

'How's thirty-five percent?'

Teigan couldn't even begin to work that out in her head so she pulled out her phone and did the calculation. As she stared at the numbers on the screen, she felt secure that it would be more than enough to survive on.

'Is that a general cut, or just for the trial?' Teigan queried.

'Let's call it a general term for now. If sales are as good as you state, then we can possibly renegotiate in the future,' Frank said, swinging gently on his chair. He hadn't yet sipped from the whisky chaser coffee.

'Let me just step outside to make a call, and I'll be back in a few minutes.'

Frank gestured to the door, without getting up, and kept his eyes on Teigan as she rose from her seat.

Stepping out of the office, Teigan crossed the floor of the club, walking carefully due to the floor being wet from the woman mopping. The woman raised her eyes and stared at her. Teigan frowned and then gave a tight lipped, polite smile then looked down at her phone. As she moved towards the exit, she felt the woman's eyes on her. She wanted to ask what the woman was staring at, but in the grand scheme of things it didn't matter. Teigan had a pressing call to make and a weirdo cleaner who was staring at her was not at the top of her priorities.

Pushing open the door, Teigan took a deep breath and called her dad.

Chapter Fourteen

As she lay in Ricky's arms, Danica was dozing off when the shrill ring of Ricky's phone made her eyes shoot open.

'*Jesus*, Ricky, that bloody phone,' Danica said. 'It's always so bloody loud.'

Ricky didn't say anything as he picked it up from the bedside table and answered it. Danica knew it would be Teigan, her soon to be stepdaughter, even though Teigan was only a few months older than her.

'Teigan?' Ricky said, as he pulled his arm out from under Danica and sat up. Danica readjusted her position and stared up at the ceiling. She could hear Teigan's voice but couldn't make out what was being said.

After a few moments, Ricky said, 'Aye, good work Teeg. I'll speak to you soon,' before hanging up.

'Everything okay?' she asked, waiting for him to fill her in.

Ricky smiled. 'Better than okay.' Then he pulled Danica in and kissed her hard. The same way he'd kissed her for the first time four years ago in his club.

'Teigan did good on the deal?'

'Teigan *always* does well. She learned from the best,' Ricky replied.

'And what about me?' Danica asked.

Ricky frowned. 'What about you?'

'My place in the business. Where do you see me once we're married?'

Ricky's frown deepened. 'I see you here. In our home.'

Danica stared at him for a few seconds, wondering if he was joking. When his expression didn't change, she said, 'You see me as a house-wife? At twenty-seven years old?'

'I'd have thought you'd love to stay at home all day? You can shop, swim in our brand-new heated pool. What's not to like?'

Danica blinked in quick succession. 'Well, when you put it like that, nothing I suppose. But I'll get bored, Ricky. I have never envisioned my life as being a stay-at-home wife who cooks and cleans.'

Ricky let out a loud laugh. 'You don't have to. We have a cleaner and I can hire a cook if that's what you want.'

'What I want is to play an important part in the business. In any of them, really. I've got a lot to give, Ricky.'

Ricky raised a brow and slipped his hand over her bare stomach. 'Oh, I know that for sure.'

She rolled her eyes. 'I mean it, Ricky. Once we're married, I don't want to just sit around here all day doing nothing. After we met and I decided to take a year out from studying, I suppose I was excited to spend all my free time with you. I got carried away with being in love and I never got back into it. But I'm bored now, Ricky. Bored of doing nothing all day and watching you and Teigan work together when I could be a part of it. You put me in the know about your business quite quickly, Ricky, so I *know* you trust me. Make use of the fact that your fiancée was halfway through her accountancy degree before she met you. I *still* want my own firm one day and I know I need to finish my degree first, but maybe that's something you could think about? Maybe I could be the Fyfe firm accountant, unofficially until I complete my studies?'

Ricky pulled his lips into a tight line and looked off to the opposite end of their bedroom, thinking.

'What's to think about?' she asked. 'I mean, I'm young, I'm smart and the most loyal person by your side; plus I'm an absolute wiz when it comes to numbers. Who *better* than to do the books?'

Ricky raised a brow. 'Don't say that in front of Teigan or she'll take one of my guns from the lock up beneath the house and shoot you.'

'Just a tad of an overreaction,' Danica replied, staring at her fiancé with trepidation, even though she knew it was a figure of speech. 'Like I said, Teigan and I never got on, but I doubt she'd try to kill me if you put me in charge of the accounts.'

Ricky sighed, tapping his fingers on her arm gently. 'Look, I get it. After what you've been through, I understand wanting to be part of something.'

A pang of sadness and grief hit her out of the blue. She hadn't expected him to say that.

'Growing up in care and thinking I would amount to nothing was a lot to take through life, Ricky. When my parents died, I was on my own. No extended family, no grandparents or aunties and uncles. So, straight into the system I went. I had to be strong going through school because of that. There is no other way to deal with life once you've suffered the loss I did. In fact, I was too strong and evidently became a top-class bitch and people either loved me or hated me because of it, which is why Teigan and I never got on. Meeting someone like you and being swept off my feet was never something I'd imagined would happen. I mean, people like me generally don't have good luck.'

'Well, you don't have to be a bitch to get by anymore. You've got me now. I'll be your shield against all the shit.'

Danica stared at him and tried not to cry. 'I just want to do something in life that gives me a purpose. I want to do the thing I'm half trained in. I know I only half part of my degree, but that doesn't mean I can't do the job for you.' She stopped and took a breath, realising that her words had come out in a flood and Ricky's eyes widened as she spoke each one with urgency. 'Just let me show you that my skills would be beneficial to the business.'

Ricky nodded, bit his lip and said, 'Accountancy sounds like a great way to go if that's what you say you're good at. But in the meantime, you're planning our wedding. I'm sure *that* will keep you busy.'

Danica smiled, hiding her annoyance. She knew fine well that he had no real interest in letting her into the business. All she was to him in business was a trophy wife. Yes, he loved her, but that was as far as it went. 'Yeah,' she said, not wishing to start an argument. 'Busy is one word for it. Apparently planning a wedding is just as stressful as moving house.'

'Well at least you don't have to worry about us moving. I've too many bodies buried here, I can't leave them all behind, can I?' Ricky laughed and Danica felt a tingle up her spine. To anyone else, that comment would just be a figure of speech. But knowing the line of work Ricky was in, Danica knew that there could be some truth to what he'd just said.

Chapter Fifteen

She stood by the bar, wiping furiously as she went over it in her head, again and again. No, it couldn't be. It just wasn't possible. But then again, in this world Elle had learned that just about anything was possible.

'I think it's clean,' a voice interrupted her chaotic thoughts. Elle looked up to see Frank Cranwell standing in his office doorway, holding a mug in his hand. He was staring at her with curiosity in his eyes.

She glanced down at the bar and realised she'd been wiping the same spot for several minutes.

'You know me, like to be thorough.'

'Or, like I suggested earlier, you have the weight of the world on your shoulders?' Frank said again and this time it made Elle's stomach roll. Was she *that* transparent? She'd known him for a long time, why could he suddenly see that she had something on her mind now, when in fact, it had always been there?

'I'm fine, Frank. I promise.'

She could tell by the look on his face that he didn't believe her, but she wasn't about to spill the tea now.

'Ah,' Frank said, as the entrance door of the club opened and a woman walked in. 'Good news I hope?'

Teigan glanced briefly at Elle and then back to Frank and smiled. 'Shall we?'

Frank allowed Teigan into the office first and went in behind her, before closing the door.

Elle felt sick. That name had made her feel sick. Fyfe. Her husband's surname from a long, long time ago. The man who'd tried and failed to kill her and didn't know she wasn't dead. But that wasn't what made her feel so ill. She'd just been standing in front of her own daughter, Teigan Fyfe, who she'd walked away from twenty-seven years ago. And the woman had looked right through her because she had no idea who Elle was. No clue that she was in the presence of her own mother. Jesus, if Frank hadn't greeted her by name, then Elle herself may not have made the connection at all. Why would she? Teigan was an adult now, no longer resembling the tiny baby she once was.

Jesus Christ. Breathe. Just breathe.

Elle placed a hand on her chest and struggled against the spasms. Of all the places in the world she imagined running into her daughter, a casino bar in Chigwell certainly wasn't one of them.

The office door opened and Teigan stepped out, with Frank at her back. Elle straightened herself and tried to look calm, even though deep inside she felt as though her organs were twisted and spasmed out of control.

'Thank you for seeing me, Mr Cranwell,' Teigan said, and Elle's urge to vomit intensified.

'Ah, call me Frank. We'll be in contact about the details we just discussed. Oh, and pass my best on to Ricky.'

Elle's heart jumped in her chest. Ricky. Ricky Fyfe. Jesus.

'I will do,' Teigan replied with a smile.

Frank saw Teigan to the door, and she didn't even look back at Elle. Of course she didn't. Why would she?

This is ridiculous, Elle tried to reason with herself. This isn't *real*. There was no proof that girl was her daughter. The world was a very big place. People possessed the same names all the time. She tried hard but it was difficult to convince herself that there could be two Teigan Fyfes in the world, both from Glasgow and in the club business. Especially one whose father was also named Ricky Fyfe.

Frank closed the door and turned, looking very pleased with himself. When he met Elle's eye, she tried her damnedest not to look as flustered as she felt.

Her heart banged so loudly in her chest she wondered if Frank would hear it. Throat dry and unable to swallow, Elle took a breath.

Frank placed his glass down on the counter and shook his head. 'Right, Elle. Spit it out. What's wrong?'

'Nothing,' she said as calmly as possible.

'I don't believe you, Elle. If I'm honest, we both know you've been sitting on something awful from your past and I've known this since the moment I met you all those years ago. You know you can trust me. I may be your boss, but first and foremost, I'm your friend. I took you in when you were at your lowest. I'd never let you down, Elle. You know that.'

She did know that. Elle trusted Frank Cranwell with her life. But she'd had no idea that he was in business with Ricky. Even after all these years, she was still in Ricky's clutches. Still under his control. Could she trust Frank with that information? Could she trust *anyone* with it? It wasn't a risk she was willing to take.

'I do trust you, Frank. Of course I do. If it wasn't for you, I wouldn't be standing right now.'

Frank nodded, as if remembering the state she was in when she'd first walked through the door of the Ace Lounge Casino. He'd seen something in her: her desperation to drink so much she was numb, or unconscious to the pain. And he'd helped her. Offered her a job, a place to live. He'd given her a way out of the darkness that had swallowed her whole. She'd never be able to repay him, and he'd never know just how grateful she was.

'Then talk to me,' he said. 'You're like a daughter to me, Elle. I will have your back no matter what is going on with you.'

Licking her lips, Elle swallowed hard and forced a smile. 'I promise you, Frank, if there was something to tell, then you would be the first to know. I'm just having a rough couple of days. I'll be fine once I get a decent night's sleep.'

She felt Frank's eyes burning into her skin. He didn't believe her and she didn't blame him. She'd been able to keep her secret for twenty-seven years. But how much longer could she keep this up?

Frank sighed but Elle knew he wasn't annoyed with her. 'Fine. Just know that there is nothing you can say or do that would make me think badly of you, Elle. You're looking at a man who is guilty of a million things you'd never dream of thinking about. Whatever you've done in the past to put you in such a dark place, then I can guarantee it won't shock me.'

Elle couldn't help but smile. She wondered if he'd say the same if he knew she was supposed to be dead.

'Whatever you're guilty of, Frank, I'm sure you shouldn't be talking about it with me.' She winked, trying to inject some humour into the conversation, and steer it in a different direction.

He laughed loudly. 'Yes. You're probably right.' Then he placed a hand over her own and leaned in. 'Remember, you can trust me. Always.'

Chapter Sixteen

Danica picked up the dead flowers on her mother's grave and slipped them into the bin bag at her feet. She'd already cleaned the headstone with some antibacterial wipes, but it still looked dull and worn.

Danica had read the script so many times she'd memorised it. Her mum's memory now just words on a granite headstone. She barely remembered her mum, who'd passed away when Danica was just six years old, but at least the memories were there, unlike those of her dad, who'd died when she was just a baby. Growing up in care hadn't been easy. In fact, it had been horrid from day one. Not because she'd suffered abuse, but purely because she felt like she didn't belong anywhere. The feeling of displacement had been deep rooted the second she stepped through the doors of her first foster family's home.

Danica sighed and placed the fresh bunch of flowers in the integral vase on the headstone. She had no idea if Georgia had ever liked lilies, but those were the ones Danica chose every week, since she was thirteen and old enough to venture out by herself to buy the flowers. Her ritual was the same each time – purchasing the lilies before walking to the cemetery to visit her dead mum's grave. It was something no one knew about. Not even Ricky. She wanted this moment just for herself.

Her phone buzzed in her pocket and she pulled it out to see a text from her fiancé.

> We still good for dinner tonight? I'd like to discuss wedding plans. R

She stared blankly at the screen for a moment and then smiled. Yes, there were definitely things that needed to be discussed. Plenty, in fact. Teigan was one of those subjects. The strained relationship between her and Danica was going to make things difficult if it wasn't dealt with properly.

She typed out a reply, telling Ricky that she would meet him at their favourite restaurant at the agreed time and slipped her phone back into her pocket.

Danica stared down at her mum's name once more and pulled her lips into a thin line, thinking about how awful her death had been. A sudden death after a short illness was what she'd been told as a child. Something a six-year-old should never need to go through.

'Bye mum,' Danica whispered. 'I've got lots to do and I want to tell you all about it. I'll be back soon.'

She kissed the tips of her fingers, then gently rested them on top of the stone for a few seconds before leaving the cemetery and heading back to her husband-to-be.

Chapter Seventeen

'Good afternoon, Mr Fyfe.'

Ricky stood by the front door of the crematorium and stared towards the door that led downstairs to the mortuary. The last place he'd ever seen his brother alive. And the place Ricky had cremated him. Closing his eyes, he tried to forget that day. It was his one and only regret in life. Brothers stick together but instead Chris had confessed to the ultimate betrayal. In turn, Ricky had killed him.

'Mr Fyfe? Is everything okay?'

Ricky turned, the voice bringing him back from his very real nightmare. He looked at Tim Crawford, owner of the crematorium and funeral home and friend to Ricky. More than a friend, a confidant, someone Ricky trusted more than anyone else in the business. Tim knew how to keep a secret; after all, he knew a lot about Ricky and hadn't uttered a word for all these years.

'Yes, Tim,' Ricky smiled, 'I'm fine, thank you.'

'You seemed very far away,' Tim replied, sounding unconvinced.

Yeah, Ricky thought, *twenty-seven years in the past.*

'It's Chris's anniversary,' Ricky said, and he felt the air turn ice cold. 'Elle's too, obviously.'

Tim knew everything about that time, including the fact that Chris was Teigan's biological father, and not to mention that he'd been involved in the clean up after Ricky had put a bullet in his brother's chest. Tim was paid handsomely to keep things quiet about it all. He'd have trusted him with the information without payment, but a lump sum secured his knowledge even more. Tim had done his job well. No police came knocking, no one asked questions. Tim ran Crawford Funeral Care without any issues, and that made Ricky's life so much easier. Having a funeral director on a cash-only payroll was very handy in his line of work. The fact they'd become friends was just an added bonus.

'Ah, yes,' Tim replied in such a professional tone, it almost made Ricky feel better. There was something about Tim that calmed Ricky. His voice was smooth, made him feel relaxed even in the worst situations. 'Such a sad set of circumstances. Can I get you anything? Tea, coffee? Something stronger?'

'No, thank you, Tim, I'm going to go downstairs for a bit. Gather my thoughts, if you don't mind.'

Tim nodded and gestured for Ricky to go where he pleased in his own time. Ricky liked Tim a lot. There was never any judgement from him.

Unlocking the door to the mortuary, Ricky headed downstairs and switched on the lights. The low hum of electricity above him was a comfort as he took slow, steady steps across the floor of the room that held, most likely, several dead bodies in the fridges. The cremation chambers were off. No one was being turned to ash today.

Ricky stopped, the click of his shoes on the floor echoing a second longer. He stared at the storage lockers, number nine in particular. He was still, his breathing steady.

'It's been twenty-seven years,' he whispered. 'That's a long time.'

Ricky moved closer and found himself standing in front of the locker and remembering how Chris helped him get rid of Jordan Burns. Remembering how Chris kept his darkest secret until the very end, speaking the words no one should ever hear from his own brother on his last breath.

Ricky pulled a small key from his pocket and opened the door. He stared at the bag inside, which contained Elle's dress. And Jordan's wedding ring.

He knew he should feel guilty. The man had died for no reason. But at the time, Ricky didn't know that Jordan was innocent. He had a legitimate reason for killing the man. He'd genuinely believed him to be Teigan's biological father. Elle had been friends with Jordan for years. Guys are not friends with girls without expecting benefits. And they'd always been close. Too close for Ricky's liking. But he'd been wrong.

Pulling the bag out from the locker, he stared down at the bloodied dress and the wedding ring. The evidence he'd created in case Elle ever threatened to leave. Evidence he'd never needed to use.

And yet, even now, he still couldn't bring himself to dispose of it. Having it in his possession, even after all these years, still made him feel validated for what he'd done. He'd had good reason at the time to get rid of Jordan. And it wasn't as if he'd wanted the ring as a trophy. That was the sort of thing psychopaths did – Ricky *wasn't* a nut job. The wedding ring would have been a way to identify Jordan's body if it was ever found. Ricky, however, had made sure that would never happen. But that ring had to be taken from Jordan as an extra precaution.

Closing his eyes, the faces of the ghosts from his past came flooding into his mind, and he quickly opened them again. He slipped the bag back into the locker, closed the door and slid the key back into his pocket.

Chapter Eighteen

Danica sat on Ricky's office chair and rested her bare feet on the desk. Having just come back from her visit to the cemetery, her emotions were at their height. Danica was very good at hiding how she really felt, even if she was on the brink of tears; a skill she'd acquired over years of living in the system after she'd become an orphan.

'Get your feet off my desk.' Ricky smiled up at her from the maroon Chesterfield against the opposite wall.

'I'm comfy,' she teased. 'Unlike how you must be feeling sitting on that *shit show* of a sofa.'

'Oi,' Ricky laughed. 'This is a belter of a sofa.'

Danica pulled a face. 'It looks wet. And ugly. Like an ugly duckling. It doesn't even go with anything in here.'

Ricky rolled his eyes and glanced down at his phone, concern etched on his face.

'You're still thinking about who's selling on your patch?'

Ricky shook his head. 'It'll just be some wee ned who doesn't realise there's someone bigger he'll eventually have to deal with.'

Danica eyed him from behind the desk. She knew that wasn't how Ricky truly felt. He'd be furious that someone was trying to push their way in. It would distract him from everything else going on.

'So, the wedding?' Danica said, changing the subject.

'Aye, what about it?' he asked, without looking up.

'Do you want to wear a kilt or suit?'

'Kilt, obviously.'

Danica smiled. 'Good answer. And don't be bothering with boxers. I want easy access after the ceremony.'

Ricky let out a loud laugh and it seemed to ease his tension because his shoulders relaxed a little.

'And the venue,' Danica continued. 'I've booked The Art House in the city centre.'

'Hmm,' Ricky said, tapping away on his phone. 'That's a good one.'

'Yeah, it's stunning. And they completely close it off to the public for the entire day, so we have the whole place to ourselves. We get married in the main hall upstairs and then the dinner is in the art hall before the evening reception, which takes place in the Gold Room.'

Ricky raised his eyes and looked at her expectantly. 'You're within budget?'

'Of course, I am. I'm not a gold digger, regardless of what your daughter thinks about me.'

'And all this is happening when?' Ricky asked.

'Well, I took the liberty of going through your diary to check your availability and one date stuck out to me so I went ahead and booked everything. So...' Danica stood up and extended her arms as though she was about to welcome in a celebrity. 'We get married in two weeks. Saturday the ninth of March at two in the afternoon.'

Ricky stood up quicky and glared at her. 'You booked our wedding day for the ninth of March?'

Danica frowned. 'What's wrong with that day?'

Ricky looked down at the floor and took a deep breath. 'That's Teigan's mum's birthday.'

Danica widened her eyes in shock. 'Oh *shit*. I didn't know. I can change it.'

Ricky waved a hand. 'No. You'll lose out on deposits with it being so soon.'

'We can't get married on that day, Ricky. Teigan might think I'm a bitch but if we do this, she'll never come around to the idea of us. And she might fall out with you over it. I don't want *that* on my conscience.'

Ricky was quiet again, as though he was thinking things through. She stared at him, eagerly waiting for what he would say next.

'I'll talk to her. If I'm honest, it'll be a good thing to have something else to think about on that particular day in the future,' Ricky said. 'And it's not like we've ever celebrated that day, you know? I mean, I've always made a fuss of Teegs on that day, but never actually marked the day as Elle's birthday.'

'Are you really sure about this, Ricky? I don't want our day tainted by this.'

Ricky nodded, got to his feet and moved towards her. He kissed her on the head and smiled. 'Keep planning. I'll talk to Teegs.'

She tried to read his expression. Was he sad? Annoyed? It was hard to tell. She didn't know for sure how he truly felt about his ex-wife.

'And you've picked your wedding dress?' Ricky said, bringing her out from her thoughts. 'You're wearing white?' he teased.

Danica forced a smile. 'I *am* wearing white. And no, I haven't picked it yet. That's next on my list. Along with a bridesmaid's dress.'

'Who is your bridesmaid, by the way?' Ricky asked, sitting back down on the Chesterfield sofa as though nothing had happened.

'I haven't picked one yet,' Danica said, running through the minimal options in her head. Yes, she had friends. But were they true friends, people she could confide in, who'd known her throughout all the hardship she'd gone through in life? She wouldn't have said so. Emma and the other girls were just social acquaintances, people she went on a night out with. They knew nothing about her life, nothing of importance at least.

Ricky nodded. 'What about Teigan?'

Danica laughed harder than she intended. 'That would go down like a lead balloon.'

'I don't think so. I think she'd say yes.'

'Aye, only to please you. No, I'll ask one of the girls. Emma, probably. Why don't you have Teigan as your best man?'

'You mean since my brother isn't around to do the honours?' Ricky scoffed and then he fell quiet again and Danica closed her eyes momentarily, knowing that her mention of a best man had brought back some bad memories.

'Shit, sorry. You know what? I think I'm just going to shut my mouth and get on with things before I say anything else that's going to upset you.'

'No, it's fine. It's not your fault my wife and brother ran off together before you were even born.'

Danica puffed out her cheeks and sighed loudly. 'That wasn't something anyone should have to go through. Ever. I'm sorry you did.' She reached over and gave his hand a squeeze.

'Let's not talk about this again,' Ricky said. 'Neither of them deserves my head space, especially not now.'

'Okay,' Danica replied almost in a whisper. 'Right then, I suppose I'll get back to it.'

'Just one thing,' Ricky said before Danica went back to the laptop in front of her. 'Make the wedding cake a sponge, eh? None of that fruit shite.'

Danica smiled. 'Fine by me.'

Ricky began tapping away on his phone and then said, 'I need to go.'

'Yep, do what you have to do. I'll stay here and keep planning.'

She looked up, waiting for him to kiss her goodbye, and saw him standing at the door, holding it open, his eyes on her expectantly.

'What?' she frowned.

'I need to lock up.'

'The office in your *house* needs locking up?' she asked sarcastically.

He nodded without saying a word and she knew that he wasn't going to leave her alone in there. He didn't let *anyone* in the home office without his presence. Was that a trust issue, or just the way of it? Come to think of it, Danica had never even seen Teigan in there without Ricky.

'Where are you hiding the bodies? Under that ugly sofa?' Danica laughed.

'Too many skeletons to fit under that thing.' He winked, and Danica stood up, knowing fine well there was no point in arguing. Ricky was very protective of his private space and she had to respect that.

'Fine. I'll go to Starbucks and plan from there. Unless you're going to make me take the price of the coffee out of the wedding budget?' she teased.

She felt Ricky's hand playfully tap her behind as she brushed past him out of the office and onto the landing, watching as he carefully locked the door.

'Right,' Danica said, reaching up and kissing him. 'I'll be a few hours. Might even pop into the florist on the way back to get an idea of centrepieces and bouquets.'

Ricky nodded sarcastically as they headed downstairs to the large, circular entrance hallway of the house. Danica slipped her shoes on and slid the laptop into her Chanel bag before heading out the door. She unlocked the Mercedes GLC that sat in the centre of the black resin driveway and opened the passenger door before placing the bag on the seat.

'Don't kerb the alloys,' Ricky warned.

'Oi,' she turned. 'I'm a better driver than you.'

'No one's a good driver in a brand-new Merc,' Ricky smiled. 'I mean it, drive that thing like you've got the queen in the back.'

'News flash, Ricky. Lizzy died in twenty twenty-two.'

'The fucking king then,' he scoffed. 'I mean it. That thing is only a week old. I'll see you later.'

She waved him off as he drove down the half-mile-long private road in his Audi Q7 and disappeared out of sight.

Chapter Nineteen

Pulling into the designated space outside her building, Teigan looked up at her flat and was so glad to be home, yet she knew the hard work with the Frank Cranwell deal hadn't even got started yet. Teigan had done her bit; she'd secured the deal and a good one at that. She hoped that her dad would see how good she was at her job, and he'd understand that once he was gone, she'd be able to take over.

The one worry Teigan had was that Ricky may be so blinded by love that he would want Danica to take the reins one day. Teigan didn't trust Danica, not one bit, and she never had. Back in their school days, Danica was the biggest bitch Teigan could ever imagine – the typical school bully and the type of person now that Teigan would usually avoid. Danica loved putting people down back then and had tried it with Teigan, time and time again.

Everyone knew Teigan and who she was, and who her dad was. She didn't want to bring attention to herself, but Danica either didn't know or didn't care. She pushed and pushed with her bitchy comments, teasing her about her hair, her shoes. Not that there was ever anything wrong with how Teigan looked. Danica was nothing more than a bully and Teigan had seen her do this to multiple people in her school years. One day, Teigan snapped. Danica hadn't factored in how brutal Teigan could be if she was backed into a corner; she supposed no bully ever took into account that they could pick on the wrong person. One hard slap across the face and the threat of another in front of her cronies, who'd never once attempted to provoke Teigan, had been enough to deter Danica from bothering her again. It was like the girl thought she was invincible. She found it strange that no one told Danica about who Teigan's dad was and actually, in that instant, Teigan hadn't needed the backing of her name. She'd dealt with her all on her own, like she'd always been capable of.

Then, seven years later, Danica sauntered back into Teigan's life on her dad's arm. She'd been all over Teigan, expressing fake excitement that she couldn't believe Ricky was Teigan's dad. Teigan had shut it down immediately, telling Danica to stay clear; she didn't want a bully or a bitch to be part of her life. Ricky had managed to cool things down, but Teigan made it clear from the outset that she wasn't happy. Teigan was certain it would never last. Her dad's head had been turned by a young woman and he'd been flattered. She'd been blatantly open about how ridiculous the relationship looked from the outside. How Danica being with Ricky screamed gold digger. Teigan had gone one step lower and said that she understood why Danica would want someone like Ricky based on her upbringing. Danica had tried to make amends, apologise for her behaviour back in their school days – blamed it on her difficult life growing up – but Teigan was having none of it. Especially not when she faced the prospect of this bitch being in her dad's life for the foreseeable. Danica continued to offer her apologies, but it didn't get through. Finally, the two were at loggerheads and Ricky had sat them down, said that he wanted to try to get them to make peace. He loved them both and he couldn't live with one and not the other. Finally, Teigan agreed to be civil but it wasn't without difficulty.

Now, the bitch was marrying him. Teigan couldn't get her head around it at all. Why couldn't Ricky see what was so glaringly obvious, that Danica was in the relationship for the money.

Getting out of the car, she moved around to the boot and pulled the small, black case out. Darren got out and walked around to the back of the car to stand by her. He offered his hand to take the case from her but she shook her head.

'Oh yeah, you don't do the whole traditional thing, do you? A man taking your case for you? No chance.' Darren smiled.

'You can't even manage your own half the time,' Teigan teased back as she pulled his out for him and closed the boot.

He'd never admit it, but she knew it was one of the things Darren loved about Teigan, that she wasn't a traditionalist. She wasn't one for allowing men to hold doors open for her, carry her bags or refer to her as Miss or Madam. It always made him smile when he tried to be gentlemanly, and she told him to fuck off with a sly smile on her face.

They reached Teigan's flat and she opened the door. The place smelled like home. It was always something she looked forward to. The smell of success and the fact that she had the ability to stand on her own two feet. She didn't live off Daddy's money. She earned her own, even though it was through her dad's business. But one day, that business would be hers and if she worked hard now, she would reap the benefits of it later in life. She'd just have to make sure Danica didn't see a penny of it.

'Shove the kettle on, Darren,' she said, kicking her boots off and relishing the feeling of the soft plush carpet beneath her feet. She made her way through to the lounge and sat down on the seat by the window. She stared out at Anniesland station and watched as the train approached the platform. Teigan had become so used to the sound that she barely heard it anymore.

'Tea or coffee?' Darren asked and she didn't take her eye off the train.

'Coffee, two scoops please. I'm going to need it,' she replied.

'I always thought a gangster would throw a shot of whisky in there,' Darren said.

'Don't call me that.'

Darren shrugged as she glanced up at him. 'Okay, then. How's apprentice gangster?'

She raised a brow. 'Just make the bloody coffee.'

People poured on and off the train, and she watched them, homing in on one person in particular. A woman, around the same age as Teigan. She wondered what her life was like. Was it simple? Carefree? Or did she have the weight of the world on her shoulders, while she went about her day like everyone else? A bit like herself, she supposed.

'You're thinking about her again, aren't you?' Darren asked, setting the coffee mug down on the side table next to Teigan.

'Who?' she said, picking up the mug and blowing onto the steaming hot liquid before taking a sip.

'Your mum.'

Teigan sighed loudly. 'Well, I wasn't, but I am now, so thanks for that.'

Darren pulled his lips into a thin line but didn't respond.

'I was actually thinking about this bloody wedding. I don't know if I can attend.'

'You can't *not* go.'

'But how can I stand there and watch my dad marry Danica when I don't agree with their relationship?' she asked, sipping the coffee and keeping her eye on the train.

'You *have* to go to your dad's wedding. How would it look if you didn't? It would cause problems.'

Teigan shrugged. 'Maybe that's not such a bad thing. Maybe if I don't go, he won't go through with the marriage.'

'But he *wants* to marry Danica. Do you want to hurt him like that? You're both so close, it could really drive a wedge between you. Do you want that?'

'Since when did you become a bloody counsellor?' Teigan scoffed, but she knew that Darren was right. It could cause problems and perhaps not for his relationship with Danica. It could push him closer to her rather than the other way. And if that happened, Teigan could lose everything. It was bad enough that her family was already so small. No mum. No extended family. The only family she had was her dad.

'You know I'm right,' Darren said softly, still standing over her.

The train started to move out of the station and the hum of the electricity on the line above it reverberated in her chest. She wondered if anyone else felt it.

'I just wish I had other family members to be able to tell me if I'm being a brat or just over-protective. I mean, it's no secret that my mum and my uncle left together, or at least that's what my dad thinks happened. I mean, it makes sense. What other explanation is there?'

Darren shrugged. 'Have you ever tried to look them up on social media?'

Teigan shook her head. 'A couple of times, but nothing showed up. If they ran off together, I suppose they'd want to stay hidden from my dad. But from me? Doesn't she wonder about me? Doesn't she want to know how I am?' She stopped, sighing at the realisation of why Elle had never tried to contact her. 'I suppose not, considering she left me when I was a newborn. If she didn't give a shit back then, she really won't give a shit now. And Danica doesn't even have a family. So, who the hell is even going to be at this wedding? Them, us and who? Business associates? How *very* special.'

'That's a lot of thoughts for someone who wasn't thinking about their mum,' Darren replied.

'I wasn't, not really. I suppose I just have those thoughts all the time. I was more worried about my dad getting married to that little gold digger.'

'You disapprove?' Darren asked sarcastically.

Teigan rolled her eyes. 'Danica is in this for the money.'

'I think even the dead folk up at the cemetery know you think that – you've not exactly been quiet about it. I can understand why you think it and, in all honesty, I do too. But it's up to him to make sure she doesn't get her claws into his cash. He's a clever man, Teigan. He's not going to let a woman take advantage of him. And they have been together for four years. It's not like she's just woken up in his bed after a one-night thing and they're walking down the aisle. If your dad didn't trust her, she certainly wouldn't have a ring on her finger.'

Silence fell between them and Teigan watched as the train disappeared along the track, leaving the station empty. Was that how Ricky felt and why he was marrying Danica? He'd been unable to hold down a relationship for several years; Teigan remembered them all. They'd all seemed nice. Maybe *too* nice, too soft for Ricky. No one stuck around. But Danica seemed different. She was fiery. Determined. And Darren was right, they'd been together for four years. That was staying power if nothing else. Maybe she was the challenge he needed.

'I need to talk to him.'

'Maybe it's not him you need to talk to?' Darren suggested.

'Yeah,' Teigan replied. 'I think you're right.'

Pulling her phone from her pocket, Teigan searched for Danica's number and hit call.

'Hi. It's Teigan. Can we meet? I want to talk to you about my dad.'

Chapter Twenty

Danica kept an eye on the coffee shop door as she attempted a first draft of a seating plan while awaiting Teigan's arrival. The meeting wasn't going to be an easy one, and she knew fine well that Teigan was going to do and say everything she could to change Danica's mind about marrying Ricky. Did Teigan know the date of the wedding yet? Maybe Ricky was leaving that revelation to Danica. Another reason for Teigan to hate her – not that it took much.

She noticed Teigan's car pull up outside the coffee shop and her heart lurched a little. She strode through the door towards her. She didn't look much like her dad. Perhaps she looked more like her mum.

Danica couldn't miss the large diamond on Teigan's ring finger, and it sent her back to that time at school when Teigan had slapped her so hard she'd almost been knocked off her feet. She'd been wearing a ring that day too, although not the diamond she sported now. It was a memory Danica wished she could wipe; it wasn't her finest moment.

'Hi.' Danica smiled up at Teigan sweetly.

Teigan pulled her lips into a thin smile but there was nothing friendly about it. She sat down opposite Danica and placed her bag on the floor.

'Do you want anything?' Danica asked.

'No, I'm fine thanks. I'll just get right into it,' Teigan said, flicking her long, brown hair over her shoulder and looking Danica dead in the eye. 'I don't think you should be marrying my dad.'

Danica's eyes widened and she let out a humourless laugh.

'Wow, straight to the point.'

'Yeah, sorry for being so blunt. What I meant was, well…' Teigan stopped, as though she was thinking about what to say next, or how to say it. 'Do you think getting married is a good idea?'

Danica narrowed her eyes and stared at Teigan with scrutiny. 'A good idea for who? For me and Ricky, yes. Yes, I do.'

Teigan bit her bottom lip. 'I beg to differ.'

'And why is that?'

'I don't think you're right for each other,' Teigan said.

Danica sat back on her seat and watched as Teigan fiddled with her diamond ring. 'After four years, you're only coming to this conclusion now?'

Teigan shook her head and sighed. 'Well, I didn't think it would go this far, if I'm honest. He's my dad, right? So, I'm not going to go into detail, but he's had women before you, Danica. A lot of women. And they've never resulted in more than a bed partner and someone to be on his arm during lavish events.'

Danica couldn't help but laugh. 'Casual flings don't last four years, Teigan. I'm more than that to Ricky and you know fine well that's the case.'

Teigan closed her eyes briefly and when she opened them again, she was staring straight at Danica.

'He's closing in on sixty, Danica. He has a daughter the same age as you. If you're thinking of expanding your family, then you might want to give that some thought. Do you think a businessman of my dad's standing is going to want to have a baby again? And that's not to mention his age. He's already done that once, and it wasn't easy.'

The words were on the tip of Danica's tongue, and she knew she shouldn't say it, but she just couldn't help herself. 'Yeah, well, the mother of our kids would stick around this time. And not that it's *any* of your business, but kids aren't exactly in our plans as soon as we get married. I think he made that mistake once before, didn't he?'

Teigan's eyes grew darker by the second, her jaw tensed. For a moment, Danica wondered if Teigan was going to launch herself across the table and attack her. With a ring that size, the slap would leave a black eye the size of Mount Everest.

Instead of getting angry, Teigan leaned back in her seat, composed herself and said, 'Like I said before, he's nearly sixty, Danica. You're the *same age* as me – his daughter. What's that about?'

'What's that *about*?' Danica repeated. 'It's about me being in love with a guy and saying yes to a proposal. I genuinely don't give a shit what age he is, if I'm honest.'

Teigan narrowed her eyes and her brow furrowed so hard that deep lines appeared. 'I don't believe you. I think you saw pound signs and knew you'd be able to make some money out of the marriage because you came from care and have grown up with fuck all.'

Danica scoffed loudly and noticed that a couple two tables away were watching them out of the corner of their eye. She straightened her back and lowered her voice. 'And there it is, the reality about how you feel. You came in here trying to be all nicey nicey, trying to appeal to my good side. Didn't take long for the real you to come out. And thanks for that lovely observation about my life, which by the way, you know nothing about. But I'll let you off on that one. And just so you know, you're wrong about me.'

'Am I?' Teigan pressed, her jaw still tense. 'Doesn't it feel weird that you're marrying someone old enough to be your dad?'

'Not at all.'

Teigan leaned forward and tapped her long, manicured nails on the surface of the table. 'Ah, is that what this is about? Are you marrying him because you grew up *without* one? Is this some sick, sugar daddy fetish to fill in the gaps from your childhood?'

Danica closed her eyes briefly as her fingers twitched to the empty mug in front of her. She wanted to smash it across Teigan's face. How dare she say such horrid things about a situation she knew nothing about. Teigan had no idea how lucky she was to have a dad all her life and she was mocking someone for not having that experience.

She glanced down at the mug beside her hand, imagined how satisfying it would be to use it to shut Teigan up. Instead, she composed herself and said, 'The words that just came out of your mouth show the type of person you are, Teigan. Jealous and cruel, among other things.'

Teigan raised a brow but said nothing.

'And no, my relationship with Ricky is not a fetish. But I'm sure you don't want me going into detail about that kind of thing when it comes to *me* bedding *your* dad.'

Danica noted the fury in Teigan's eyes. Her cheeks flushed with anger.

'You're an arsehole, Danica.'

'Takes one to know one, Teigan.'

'I know you're only in this for the money. And I won't have you take the piss out of him. Or me. You won't have any access to our business or funds. I'll make him get an agreement to secure it all so that you won't get a penny.'

Danica was nodding slowly. 'Ah, the prenup. Happy to sign one, Teigan. Never doubted it would crop up.'

She wasn't lying. Danica knew that a prenuptial agreement was something that Ricky would probably put on the table. 'On that note,' Danica continued, 'we've secured a date to get married, Teigan. So, if you don't like the idea of me and your dad being together, that really is a *you* problem.'

Teigan stared right through Danica, her eyes darker than she'd ever seen them.

'And when is this *wedding* happening?'

Here goes, Danica thought, preparing herself for the explosion. 'Saturday the ninth of March at two in the afternoon.'

Silence fell between them and Teigan's mouth was agape.

'Are you fucking kidding?'

'Our wedding isn't a joke, so no. I'm not kidding.'

'You do know what that day is, don't you?' Teigan said and Danica saw Teigan bare her teeth.

'I didn't, at first. But when I revealed it to Ricky, he said it would be a good idea to go ahead because it would mean we'd have something good to think about on that day in the future, instead of... well, you know?'

Teigan blinked. 'Wow. Just... wow.'

Danica frowned. 'What?'

'You really haven't changed at all, have you? You're still the same cold-hearted bitch that you were back in the day. Care really fucked you up.'

'Your dad doesn't seem to think so,' Danica replied, and she couldn't keep the smile off her face.

Teigan got up so suddenly her chair fell backwards and the sound of it hitting the floor made Danica jump. She placed both hands down on the table and leaned forward.

'He'll see it one day. Just trust me on this, Danica. You step out of line, you hurt him, you try to screw him over or even consider getting involved in the family business, I'll slap you a lot harder than the last time and this time, you won't get back up.'

'I'm not sure your dad would approve,' Danica replied. 'Oh, and just so you know, I would get back up and put you on your fucking arse. You don't get to speak to me about my personal life this way and get away with it. Hopefully, it doesn't come to that for Ricky's sake. It would hurt him a lot to have to choose between us. And he'd choose me, Teigan. We both know that.'

'Aye, we'll see about that,' Teigan sneered, turning her back and leaving the table, but not before swiping the wedding notebook and empty mug and plate, letting them fall to the tiled floor with a smash. Danica watched her go, a little triumphant that she'd pushed her buttons. Good. Who did she think she was to say the things she'd said?

'Nasty bitch,' Danica whispered as she leaned down and picked up the notebook.

'Are you okay?' a voice interrupted her thoughts.

Danica turned to see a woman to her right with a concerned look on her face.

'I'm fine, thanks. Just a misunderstanding.'

The woman looked worried, and Danica smiled to reassure her, before pulling her eyes away and noticing Teigan's car pulling out of the car park.

Danica decided to help clear up the broken mug and plate before heading out to her own car.

Chapter Twenty-One

'I can't believe her, Darren,' Teigan said through gritted teeth as he picked up the call. She replayed her encounter with Danica in her head and the fury only intensified. 'She's a fucking gold digger and it's so obvious. I don't know how my dad doesn't see it. She's going to get her manky little fingers on my dad's money if he doesn't make her sign one of those prenups.'

Teigan gripped the steering wheel so tightly her knuckles hurt. 'You should have seen the smug look on her face. Honestly Darren, if we weren't in public I'd have ripped her mouth off instead of swiping the stuff off the table.'

'Take a breath,' Darren said. 'Getting yourself all worked up isn't going to change it.'

'I just can't believe she would do this. Booking the wedding on my mum's birthday. It's like she's doing it to try to hurt me. What's worse is she said my dad *agreed* to it.'

There was a pause, as if Darren was hesitant about how to respond. And then he said, 'Did she know it was your mum's birthday? I mean, I can't imagine she would. Ricky probably doesn't speak about your mum to his fiancée. And maybe agreeing to the date is his way of moving on after she left you both? Maybe now, that day won't bring such bad memories anymore?'

'Nah,' Teigan said. 'Danica has him wrapped around her finger. He'll do whatever the fuck she wants. He's being fucking brainwashed by her.'

'Talk to him,' Darren said, slowly this time. 'Tell him what you're thinking, how you're feeling about it all. He will understand. He's your dad.'

Teigan sighed loudly, feeling tears prick her eyes. She'd always been close with her dad and she'd never known if it was because of the absence of a mother figure, or if that was just how it was. Either way,

Teigan was furious about the way Danica was pushing herself between them. The disrespect on Danica's part for having the wedding on a day that was a sore spot for both Ricky and Teigan was on another level.

'Jesus, she had three hundred and sixty-four other days in the year to choose and she picked that one. She said she didn't know at first, but I don't believe her.'

Darren was quiet, allowing her to rant until she felt ready to stop. Was Danica that much of a bitch that she would do something like that on purpose? Why would she want to hurt Teigan that much? Surely not because of what happened between them at school all those years ago? But what else would be the reason?

'I'm going to talk to Dad. He needs to see what a manipulative little bitch she is.'

'Best not to word it that way, otherwise you'll end up sounding like the manipulative one.'

Teigan gritted her teeth. Why did Darren always have to be right?

–

Teigan pulled into the driveway at her dad's house and stepped out of the car. She knew he was home because she'd already been to the club and he wasn't there.

As she was walking up to the door, ready to ring the bell, the door opened and Ricky was standing there with a smile on his face.

'Hello,' he said, opening his arms and pulling her in, hugging her tight. 'How are you?'

He released her and Teigan frowned. 'What are you looking so chipper about?' she asked.

'Come in, come in,' he said, the smile on his face widening.

Teigan stepped into the house and removed her shoes, a habit he'd instilled in her from as far back as she could remember. Don't dirty the floors or the carpets.

'I need to talk to you about Danica, about what we discussed today,' she said, eager to start the conversation.

'She's already told me,' he said.

'Oh, has she now?'

'I think it's *brilliant*. I didn't think you'd go for the idea, but I'm *so* glad you did,' he replied, cupping her face in his hands. His eyes sparkled and she saw something in them she rarely got to see. Happiness.

Teigan frowned, the confusion washing over her as he let go of her. 'What idea?'

'I mean, I was thinking of having you next to *me* on the day,' Ricky continued, seemingly not having heard Teigan's question. 'But seeing you coming down the aisle as a bridesmaid would be even better, don't you think? My two girls walking together on my wedding day – doesn't get much better than that.'

Teigan felt a twist of dread inside her. '*Bridesmaid?*'

Ricky parted his lips to speak but then, out of the corner of her eye, Danica appeared from the dining room in a robe with two champagne flutes in her hand. She strode across the wooden floor in her bare feet and handed one to Teigan.

'I just couldn't wait to tell him that you agreed to be my bridesmaid. Honestly, I feel like we've really turned a corner, you know?'

Ricky slid an arm around Danica's waist and his smile grew wider.

Teigan's throat had dried up so much that she couldn't speak. She just stood there, holding the champagne flute in her hand, trying not to show how angry and confused she was. Danica had made her look like an idiot and if she let her anger out now, that sparkle in her dad's eyes that rarely shone would disappear. And that would be down to Teigan.

'I know the wedding date is a bit controversial, Teegs. But what better way to get rid of bad memories than getting married on that day? Honestly, I couldn't be happier about the whole thing,' Ricky said. 'And like I said, seeing my two girls as they walk down the aisle one after the other…' His voice trailed off, like he was going to become emotional, and Teigan had to refrain from rolling her eyes. Danica really *did* have a grip on him.

Teigan stared at Danica in amazement. How did she know that Teigan wouldn't say anything? Likely because Ricky would take Danica's side regardless. As much as Teigan was close with her dad and always had been, she knew deep down that he'd fallen hard for Danica and he wasn't going to let anything spoil their happiness.

Painting on her biggest, fakest smile, Teigan raised her glass and clinked it against Danica's – a little harder than necessary – and said, 'Here's to the wedding.'

Ricky, blissfully ignorant or just a blind idiot, drank his champagne greedily as Teigan glared at Danica, who was grinning ear to ear. Teigan wanted to chuck champagne in her face and call her out for being a lying bitch but there was no point. It would only reflect badly on Teigan.

'I can't wait to buy you a bridesmaid's dress, Teigan,' Danica said. 'We'll need to arrange a shopping trip soon. The wedding isn't *that* far away, you know?'

Yes, she did fucking know. Not a year went by where that date didn't go unnoticed. As much as her dad had been hurt by what her mother had done, he'd always made sure he and Teigan did something on that day to mask over the horrible fact that her mother had left her. Not that she'd ever forgotten. When she was younger, it was ice skating, cinema trips. As she got older, it was simply a dinner in a restaurant. They never spoke much of her mother, but Teigan was always appreciative of the fact that her dad made an effort to make her feel better. She often spent that day silently wondering who her mother was, what kind of mother she might have been and where she was now? But Danica was right. The wedding date was literally weeks away. Teigan bit the inside of her bottom lip and inhaled slowly.

'Yep. Can't wait,' she replied sarcastically, although her dad didn't seem to notice.

'This is it.' Ricky glanced down at Danica, who still had that smug smile on her face. 'The real deal. We're getting married and we are going to spend the *rest* of our lives together. Cheers.'

He raised his glass, as did Danica, and they both looked expectantly at Teigan.

Clearly Danica had her claws sunk a little deeper into Ricky than Teigan had first imagined. Teigan had to hand it to Danica, but she'd played this very well. She'd managed to manipulate the whole situation for her own gain and Ricky was utterly blind to it.

Teigan glanced at her blissfully happy dad and for a moment, she wondered how he could be the boss of the Glasgow underworld: setting up major deals with other bosses and running the city with an iron fist, yet he had no clue what his new wife was truly capable of.

Raising her glass, Teigan forced a smile. 'Cheers.'

'Cheers to the wedding of the year,' Danica said as she raised her glass and clinked it against Teigan's. She glanced up at her husband-to-be and kissed him on the cheek. This was it. Her plan was working. Teigan, as much as she clearly despised Danica, would be bridesmaid. Ricky her husband. Then she'd *finally* be part of the family like she'd always wanted.

Chapter Twenty-Two

Parking the car behind the Rotherwood flats in Knightswood, Danica unlocked the doors and he got in quickly, his hoodie pulled up over his face, his cap barely revealing his eyes.

'*Very* inconspicuous, Aidan,' she said, staring at him.

'I can't exactly walk around with my head held high, can I? Your fiancé would hang me from the fucking lampposts if he found out I was still around.'

Danica rolled her eyes. 'Don't be so dramatic. He's not the bloody cartel, although he likes to think he is. Just calm down, will you. You were once the big-time operator of the whole thing.'

'Aye, and now I'm on the run. I can't access my money. I don't have my passport so I can't leave the country. When you're flying high, the fall is always greater,' he said, his entire body trembling. She almost felt sorry for him.

'Here,' Danica said, taking an envelope from her Michael Kors bag and thrusting it into his hands. 'There's two hundred in there. That should see you right for a week.'

Aidan shot her a look and pulled his hoodie down, revealing acne scars that could be seen a mile away. 'Two hundred? You told me Ricky wanted me to set the factory on fire because it was an insurance job. Then I find out you were bullshitting me and you're telling me everything I did was worth two hundred quid. What the fuck, Danica? You told me if I did all this for you, I'd get twenty grand and a new passport and then I'd get to walk away without the worry of Ricky or the polis coming after me.'

She stared out of the front windscreen. Aidan was flustered. Of course he was. In his situation she would be too. And if Ricky found out what she was doing, his own fiancée, then she too would suffer his wrath.

Setting fire to the factory had seemed like a good idea at the time. No factory meant no production and no production meant no income for Ricky. She'd genuinely thought that he'd start to suffer after the fire. But instead, he'd gone straight to Frank fucking Cranwell and started up a brand-new business deal. She'd had to resort to plan B, which was nowhere near as good as plan A, but that had gone to shit.

'And that will still be the case,' she replied. 'But I have another idea and if you pull it off then you'll get your twenty grand. I want you to inform the police about Fyfe activities.'

Aidan frowned and then his eyes widened. 'Are you on medication that sends you fucking loopy or something?'

'Not in the slightest. My head has never been clearer,' Danica replied, staring at him without blinking. It was true; her mind was the clearest it had ever been. Of course, she was putting herself in danger – what she was doing could result in her own death. But after what Ricky Fyfe had done, she couldn't stop now. Not until she'd done what she'd set out to do.

'Do I need to remind you that I'm on the run? The second I walk into a polis station, they'll not listen to a word I have to say. They'll put me in a cell and chuck the key down the drain. And when Fyfe associates on the inside get wind I'm locked up, I won't last five minutes. I should slice your fucking throat *right* now for even suggesting this,' Aidan said through gritted teeth. 'You've fucked me over.'

'And if you so much as breathe on me, I've made sure that Ricky knows exactly where to find you. If you walk away from me without following through on my instructions, I will make sure you don't get very far. The police will be the least of your worries.'

Aidan Doyle looked defeated, but she knew that he would do whatever she told him to because he didn't want to go to prison or end up at the bottom of the Clyde because Ricky got hold of him.

'There must be something else I can do that doesn't involve the polis?'

Danica stared out of the front window again and thought about it. Maybe he was right. If he did go to the police, he'd never see the light of day again. Without thinking it through, she said, 'Okay. You're going to deal for me instead.'

'Eh?'

'I'll deliver some of Ricky's gear to you, then you cut it with whatever crap is around to get the attention of the police, you deal it for me and then we tip off the police that Ricky is the supplier.'

'And how am I going to do that without someone clocking my face and grassing me up?'

'People who buy drugs don't grass up the dealer, Aidan. Come on, you're smarter than that.'

Aidan turned to look out of the window and shifted in his seat.

'You must know someone who's in need of some extra cash who would do the job to save you putting your face out there?'

Aidan turned back to face her. 'Aye, I know one guy.'

'Good. Get in touch with him, tell him the deal and that he'll get extra cash in hand if he does this.'

'Why can't you just leave me out of it. I'll give you the guy's name and he can do it all?' Aidan pressed.

'That's not how this is going to work, Aidan. You're the best in the business, Aidan. That's why Ricky hired you and why you're working for me now.'

Aidan sighed and closed his eyes. 'What's in it for me?'

'My initial offer of the money and a passport still stands. I can get that done on the sly. Ricky doesn't need to find out because there're plenty folk out there who do that sort of thing who aren't linked to my fiancé,' Danica replied steadily.

'I don't get any of this, Danica. Aren't you supposed to be *marrying* this guy? What's this all about? I don't want to get caught up in some domestic shit.'

Danica blinked and the images of what should have been her life played out in front of her like it was being projected onto a screen.

'You already are, Aidan.'

Aidan turned back to face her and narrowed his eyes. 'You really are determined to take him down, aren't you?'

'Yes,' she said bluntly and her mother's gravestone came to mind. She knew the inscription on it word for word, and she felt as though she was stood in front of it now.

Here lies Georgia Burns, died 2 April 2003.
A loving mother to Danica. Reunited in heaven with her
husband, Jordan.

She felt sick every time she thought about it. Aged six with two dead parents. No child should have to go through that and especially not because someone else had a hand in their deaths. Georgia died because of alcohol and poor mental health after the death of Jordan, Danica's dad. But Jordan Burns had been murdered by Ricky. And Danica had been left with unanswered questions, a childhood spent in foster homes, a social worker and insurmountable trauma.

Danica cleared her throat. 'All you have to do is follow my instructions. If you do, you get to walk away with your freedom like I said. And Ricky Fyfe will never come looking for you because by the time it's done, he'll be in prison, or dead. Hopefully the latter.'

She leaned over and pulled open the glove compartment before slipping her hand in and retrieving a small burner phone. She handed it to Aidan. 'Answer this when it rings. Only I have the number so you won't get a call from anyone else on it. And yes, I have one too. It's the best way to keep what we're doing quiet.'

'And what if I don't?' Aidan challenged.

Danica eyed the envelope she'd handed to him. 'You will. I'm your only road to a passport.'

Aidan lowered his eyes and his shoulders slumped. He was defeated.

'Like I said, keep that phone on you and when I call, listen carefully to my instructions. Do that, and you'll do well out of this.'

Danica started the engine and that was Aidan's cue to get out of the car.

'How do I know I can trust you?' Aidan asked as he stepped out of the car.

'You don't. Same way that I don't know if I can trust you. But I'm choosing to. You'd do well to do the same.'

Aidan closed the door and walked away. She watched him go and let out a shaky breath. That could have gone a very different way. But she was glad that it didn't.

Once Aidan was out of sight, Danica slipped her hand into her bag and pulled out a plastic wallet; one that had been given to her by her social worker, who'd been instructed to hand it to her when she turned eighteen. Apparently, no one knew what was inside. Danica's sixteenth birthday had been hard enough. No family or real friends to celebrate with. Instead, all she had was a plastic wallet. Hands shaking with anticipation as she'd opened it up and stared inside. What was in there that had to wait until she was eighteen? The fear of the unknown had been like a chokehold and it had taken a lot of strength to get through that first moment of opening it up to see what was inside.

Now, as she sat in the driver's seat of the car, which was worth tens of thousands of pounds and paid for by her soon-to-be husband, she flicked through the items for what felt like the millionth time. She'd gone over them all, time and time again. Mostly newspaper clippings following the trial of Ricky Fyfe in the case of Jordan Burns; missing, presumed dead. It had always struck Danica as strange that someone could be tried for killing someone when there was no body to prove that a murder had taken place. Yet, he *was* tried, and the verdict had come back as not proven. So, he walked free.

As Danica looked down at the clipping of the day Ricky walked out of court a free man, she stared into the face of her mother in the background, with Danica as a baby in her arms. She looked distraught, helpless. The image had always haunted her.

Unfolding the letter from her mum, which she'd read a million times over, she scanned the words once again, only this time, she wasn't reading, but mouthing the words from memory.

My dearest daughter, Danica,

If you're reading this, it's because you've been given the letter on your sixteenth birthday. I left instructions for whoever would care for you to give this to you when the time came.

First of all, happy birthday, my beautiful girl. I am so, so sorry that neither I nor your dad can be with you today. I always intended you to know every single detail about your life and how you came to be where you are today. I wanted to tell you in person, but I lost control. The bottle got me. You were too young to understand it all. I tried to get better for your sake. But in the end, I was useless to you.

In this wallet, you'll find newspaper clippings covering the trial of the man who murdered your dad when you were a baby. I want you to know that just because he walked free doesn't mean he is innocent. He did this, Danica. Your dad was killed by Ricky Fyfe and you deserve to know the truth.

We all used to be friends, believe it or not. Your dad's best friend, Elle, was married to Ricky. We all got on well, for a while. Before your dad and Ricky fell out. He was being abusive towards Elle and we tried to warn him off. But instead of backing off, he became worse and, in the end, your dad's friendship with Elle became distant. Then Ricky accused Elle and your dad of having an affair, which is utterly ludicrous. It would never have happened, and I had every faith in your dad that he would never hurt me like that, nor would he sabotage his long-term friendship with Elle. I believe that's why your dad is dead. I think Ricky killed him in a fit of rage because he truly believed they were having an affair.

I never saw Elle again, after your dad went missing. I reported his disappearance to the police, along with Ricky's claims that Jordan was having an affair with his wife, Elle, which wasn't true, Danica. I promise you that. He'd never have done that to me, to us. But it just wasn't enough. Elle had disappeared too. I think he killed her. She would never have left Teigan behind. Not willingly.

You're probably wondering why I'm telling you all this. You've probably moved on with your life. I hope so. I truly do. But I want you to know that your dad and I loved you more than life. Having you was the most amazing thing to happen to both of us. And Ricky Fyfe destroyed it all.

He doesn't deserve to be free, Danica. Not after what he did to us.

I hope you can live your life fully and with happiness. And I hope that you'll always have a piece of your dad and I with you.

I've left some things in the wallet that might be of comfort to you.

All my love and regret that I couldn't be better for you.

Your mum, Georgia Burns

It didn't matter how many times Danica read the letter, it still brought tears to her eyes. She'd never be desensitised to the words, or the truth behind them.

The wedding ring belonging to Georgia sat inside the wallet and she slipped it onto her finger. The date of their wedding was engraved on the inner side of the band with the initials G and J still clearly visible.

She flicked through the photographs inside too. One of which depicted the four of them, clearly before things turned sour. Elle and Ricky on one side of the image, Georgia and Jordan on the other. On the reverse side of the photo was a handwritten description.

Bride, groom, Elle – bridesmaid and Ricky – guest. Georgia and Jordan's wedding at Partick bowling club.

Danica sighed and shook her head. Things could have been so different. She could still have her parents. Danica and Teigan may even have grown up together. Been best friends, perhaps.

Slipping the items back into the wallet, Danica closed her eyes before tilting her head back and resting it against the leather headrest. She knew her mum never intended for Danica to carry out what she was doing. Or maybe she did. Maybe she wanted Danica to get the justice they all deserved because Georgia wasn't strong enough to do it alone back then. Either way, Danica was going to do what was right.

'I'll get them for you both,' she said quietly. 'I'll get the bastards that destroyed our family. I'm going to make sure that Ricky Fyfe pays for what he did to us. But before I do that, I'm going to become his wife, and take him for everything he fucking has.'

Chapter Twenty-Three

Still reeling from seeing her daughter in Frank's club, and hearing how she was very deep in Ricky's business world, Elle's mind was doing overtime. She couldn't get her daughter's face out of her head. That moment, where Teigan walked into the club for the first time, replaying again and again. The baby girl she'd left behind all those years ago, simply walked back into Elle's life and she had no idea. She'd only looked at Teigan for a few moments, but she could remember every detail about her, what she was wearing, how tall she was, her hair colour. Elle's heart ached.

After all these years, upon setting eyes on Teigan, her motherly instincts had well and truly kicked in and all Elle could think about was taking action. She needed to see Teigan again, she needed to know that she was okay, even if she was now an adult. But attempting any sort of contact was dangerous. She would be putting herself at risk of Ricky discovering that she was still alive. He could come after her and finish the job he started all those years ago. She'd even considered asking Frank for help, but knew that was just as risky. He was in a business deal with Ricky. There was every possibility that he'd put that before Elle. After all, Ricky had proven that his business was everything to him, so why would Frank be any different?

At a loss, there was only one way she could look into Teigan's life without Ricky stumbling across her and that was through the internet. Heading into her local library, Elle stood in the middle of the floor, surrounded by shelves filled with books. She felt out of place. She wasn't a reader – her mind was often occupied by other things, and there wasn't much space for reading fiction, or anything at all.

'Can I help you?' a woman asked from behind the desk just a few feet away.

Elle stared at her briefly. The woman was merely trying to be helpful. But the answers Elle needed certainly didn't lie with the library assistant. Like, what had happened to Chris? What had stopped him from bringing Teigan to her? It must have been awful. He must be dead. Had Ricky discovered their secret? Had he been killed due to the business Ricky ran with an iron fist? There was no other explanation.

The woman looked on at her expectantly and Elle realised she'd been silent for a few seconds too long. 'I'm looking to use one of your computers to access the internet,' she finally managed.

She waited for the woman to ask why she didn't have the latest smartphone, expecting judgement, but the woman simply smiled, got up from the desk and led Elle to a small cluster of tables at the back of the library.

'If you need any help with it, just let me know. The computers in here are a bit ancient, but they should get the job done,' the woman said with a smile, before leaving Elle alone.

She stared down at the computer and sighed. She had only ever used Frank's computer in the office to order cleaning supplies for the club and had steered clear of social media. Not just for the obvious reason, but also the fact that Elle had no friends, no one to keep in touch with. The only friend she'd ever had was dead.

She sat down in front of one of the desktops and opened up Google Chrome, the browser she was familiar with.

Heart pounding so fast she felt sick, Elle typed in *Ricky Fyfe Glasgow.* What showed up on the screen at first made her blood run cold.

November 1997

The man accused of the disappearance and murder of Jordan Burns has walked away from court a free man after the jury delivered a not proven verdict. Richard 'Ricky' Fyfe was accused of the disappearance and murder of Burns, after an altercation between the two. No witnesses came forward to testify in the case and today, Fyfe walked free. When approached for comment, Ricky Fyfe had nothing to say in regards to Jordan Burns's family, but did mention that he was looking forward to getting home to his own daughter. Fyfe had served four months in prison for the alleged crime.

Elle's eyes burned as she read the report over and over again. Shaking her head, she leaned forward and placed her head in her hands. How could she have let this happen? The night Ricky attacked her, he'd told her Jordan was dead. She'd always wanted him to be caught for it. But now, reading that report, knowing that he got away with it, how could she live with herself? How had she lived with herself all these years? Jordan Burns had been her best friend growing up and when she'd started seeing Ricky, the two had got on to start with, until Ricky's abuse started. Jordan had warned Elle against Ricky, but she'd been smitten and fallen fast for him. So fast that when she'd experienced the real Ricky Fyfe, it was far too late to get out.

And then came the accusation that Jordan Burns was Teigan's biological dad, right before Ricky had tried to kill her. It was utterly ridiculous. Jordan had been like a brother growing up. She and Georgia had their babies at the same time. Elle had always dreamed of the two of them growing closer and raising the girls together.

Ricky had said he'd set her up for Jordan's murder. He'd planted evidence. Now, twenty-seven years later, would that still be the case? Would he still try to pin Jordan's death on her after all this time? She recalled what he'd said – that Jordan's blood was on her dress. Not only that, but she'd also disappeared after Jordan was killed. Ricky could use that to make her look more like a suspect.

She felt the sudden urge to throw up and got up from her chair so quickly it nearly fell over. Turning, she glanced towards the reception desk and saw the sign for the bathroom to the right. Rushing past the desk, hoping she would make it in time, she pushed the door open and almost launched herself into a cubicle just as she started to retch.

Grabbing some toilet roll, she wiped her mouth and flushed the toilet before attempting to get up and sit on the seat.

Jordan was dead. He'd been murdered by Ricky. And it was her fault. If she hadn't been such a coward back then, she could have played a part in putting Ricky away. Then the memories of just how terrifying Ricky was came flooding back and she remembered that she wasn't a coward, but a victim. Like Jordan was. And most likely, Chris too.

Eyes flooding with tears, Elle took some deep breaths. She couldn't crumble. Not now. She had too many questions in her mind. Where was Jordan's body? What happened to Georgia and their daughter? And what in hell's name had Ricky Fyfe turned her daughter into? The shame of leaving her behind with a man like that hit her like a freight train and she couldn't believe she'd allowed him to do what he did.

Composing herself, Elle opened the cubicle door and washed her hands at the sink before returning to the computer and continuing her Google search of Ricky Fyfe.

Chapter Twenty-Four

One week had passed since Teigan's meeting with Frank Cranwell and now, Ricky was standing outside the back entrance of Fyfe Cabs while a fleet of brand-new taxis pulled up. Five in total.

He rubbed his hands together and nudged Teigan's arm with his elbow. 'You're a fucking genius for securing this deal, Teegs. I honestly couldn't be prouder that you've done this for the business.'

Teigan didn't reply, only smiled and kept her eye on the taxis as they each pulled into a space. The drivers all got out and approached Ricky and Teigan. One at a time, they each shook his hand and headed inside.

'That's some amount of gear we just had transported,' Teigan finally spoke as she turned to face him.

'Successfully, I'd say.'

She nodded. 'And very, *very* risky. Just because they arrived safely here in Glasgow, doesn't mean they've not been followed, or watched, or photographed.'

Ricky narrowed his eyes. 'Our arrangements were made very carefully. Both Frank and I vetted the drivers ourselves.'

'And what about that rogue dealer on your patch, Dad? What if he gets wind of this and snitches to the police?'

The concern in her voice was very clear and Ricky felt a sudden pang of apprehension himself. 'A little fucker like that won't want to do that because it would jeopardise his own income. And a grass would be punished far worse than a trespasser in my city. Anyone in our game knows that. Also, I've heard nothing since that shit Danica's pal had in my club. It's likely the wee guy's shat himself when he discovered whose turf he'd dealt on. I don't think it goes any deeper than that.'

Teigan pulled her lips into a thin line. 'I just think that we need to be extra vigilant. With the factory fire, Aidan Doyle on the run and now a lone dealer, even if you think it was a one-off, we can't be too careful. We can't trust anyone, and I mean *anyone*.'

Ricky raised a brow. 'If by *anyone*, you mean Danica, then I'd advise you to stop before you say something that's going to end in an argument. You've already agreed to be her bridesmaid. Let's not start up any animosity again when we've just got back on track. I know you two have never seen eye to eye. I haven't forgotten the shit between you both that happened years ago. I know you have bad history. But I can't help who I fall for, Teigan.'

He saw a flicker of distaste cross Teigan's face.

'She's not blood, Dad,' Teigan replied. 'Doesn't that worry you?'

Something twisted inside him then. Teigan wasn't blood either, not Ricky's anyway. Not that anyone alive knew that and he intended it to stay that way. In all other ways possible, Teigan *was* his daughter and always would be. She was all he'd had until he met Danica. Of course, there had been other women between Elle and Danica, but none of them could live up to what he needed. Elle certainly couldn't and he never wanted to make that mistake again. It had taken him a very, very long time to be able to trust anyone after what Elle had done. And Chris, his brother? They'd both committed the ultimate betrayal. As much as there were issues between his daughter and Danica, he loved and trusted his wife-to-be.

He wasn't stupid though; he was a wealthy businessman and there was a huge age gap between them. It was highly likely that Danica was first attracted to his money. But four years down the line, she'd proved that she loved him. She gave everything to him. She didn't judge his line of work, never passed comment. She merely stood by his side and accepted him for who he was. He'd never known a relationship like it, and he had no intention of giving that up. He'd make sure that Teigan and Danica settled their differences if it killed him.

'It doesn't worry me at all,' he replied. 'But she *is* going to be my wife. There can't be any animosity within our family or the firm. I know you don't think she deserves a seat at the table because she doesn't share our bloodline, and you have your issues with her, but I can't marry her and make her sit back and not involve her in my life, Teegs. And this business, everything I've ever built for us, is my life.'

'And how are you to know she's not just with you *for* your money?' Teigan asked and the question didn't take him by surprise. 'How do you know she's not just planning to bleed you dry once you marry her? You could lose everything you've ever worked for because you didn't have your guard up. You should get her to sign an agreement that states she gets nothing when you finally pass, which I'm hoping isn't for a very long time, of course.'

'*Enough*,' Ricky said, lowering his voice. 'This is my life, Teigan. I'm an adult and I make my own choices. I'm a businessman, a good one at that. You don't have to tell me what I should and shouldn't do to protect my assets. I don't appreciate you making out as though you think I'm thick.'

'I don't think you're thick, Dad – far from it. I just want you to be careful. I want you going into this with both eyes wide open. You're the only parent I have. I just don't want you to get hurt, that's all.'

'Don't you worry about me. I'll be fine,' he replied, trying to swallow down his frustration. It was nice that Teigan cared, but he knew what she was like. She had an ability to push too far. A little like her mother had.

Teigan stared at him blankly and rolled her eyes just slightly. 'Fine. It's your funeral.'

Ricky let out a snort and then said, 'Wedding, actually.'

Teigan smiled in response but he knew it was forced.

Ricky gave a nod, pushed back his shoulders and headed into the taxi office, with an anger burning inside him that he needed to keep hidden. He loved Teigan, and he loved Danica. It was typical that when he'd finally found real happiness, there was a heavy cloud of doubt hanging over it.

Chapter Twenty-Five

Danica rested against the highbacked chair at Ricky's desk in the home office and watched the screen in front of her. Copying the only key he held to the office had been one of Danica's best ideas. That way, she could watch what was going on at his various businesses through the web-linked CCTV he'd had set up. He'd paid for a top-of-the-range system that recorded not just footage, but sound too. Only the best for big time gangster Ricky Fyfe. He needed eyes and ears everywhere if he was going to be able to trust his employees.

So now she was sat back, a glass of wine in hand as she took in the scene in front of her. On the right-hand side of the screen, Ricky stood in his taxi office, Teigan by his side. He was giving instructions to several men, who she assumed were taxi drivers, or at least acting like they were. Danica wasn't stupid. Far from it. She knew they were drug dealers because she'd overheard a conversation between Ricky and Teigan about it all. As much as she knew about Ricky being a gangster and securing a new deal with Frank Cranwell, he didn't tell her much else. He trusted her, but it seemed that in business, he kept her at arm's length.

'Aye, Ricky,' Danica said in a low voice before taking a sip of wine. 'You think your good little fiancée doesn't have a clue what goes on in your business ventures. Thanks to your CCTV and lack of security on your computer, I know it all.'

She listened carefully as Ricky gave clear instructions about what was to happen with Frank Cranwell's drugs. If the first delivery sold well, the men would be paid well, and if that happened, it would mean long-term income for both the Fyfe firm and the men employed by Ricky.

Danica imagined her dad stood in front of Ricky all those years ago. She imagined how it all went down before her dad was killed. She'd considered the possibility of a hit man arranged by Ricky to kill Jordan, which could be why the jury had struggled to agree on a verdict. She'd wondered if it had been accidental, and Ricky had perhaps panicked. But then, knowing him the way she did now, and knowing that he had a violent and aggressive side to him – he had to in his line of work, according to Ricky – she knew that wasn't the case. First of all, Ricky wasn't the type to panic. Secondly, if he *was* the type to panic, or at least had a conscience and it had been an accident, surely Jordan's death would have eaten Ricky up years ago. The court case could have broken him if there was any sort of remorse there. And it seemed there wasn't. None whatsoever.

'Because you fucking murdered him,' she whispered at the screen.

Getting to her feet, Danica began pulling open drawers, peering inside at the organised files. The *legitimate*, organised files. Ricky wasn't going to have anything incriminating in a desk drawer that just anyone could access, door locked or not, wife-to-be or not.

She padded across the plush, grey carpet, feeling its velvety softness beneath her bare feet and headed to the other side of the room. As a businessman who claimed to be big on family, he really only had Teigan. Ricky had spoken vaguely of Chris, his older brother who Ricky had claimed did a bunk with his wife and left Teigan behind. He lived and breathed his businesses, and it was safe to say that he and Teigan were very close. It was a bond that Danica thought she might struggle to break. And if she didn't break it, that was fine. It would just be an added bonus if she did. What she was *certain* of was that she would break him. In every way she possibly could.

Danica stood in front of a picture on the back wall, taking in the image. A family portrait, she supposed. Ricky and Teigan, smiling widely and staring down the lens of the camera. It wasn't a professional photo; it was barely one Danica thought worthy of a frame, let alone blown up to the size that it was and displayed on the wall. Yet there Ricky was, standing in his kitchen in front of the sink, his arm round his daughter's shoulders and looking like the doting, trustworthy man anyone would count themselves lucky to be marrying.

Something about the photo made her skin prickle. Maybe it was because now, as she stared into the eyes of Ricky Fyfe, the man she was about to marry, she suddenly realised what she'd got herself into. This was one hell of a dangerous game, and she was four years deep. One that, if it went wrong, could see Danica end up dead too. How she'd managed to keep up the pretence for this long was impressive even to herself.

Biting her bottom lip, Danica took a step closer and raised her free hand, running her fingers over the glass that encased the photo. The frame moved, tilted on its hook. Danica placed her glass of wine on the table to her right and raised both hands to fix the frame back into place. But as she gripped the bottom corners, the frame came away from the wall and she was left holding it.

'Fuck's sake,' she muttered, lowering it to look at the hook. Maybe it had fallen out of the wall completely.

Glancing up at the wall, she was surprised to see a safe. Carefully placing the frame down on the carpet, she took a closer look. It wasn't a modern safe. There was no digital keypad or fingerprint recognition plate. It was a simple lock and key.

'And what do we have hiding in here?' Danica raised a brow. She knew it was likely cash that still needed cleaning. Or maybe something else? Evidence of her dad's murder?

Wishful thinking, she thought.

Staring at the safe, Danica wondered how she was going to get into it. Because she *would* get into it. Without any doubt, she would make sure she unravelled every single piece of information that could ruin Ricky. But not until after she'd married him, of course.

'Right,' Ricky's voice boomed out from the speakers on the computer, making Danica jump. 'Now that we all know what's what, it's time to get out there and get it done.'

Danica looked up at the picture hook on the wall and noticed that it was a little loose. She picked up the oval-shaped paperweight on top of the drinks table – why it was there and not on the desk, she had no clue – and gently tapped it against the hook until it seemed more secure. Then, she hung the picture back on the wall and found she could hardly look at Ricky's face. Four years and she was so close. It was becoming increasingly difficult to pretend to love, or even like, someone like Ricky as time went on. But she couldn't fail now.

Swallowing back the last of the wine from her glass, she walked across to the computer, shut it down and left the office, locking the door on the way out.

Chapter Twenty-Six

She'd fallen down a Google rabbit hole of Glasgow gangsters, criminal activity and unsolved cases. She'd been sat at the desk in the local library for almost two hours and she had no intention of stopping.

'The urn has just been filled if you want another cuppa?' the woman behind the reception desk said.

Elle looked up and gave her a smile. 'Thank you.'

What she really wanted was a drink – a proper drink. But making her tea Irish wasn't an option. She'd have to wait and have a half at home before heading into work.

Glancing back at the computer screen, she shut down the multiple Google tabs, leaving just one open. Facebook wouldn't let her look for people unless she opened an account.

Sighing, Elle clicked to sign up and worried she would need some form of I.D. But it was a lot simpler than she expected. She was able to not only set up a page, but set up a page that was utterly fake.

She glanced around the library and picked a forename from one book and a surname from another and set it as her username. Sarah Parks. She didn't add a profile picture, and didn't fill out a lot of the information. The page was up and running very quickly, and then she started to search.

First, she typed her daughter's name in the search bar. She was the first suggestion to appear, and Elle felt strange. She was excited, yet terrified. Instant pride at how beautiful Teigan looked, and immediate heartache that she'd missed out on being her mother.

The profile picture featured only Teigan. Her rich, chocolate brown hair was just like Elle's when she was younger. Her matching hazel eyes stood out and Elle couldn't stop looking at her. She was perfect.

Her eyes stung a little from threatening tears, but she refused to give in to them. In order to carry on looking into her past, which now felt very much in the present thanks to the powers of social media, she had to be strong.

She began scrolling through the images that were available to be viewed without having to send a friend request. And sure enough, Ricky Fyfe popped up almost immediately. The image she was now looking at made her feel sick to her stomach as she read the caption.

He's only smiling because I did the dishes.

The image of Ricky, standing next to Teigan with his arm around her shoulder, made Elle sick and angry. What's more, they were standing in the very spot in the kitchen where Elle was supposed to have died. When he'd hit her over the head with the bottle he'd been drinking from, it was like someone had flipped a light switch. Everything had gone dark. Next thing she knew, she was in the boot of Chris's car, utterly terrified and no longer with her baby. That was the moment her entire life had shifted. Now, she was here. On her own. Hiding from her past and barely surviving every day.

As Elle studied the image, she could see that the layout of the kitchen was much the same, although it had been decorated. New worktops, new tiles. It seemed Ricky had modernised the place. He'd likely poured more money into the house after she'd gone. It was his dad's house originally, and he'd never said it out loud, but Ricky would never have moved from it. That's why he'd extended it back when Elle was still around. The place had always been too big for her. It had never truly felt like home. Nowhere ever did.

Closing her eyes for a brief moment, she tried to breathe through the panic, trying to remind herself it was only a memory and she wasn't living in that moment right now.

She moved on to the next picture and felt herself smile a little. Teigan, with a man her age. She was holding up her left hand, showing off a diamond and the caption read:

Of course I said yes!

Elle eyed the date on the post. It was two years old, give or take a few days. There didn't seem to be any pictures relating to a wedding plus she hadn't changed her surname. She breathed a sigh of relief. Her daughter wasn't married yet. Then it occurred to her that the relief was irrelevant because no matter what, she'd never be able to attend her daughter's wedding. She was supposed to be dead.

Supposed to be, she thought.

She shook her head. No. Nope. Absolutely not. There was no way in hell she would be able to watch that ceremony, even in secret. The second she crossed the Scottish border, she would be in danger. And now that she thought of it, did Teigan know anything about Elle? What had Ricky told her about her mother? A pack of lies, painting her in the worst light he possibly could? Or had he allowed Elle's existence to disappear, allowing Teigan to grow up thinking nothing of the woman who'd carried her? Birthed her? Loved her so uncontrollably that it hurt in places she didn't know existed?

She wiped a lone tear from her cheek and clicked along, but there were no more accessible pictures.

Moving back to the first image, she noticed that Teigan had tagged Ricky in the picture.

Taking a deep breath, Elle clicked on his name, and a new page filled the screen. And there he was, smiling out at anyone who would look at him. But this time, it wasn't Teigan in the picture with him. It was another female. A second daughter, perhaps? Then, she took a closer look. The body language, the way the woman was looking up at him.

'Jesus,' Elle said out loud. She knew the woman at the front desk would have heard her, and decided to stay quiet and not draw any more attention to herself.

She's young enough to be his fucking daughter, Elle thought as she glanced down at the bio and saw that this girl was, in fact, his fiancée. The name stood out to her like a newly sharpened blade.

Danica Campbell. Narrowing her eyes, Elle took in the girl's features. There was something very familiar about her.

The name, Danica, it was rare. She'd never come across anyone with that name in her life. Except one. Jordan Burns's daughter was named Danica.

Clicking on the girl's name, it took Elle to her profile page. She shook her head. This *had* to be a coincidence.

As she scrolled through Danica's page, she couldn't find anything obvious to link her to who Elle suspected she was. But as she looked closer, she began to see, or at least think, she saw a resemblance to Jordan.

Letting her hand fall from the mouse onto her lap, she stared a little open mouthed at the screen. No way.

Why the hell would Ricky Fyfe be engaged to Jordan Burns's twenty-seven-year-old daughter? Was it Ricky's warped way of keeping the truth from Danica? Or was it some kind of trophy? Almost like he was laughing at Jordan. *Haha. I murdered you and now I've got your daughter.*

Elle puffed out her cheeks and released the air slowly from her lungs.

Whatever his motive, Elle felt an overwhelming need to contact Danica to have her suspicions confirmed, and if they were, she would have to warn her about the kind of man she was becoming romantically involved with. But that could mean heading back up to Scotland. That could mean potentially coming face to face with the man who tried and failed to kill her.

Ricky thought Elle was long dead. Would he even recognise her now? It had been almost three decades since he'd last clapped eyes on her. She'd changed. A lot. She'd lost weight because of the alcohol she consumed regularly and from eating too little. And she'd aged through stress, depression and grief that she never got to be a mum to Teigan.

Elle gritted her teeth as she stared at the picture of the two of them together. How many more lives did that man have to ruin before someone said enough was enough?

'No. No more, Ricky,' Elle whispered. 'This stops, now.'

Chapter Twenty-Seven

Closing the door to her flat, Teigan leaned her back against it and took a steadying breath. The words Ricky had spoken to her didn't give her the relief he'd probably wanted them to. 'Don't worry about me.' But she did worry. Because it seemed as if he wholeheartedly trusted Danica. He had no suspicions whatsoever that Danica was only with him for his money. If he did, he certainly didn't show it.

'Hey,' Darren said, stepping out from the bathroom with a towel wrapped around him. 'I'm guessing by the look on your face, you talked to your dad?'

'Is it that obvious?' Teigan rolled her eyes and hung her bag up on the hook by the door.

'What did he say?'

'Not a lot, although what he did say confirmed to me that he fully trusts in his relationship with Danica and he will be going ahead with the wedding regardless of my concerns. He said I've not to worry about him, he's an adult and he doesn't like that I think he's thick. Or words to that effect.'

Darren's eyes widened. 'That's... straight to the point then?'

'I need a drink,' Teigan said, moving through to the kitchen. 'I can't stress enough how worried I am about the business and about how she's going to break his heart. I can just see it now, she's going to get, what, a year or so into the marriage and then she'll walk away and she's going to get half of it all, Darren.'

Teigan opened the cupboard and took out a gin glass.

'That's quite the picture you've painted there, Teegs,' Darren said, coming into the kitchen behind her and handing her the bottle of Ben Lomond Raspberry and Elderflower gin. 'You really think he's naïve enough not to make her sign a prenup prior to the wedding?'

'Thanks.' She smiled, pulling the top off and pouring a generous amount of gin into the goblet. Then she sighed. 'I don't know, Darren. I hope not.'

She stared down at the personalised bottle, which Darren had made and presented to her on the day he'd proposed. The memory would never leave her. The private dinner table on the beach down at The Lodge on Loch Lomond. The waiter had brought the bottle to the table and placed it on the table. Darren had got down on one knee in the sand as the sun began to set over them, holding the ring in his hand.

Darren poured some tonic into the glass and Teigan immediately took a long drink. She felt his eyes on her and she looked up at him.

'Are you okay?' he asked.

Another long drink. Swallowing hard, she said, 'No. But I will be. I'll just have to... I don't know. Accept her?'

Darren shrugged, placing the bottle of tonic on the kitchen counter. 'If you don't want there to be any animosity between you and your dad, I'd say so. Obviously if you see anything that you think is a red flag, then act on it. But act smart, not rashly.'

She felt the gin slowly begin to flow through her and she was already beginning to feel calmer. She didn't know if it was the gin, or Darren. He was always good at putting out the fires and helping her see through the chaos in her mind.

'Yeah,' she said. 'I will.'

'So, you're going to go ahead with the bridesmaid thing?'

'I suppose I'll have to. But knowing Danica, she'll have me in some fucking toilet-roll-holder dress from the Eighties and I'll look ridiculous just for her entertainment.'

Darren laughed and shook his head. 'Well, let's hope it's your colour, at least.'

Teigan couldn't help but laugh with him. She drank some more of the gin and then her phone pinged. Glancing down at it, there was a Facebook notification. A friend request.

Opening the app, she looked at the request and frowned. There was no profile picture and barely any information.

'Sorry Sarah Parks, don't know you,' she said, and went to hit the delete button, but before she did, she realised that this Sarah Parks person had just one other friend. Danica Campbell.

Frowning, Teigan wondered who she was. A random family member? But Danica didn't have any family. She'd been raised in care. A friend from school? No, that wasn't it. If it was someone from school, Teigan would know who it was as they'd been in most of the same classes.

Curiosity got the better of her and she clicked accept. Not much on the page changed, other than a few more pieces of information. Nothing that could really identify who Sarah was.

There were no workplaces listed. No date of birth. No schools or universities. There was one, though. Places lived. Glasgow. And Essex.

Teigan frowned. She couldn't figure out who this person was, and quickly got bored. She walked through to the living room and threw her phone down onto the sofa.

'Do you know anyone called Sarah Parks?' Darren asked from the kitchen.

'Why?' Teigan asked, frowning.

'She's just sent me a friend request and I noticed she is friends with you and Danica, but no one else.'

Teigan shook her head. Whoever it was, clearly knew them. Or maybe not? Maybe it was a spam account.

'I don't know who it is either,' Teigan replied. 'Just delete. I'm going to.'

Picking up her phone, she went back into the app and when she opened it, there was new information. Pages liked: **Glasgow Crime, Unsolved Glasgow, Glasgow Gang Wars.**

'What the fuck?' Teigan said quietly. And then a message request came through.

> I'm sorry for leaving you.

Teigan's stomach lurched and she sat forward. 'Darren, did you just get a message from this person?'

Darren appeared in the living room, now dressed in jeans and a t-shirt. 'No. Why? Did you?'

Teigan nodded and held her phone out to Darren. His face contorted.

'Sorry for leaving you?' he read out loud. 'What does that mean?'

'I don't know. But my stomach went funny when I read it. Do you think…' She stopped, hesitating to say the words sitting on the tip of her tongue.

'What?'

'No, I'm being stupid.'

Darren's eyes narrowed. 'Tell me. What were you going to say?'

Teigan swallowed down the growing lump of anxiety in her throat and took a breath. 'It's just, the words. Sorry for leaving you. Darren, no one in my life has ever *left* me except my mum, when I was a baby.'

Darren met her eye. 'But your mum's name isn't Sarah Parks, is it?' He sounded genuinely confused, as though he was second guessing himself.

'She could be using a fake name? What if she's suddenly feeling guilty for leaving me when I was so little? She broke my dad's heart, you know? And even though I never knew her, and have no memory of her whatsoever, I still wonder about her. Every day, in fact.'

Darren sighed. 'Teigan, that's a wound you really don't want to pick at. It could really upset you and your dad. And what if it's not her, and you've opened that door? I'm worried it'll break you.'

She knew that was a risk; of course it was. Ricky never, ever spoke about Elle. Never. And why would he? She'd left him and run off with her Uncle Chris. Why would *any* mother do that? It had baffled her for years. Consumed her at night when she couldn't sleep. Thinking about who she could be. Was she still out there, living her life like she didn't have a past? And where was she living? Still in Scotland? In Glasgow, even? Teigan could have walked past her mother in the street, and she would never know.

'You're right,' Teigan said. 'I'm being ridiculous. She wouldn't contact me after all these years. Would she? I mean, if I was her, I wouldn't want to risk the rejection.'

Darren shrugged. 'I don't know. But if she did, why would she use a fake name? If she was going to apologise for leaving you as a baby, why not just be truthful about who she was from the start? And why now?'

Darren was right. What he was saying made sense. Yet, there was still a niggling feeling in the back of her head, a strong sense in her gut that this really could be her mum. Who *else* could it be?

Teigan stared down at the message, fingers poised over the screen, thinking about how to reply.

Chapter Twenty-Eight

Ricky still hadn't come back from the taxi firm and it annoyed Danica because she could have done some more digging in that office of his. She could have tried to find the key to that safe.

Sitting on the sofa, legs crossed, Danica stared up at the seventy-inch television on the wall. The Amazon Fire home screen displayed the apps – Netflix, Disney Plus, Apple TV. None of which appealed to her.

Sighing, Danica set down her wine glass and when she glanced at the bottle, seeing it almost empty, she realised it was the third night this week she'd had a full bottle. She blinked, closing her eyes a little longer than normal and felt the room spin.

Getting to her feet, Danica went to the recycling bin with the bottle and threw it inside. The clatter of the glass against the side of the bin made her flinch.

'No more drink, Danica,' she whispered to herself. Then she glanced at the clock. It was only just gone lunch time. Day drinking sessions were different if you were out enjoying them with friends. Drinking alone in the house when the only thing keeping you company was your dark thoughts was an entirely different ballgame. And if she was going to fuck up Ricky's life, she needed to be sober to do it.

She filled a glass with water and began sipping it slowly. She needed to sober up, not because Ricky would be annoyed she was drunk, but so she could put on her fiancée persona when he got home.

Her phone vibrated in her pocket and when she took it out, she expected to see a message from Ricky. Instead, she saw a private message from Sarah Parks on Facebook. She opened it, the words swimming around the screen.

> Are you originally a Burns?

The words jolted her, and suddenly she felt a little more sober. Blinking in quick succession, Danica re-read the message and felt her heart begin to thump inside her chest.

Clicking on the profile, she saw that she was friends with this Sarah. Danica didn't remember linking with this profile. But then, she'd sunk almost an entire bottle of red wine, so maybe she'd accepted it without consciously thinking about it. Sometimes social media added people to your list without informing you, maybe that was it?

She tapped out a reply.

> Who are you?

Three little dots flashed on the screen to indicate Sarah was typing.

> No one if I have the wrong person.

Danica's stomach flipped and the red wine almost came back on her. Who in the *fuck* was this person? How did they know she used to be named Burns? The only people who would have known that would be her dead parents, her social workers and the foster families who cared for her in her younger days.

Danica typed out a second question.

> Why are you asking me that?

She watched as the three dots danced on the screen again and then a reply came through.

> Because I think you are Jordan Burns's daughter and if you are, you're in danger.

Danica's head was swimming as she read her dad's name over and over. Who the bloody hell was this person? She looked at the profile name. Sarah Parks. She had never heard of that name before.

> I have no idea who you're talking about. You must have the wrong person.

Denying who she was racked her with guilt. She hated lying about where she'd come from, even to Ricky.

Nothing for a few moments, and then the three dots again.

> You're engaged to a very dangerous man, Danica. My advice would be to get out while you can.

Another flip of the stomach and this time, it made Danica retch. Saliva pooled at the back of her throat and she ran to the bathroom, taking deep breaths and hoping she would be able to suppress what was threatening to happen.

Her phone was still in her hand as the red wine came up, hitting the white porcelain toilet. Danica trembled as she tried to process what she'd just read.

Composing herself and wiping at her mouth with some toilet roll, Danica read the message again before typing out a reply.

> Like I said, you have the wrong person.

Chapter Twenty-Nine

Elle stared at the screen and an intense nausea began to creep in. What the hell was she doing? How was she to know that Danica wouldn't tell Ricky about the messages? Or Teigan? If he found out, he could put two and two together. He could realise who Sarah Parks really was. He could come looking for her.

Shit, what have I done?

She quickly logged out of Facebook, closed down the browser and got up from her seat. This was a bad idea. A *very* bad idea.

Stepping outside and into the fresh air, Elle started walking back towards her flat, her heart thumping in her chest. There was no going back now. She couldn't just forget that she'd spoken with Teigan, even if it was through a fake profile. But saying something that could lead her to think it could be Teigan's mum was a stupid move. Both Teigan and Danica could go into panic mode for their own reasons and tell Ricky. If Ricky was still the same person he was when Elle left, he could have access to Danica's messages. He could have been the one replying and not Danica.

The very idea made her feel sick. She'd have to move, start again somewhere else. Ricky was a resourceful man. If he even slightly suspected that Elle was alive, he'd find her, without a doubt. She'd have to tell Frank that she was leaving. But he'd ask her why so suddenly and she couldn't lie to him. Not after everything he'd done for her over the years. He'd been like a dad to her.

Elle reached the flat and went inside, rushing up the stairs and locking the door behind her. Her breath caught in her throat. They could have told him already. He could already be making inquiries. In this day and age, with modern technology, it wouldn't be hard to find her.

Hanging her keys up on the hook by the kitchen door, Elle went into the kitchen and fished a bottle of gin from the drinks cupboard.

She needed a quick solution to numb her fear. Taking off the lid, she raised the bottle to her lips and saw her trembling hand. The liquid swished around inside the bottle as she tried to steady herself, but the more she did, the more she trembled. Was it through fear, or through her need to have a drink?

Slowly, Elle placed the bottle down on the kitchen worktop above the fridge and stared at it. It had been the first thing she'd done when she'd arrived home. Reaching for a drink. It was the first thing she did every morning, and every evening. In fact, it was what consumed her thoughts every single day. *Just a little to get me through. Just one to help calm the shakes. Just one more. Just half the bottle tonight.*

Tears pooled in her eyes and Elle saw what she'd become. An alcoholic. Through years of trying to cope with what she'd done, of what she'd gone through with Ricky, she'd turned to the bottle as her coping mechanism. And now, she didn't know how else to deal with her traumas.

'Fuck!' she screamed, taking the bottle into her hand and raising it to her mouth once more. Poised at her lips, she could smell the gin, ready to take it into her mouth and let the alcohol do its work. But something stopped her. Something in her mind told her that she shouldn't do it.

With the bottle still in her hand, she picked up her phone and called the only person she had in her life. Frank Cranwell.

Chapter Thirty

'Are you throwing up in there?' Ricky asked as he stood outside the bathroom door.

'I'll be okay,' Danica called back. 'I think I just ate something that didn't agree with me.'

With a raised brow, Ricky sighed. 'Can I get you anything?'

The sound of the toilet flushing made Ricky stand back and the bathroom door opened. When he saw Danica, face grey and eyes dark, he knew instantly that she'd been drinking, and that was aside from the fact that the bathroom stank of the red wine that Danica enjoyed regularly. She always had the same faraway look in her eyes when she'd had a skinful.

'The food that didn't agree with you wasn't a bottle of red, was it?'

Danica blinked and pushed past Ricky before making her way down the stairs. 'No, you cheeky bastard, what do you think I am, some kind of alky?'

Ricky stared down at his TAG Heuer watch and noted the time. One thirty in the afternoon. He raised a brow. The word *alky* echoed in his ears.

'That's not what I said,' Ricky replied, following Danica down the stairs. 'But, yeah, okay. If you really want to know, then yeah, I do think you're drinking a little too much.'

Danica spun on her heel at the bottom of the stairs and glared up at him. 'I told you, it was something I ate.'

Ricky slowly descended the stairs and stood in front of Danica, taking her chin in his hand. 'Don't lie to me,' he said. 'I'm not stupid. I've been around a lot longer than you, and I know a drinker when I see one. I own a nightclub, remember? I've picked many a drunk off the floor.'

Danica closed her eyes as though she was trying to stay calm. His accusation had clearly hit a nerve.

'Look, I'm not judging you…'

'Funny way of showing it,' Danica butted in before heading into the kitchen.

Ricky reached out and grabbed at Danica's hand. 'I promise I'm not having a go at you. I'm just worried. You're young, Danica. Drinking as often as I think you are, it won't do you any good. Or us for that matter.'

Danica's expression soured, with the hint of a sarcastic grin on her face. '*Us?*'

'Well, when we're married, I'm assuming you're going to want to start trying for a kid and alcohol could hinder that.'

He tried to ignore the little voices in his head that kept whispering how he had been diagnosed as infertile almost thirty years ago. He hoped that having kids wasn't something she wanted. Because he simply couldn't give it to her.

'Excuse me?' Danica said, her brow furrowing.

'If you want to get pregnant then I don't think you should be drinking. It's not good for you.'

Danica glanced around the room with a confused look on her face. 'I'm sorry, did I miss a conversation?'

'What do you mean?'

'The conversation about us *having a baby*. Did I miss that?'

Ricky stared at her, feeling anger slowly building in the centre of his chest. She was acting like a bitch. A side of her he hadn't experienced before.

'That's what people do when they get married, Danica. I just thought you'd want that.'

Danica smirked. 'Well, I'm not *people*. And you're old. Teigan said as much herself. That you won't want a kid because of your age and that suits me just fine.'

Ricky was so taken aback he didn't know how to respond. Had Teigan truly said that? When did that conversation take place?

He watched as Danica grabbed her car keys and left the house via the side door in the kitchen. Realising that she was about to take the new car out while she had alcohol in her bloodstream, he moved quickly after her. Reaching out, he snatched the keys from her hand, and she spun around so fast she almost fell over.

'Give them back,' she said, her voice quivering.

'What the *fuck* is wrong with you today?' Ricky spat the words at her. 'You're like a different person.'

Danica tried to grab the keys but Ricky held them behind his back and felt himself suppressing a laugh, not in humour but disbelief.

'Give them to me,' she said through gritted teeth.

'No. You're hammered and you're *not* driving my car.'

'Oh, it's *your* car. Same as this,' she gestured to her body, 'is *yours* too?'

Ricky looked her up and down and couldn't work out where the attitude was coming from. Was it just the drink? Or something else?

'So you get to decide when and what I drive and when I have a baby, without consulting me first?' she persisted, only this time her speech was beginning to slow and slur.

Biting his bottom lip to stop himself from exploding, Ricky shoved the keys into his pocket and turned his back on Danica.

'Where are you going?' she called.

'I'm not going to stand on my drive and argue with a drunk person. If you want to leave, off you go. But you're walking. No skin off my nose.'

He headed back into the house and into the kitchen. He eyed the recycling bin by the door and pulled the lid up. The empty Merlot bottle stared up at him, with two more beneath it. He shook his head and let the lid fall shut before looking out of the window onto the drive. Danica was gone.

'Fucking idiot,' he whispered.

Thinking back to when he was with Elle, if something like this had happened, he'd have punished her for it. Why was he so calm with Danica? What was so different about her? Her age? And the fact that he had this chance at real happiness, and he didn't want to mess it up. He genuinely felt a love for Danica he'd never experienced before. He'd never wanted to be careful with Elle. But he was older now, wiser. He knew that if he didn't behave well, Danica wouldn't want to stick around.

As he contemplated his feelings and the differences between then and now, he headed upstairs to his office, knowing full well that when Danica got to the bottom of the driveway, she'd turn around and head back up to the house. In the beginning with Elle, she'd threaten to walk away, but she always came back.

It wasn't until Teigan was born that Ricky decided he wasn't allowing Elle to go anywhere. She was not going to take his child from him. Because of that decision, Elle was dead. Chris was dead, Teigan's biological dad. Teigan had been living a lie her whole life, and had no idea.

Ricky sat down at his desk and stared up at the picture of him and Teigan. Even for a hardened criminal like Ricky Fyfe, the hardest thing he'd ever had to do was keep up the lie. Not because he felt guilty. He couldn't give a fuck about Elle. He only worried that one day the truth would come out and life as he knew it would come to an end.

Chapter Thirty-One

What the *hell* had she just done? Perched on the wall at the bottom of the driveway, her phone in her hand, Danica sobbed silent tears as she went over in her head what had just happened between her and Ricky. She'd broken character and it was because she'd sunk a couple bottles of wine, during the day.

She rubbed at her eyes furiously, desperate to sober up and wishing she had a decent gram of coke to shove up her nose. That would have sobered her up immediately. Ricky wouldn't be happy with her behaviour. She could barely remember the content of their argument. All she could remember was the look on his face. Sheer rage. But he'd kept it in. She'd never seen that in him before.

Sighing, Danica stood up and looked up the driveway. Anxiety about what awaited her in the house almost crippled her to the point she didn't want to go back up. Then she remembered the reason why she was marrying Ricky in the first place. She pictured her dad, the man she should have had in her life. The mum who died from alcoholism when she was just a child all because Ricky got away with murder, and she didn't know how else to cope.

They both deserved justice. Danica was the only one left who could serve that. Putting one foot in front of the other, Danica began walking back up to the house, taking deep breaths and focusing on getting into the zone. Danica Campbell. The sweet, slightly edgy, sexy fiancée that Ricky adored. Not Danica Burns, the broken, anxious and grief-stricken orphan. He didn't know she existed and she'd make sure it stayed that way for as long as possible. That was unless she'd already ruined it.

The house came into sight and Danica slipped back into character, although her head still swirled from the wine. She wouldn't have thrown up if she hadn't got that message on Facebook. Someone out there knew who she was and who she was engaged to. It must have been someone from her dad's past. But who was it? And what were their intentions?

She crossed the threshold of the open gates, glad that Ricky hadn't closed them and locked her out, and walked up to the side door of the house. Resting her hand on the door handle, she almost jumped when it opened, and Ricky stood in the doorway.

'You're back then?' he said, his voice smooth. He didn't look angry. Thankfully.

'I'm sorry,' she said, trying to keep the quiver from her voice.

Ricky gave a nod and stood to the side before Danica entered the kitchen. What was she going to say? About his plans for their future? About how she'd behaved, and what she'd said?

'Just so you know, if you don't want to have a baby, that's fine,' Ricky said. 'I'd never force the issue if it wasn't something you wanted. No child deserves to be born unwanted. Also, I'm not exactly young enough to be having more kids. I just assumed you'd want them. I'm sorry.'

Danica turned and smiled. 'Thank you. I just think it's something we should discuss. But I shouldn't have reacted in the way that I did. And you're right. I *am* drinking a little too much. I see that now. I'm more aware of it.'

Another nod and a smile. 'We can discuss it later. I'm going for a bath. Fancy joining me?'

There it was. That cheeky smile, the sparkle in his eye that could charm anyone. But not her. She was good at pretending. She'd had four years' practice.

Danica fixed him with her best seductive smile and said, 'I'll get the water running.'

Chapter Thirty-Two

Frank opened the office door and Elle had to stop herself from launching into a full-scale panic attack. The expression of concern on his face told her just how fretful she must look.

'What is going on?' Frank said with apprehension. 'You sounded really worried when you called me.'

'I don't know how else to say this, but I think it's time for me to leave Essex,' Elle said, trying not to let the fear break her.

Frank ushered her into the office, and she sat down on the chair opposite his. Placing her hands on the desk in front of her, she leaned forward and took some deep breaths.

'Why do you need to leave Essex? And why do you look so panicked?' Frank asked, crouching down beside her.

'Believe me, Frank. I want to tell you, but I really can't,' she said, her voice and hands trembling.

Frank took her quivering hands in his. 'Elle, love, you look fucking terrified. What on earth is going on? What's happened? I can help you if you let me.'

She looked at him, full of hope that she could reveal all to him. But Frank was in business with Ricky. How would he react to it all? It could mess up the deal and Frank could lose a lot of money because of her.

'I can't,' she whispered in defeat, tears dropping off the end of her nose. 'It's too big.'

Frank leaned back and gave an obnoxious yet gentle smile. 'Hey, *nothing* is too big for Frank Cranwell.'

Elle forced a smile in return. 'No. It really is too big. Especially after the amount of time I've kept it quiet. I just need to go away for a while.'

Frank narrowed his eyes. 'You know I'd never let anything happen to you, Elle. You're like a daughter to me.'

Elle nodded. 'I know.'

'Whatever it is that you've held on to by yourself, I can try to fix it. I can try to make it go away.'

Elle closed her eyes. Even Frank couldn't sort this. The only way to fix this was to see Ricky Fyfe pay for what he'd done. The only way for justice to be done would be with Ricky's death.

'Thank you, Frank. But no one can fix my life except me.'

'I wish you knew how untrue that is,' Frank replied.

She threw her arms around Frank and held him so tight that she never wanted to let go.

'You'll always have a home here with me. You know that. No matter what,' Frank said, holding her just as tight. 'Where are you going?'

Elle held her breath as she thought about it. The only place she could go. To Glasgow to see her daughter. She couldn't do this anymore. Not after seeing Teigan in the club the other night. Not after making contact. Teigan was out there, living her life believing that Ricky was her real dad. A man who'd scared Elle into staying away for almost three decades.

'As far away as I possibly can,' Elle lied. No one could know she was travelling to Glasgow. No one could know she was alive.

'Here,' he said, getting to his feet and opening the digital safe under the desk. 'Take this. There's about four grand there. That should do you for a while until you get settled, wherever you're going.'

He handed her a bundle of cash and Elle's mouth fell open. 'I can't take all this.'

'Yes you can. And if you run out, and you need my help, do not hesitate to call me. I'll always be here to help you, Elle.'

As her eyes pooled with tears, Elle thanked Frank and wondered if she'd ever see him again.

Chapter Thirty-Three

Waking up the next morning, Teigan glanced at her phone to see the time. It was only five thirty. Why was she awake so early, again? She hadn't been sleeping properly for weeks and it was slowly beginning to break her down. Her head had been full of so much: her dad's imminent wedding to a fellow school pupil, which still baffled her; the mysterious message from Sarah Parks; and then the deal with Frank Cranwell. It was a huge amount of money and the biggest contract the firm had had to date. She needed to be focused on that. Instead, she was distracted, and it was beginning to get to her.

Darren snored softly beside her as she rolled out of bed and went to the kitchen. Coffee. She needed coffee, and lots of it, if she was going to survive another day on very little sleep.

As the coffee machine was doing its thing, Teigan looked at her phone. She hadn't sent a reply to Sarah Parks and it seemed the account hadn't been active since the message had been sent. Teigan couldn't get it out of her head. The words meant something. A random person wouldn't just send that for no reason. It had real conviction behind it and something in Teigan's gut told her as much. And why was Danica the only other person on Sarah Park's friends list? What was the connection?

Taking her coffee through to the living room, Teigan sat down on the sofa and stared out of the window at the train station. The first train would be due through soon. People starting to go about their day, getting to work. It always made her think about what was going on in their lives. Who grew up without a mum like her? Who went through life wondering about who their mum was? Where had she gone? Why did she leave?

There were only two people in the world who could answer those questions for Teigan. Her dad and her mum. She wanted to message

Sarah Parks back more than anything, but she was terrified of the response she might get. What if she didn't get the answers she wanted? What if she didn't get a reply at all?

Sipping her coffee and staring out at the station, Teigan considered speaking to her dad. He'd never said more than what she already knew. That her mum and uncle ran off together.

Something about that niggled at her. It always had. Was an affair worth leaving your baby girl for? Your *newborn* baby girl? Of course, Teigan wasn't a mum herself, but she could never imagine walking away from her child for a man, no matter who it was. As much as she tried, she couldn't stop wondering whether her dad was more involved in the reason her mum disappeared. It wasn't exactly a secret that he used violence in his line of work; was it really that impossible for him to have used that at home?

Ridiculous, she said to herself, pushing such ludicrous thoughts from her head. He'd been nothing but kind, loving and caring as a dad. She scolded herself for thinking such a horrible thing.

She drank her coffee in silence and watched as the first train pulled into the station. The sound of the wheels on the track coming to a screeching halt was a comfort to her. It meant the city was beginning to wake up. She was no longer alone in her fretful, insomnia-ridden mind.

The sound of Darren rolling over in bed made her tense. She wasn't ready to talk to anyone yet, as much as she was glad that he would be starting to wake up. He'd ask her questions about how she was feeling, about if she was going to reply to Sarah Parks. Was she going to talk to Ricky about the message? Would she go dress shopping with Danica? It was all too much, and she just wanted to disappear for the day, collect her thoughts and figure out how to deal with it all.

'Morning,' Darren said as he appeared in the living room.

'Hey,' she said gently. 'Sleep well?'

He raised his arms above his head, yawned loudly and said, 'Like a baby.'

Teigan smiled and said, 'I've never understood that saying. Babies never sleep. At least, I didn't, according to my dad. Although I don't know why he complains about it. I was brought up by a million different nannies.'

Darren rubbed at his eyes and collapsed onto the sofa beside her. 'That's deep for six in the morning.'

'I always do my deepest thinking before the world wakes up,' Teigan replied, setting her now empty coffee mug down on the side table.

'I can't function for at least two hours after my first coffee, so deep thoughts are a no go for me.' Darren yawned again and got to his feet. 'Speaking of coffee. You want another?'

Teigan shook her head. 'No, I think I'm going to go for a swim, actually.'

'Ooft, that's dedication. I'll be cheering you on in my head while I attempt to wake up properly.'

Teigan laughed and got up before heading to the bathroom. After a quick leg and bikini tidy-up, she grabbed her swim bag and headed out the door. Swimming was the only thing that helped clear her mind. All she could focus on was counting her lengths, attempting a mile with each visit to the pool. Seventy-two lengths were a killer on the thighs, but she always felt incredible after it. She hoped that today would be one of those days.

In the car, Teigan couldn't stop her mind from wandering back to her mum. *Why did she leave me?* She intended to find out.

Pulling into the almost empty car park, Teigan pulled out her phone, opened up Facebook Messenger and went to Sarah Parks's message.

> Question one. Are you my mum? Are you Elle Fyfe? And question two, how do you know Danica Campbell?

She hit send immediately, realising that hesitating wouldn't bring her the answers she needed. As soon as she did, she threw the phone into her bag, got out the car and went into the leisure complex. It was time to clear her head and her phone would still be there when she got out.

Chapter Thirty-Four

Ricky was already in the shower when Danica woke up. She'd had the hangover from hell the night before and today she vowed not to touch a drop of alcohol. It made her feel awful, and she couldn't risk another break-of-character incident. He could start to suspect something was wrong and Danica had plans that she needed to execute.

She sat up slowly, hopeful that the wine headache from last night wouldn't return. Thankfully, her head felt a lot clearer than she'd expected and she rested back on the headboard.

Ricky was in fine form last night. He had high expectations when it came to sex. Although she'd learned to remind herself that she was playing a role, and that sex was just a part of the script. It got easier the longer they were together. If she gained anything from this it was her newfound acting skills, all developed over a four-year period.

Some days, she questioned whether she was strong enough to get through to the final act. Other days, she knew she was. Today was a questionable day but she would push through. The more Ricky loved Danica, the easier it would be to fool him, and the more satisfying it would be to watch his world crumble when he realised that she was Danica Burns, vengeful daughter of the man he had murdered. She pictured that moment in her head every day. Even when she was on top of him in bed, or he was behind her in the shower, she would imagine his expression when it all came out. *How* it would all come out was a detail she hadn't finalised yet. Neither had she worked out how she was going to make sure she got all his money.

Danica got up out of bed and picked her underwear up from the floor, where Ricky had discarded it the night before. Even after their bath session he'd wanted more, and she had been exhausted with the hangover. But she couldn't very well say no. She had to keep on his good side.

The en-suite shower stopped running and Ricky opened the door. He smiled at her widely and she hoped he wasn't going to suggest more sex. Instead, he said, 'How's the head?'

Relief flooded through her and she smiled back. 'I'm fine, thank you.'

'Good,' he said, wrapping a towel around his waist and running his hand through his wet hair. 'Don't pull a stunt like that again.'

Danica blinked and for a moment, she thought he was being funny. When his expression darkened, she realised he was being serious.

'What do you mean?'

Stepping onto the thick carpet with his wet feet, he moved closer to the bed and stopped beside her. 'I mean, don't ever get pissed and threaten to drive my fucking car again. Got it?'

Danica's heart started to pound in her chest. Did she do that? She couldn't remember. Maybe she had been a lot drunker than she'd realised. Or maybe he was lying?

'I won't,' she replied submissively. 'And I'm off the drink.'

'Good,' he leaned down and for a moment, Danica thought he was going to raise his hand to her. Instead, he kissed her lightly on the cheek and said, 'You were a dirty little bitch last night.'

The hairs on her body instantly prickled and she felt the words crawl across her skin. 'Just being a dutiful wife-to-be,' she forced the words out with a smile.

'Keep up the good work. Although, you ride me that hard again and you might kill me.' He laughed loudly and went back into the bathroom.

If only, she thought. *If he could die of a heart attack during sex on their wedding night, then all this would be over a lot sooner than planned.*

Chapter Thirty-Five

Elle stared at her reflection in the bathroom mirror at the train station and could hardly see herself anymore. The transformation from natural mouse brown to black box dye and a self-cut fringe had rendered her unrecognisable. *Good*, she thought. That was the way she'd wanted it. Even after almost three decades, she could not risk Ricky Fyfe recognising her.

Leaving the bathroom, she stood in the centre of the train station and dropped the bag containing all her worldly possessions at her feet. Elle realised just how pathetic her life was, and just how terribly she'd behaved over the years. She'd left her daughter, her *only* daughter, behind and fled from a man she was terrified of. What kind of woman, let alone mother, was she?

Sighing in annoyance at herself, Elle glanced up at the boards and scanned the times and destinations of each train, specifically looking for Glasgow Central. She had to see her daughter. She couldn't do this anymore. She wanted to explain her truth. Would Teigan believe her? Would Teigan even listen? Elle hadn't been able to log on to her fake Facebook account since sending a message from the library, so for all she knew, Teigan may not have even read it. Or on the other hand, she could have read it, showed Ricky and by now he may know she was alive, or at least suspect.

Her stomach flipped at the idea of just stepping onto the train. Finding a seat. Watching the doors as they closed. The train slowly pulling out of the station and beginning her journey back home to Glasgow. To see the daughter she never got to watch grow up.

Blinking at the digital words as they now danced around on the board she'd been staring at for so long, Elle bent down, picked up her bag and headed towards the ticket office. She wanted to deal with a real human; the idea of using one of the machines horrified her. Technology itself horrified her, but she was sure it was only because it would make it so easy for Ricky to find her. Although she'd somehow seemed to shed some of that fear when she'd decided to contact Teigan. And Danica.

God, what the fuck was she doing? She'd managed to survive twenty-seven years without Ricky finding her or even knowing she was still alive. Why was she risking her safety now?

She already knew the answer. If Teigan hadn't walked through the door of Frank's club, Elle would still be living out her miserable, yet safe, albeit somewhat drunken, days in Essex without that gut-wrenching feeling that she had unfinished business.

Glasgow was the only place she could go. There was no point in going anywhere else. If she did, she'd be wasting time. And she'd already wasted just short of three decades.

There were so many questions she wanted the answers to, and the only city in the world where those answers lay was Glasgow.

'Can I help you?' a woman on the other side of the glass said.

Elle nodded, fumbling around in her purse for cash. 'The nine o'clock to Glasgow Central, please.'

'Oh, you'll have to be quick. It leaves in three minutes,' the woman said, printing off the ticket and pushing it through the gap at the bottom.

Elle handed over the money, grabbed the ticket and headed for her platform. If she did this quickly, she wouldn't look back. That was her logic at least. She approached the barrier, slipped her ticket into the slot and grabbed it when it was spat back out at her from the top.

Breathe, breathe, breathe, she told herself as her stomach threatened to release its contents. *Glasgow is a big city. It's not like you're going to step off the train and the first person you're going to see is Ricky.*

But what if that really did happen? What if he'd discovered she was still alive? What if he knew she was coming?

All thoughts emptied from her head as Elle stepped onto the train, found a seat with a table and slipped her bag into the overhead compartment. She let out a breath and glanced up the carriage. There was an on-board shop. Not that she was hungry, or could imagine getting hungry. A drink on the other hand would be a good idea. Just to steady the nerves, and the stomach.

Then it was happening. The train doors were closing with a bleeping sound, shooshing as they slid shut. That was it now. She was doing this. She was on the train to Glasgow.

Resting her head back against the chair, Elle looked out of the window as the train slowly exited the station. The gentle thrum of the electricity lines above was oddly soothing.

Would the on-board shop sell wine at this time of the morning? Perhaps not. But to crack out the two small bottles of wine she had in her bag at this time, while travelling alone, was something she questioned whether she should or shouldn't do.

Have some bloody self-control, Elle. It's a six-and-a-half-hour journey. You won't die without a drink.

But Elle knew that the feeling would only get worse if she *didn't* at least have a sniff. She rolled her eyes at the sheer ridiculousness of the fact that all she could think about was having a drink, when she was heading into Glasgow and potentially coming face to face with her past traumas.

Elle closed her eyes and bit the tip of her tongue a little. She wanted to tell herself it would all be over soon. In reality, it was just about to begin.

Chapter Thirty-Six

Teigan walked towards Danica with such a scowl on her face that she resembled a scolded child. In that moment, it occurred to Danica just how pathetically sad this whole scenario was, with no family or real friends between them to truly enjoy what should be a joyous occasion.

'Hi,' Danica said. It came out a lot sweeter than she'd intended. 'How are you?'

Teigan narrowed her eyes and said, 'How am I? Hmm, let's see. I'm being forced to shop for a bridesmaid's dress I don't want to wear for a bride I don't like, who doesn't like me, and all just to keep my dad happy. You really fucking outdid yourself by telling him I'd agreed to this shitshow.'

Just as Danica was about to hit back, the door to the bridal shop opened and a bright-eyed woman smiled widely at them both. 'Welcome to Mandy's Bridal. Danica?' she asked, staring at Teigan.

'I'm the bride,' Danica replied.

'Unfortunately,' Teigan said under her breath and the woman's eyes darted between the two.

'Would you ladies like a glass of fizz?' the woman asked, seemingly trying to break the tension as Danica crossed the threshold of the shop with Teigan closely behind.

'Shall we just get this over with?' Teigan suggested.

'Couldn't agree more.'

The look on the dress fitter's face said it all. Raised brows and a stunned expression quickly dispersed as she handed Danica a glass of fizz and smiled.

'So, you know what kind of style you're looking for?'

Danica stared at Teigan and then said, 'Well, I think we should start with the bridesmaid's dress.'

Teigan rolled her eyes. 'You put me in something that resembles anything other than elegant and I'm out of here, Danica. I couldn't give a sh—'

'Why don't we pick out something you both like,' the dress fitter interrupted, as though she hated the idea of colourful language tarnishing the elegance of the bridal shop. 'And we can go from there.'

Both Danica and Teigan nodded and the woman headed to the back of the shop, leaving them on their own.

'You could at least pretend you're excited about the wedding, for your dad's sake,' Danica said, without looking at Teigan.

'Pfft, aye right,' Teigan scoffed.

Danica remained silent. She didn't want this as much as Teigan. Danica was forcing herself into this wedding, this marriage, all for the greater good.

'You can choose which kind of dress you want to wear. I don't mind,' Danica said softly.

Frowning in confusion, Teigan turned and stared at her. 'What's the catch?'

Pursing her lips, Danica replied, 'No catch. I just think that, well, Ricky wouldn't want us being catty with each other, would he? And let's face it, we don't have any family or friends here. Shouldn't we just try to get along for Ricky's sake?'

Teigan's expression softened. 'Fine,' she replied a little less sternly.

Danica tried to stop herself from looking smug. Once again, her acting skills had worked. Both Teigan and her murderous dad were highly gullible, she'd give them that.

'Oh, by the way. Do you know someone called Sarah Parks?'

Danica's stomach flipped and she froze. 'No,' she lied. 'Why?'

'I saw she was a mutual friend of yours on Facebook,' Teigan replied.

Frowning, Danica wondered if there was more to it but was too nervous to ask in case it was a trap. Perhaps Teigan knew about the nature of the messages between Sarah and Danica and wanted to question her.

'If she's on your friends list, and you don't know her, then why is she on there?' Teigan pushed.

'I don't even remember adding or accepting her if I'm honest. Too much wine,' she joked, even though it wasn't funny. The memory of the messages from Sarah Parks, the warnings, they haunted Danica. That person said she was in danger, something that Danica already knew. The risks involved in her plan were huge, but not as huge as the rewards if things went according to plan. But the message was a good reminder to Danica to tread lightly. If Ricky found out what her intentions were, he could end her. All three members of the Burns family, dead because of him.

Just as Teigan parted her lips to speak again, the dress fitter reappeared with a smile on her face. 'I have some dresses for you to try on. Why don't you both come through?'

They followed her through to the back of the shop and took a seat on oversized, cream velvet sofas. Three ivory wedding dresses hung proudly on a rail in front of Danica, and she couldn't help but admire their beauty. A further three bridesmaid's dresses hung on the rail next to them and Teigan stood in front of them, reaching out and running her fingers across the material. Each one was a different colour. One black; very apt for the situation right now. The second was royal blue and the third was a deep red.

'Each dress comes in every colour,' the dress fitter said. 'These are just to give you a sense of the style and how they fit.'

Danica stared longingly at the red dress. Blood red, she thought.

'I thought you said I could pick my own dress,' Teigan asked, her tone blunt.

'Yeah, I changed my mind,' Danica replied. If she was going to take down the top man, she had to be firm with the daughter too. 'But surely one of these takes your fancy?'

A silence followed but not in Danica's head. All she could think about was the end result. Ricky dead.

'Fine. Never thought I'd say this,' Teigan's voice crept in and jolted Danica from her thoughts. 'But I really like all of those.'

Danica glanced at Teigan and gave a smile. A sadness crossed her then. In any other life, Danica wondered if she and Teigan could actually be friends. It wasn't Teigan's fault she was bred by a monster. Not at all. But she was involved in his world. A world that turned a blind eye to the deaths of innocents.

'Yeah,' Danica replied, switching back into character. 'Elegant enough for you?'

Teigan glared at her upon hearing the tone. 'They'll have to do.'

Raising a brow, Danica said, 'I'd like to try on my dresses, please.'

A thought occurred to her then. The next time Danica would be wearing her wedding dress would be when she was marrying Ricky. Marrying the man who murdered her dad and caused the death of her mother. The red bridesmaid's dress caught her eye once more.

'I think the red dress is the one I like the best. Try it on, Teigan. Because it's what you're wearing on the day.'

They stared each other down and Danica needed to be the one to hold on. She couldn't look away. If Teigan Fyfe could break Danica down with a look, then she had no chance being married to Ricky. Because that marriage could last a long time if Danica couldn't bring him down quickly enough. And the longer she was married to him, the harder things were going to get.

Chapter Thirty-Seven

Teigan had never felt anger like it. So much so that her face was almost the same crimson shade as the bridesmaid's dress Danica had *insisted* Teigan would wear on the big day. It was out of spite, surely? The dress itself was nice, but the colour? What was the theme? Massacre wedding?

With her measurements taken, Teigan was now sat on the cream velvet sofa, her almost empty glass of prosecco on the table in the centre of the seating area. Danica was in the changing room, trying on wedding dresses and Teigan needed a distraction.

Pulling out her phone, Teigan opened up the Facebook Messenger app and scrolled to Sarah Parks. There was no reply. The message Teigan had sent hadn't been read from what she could see. The questions just sat there, unread, unanswered.

Teigan felt her mind swirl back to the other question. Why did Danica have this woman as a friend? Who was she to them all? If she was Teigan's mum as she suspected, then why add Danica as a friend? Was it because she was engaged to Ricky? Or was it something else?

Fingers hovering over the screen, Teigan debated deleting the message and removing the woman. But curiosity wouldn't allow it.

Just then, the curtain drew back, and Danica stepped out of the changing room in dress number one. A plain, sleek, body sculpting ivory dress that flowed beautifully from knee to floor. Teigan kicked herself for thinking Danica looked incredible.

Danica stepped up onto the box in front of the full-length mirror and stared at herself. She had such a resting bitchface, it was difficult to tell if she liked the dress at all. Not that Teigan cared. If Danica pulled out of the wedding at that moment, Teigan would pop another bottle of fizz. Of course, that was never going to happen. She was never going to give up her meal ticket that easily.

'What do you think?' the dress fitter asked with a beaming smile.

'It's beautiful,' Danica said, her voice cracking with emotion. Teigan couldn't help but roll her eyes.

'Is that the kind of style you wanted?' Teigan asked, trying to be as nice as possible. She didn't want her dad giving her grief for not being enthusiastic about anything to do with the wedding.

'I definitely think it's something Ricky would like,' Danica replied.

'But what do you think?' Teigan interrupted.

Danica narrowed her eyes and stared at Teigan in the mirror.

'Careful, Teigan. You almost sound like you care how I feel. And we both know that isn't the case.'

Raising a brow, Teigan replied, 'You're spending my dad's money on this dress. You should at least like what you're wearing.'

The dress fitter's face was a picture, the corners of her mouth rising slightly in what Teigan could only imagine was nervous humour. Teigan wondered if she'd had worse bridal parties than what she was faced with now.

'I do like it,' Danica replied, straightening her back and pushing back her shoulders. 'It's beautiful. But I'd like to see the others too.'

Snapping back into her role, the dress fitter nodded and helped Danica down from the box and back into the dressing room.

Teigan sighed and tried to convince herself to be kinder. This whole situation would be a lot easier if she could get along better with Danica. They both had their guard up. Although, when Teigan considered it, what was there to be guarded about on Danica's end? She was marrying a millionaire. She didn't have to worry about working for a living. She'd be able to live a life of luxury until her dying day.

Glancing down at her phone, there was still no response from Sarah Parks. So, Teigan decided to ask another question. She began typing.

> And three, if you are who I think you are, can you explain to me why you left? Why did you leave me when I was a newborn? Why did you have to break my dad's heart by running off with his brother?

Something caught her off guard then. A sadness that she had not expected to feel. Because no matter whether the person on the other side of the message window was her mum or not, she didn't know her. She could walk past her in the street and never know it was her. There was no love lost because she'd never had it to begin with. Maybe that's where the emotion came from. The idea that she'd grown up without a mother figure because Elle had put her own needs first saddened her. It also brought anger to the surface.

As she glanced down at the screen, she hoped to see a blue tick. In its place was a grey one. Sent, but not read.

Maybe Sarah Parks would never read them. Maybe Teigan would never get her answers. But now she'd started asking the questions, having them unanswered for the rest of her life wasn't something she was sure she could accept.

Maybe it was time to start looking for Elle herself. Properly, this time. Not just a meagre social media scroll. Maybe she needed to do some proper investigations. The only problem was, she didn't know where to start.

POSSIBLE DRUG DEATH IN GLASGOW

A teenage girl has died outside a nightclub in Glasgow. The nineteen-year-old was found unconscious by friends, who raised the alarm just after two in the morning, outside Club Margharita, in the Merchant City.

Police are looking at drugs as a possible line of inquiry, as it was reported the teenager had been seen taking cocaine just moments before her body was discovered.

A spokesperson has said that her next of kin have been informed, and inquiries are ongoing.

Chapter Thirty-Eight

Ricky Fyfe stared at the report in the newspaper with suspicion. It was tucked away in the corner of the page, seemingly almost not worthy of a report at all. But Ricky saw it. And he knew that it could possibly come back on him. He'd only just done a deal with Frank Cranwell, a matter of days ago. Distribution done just after. Now there was a possible cocaine-related death in the city. It could just be coincidence. But then, what a shitty coincidence it was.

Picking up the burner phone from the desk, he sent out a message via the encrypted app he made all his employees use.

Drug death report. Keep your ears to the ground.

Chucking the phone down onto the desk, he sighed angrily. Was Frank Cranwell's product a bad batch? Or had this girl just been unlucky? Ricky would have to keep his eyes and ears open. If there were any more issues, any more reports on other users dropping dead, he'd have to pull the deal. It was a conversation he didn't want to think about having. Frank would be fucking raging, to say the least.

Then he heard the front door open, and the sound of his favourite people walking into the house.

He got up and went to the landing of the hallway outside his home office. Leaning over the banister, he shouted, 'Success?'

He heard his daughter grunt something in annoyance while Danica sounded like her usual, chirpy self.

'You're going to die when you see me in this dress,' Danica called back in a sing-song tone.

'And I'm going to fucking die wearing mine,' Teigan said, with a little too much venom. Ricky rolled his eyes and headed downstairs.

'It can't be that bad,' Ricky said when he reached the bottom. 'I mean, the fact that you're both here together speaks volumes. Let's face it, you can't stand each other, but you went dress shopping together. That's progress.'

'Not like I had much choice,' Teigan muttered. Danica seemed to ignore her and strutted happily into the kitchen.

'Drink?' she called back.

Ricky glanced after her. There was no way she was opening a bottle of wine. Not after the other night's antics.

As if hearing his thoughts, Danica turned back and smiled. 'Tea, coffee?'

'Coffee, thanks,' he replied, turning to Teigan, whose face was like thunder.

'I'm being serious, Dad. It's fucking hideous.'

Ignoring the comment, Ricky said, 'Have you heard?'

'Heard what?'

'A teenager died in the city last night and they suspect it's cocaine-related.'

Teigan's face paled. 'Are you sure?'

'Yes. I've sent a message to the team to keep their ears open. It could just be a coincidence but it's strange considering this has happened almost immediately after the first batch of Cranwell coke went out.'

Teigan's brows crept up her forehead. 'But there was only one? Surely if it was a product issue, then there would be more deaths, or at least illnesses?'

Ricky ran a hand over his stubble and nodded. 'Yeah, I'm hoping it was a case of bad luck. Or maybe it's that lone dealer?'

Teigan shook her head. 'I don't think so. It's too close to when we did the deal with Frank.'

Ricky nodded, his face darkening.

'What if it happens again?' Teigan asked.

'I'm pulling the plug on the deal with Frank. First the factory fire, then this? Police will be crawling the streets looking for the dealers, hoping it will lead them to me. I'm not risking it.'

It was Teigan's turn to nod. 'Frank won't be happy about that.'

'I don't give a fuck. If he's pedalling a product that's killing folk, I don't want anything to do with it.'

'Do you really think that's what it is?' Teigan asked.

'Like I said, I'm hoping that girl was just unlucky.'

Teigan puffed out her cheeks. 'Poor girl.'

'Nope,' Ricky said. 'Don't make that connection.'

Teigan's brow furrowed. 'Eh?'

'You're connecting what we do to the person buying our product.'

'You've lost me.'

Ricky sighed and placed a hand on his daughter's shoulder. 'You're not the one who needs to worry about what happens once the product is sold. The people who are buying from us are adults. They know the risks involved. Once it's out of our hands and into theirs, it's nothing more to do with us. If they have a bad reaction, it's not our responsibility. Keep that in mind.'

'She was a *teenager*, Dad. Someone's daughter, granddaughter. An actual person.'

'Yes, but she was also an adult who was old enough to know the risk she was taking. Seriously, Teigan, if you're going to go far in this business, you need to grow a stronger backbone.'

Teigan stared at him and Ricky could tell she was shocked by the way her mouth fell open slightly. It frustrated him that Teigan was looking at the human side more than the business side of things. She was becoming more and more like her mother, the older she was getting. Another annoyance he'd have to ignore.

Chapter Thirty-Nine

Stepping off the train at Glasgow Central, Elle felt immediately exposed. Even though she was almost three decades older, with a lot more lines around the corners of her eyes, she still worried someone would recognise her and immediately run to Ricky. She was worried that would happen before she got a chance to see Teigan and put things right. She needed to know the truth.

Stepping out of the train station onto Hope Street, the sudden and familiar smell of her home city hit her like a ton of bricks. It was almost as if she'd never been away and yet it felt like a lifetime since she'd left.

Across the road she noticed a small shop tucked away in the corner of the street. The window displayed used mobile phones. She would be needing one of those if she was going to make contact with Teigan. Checking the road was clear, Elle crossed over and went inside.

Around half an hour later, she was back outside with a new smart phone and one hundred and fifty quid lighter. She was going to have to teach herself how to use it. It wouldn't be difficult. Not if she put her mind to it. The man inside had set it all up for her, installed the Facebook app and put the sim card in before giving her a copy of the mobile number and network details.

Glancing up the street she froze. What was she supposed to do now? She had nowhere to stay and no idea of where to find somewhere that wouldn't quickly eat up the cash Frank had given her.

She ran through some ideas. Even a basic budget hotel wasn't cheap these days. Perhaps a hostel? But then she would have to share with strangers. Not her idea of safety, especially not in a city where most criminals would know or know of Ricky Fyfe. Then she remembered some of the girls back in Essex who she worked with talking about Airbnb and how they'd found holiday accommodation for a good price. They'd talked about renting entire homes for decent money. Maybe she could use that?

Realising that she was starving, Elle decided to find somewhere to have food and become familiar with her new phone. If she could get it going, maybe she could book somewhere for tonight and the next few weeks. Just to help her get settled.

Around twenty minutes later, Elle was sitting at the back of a McDonald's, with her cheeseburger meal in front of her and phone in hand. She switched it on and hoped that it was good to go.

As she took a bite of her burger, she opened the Google app already on the screen and searched for Airbnb. Before she knew it, she had booked a house in the West End of Glasgow for fourteen nights. It had been so simple she worried she'd messed it up.

Finishing her food and wondering how greedy it would be to order the same thing again, Elle opened the Facebook app and saw that she had two messages from Teigan. Her stomach flipped and suddenly, she wasn't as hungry anymore.

She read over the questions and her heart sank. On some level, Teigan knew who Elle was. Of course she did. She couldn't read the message Elle had sent and not suspect, could she?

How was she going to answer? How did Elle know that Teigan wasn't going to tell Ricky? How did she know it wasn't Ricky himself sending the messages?

Then she read the third question. She had to read the last part twice and still couldn't comprehend what Teigan was asking. Why had she broken Ricky's heart and left with his brother? Chris had helped her get out of Scotland and away from Ricky. The question suggested that Chris was no longer in Ricky's life. And if that was the case, then there was only one reason for that. Chris must be dead.

If Chris *was* dead, then there could be one or two reasons.

Ricky found out that Chris had betrayed him by helping her get away, and in a fit of rage had killed him.

Or, Ricky had found out that Chris was Teigan's biological father. Either way, the outcome for Chris would have been the same. Ricky would never have let him away with either.

Elle closed her eyes and even with almost three decades between them, she felt that same fear she did on the day she left.

Ricky Fyfe was ruthless. But she'd been absent in her daughter's life for too long because of him.

Enough was enough.

Chapter Forty

Laying back in a bath overflowing with bubbles, Danica stared at the phone in her hand and she couldn't stop the feeling of dread as it crept over her, pricking her skin even in the warm water. She hadn't expected to feel this way. To know that a teenage girl had died because of the plan she'd executed with Aidan Doyle made her feel like the shittiest person in the world. That was because she had a conscience. Unlike Ricky, who had killed her dad without even thinking about it.

She took a deep breath, inhaling the lavender scent from the bubble bath. She should feel relaxed. But with the report in front of her, and the knowledge that it was probably going to happen again, she just couldn't keep the tension away.

Sitting up straight and glancing at the bathroom door to check that it was locked for the millionth time, Danica reached for the burner phone sitting on the side of the sink and texted Aidan.

> Do they have to die? Can't they just become really sick?

Danica waited for a reply, which came through very quickly.

> I don't get to choose who dies or who gets sick. I tampered with the products, putting my own life in danger by the way. You are welcome for that. The sooner more people suffer because of Ricky's drugs, the better. You started this Danica, not me. You think I want people to die?

She stared at the words Doyle had sent. Danica didn't want people to die. Of course she didn't. She herself was the victim of horrific loss.

But she didn't know another way to stop Ricky other than to bring his empire down.

> I know you don't. Maybe you could make an anonymous call to Frank, let him know what's happened?

Frank Cranwell would kill Ricky if he thought his own reputation was on the line because of drug-related deaths in Glasgow. But Danica didn't want Ricky dead before she had the chance to marry him.

> Are you serious? You know what will happen if I do that. Just do whatever it is you're doing, get me my money and passport so I can get the fuck out of the country.

Danica pulled her lips into a thin line and nodded. She knew it was best to keep Aidan on side. If she didn't pay him what she'd promised for his part in the crash of the Fyfe empire, he could grass her up to the police himself. He was flying under the radar since the factory fire and she was the only person from the Fyfe family to even know where he was. If she put a foot wrong in his direction, he could expose her and disappear. She'd left herself open to more risk with Aidan's involvement.

> I'll be in touch when I have the passport and cash.

She set the phone on the edge of the sink and slid back down into the water, praying that the next person to fall victim to Ricky's drugs didn't die. Otherwise, Frank would take matters into his own hands and the wedding wouldn't be able to go ahead because Ricky would, at best, lose a limb.

Just a few days until the wedding. Anything could happen in that short time. Not long to wait now.

Chapter Forty-One

Now settled in her Airbnb rental, Elle felt at a loss as to what to do next. She had no plan, no real idea of what to do when she got there. She was, however, back in Glasgow. Her home city. And in an odd way, it felt wonderful. Freeing. But also terrifying. *Mostly* terrifying.

She stared at the messages from Teigan and found herself typing out a reply, asking if she would like to meet but to keep it secret. Her stomach rolled and flipped with each new letter appearing on the screen. This was not a good idea. Not one bit. Teigan could very well tell Ricky that she suspected she was talking to her runaway mum.

Wine. Elle needed wine.

Getting to her feet, she grabbed some cash from her bag and the key for the rental and headed out to the street. She was in the West End of Glasgow. A high end, beautiful part of the city. She should enjoy the walk. But all she kept thinking was to keep her eyes to the ground, get the wine and get back to the rental.

Elle headed up Byres Road, desperate to savour it, take it all in. She'd missed her home city a lot, more than she'd realised. The smells, the sights, the conversation. The familiar accent. But she knew she had to be quick. She was dangerously close to her old street, Cleveden Drive, where she once lived as a gangster's wife. An abused gangster's wife. This was stupid. Picking a rental so close to Ricky's home. But then, Glasgow itself was close enough. He could be around any corner, across any street.

Turning onto Chancellor Street, she went into an independent off-licence and grabbed two bottles of Merlot without much thought. She didn't care. The stronger the better.

She paid for her wine and headed back to the rental. Her stomach churned as her phone buzzed in her pocket; the buzz itself almost ringing in her ears. Glancing down at the message, she saw that it was

Teigan, as expected, and she had agreed to meet. She had also agreed to keep their meeting quiet. But could she trust she was telling the truth?

Elle arranged to meet Teigan in Kelvingrove Park the next day at three o'clock. Schools would just be getting out and that meant a busy, neutral spot that would provide camouflage for Elle. Plenty of places for her to hide if things got too much or if Ricky showed up.

Ricky. She never forgot a face, especially not his. But if the years hadn't been kind to him the way they hadn't been to Elle, then he would have aged a fair bit. If that was the case, at least she knew what he looked like now in order to be able to avoid him if he showed up, thanks to having a look on Danica's page.

Once Elle arrived back at the rental, she headed into the kitchen, poured a large glass of Merlot and sank down onto the black leather sofa in the lounge area. Looking Ricky Fyfe up on Google proved to be interesting. A man with many business ventures, some of which screamed that they were a front for all sorts. A man like Ricky didn't do legit. Ever.

When she locked eyes with his image, it felt strange to know that she was still technically married to him. The fact that she had ever married him in the first place baffled her now. A handsome man, with dark, sadistic eyes and a hypnotic smile. It was no wonder he'd managed to charm Danica.

Taking a large gulp of wine, Elle felt her jaw tense. Sadistic really was the right word for him. Getting into a relationship with the daughter of the man he'd murdered truly made him bottom of the barrel scum in Elle's eyes. But it made sense purely based on the person he was.

'Bastard,' she whispered as she scrolled along to the next picture. This time, he was smiling out at the camera and Elle read the caption. It was an image taken of him after he'd got away with a not proven verdict in Jordan Burns's murder. A murder case that had gone unsolved in the eyes of the courts. But Elle knew who had done it. And she knew that even now, after all these years, he'd still try to pin it on her if he knew she was back. It was his insurance policy.

But Elle had her own insurance policy now. She wasn't going to cower away and be that terrified little wife anymore. She was taking back her life. Not only that, she was seeking justice for the lives that Ricky stole from Teigan and Danica.

Chapter Forty-Two

Kelvingrove Park at three in the afternoon was heaving with kids, even though the weather wasn't great. Grey clouds threatened heavy rain and Teigan's stomach wouldn't settle. She stood by the gate at the west entrance, opposite the Kelvingrove Art Gallery and scanned the surrounding area. She had no idea what her mum – Sarah Parks – looked like, so didn't know who she was supposed to be watching out for.

Rolling her eyes at the ridiculous idea that this person was her mum, she shook her head and considered leaving. But what was she going back to? A life that was slowly beginning to change – and not for the better. Danica was beginning to phase Teigan out. She was the only one who could see it coming. It would only be a matter of time before her dad would want his wife by his side in business meetings and deals. Ricky was deep in love with a woman the same age as his daughter. He was thinking with his bloody crotch but he'd never admit that. He probably didn't even realise that was the case.

The clouds above her darkened and she felt her skin prickle against the cooler temperature. Glancing around, she looked at every passing woman, wondering if it could be her. Elle.

And then she spotted someone down by the skatepark. A woman who could possibly be her. She fitted the idea of what Teigan imagined her to look like. Around five feet, four inches tall. Slim. She looked around the right age too.

Narrowing her eyes as she watched the woman walk towards her, Teigan's hope died a little when the woman walked up the hill and out of the gate, heading in the direction of Sauchiehall Street.

She spied another woman, but she quickly disappeared too and Teigan was beginning to wonder if this Sarah Parks was hiding in plain sight, or if maybe, she wasn't coming at all. What if it was all a hoax?

Why would they do that to her? Or maybe they were doing it to wind Ricky up. But Teigan hadn't told her dad about this. She didn't want his input, his opinions. He still held some kind of anger towards Elle. And why wouldn't he? She'd left them for his brother.

Her uncle came into her thoughts as she continued to watch the crowds of people in the park, some passing her by as they came and went. What if he was back too? What if they were here to try to explain away what they did?

Teigan imagined the moment she came face to face with her long-lost mum. How would they greet one another? What words would be exchanged? How would Teigan feel?

Glancing down at her watch, she noted that it was now half past three. This person, whoever they were, wasn't coming. That was obvious. This had been some sick game and she'd fallen for it because she was vulnerable.

Turning her back to the park, Teigan faced the galleries and took a long, deep breath, trying not to cry.

She didn't *need* another parent. She had her dad – the one who *hadn't* abandoned her as a baby, although how long that would last was questionable. However, he'd been the one who'd been there throughout her entire life. Elle had fucked off all those years ago to be with her brother-in-law. Why should Teigan give her the time of day even if she did come back?

Teigan held her head up high and decided she wasn't going to look back. She'd managed to get through her entire life without a mother. She didn't need one now.

Chapter Forty-Three

Elle entered the coffee shop and glanced over to the back corner. She'd followed Teigan from the park, having been too full of fear to approach her. It had all been too overwhelming, the idea of coming face to face with her. She didn't want to see Teigan's reaction to having a mother who looked the way she did. Haggard by years of alcohol abuse and living in fear that she'd be found. Teigan was young, healthy and beautiful. And Elle looked like she'd just crawled out from under a rock.

Having to explain her absence wouldn't be easy. It would mean having to tarnish the perception Teigan had of the man who'd brought her up, who'd called himself Dad. Even though it killed Elle to think that she'd allowed that to happen, she couldn't hurt Teigan that way. She couldn't tell her daughter that the man she thought was her dad all her life, was not her real father.

Elle ordered a coffee and sat down at a table on the opposite side of the cafe, but with a good view of Teigan. She studied her face, her hair, her height. She was beautiful and looked a lot like Elle did back in the day, before Ricky got his claws into her and she stopped putting so much effort into her appearance.

A waitress brought the hot drink to Elle's table and smiled down as she placed it in front of her. Elle took her eyes off Teigan, thanked the woman and took a breath. Teigan was drinking a large latte and staring out of the window. She looked deep in thought. Most likely wondering why she'd been stood up. The guilt was unbearable; it felt like she'd abandoned her daughter twice.

But she just couldn't bring herself to stand in front of Teigan and tell her who she was. Would Teigan even believe her? Who knew what kind of crap Ricky had fed her over the years about who her mother was and the kind of person she'd been. Teigan could have a mountain of false information, all negative and toxic. Or she could simply know nothing. Knowing Ricky, it would be the former.

The coffee shop was playing music, which Elle had barely noticed until now. The song made her stomach lurch. The coincidence was utterly ridiculous. She hadn't listened to Wet Wet Wet since she'd left Glasgow. 'Love Is All Around' had been the song playing on the radio in the hospital when Teigan had been born, and now it was playing in the coffee shop, while she was sitting just feet away from her daughter.

She lowered her head and tried to stop herself from crying. Taking a few deep breaths, she raised her eyes and glanced at Teigan. She was mouthing the words. Every single lyric, as she stared out of the window.

Elle watched and her heart ached, yet she felt warm. She was breathing the same air as her baby girl. She had thought she would never get to see her again.

Marti Pellow belted out the last of the lyrics as the song faded and Elle pushed back her seat and left.

Chapter Forty-Four

Teigan stared out onto Argyle Street, with her coffee in front of her as she sang quietly along to the music. She'd always loved this song. She loved Wet Wet Wet, but never told anyone. They were her guilty pleasure ever since watching *Four Weddings and a Funeral*, as was Hugh Grant. Something she'd never admit out loud as he was old enough to be her dad, not that it would have bothered Danica, of course.

Thinking of weddings, Teigan knew that her father's upcoming nuptials weren't far away and she didn't know what to do about it. Try to stop the wedding, or simply stand back and silently hate that her future stepmother was the same age as her.

There had been so much heartache in Ricky's life. Teigan had grown up knowing how broken he was that his wife and brother had run away together, leaving him to bring her up on his own. Maybe he was finally happy with Danica. She just struggled to believe this to be true. Danica wasn't making him happy; she was flattering him. A man fast approaching sixty, who'd been single most of his life, apart from a few women when Teigan had been younger, of course he was flattered when a twenty-three-year-old woman had shown an interest in him. Shame he couldn't see the pound signs reflecting in her eyes the way Teigan could. A smile crossed her face then. If Hugh Grant was to ask her out, would she say no? He was handsome and had money, and he was even older than Ricky. With Danica and Ricky, it was the same thing, wasn't it?

As much as Teigan tried to distract herself with other things, she couldn't get her mother out of her head.

She'd never asked about Elle, or her uncle for that matter. And Ricky had never volunteered any information. Maybe it wouldn't do any harm to ask some questions, to set her mind at ease.

Her phone started to ring, jolting her from her thoughts. Her dad's name flashed across the screen and Teigan answered it.

'I was just about to come and see you,' she said.

–

'You look like you've seen a ghost,' her dad said to her as she sat on the sofa in his office. 'What's up with you? You're not still angry about Danica's dress choice for you?'

Teigan smirked. She wished that was the only thing she had to worry about. 'It's only one day. I'll survive wearing a dress I hate for a woman I despise on the worst day of my life.'

Ricky smiled widely. 'Nice to know you're in a good place with it.'

Teigan watched as her dad carefully removed the frame from the wall, opened the safe and slid an envelope of cash inside. She saw something else in the corner. A small key hanging on the back wall of the safe. It wasn't something she'd ever noticed before. Not that she ever had access to that safe. No one did.

'Can I ask you something about my mum?' The words were out of her mouth before she'd even processed that she was going to ask the question at all.

She watched as her dad's shoulders stiffened. He cleared his throat and turned to face her, the safe door still ajar. 'What about her?'

'Do you ever wonder if she'll come back?' She didn't plan on keeping the messages from Facebook a secret from him. But she wanted to gauge his reaction to the subject of talking about her first.

Ricky frowned, deep creases lining the skin between his brows. It showed his age, that he would be sixty in the summer. An age where he'd receive his free pensioner's bus pass. The thought almost made her smile, but now was not the time. 'What makes you ask that?'

She stared at him, hoping that his eyes would reach her own. Instead, he kept his gaze on the papers on the desk. He wasn't blinking, shoulders still rigid.

'I don't know,' Teigan lied. 'Maybe because you're getting married on her birthday.' A thought came to her then, something that had never occurred to her before. 'Actually, come to think of it, if she left and you have no idea where she is and haven't had any contact, aren't you still legally married to her?'

His eyes shifted and he fixed them on Teigan. 'We're no longer legally bound.'

'How do you know that though?'

Ricky's chest rose as he filled his lungs with air. 'Because she asked me for a divorce before she left. I signed the papers and that was that.'

Teigan stared at him through wide eyes. 'Why have you never told me this?'

'Because it's not important,' Ricky replied and then he slammed a fist on the desk. 'Why are you talking about her all of a sudden?'

Teigan jumped from the sudden outburst and her heart raced. At first, she was hurt by his reaction. Then, frustration built in her chest, and she got to her feet. 'Because she was my fucking mum and I have a right to know why she fucking ditched me, that's why. And you've never fully told me what happened, Dad. I have a right to know, don't you think?'

She could see just how angry he was becoming and a pang of guilt hit her alongside her own frustrations. This would be hurting him as much as it was hurting her.

'She has no place in your life, Teigan. She was nothing but a liar and a traitor.'

His shoulders became looser then, and his eyes darkened.

'Yes, I know she left you for your brother, but why didn't she take me with her?' Teigan shouted at him. 'She might have fallen out of love with you, Dad, but why me? I was just a baby and she left me.'

She felt tears running down her cheeks that she hadn't expected, and it seemed Ricky didn't know how to deal with it.

'I don't have time for this, Teigan. It's trivial shit now. Just... just forget about her. She forgot about *you*.'

Her jaw dropped open as Ricky strode towards the door and stepped out of the office, leaving her alone.

She stared down at the large picture of the two of them which rested on the floor against the wall. Smiling. Happy. Teigan couldn't remember if she'd thought about her mum much before today, but now she couldn't stop.

Shaking her head, Teigan followed her dad out into the hallway. She stood behind him as he gripped onto the banister, staring down to the hallway below.

'It might be trivial to you, but it's not to me. You knew her well. She was your wife for... I don't even know how long for before I came along. You have a lot to be angry with her about, I get that. But I never got the chance to be her daughter. Do you have any idea how much that hurts?'

Without turning, Ricky bowed his head and said in an almost whisper, 'More than you know.'

He kept his back to her and headed downstairs and out of the house. She heard the roar of his car as it left the driveway. Danica appeared at the bottom of the stairs and glanced up at her.

'What was all that about?' she asked, sounding genuinely concerned.

'Just a fight about the wedding,' Teigan replied. 'No, actually, it wasn't about the wedding. It was about my mum.'

She kept her eye on Danica, waiting for her to say something cocky or inappropriate. Instead, her expression softened. 'Are you okay?'

Frowning, Teigan felt the adrenaline dissipating, replaced with a lump in her throat. No, she wasn't okay. Not at all. What did Danica care anyway? She'd gone and booked the wedding on Elle's birthday. She didn't give a shit. She was marrying a shit ton of money. Instead, she took a breath and decided to be the bigger person.

'I will be. I just need to talk to him.'

Danica nodded. 'Maybe he's just stressed about the newspaper reporting that drug death. I'm sure he'll come back soon, and you'll work it out.'

Teigan's frown deepened. 'No, it's not that. He's pissed off because I brought up my mum.'

'Don't worry about it. Like I said, you guys will work it out.'

'Why are you being so nice?'

Danica shrugged. 'I'd give anything to have an argument with my dad. Or my mum.'

The pair fell silent.

Chapter Forty-Five

She watched as Teigan closed the door behind her and Danica let out a sigh of relief that she was alone in the house again. She'd heard what had been said upstairs; she'd heard it all. Teigan was questioning Ricky about her mother, his ex-wife, asking why she'd left Teigan behind as a baby.

In a way, Danica got it. She understood on some level what abandonment felt like, although their childhoods had been very different. Ricky had been ruthless in his response to Teigan's questions. His dismissal of how his own daughter felt reminded Danica of just how little empathy the man possessed. It was a stark reminder that if he found out what her plan was, the game would be up for Danica. If he could be that ruthless with his daughter, he wouldn't think twice about ending Danica's life.

The notification sound rung out from her pocket and when she glanced down at the screen, her stomach flipped when she saw a reply from Sarah Parks, agreeing to meet with her. If there was someone out there who had been friends with her parents, Danica needed to find them. She needed to know more about her dad. She needed to understand why Ricky had killed him and it seemed as if Sarah Parks might know the answer to that question.

The burner phone in her other pocket buzzed. It was Aidan Doyle calling.

'What?'

'There's someone else in the hospital after taking Ricky's coke,' he said. 'I actually watched them collapse in the street.'

'Are they dead?' Danica asked.

'No. But that doesn't mean they won't die.'

Danica closed her eyes. 'Does Ricky know?'

'I don't know. I was hoping you'd tell me.'

She opened her eyes and glanced out of the window looking onto the drive. 'He's just gone out. Keep me posted and I'll let you know if he says anything.'

'You think Cranwell will come up to Glasgow?'

Danica shrugged even though Aidan couldn't see her. 'I don't know. But if he does, there will be an all-out war. I need to be married before that happens.'

'Maybe you should have waited until he put a ring on your finger,' Aidan said. She heard his words echo in her head and gritted her teeth at how right he was. But she couldn't let herself think that way. She couldn't have waited. She needed to get the ball rolling.

Danica hung up the phone and ran up to Ricky's office. Standing in front of the open door, she was surprised he hadn't locked it behind him. He never, *ever*, left the house with the office door open, let alone unlocked.

Stepping inside, Danica inhaled deeply. The safe was open. Another thing he never did. What the hell was going through his head to have left the house with not only the office unsecured, but the safe too?

Knowing she probably wouldn't have too long before Ricky returned, Danica moved quickly inside and stood in front of the safe. An envelope lay flat, which she guessed was stuffed full of cash. A gun and, oddly, two keys back-to-back hung on the rear wall. It was the keys that really caught her attention. What were they for? Not the safe. They seemed more like the kind that would open a safety deposit box or a storage locker. Slipping her hand in carefully, Danica pulled them off the hook and removed one from the keyring. She knew how risky it would be, but she intended to copy and return it as quickly as possible. The only question now was how to figure out where the lock to match the key was. Whatever it was for was clearly very important to him if he kept it in a safe.

She spun around and glanced down at the drawer in the desk. It had a lock. She tried it, but the key wouldn't even go in. Danica held it in her hand, using her fingers to flip it back and forward. And then she noticed it. The number engraved on the top of the key. Nine. It had to be a locker or security box of some kind. But where?

The sound of a car coming into the drive jolted her from her thoughts and she quickly slipped the key into her pocket before rushing back downstairs. Ricky was just coming through the door as she reached the bottom.

'Hey,' she said. 'Do you know you've left your office door open?'

He nodded and pushed past her on the stairs. 'Why were you in there?'

'I wasn't,' she frowned, the lie coming easily. 'I just noticed it was open. I know you don't like anyone being in there without you, so I thought it was odd that it was left open.'

He grunted something inaudible and went inside before closing the door behind him. Danica listened as the sound of the safe door closed and she felt another dump of adrenaline course through her. She so very nearly got caught then. What would he have done if he'd found her in there, with her hands in the safe?

She dreaded to think.

–

Danica sat with her back resting against her mother's headstone, facing out to the rest of the graves in front of her. Her heart pounded in her chest, wondering if this mystery person who claimed to know her parents would even show up. All the while, her heart pounded at the thought of what Ricky would do if he realised one of the keys from the safe was missing. He'd immediately suspect Danica.

'Danica?' a soft voice interrupted her thoughts from behind her mother's stone. Getting to her feet, she turned to see a woman standing there. She looked worn, worried and exhausted. Blemishes across her cheeks screamed too much alcohol, something that Danica knew would be coming her way soon if she continued drinking the way she had been of late.

'You're Danica Burns?'

Danica pulled her lips between her teeth and took in a long, deep breath through her nose. She hadn't heard anyone call her that for a long time and it sounded beautiful as it carried on the air.

'Who *are* you?' Danica asked. 'And how do you know my parents?'

The woman walked around the grave and stood next to Danica. She looked down at the stone and sighed. 'I knew your dad from a long time ago.'

Danica frowned. 'Yeah, but *who* are you? You warned me about Ricky. How do you know him? How do you know he's not a good person to be in a relationship with?' Her voice trailed off and in that moment she suspected – no, *knew* – who she was standing next to. She studied her face, her eyes, the shape of her jawline, how her nose turned up just a little at the tip. The exact same shape as...

The woman stood silently, staring at Danica.

'Oh my god, are you Teigan's mum? Are you *Elle Fyfe*?' The words came out in a cracked whisper, in disbelief and utter shock.

Elle nodded but remained silent.

'Fucking hell,' Danica gasped, staring at her and wondering if she was losing her mind. 'She looks exactly like you. This was not who I was expecting at all.'

'I'm trusting you to keep quiet about this, Danica. Ricky can't know I'm here, and neither can Teigan. I've only come here to plead with you to get out of that house, or you could end up dead.'

'Is that why you left? You were worried he would kill you or something?' Danica pressed.

Elle raised a brow and shook her head. 'He *did* kill me. Or at least, he thinks he did. And if you don't get out he will do the same to you, although I doubt you'll be as lucky as I was.'

'Jesus Christ,' Danica muttered as she started to pace. Wringing her hands together as beads of sweat formed on her brow, a thought sprung to mind. 'Do you know what happened between Ricky and my dad?'

Elle puffed out her cheeks and her expression was awash with empathy. 'I do. Well, he told me his version, which implicated me. If it had happened now, as the person I am today, I don't know if I'd have rolled over so quickly.'

Danica felt her stomach roll. 'What did he say happened?'

'There's a lot to it, but basically he thought I was having an affair with Jordan, which I was not. He was my friend, that's as far as it went. I was friends with Georgia too. Anyway, he told me he had killed Jordan and framed me for it.'

Danica's jaw almost hit the floor and her rolling stomach made her gag. She leaned over slightly, took some deep breaths. The thing she'd wanted to hear from the moment she'd read her mum's letter had finally been said, and all she could do was try to stop herself from being sick.

'Oh no,' Elle said, placing a hand on Danica's back. 'I'm so sorry. I shouldn't have just blurted it out like that. I didn't think.'

Straightening her back, Danica looked Elle in the eye and said, 'But he was tried for it, and got off on a not proven verdict because of insufficient evidence. My dad's body was never found.'

Elle closed her eyes. 'I know. I'm so sorry, lovely girl. You do not deserve this. None of your family did. Your dad was a million times the man Ricky ever could be. He told me that he dipped my dress in your dad's blood, and had it packed away as evidence to prove I was the one who killed him.'

Danica felt hot tears sting her eyes. How could someone so evil exist?

'And Teigan doesn't know any of this?' Danica asked, her voice trembling.

'I doubt it. What are you doing, marrying him, Danica?'

'I want to ruin him,' she said, wiping furiously at the tears on her cheeks. 'And now I have this.'

Elle's eyes widened. 'No. No, you can't tell him about this. Danica, he thinks I'm dead. He won't mess around this time. He'll finish the job properly if he gets a hold of me.'

Danica's shoulders slumped. She knew she couldn't risk someone else's life like that. She was in no way any kind of version of Ricky. She raised her hands and nodded. 'Okay. I won't mention a thing. But don't for one minute think I'm going to walk away from this wedding.'

Elle sighed in frustration and gripped Danica's hands, giving them a shake. 'Think of your dad, Danica. Imagine what he would think.'

Snatching her hands away, she snapped back, 'If my dad could think, then I wouldn't be doing this in the fucking first place.'

'Okay, so you marry him. And then what?'

'Somehow, he dies. And I get everything. I can give myself the life I should have had.'

Elle stared at her with a disbelieving look on her face. 'You think that all of Ricky's money is going to help you to move on and be happy in life?'

Danica shook her head slowly and glanced down at her mother's grave. 'No, but it would help.'

'And how do you propose he dies?'

Danica shrugged. 'I don't know. A car accident? Falling off a cliff on our honeymoon? Stabbed to death. Who the hell cares. But I'll find someone to do it.'

It sounded insane, but Danica couldn't go back on the promise she'd made to herself.

'Danica. You can't do this.'

'You can't stop me. You're supposed to be dead. And I promise you Elle, if you try to get in my way, I'll tell him you're back. Don't underestimate me on that.'

Elle looked defeated. 'Fine. Just don't say I didn't warn you.'

Elle stood up and began walking away from the headstone. Danica watched her go and called out, 'I'm sorry your life is such a mess because of him. Try to see this as justice for what he did to you, too.'

Elle didn't turn, she kept walking, her stature getting smaller and smaller until Danica couldn't see her anymore.

Danica got to her feet and stared out across the cemetery. She closed her eyes and breathed deeply. She was going to become Danica Fyfe. Ricky's second wife. The one who was going to make a difference.

Once that happened, there would be nothing she wouldn't do to make sure her husband suffered.

Chapter Forty-Six

'Mr Fyfe, are you alright? You don't usually come in here and just, well, sit,' Tim Crawford said as he made a coffee from the machine in the kitchen. Ricky sat with his back to the window and stared blankly at the wall.

'Just having a bad day, Tim. I like to come in here because it's peaceful. No one knows I'm here other than you and if I'm honest, the dead can't bother me the way the living can.'

Tim smiled softly. Ricky could never understand how someone surrounded by so much death every day could have such a cheery and calming disposition. Ricky had only ever felt stress and anger each time he was involved in a death.

'Ah, yes,' Tim replied. 'The dead are often quiet.'

Ricky raised his eyebrow and frowned. 'Often?'

'Well, you know.'

Ricky glanced from side to side and shook his head. 'Enlighten me.'

'It's been known for corpses to release gases; sometimes it can sound like a moan, or a gasp. First time it happened to me when I was just a young man, I almost had a heart attack.'

Ricky couldn't help the laugh that burst out of him. 'Ha, not what I was expecting to hear, Tim. But that did cheer me up.'

Tim smiled softly once more and went on making his coffee. It occurred to Ricky that he'd known Tim since he'd been a boy, when old man Fyfe had the reins of the business. He'd watched Tim grow into an older gentleman. It wouldn't be so surprising if Tim hung up his mortuary keys soon. Where would that leave Ricky? There were plenty of secrets Tim had kept for Ricky and he knew it wasn't by choice or loyalty, but fear. Tim had come to learn that the path of least resistance was the best way for him. And it had worked in Ricky's favour. He'd been able to keep Elle's death a secret alongside Chris. And Jordan Burns.

'Does it ever get tiring? You know, working with the dead?' Ricky asked.

'No,' Tim answered quickly. 'Never tiring. Well, not physically. Sometimes when there's a premature death, it can be difficult, especially if it's a child or a young adult.'

'And the ones you're paid extra for?' Ricky pressed, knowing that Tim would never speak ill against the Fyfe empire or what he was asked to do for it.

'It's just another job, Mr Fyfe. I don't ask questions,' he said, sipping on his coffee as he stood with his back pressed against the counter, staring back at Ricky. 'I do the job, release the soul from the shell and get on with the rest of my day.'

Ricky stared at Tim, shocked by how easily he put things. 'It's hardened you. Or desensitised you. I can't figure out which.'

Tim shook his head. 'No, I've always seen death as factual, the inevitable end we will all meet. It cannot be avoided, so why not embrace it?'

Ricky nodded and realised that Tim was just the grim reaper in a suit; much like Ricky, if it came to it.

'A very healthy way to deal with it,' Ricky said. 'Now, if you'll excuse me, I have some deposits to make.'

Tim nodded, looking down at the floor as Ricky walked past, and said nothing. Out of the kitchen, Ricky opened the basement door and headed down into the mortuary. He passed by the lockers containing dead bodies and continued to the end, where he stored the cash that still needed to be cleaned. That had always been Chris's job. Now, it was Teigan's.

Closing the drawer, Ricky turned and was faced with the smaller storage lockers. He glanced at number nine. No one else in the world knew what was in there, or that the locker even existed, other than Tim, but even he didn't know what was inside. And he didn't have to.

Elle was never coming back because she was dead, so he could get rid of the contents. But they'd been an insurance policy for so long that he couldn't bring himself to do it. They'd served a purpose back then, that if he'd had to, he could have used them to clear his name. And he'd often questioned himself as to why he never had. It was the perfect crime: Jordan's blood on Elle's dress. Elle had done a runner with Chris. Done and dusted. Yet, at the time, something stopped him. His daughter, perhaps? As much as he hated the lie he'd carried for years about being her real dad, he loved being her dad. He loved Teigan like she was his own. Treated her like it too. The fact she was not his biological daughter didn't matter to him. But now she was asking questions about Elle. Questions he didn't want to answer. Teigan had no idea Elle was dead. He didn't want to leave things as hostile as they were. He wanted to sort things out with his daughter but if she wasn't going to back down and change her feelings about his marriage, then there wasn't much hope for them. Ricky had never let the feelings of others affect his actions before, so he wasn't going to start now. If Teigan couldn't accept the inevitable, then maybe they didn't have much of a future as father and daughter.

Chapter Forty-Seven

'All done here, Mr Crawford,' Teigan said, closing down the financial records on the computer.

'Please, call me Tim,' Tim Crawford smiled.

Teigan returned his smile, and a pang of guilt washed over her. This man was so utterly kind; there wasn't a bad bone in his body. And yet he never seemed to question what she and her dad were doing. He simply nodded along. Maybe he was just happy not to be the one on a mortuary slab downstairs, the fear of questioning enough to keep him quiet.

'Okay, Tim. All funds in the safe are now included in your daily figures for the month, ready to be deposited into the business account. Nothing more for you to do than that.'

Tim nodded once, smiled and said, 'Great.'

Teigan got up from the seat behind the desk and shut down the computer. She felt Tim's eyes on her but when she looked up at him, he was staring out onto the street.

'You okay over there, Tim?'

'Hm? Oh, yes. Just thinking about retirement. Or rather, dreaming.'

'That day not coming quickly enough for you?'

'Oh, I don't know. It's just something your dad said when he was here earlier today.'

Teigan frowned. There was nothing in the diary about Ricky going to the funeral home today. 'Dad was here today?'

'Yes, he seemed fretful. Forgive me, I don't want to come across as a tell-tale. He did, however, seem a little different today. And he was asking me if I ever got tired of the business of death. I didn't think so. But since he asked, I've been wondering what it would be like to retire. Of course, it has only been a few hours, but still, it's a nice thought.'

'You've been in this game for a long time,' Teigan replied. 'It's natural for your thoughts to wander to somewhere else. Especially given what we put on you every month.'

Tim raised a brow. 'Well, we all know my position on that. See no evil, hear no evil, speak no evil.'

Interesting way to look at it, Teigan thought to herself. Evil wasn't the word she'd use for the Fyfe empire but still, everyone had their own opinion.

'Ha, I hope you don't say that to my dad when he's around,' Teigan laughed as she gathered up her bag.

'Your dad and I have a good understanding of one another. There's a mutual respect there.'

'Shame the same can't be said for me and him,' Teigan muttered.

'Pardon?'

'Oh, it's nothing. We just had a bit of a fight today.'

Tim looked genuinely concerned. 'Oh no, nothing that can't be fixed, I hope.'

'Actually, it was a fight about my mum.'

Tim seemed to stiffen up then and Teigan noticed how he averted his eyes. He cleared his throat loudly and reached for his glass of water.

'Are you okay, Tim?'

Swallowing and nodding at the same time, it seemed as though the man was uncomfortable.

'Did he tell you about our fight?' Teigan pressed.

Tim shook his head. 'Oh, no. Not at all.'

Narrowing her eyes, Teigan couldn't shift the feeling that something was off. 'Did you know my mum? Did you ever meet her? I mean, you've been in my dad's life for as long as I can remember, surely you must have known her?'

Clearing his throat again, Tim closed his eyes briefly and said, 'Yes. I did. *Lovely* woman. Very kind. She had a quiet disposition, from what I remember.'

Teigan wondered what would happen if she told Tim about Elle coming back into her life. Would he be as loyal to her as he was to Ricky and keep it to himself? Likely not if he thought it was going to lead to him getting a black eye or losing a finger.

'Did she?'

'She did, yes. You remind me a lot of her before she...' Tim's voice trailed off.

'Before she...?'

The phone on the desk rang, so sharp and shrill that both Teigan and Tim jumped at the same time. Tim got to his feet and rushed across the room, picking up the phone and giving his usual spiel in his telephone voice, which wasn't much different from his usual voice.

Teigan sighed and shook her head. She was grilling a man old enough to be her grandad about a woman she'd never met, hoping that he'd have all the answers that Ricky didn't want to give her. It was ridiculous.

She mouthed that she was going to leave him to it and stepped out of the office onto the street. The fresh air hit her like a ton of bricks, almost like it awakened her to what had gone on earlier that day. So much had happened in a short space of time. She'd turned up to meet a woman she believed could be her mum, but she never showed up. She'd questioned her dad about the past. She'd laundered money for the business. And it was only two in the afternoon.

She pulled out her phone and texted her dad.

We need to talk. Now.

Glancing over at the pub across the road, she said aloud, 'I need a fucking drink.'

Chapter Forty-Eight

Glancing down at his phone, Ricky shook his head. No, he didn't want to talk to Teigan right then and there. The argument they'd had was still too raw. He hated that they'd fought, especially about that bitch of a mother of hers. He needed time to think. Teigan had never questioned him before. Never asked about Elle. Just took his word for things. So why now?

Ricky's phone rang and he answered. 'What?'

'Boss, you're not going to like this, but you need to look at the news. You need to know what's going on.'

The sound of his employee's tone chilled him. He almost knew what was coming but hoped for a miracle that it wasn't going to happen.

He opened up the laptop. 'Okay, what exactly am I supposed to be searching for here?'

'Any local news outlet. In fact, it doesn't even have to be local. Just type in "Glasgow drug death" and you'll see.'

Ricky closed his eyes. *Shit. Shit. Shit!*

He opened his eyes just enough to be able to see the screen and his stomach dropped. He scanned the headline again and again. But there was no mistaking what he was reading.

> **Fifth death in just forty-eight hours. Police leading Glasgow drug probe.**

'Is this for real?' Ricky said down the phone. 'I thought I said to be vigilant.'

'It's happened inside two days, boss. It will have come from the first batch we put out there.'

Ricky gritted his teeth. 'This is fucked up. This is the work of an insider. I'm sure of it.'

'Or it could be bad stock from the provider?'

'Nah,' Ricky replied. 'Frank Cranwell's product has never come into question. Ever. This has happened here, in Glasgow. We need to pull product from circulation. No more goes out until I figure out what I'm going to do next.'

There was silence on the other end of the line and Ricky knew what his man was thinking. This was on the news outlets online. It would be in the papers again. Frank Cranwell was going to find out about this, and he was going to make his way to Glasgow. There was no doubt about it. Ricky had to be ready to face his wrath.

'I'll stop all distribution now, boss.'

Ricky ended the call and stared at the headline. He couldn't stop himself from thinking the worst, that someone on his team was the one causing this. Frank Cranwell was a dangerous, dangerous bastard. But he had integrity. He'd never put drugs out there that would start killing people instantly. There had never been a drug-related death down in his neck of the woods. Not one.

Frank would go to great lengths to find out what had happened to his drugs, or rather, who. Ricky needed to be ready for that. And if he couldn't give Frank a name, then it would be Ricky on the line for what had gone wrong.

He picked up his phone and dialled Teigan.

'We need to talk about earlier,' she said.

'Not now, Teigan. We have a situation. The police are in the middle of a drugs probe. There's been five deaths in the last forty-eight hours. You need to come back to the office right now. We need to do some damage control.'

He didn't wait for her response. Instead, he hung up and dialled Danica. She didn't answer, but he left a stern voicemail with the same message he'd given to Teigan.

He slammed the phone down on the desk and pinched the bridge of his nose. He had no one to turn to for help. He was head honcho. The only person in the world he knew of that would be able to fix this in one way or another was dead. His brother. Gritting his teeth, he thought of his dead ex-wife. She was the reason Chris was dead. It was her fault. All of what was going wrong was her fucking fault. If he could kill her again, he would do it in a heartbeat.

Chapter Forty-Nine

As she listened to the voice message Ricky had left her, Danica clamped her hand over her mouth. The feeling that her stomach was going to come up and out of her mouth was overwhelming. Five. *Five people.* All dead, because of her plan to take Ricky down. This wasn't how it was supposed to go. The only person who was supposed to die was Ricky. How had it come to this?

Breathing in and out slowly to get rid of the sick feeling wasn't working and her heart began to race. The feeling of sadness that there were five families out there, all mourning the loss of a loved one because of her was something she just couldn't comprehend. Was she a bad person? Was she just as bad as Ricky?

Pushing the door open, Danica walked into the house and her legs felt like jelly beneath her.

'Danica, is that you?' Ricky called out, his voice urgent and shaky. He appeared at the bottom of the stairs, and she'd never seen him look more like shit in the time she'd known him.

'What's wrong?' she asked, although she knew fine well what the problem was. He looked how she felt.

'Where the *fuck* have you been? You didn't get my voicemail?'

Danica feigned ignorance and shook her head with a sweet smile on her face, as hard as it was to do given that this was all her fault. 'My phone has been on silent. I was out running some wedding errands. Has something happened?'

Ricky took a deep, soothing breath but she could see fire burning in the back of his eyes. He was utterly furious.

'My deal with Frank Cranwell is about to come crashing to its fucking knees because someone on my team has been fucking with his cocaine!'

Danica raised her brows and took a step back. 'What the *hell* are you on about?'

'There have been five deaths in the last two days and the police are all over it. I'm fucked either way, Danica. The police are either going to figure this one out, or Frank is going to come up here and fucking kill me.'

She'd fully expected anger, but panic? She'd never seen him so concerned about anything before. Danica almost felt sorry for him. Then the feeling was gone.

'Frank isn't going to kill anyone, Ricky. And aren't you forgetting who you are? You've been at the top of your game in Glasgow for how many years? Since before I was born. Someone like Cranwell isn't going to just come to Glasgow and kill you the second something goes wrong with a drug deal. It's cocaine, Ricky. People die all the time from taking drugs.'

Ricky breathed heavily, his chest heaving. She stared at him and hoped he wasn't about to keel over and die from the stress. She hadn't married the fucker yet.

'Does Teigan know about this?'

'She's on her way,' Ricky replied.

'And I take it you've not actually heard from Frank?'

Ricky shook his head.

'Then take a breath. Maybe have a half, sit down and try to relax. You're catastrophising. I assume your next step is to kill the distribution line before there's another death?'

Ricky nodded again and headed through the hallway to the kitchen. He opened the small cabinet beneath the oven and pulled out a bottle of Jack Daniels. Opening it, he took a gulp straight from the neck and Danica watched as he slowly came back down from his panicked state.

'Yeah, I've told the team to cut it off now. But I don't know how much more of it is still out there. There could be more deaths.'

Danica nodded. 'That is possible. But let's not focus on that right now. Let's wait until Teigan gets here. She was the one who made the deal with Cranwell. Let's get her thoughts on how to proceed with this and then we go from there, okay?'

Ricky was already taking another drink from the open bottle. He was well and truly spooked by this. She felt euphoric watching him unravel. She hoped it lasted, and she could rejoice in watching him fall apart, little by little, piece by piece. She just had to hope that with the remaining cocaine still out there, that no one else died. She couldn't bear the thought of being the reason for someone else's death. The weight of that responsibility could very well put a stop to her plan. But if that happened, more people *would* continue to meet their untimely deaths because there *was* no one else to stop Ricky.

It was all down to her.

Chapter Fifty

'You look like shit,' Teigan said, as she walked into her dad's home office. Danica was sat on a chair on the back wall of the office in silence. Teigan glanced at her briefly but kept her focus on her dad.

'Thanks,' Ricky replied sarcastically as he turned the laptop towards her. 'You would too if it was your neck on the fucking line.'

Teigan stared down at the headline and raised a brow. 'Does anyone know for sure, or has it been confirmed that cocaine is the cause?'

Ricky scowled. 'Are you serious? A monkey could work it out.'

Teigan closed her eyes to stop herself from rolling them at him. On opening them she said, 'And Frank hasn't been in touch?'

Ricky bit his bottom lip and shook his head. As she looked at her dad, she wasn't sure she'd ever seen him react this way to anything. He was usually strong in the most stressful situations. He'd never so much as flinched when things got tough. But this, this was something else.

'Right, we pull out,' Teigan said.

'Already executed that. Now we need to break the news to Frank,' Ricky replied. 'And since you were the one who sealed this deal, then you can be the one to break it to him.'

Glaring at him in shock, Teigan slowly nodded. 'Wow, pulling me out of the frying pan and chucking me right into the fire there, Dad. Nice one.'

Ricky sighed. 'What I mean is, you have already got a rapport with him.'

'No, what you really mean is you know this shit is going to fuel the anger of one of Britain's biggest gangsters and you don't want to be in the fucking firing line. Are you *insane*? Frank Cranwell is going to be deadly furious about this. And you want to send me in? Your fucking daughter!'

'You started in this business as soon as you could vote, Teigan. Let's not forget you're just as capable and culpable as the rest of us in this game,' Ricky said, staring just a little off to her right.

'Wow, Dad. You know, it's good to know where I stand with you on this. I don't suppose you'd send Danica in there, all guns blazing.'

Ricky ignored her, as did Danica and he picked up a glass of amber liquid. Teigan regarded it. 'Are you sure drinking Jack is a good idea right now?'

'What are you, my mother?'

'I wouldn't know how to act like one, seeing as I've never actually had one myself.'

Danica took a sharp intake of breath and Teigan glanced at her. She didn't possess her usual bitchy expression. This one was of concern.

'What *the fuck* did you just say to me?' Ricky growled.

'You heard. Don't think I've forgotten about earlier, even with all this drug shit going on.'

Danica glanced down at the floor and Teigan frowned.

'What? You've got nothing to say for yourself in his defence?' Teigan said, her voice low like Ricky's. 'No, you couldn't give a fuck because you're already getting what you want, aren't you? You're not marrying him. You're marrying his fucking money.'

'Right, that's enough. We've got a fucking crisis on our hands here, Teigan, and you need to help me fix it,' Ricky said sternly, before throwing the Jack Daniels down his throat and slamming the glass on the table.

Teigan glared at him through narrowed eyes and shook her head. 'Nah, you know what? I'm done.'

Ricky's expression switched then, from dark and troubled to utter shock. 'Done is not an option,' he scoffed.

'Aye, not to you. This is your business, not mine. I don't have a stake in anything you own until you die. But that's only if she signs a prenup, otherwise your bit of skirt gets it all.'

Teigan turned her back. She had no clue where this fire was coming from. Was it because of all the thoughts of her mum? Or was she genuinely sick of this life? She couldn't work it out in her head. All Teigan knew was that she had to get out of the house. Immediately.

'Don't you *dare* walk away from me. No one gets to walk away from me in this game. Not again!'

The sound of shattering glass and Danica's shriek made Teigan freeze on the spot. Turning back, she saw a million pieces of glass shattered across the office floor, and amber droplets on the carpet, the remnants of Jack Daniels.

Eyeing the glass and then her dad, Teigan loosened her shoulders and watched as Ricky took a breath.

'Now, let's try to stay calm and figure this out,' Ricky said.

Teigan frowned. Droplets of blood from Danica's brow ran down the side of her face.

'Don't pick any of that up,' Teigan said to her as Danica bent down to the carpet.

'It's fine,' Danica replied, trying to scoop up the glass. What was odd to Teigan was that Ricky didn't seem too bothered that his fiancée was injured by his actions.

'No.' Teigan grabbed Danica's wrists and stared into her eyes. As much as she despised this girl, there was no way she was going to condone the violence that caused her injury, especially not from her dad. But she couldn't let Danica know what she was thinking, because that might show weakness, or that she wasn't as cold hearted as she made out. 'You're getting blood on the carpet. Go and clean yourself up and he will take care of this.'

As if her words had made him see the reality of the situation, Ricky seemed to switch back into loving husband-to-be mode and appeared by Danica's side.

'I'm sorry, Danica. Are you okay? I didn't mean to get you with it. I was angry and lashed out.'

'It's okay,' Danica replied, and Teigan heard the tremor in her voice. It wasn't okay. Not at all. This kind of violent outburst from a man around his fiancée and daughter was never going to be accepted, not from Teigan anyway. 'You're not angry with me. I know that. I was just in the way. It didn't even hit me. Just a small shard bounced back off the wall and got my eyebrow. I'm okay.'

They all got to their feet and Teigan stole a glance at her dad. His expression had softened upon hearing Danica's words, her submissive tone.

It threw Teigan. She knew Danica was only marrying Ricky for his money. But was she really going to let this one go, all in the name of a healthy bank balance?

'Dad, you need to deal with Frank if he comes knocking. I'm not the boss. And I'm leaving now. I'll speak to you later.'

Danica gave her a look, as though she was thanking her for being somewhat kind. Teigan couldn't stop herself, and she gave her a very subtle nod. Then Ricky caught her eye.

'You're going to go against my instruction to deal with Frank?' His words bore a heaviness that Teigan refused to carry.

'I'm not going against you, Dad. This is your business. You are the CEO of all things Fyfe. Cranwell will not deal with me in this scenario. He's going to want to speak to the man who deals with distribution because you signed off on those who were in charge of getting his product out on the street. He's going to grill you on this. You can put me in front of him all you like, Dad, but he won't see me. That's a fact and if you don't like it, that's a you problem, and a big one at that.'

He drew his eyes off her and for a brief second, she saw something in the way he looked at her that she'd never seen before. Something dark. Resentment? For what? The fact that she wasn't responsible for the mess coming out of the drug scene in Glasgow? Or was it something else?

'Just get out of my sight, Teigan,' Ricky said, his voice sounding drained, like he'd had enough. 'You're worse than fucking useless to me right now.'

Brows creeping up her forehead, she stared at him wide eyed. Then she pulled her mouth into a thin, dejected smile and turned her back on him. As she headed for the door, Teigan bit her lip to stop herself from crying. She hated fighting with her dad. But something had changed. In her whole life, he'd never been so cruel with his words, at least not towards her.

'Ricky,' Teigan heard Danica's voice.

'What?' he asked, his tone a little kinder towards his bleeding fiancée.

'You shouldn't speak to her like that. If Frank does show up, Teigan might be the one who can smooth things over.'

Teigan moved down the stairs, holding back the urge to take them two at a time to get out of the house as fast as she could. She didn't wait to hear his response.

Chapter Fifty-One

Ricky finished tending to the wound on her eyebrow, which turned out not to be that bad. It could have been much worse if she'd been standing just a few inches to the right.

'Are your hands okay? Did you pick up any glass?' he asked, taking her hands in his.

'They're fine.' She smiled, glancing at herself in the mirror. The small laceration was barely visible, and under some make-up no one would be able to see it.

'Good. You don't want big gashes on your hands on our wedding day,' Ricky said, allowing her hand to drop from his grip. 'Maybe we should get some Arnica on that eyebrow.'

Her heart had only just stopped thumping after witnessing the exchange between Ricky and Teigan. As soon as she'd gently called him out on the way he'd spoken to her, Danica had worried he'd turn his anger on her. Thankfully, he'd been nothing but attentive since Teigan had left and the relief that flooded her veins had surprised her. Danica had never felt scared of Ricky in the time they'd been together. Nervous perhaps, but never scared. Until tonight. There had been a darkness to every part of him. His voice, his stare.

'Arnica?' Danica smiled. 'You don't seem the type to use herbal remedies.'

'Trust me, it works a treat.'

'Not on cuts,' Danica replied. She was about to suggest Sudocrem but thought better of it as it might get him talking about babies again. 'I might get an antiseptic cream or something. But I'm sure it'll be fine for the wedding. Make-up will cover it.'

Ricky nodded and turned to pick up the small dustpan, which had the shards of glass sitting on it. He tipped it into the little bin beneath the desk and the sound of the glass hitting the bottom was louder than expected, causing Danica to jump a little.

'I need to make things better with Teigan,' Ricky said, staring up at the canvas on the wall. 'I shouldn't have treated her that way.'

Danica stared at the back of his head through narrowing eyes. 'What happened back there?'

Ricky shook his head and turned around, running his hand over his face. 'I don't know. It's the stress of everything with the drug deaths. I just snapped.'

Danica stared at him blankly. 'But that's not Teigan's fault. Nor is it yours. Frank will want to do whatever he thinks will weed out the bad seed.'

'Bad seed?'

'By the sounds of it, you're convinced someone has messed with the product and put something in it to cause these people to drop dead while out clubbing. He's not going to think that's you, surely? Not when it's your name on the line with him.'

Concern etched on his face, Ricky began pacing the room. 'If someone was distributing *my* drugs and this happened, I'd want the man at the top to pay. This is going to be war, Danica. Do you understand that?'

Good, she thought. Not wanting her thoughts to transfer to her face, she gave a look of concern herself, reaching out and wrapping her arms around him.

'Don't you want to find out who is sabotaging you?' she asked.

'Yes,' he said, a little too fiercely. 'But how am I meant to do that?'

Danica forced a sympathetic sigh. 'I know. It'll be hard to work out who it is when everyone is so loyal to you. You're such a good boss to these people. Why would any of them want to harm your business?'

He didn't look angry. He looked concerned that someone was betraying him. It was highly entertaining to know that he had no clue that the bad seed was his very own fiancée.

'I don't know. I've probably earned myself a few enemies over the years in this game. It could be anyone, from the big time or the street guys. I doubt I'll ever find out unless I happen to catch them red handed.'

'Is there anything I can do to help? To take the pressure off?'

Ricky shook his head. 'No. I don't think so. Just keep planning the wedding. God, with Teigan asking questions about her mother on top of this shit, I need something good to look forward to.'

Danica closed her eyes and thought about Elle Fyfe. The Elle Fyfe who Ricky thought was dead. The *first* wife.

'Can I ask you something? And it may sound stupid, but I suppose I need to ask because we've never actually discussed it.'

Ricky narrowed his eyes. 'What is it?'

'You and Elle, you did get divorced, didn't you? You know, before she left with Chris?'

Ricky let out a long, laboured sigh. 'Well, I wouldn't be marrying you if I didn't, would I?'

'Yeah,' she forced a smile. 'Of course. Silly of me to ask. Our wedding will definitely give that date a new meaning. Every year from now on. And there's not much planning left to do. Everything is pretty much taken care of. We're good to go.'

Ricky nodded distantly. His head was likely too busy with everything that had just transpired. That was a good thing. It would mean distraction in its highest form. Exactly what was needed.

'Our wedding is going to be the most memorable thing in your life, aside from the day you became a dad, obviously,' Danica said, leaning up to kiss him.

His eyes flickered towards her then and he frowned.

Narrowing her eyes, Danica gave him her sweetest smile. 'What?'

'Our wedding *will* be the most memorable day of my life, full stop.' Then he pulled away and left Danica standing on her own. 'I've got things to deal with. You can go back to what you were doing before all this.'

She scoffed silently. *Chatting with your ex-wife who's come back from the dead.*

Chapter Fifty-Two

Teigan's eyes shot open, and she sat bolt upright in bed, her heart pounding and her head swimming from the nightmare, Although she was terrified, she couldn't quite recall it. Was it about Frank Cranwell showing up and threatening to kill them? Or was it about her mother? Something in the far corner of her mind told her it was both, but she couldn't quite picture the events of the dream.

Taking a deep breath, she swung her legs around and dangled them off the edge of the super king-sized bed. She wiped clammy palms on the legs of her pyjama bottoms and placed her feet on the thick carpet.

'You okay?' Darren asked as he placed a hand on her back. 'You were thrashing about the bed just before you woke up.'

'Bad dream,' Teigan replied, clearing her throat and getting to her feet.

'How are you feeling? You know, after your fight with Ricky last night.'

Teigan sighed as she remembered the events that had unfolded in her dad's office the previous evening. 'He got so angry when I said I wanted out. I turned to walk out, and he threw his fucking glass at the door, Darren.'

Darren's eyes were wide with shock. 'Who the hell did he throw it at? You or Danica?'

Frowning, she replied, 'Does it matter? The fact is he did it. And a bit of glass bounced off the wall and hit Danica in the face. She had blood running down from her eyebrow. She looked pretty shaken up by it.'

Darren puffed out his cheeks. 'That's bang out of order, Teigan. You need to tell him straight you won't put up with that. And I know you're not Danica's biggest fan, but she shouldn't have to deal with that kind of violence either.'

Teigan grabbed at the roots of her hair and closed her eyes briefly. 'I know, I'm still fucking livid with him. Which makes me sad, because he's my dad and he has never been anything but kind to me. Until fucking Danica came along that is. Now he's just some Jack the lad who's all consumed by his bit of skirt and I'm only good enough for dealing with the fuck-up of the drug deal with Frank. He's not thinking straight. He's never been violent in front of me. Ever.'

She turned, feeling Darren's eyes on her, a little wider than normal. 'Why are you looking at me like that?'

'I'm just worried about how the wedding is going to go, Teigan. You're not going to do anything to sabotage it, are you? I mean, I get why you would and I'm absolutely on your side with this, but I don't want you to do something you'll regret,' he said, dropping his hand from her back and sitting up straight against the leather headboard.

'I'm not going to the wedding,' she replied bluntly.

'Like I said, it's something you'll regret,' Darren responded, narrowing his eyes. 'He's your dad.'

'Yep. I know that. But after last night, I don't know. There's something different about him.' She recalled what he said before throwing the glass. '*No one gets to walk away from me. Not again.*' It made her wonder if violence was one of the reasons that Elle left in the first place.

Teigan moved around the huge bed, which took up most of the space in their bedroom, and opened the door. She stepped into the bathroom and just as she sat down on the toilet, she heard her phone ring.

'Screen that for me,' Teigan shouted, reaching for the loo roll.

'It's Frank Cranwell,' Darren called back solemnly. 'Should I answer it?'

Fuck. What the hell was she supposed to do? 'No, don't,' she called back.

The phone stopped ringing, and Teigan didn't have the capacity to feel relieved. He'd call back again and again until she answered. He'd likely have called Ricky too.

Flushing the toilet and washing her hands, Teigan stepped back into the bedroom and saw Darren pulling on a pair of jogging bottoms, her phone on the bed next to him.

'You can't ignore this, Teegs. If you don't answer, he'll think you all have something to hide, and he'll just show up. Maybe at our flat.'

She let out a long, slow breath and just as she was about to reply, the shrill ring of her phone made her jump as Frank's name flashed up on screen again. Quickly reaching for the phone with a shaky hand, Teigan plastered on her business smile and swiped the answer icon across the screen.

'Frank, how are you?' she said, a little chirpier than she'd intended.

She kept her gaze on Darren as Frank spoke. Her heart thumped in her chest as she listened to his instructions. It seemed she had no option to decline his request.

'Okay Frank,' she finally spoke as Darren looked on expectantly. 'I'll see you there.'

Ending the call, Teigan looked up at the ceiling as she threw her phone onto the bed. 'Fuck!'

'He wants to meet you, doesn't he?' Darren said speculatively, but he was bang on it.

Teigan composed herself. 'Yep. Today. He's in Glasgow. Now. I have an hour.'

Darren got to his feet. 'Shit. Did he sound angry?'

Teigan bit her bottom lip and shook her head. 'No and that's what's worrying me. At least when my dad said I had to meet with Frank to smooth this out I had the freedom to refuse and tell him to fuck off. But with Frank, that's not an option.'

'But why you?' Darren asked, his voice almost whiny, like a petulant child. 'You told your dad last night you were out.'

'Ha,' she scoffed. 'You think I really have a choice now? Like my dad said, it was me who set up the deal. Also, I think Frank knows I'm straight – well, as straight as you can get in this business. I get the impression that a sit down with my dad wasn't on the cards because he knows that it would end up in my dad being defensive, rather than logical, which could cause a fight.'

Darren fell silent, a look of fear crossing his face.

'What's wrong?' Teigan asked, as though the whole thing was normal. In her world, she supposed it was.

'This guy is a big-time gangster, Teegs. I'm worried you're walking into the lion's den.'

She forced a smile. 'Frank isn't going to hurt me, Darren. He just wants to talk. And he's hardly going to shoot me in a bloody coffee shop, is he?'

He raised a brow. 'I don't know. I mean, you hear about people being shot in the street in gang wars all the time, don't you? What's so different about this?'

Teigan felt a bubble of laughter rise to her throat. 'Darren, the top man of an organisation like his isn't going to pop me in the middle of the day in front of hundreds of witnesses. If he wanted me and my dad dead, we'd be dead already. And anyway, if he did plan our deaths, then it wouldn't be him pulling the trigger. It would be some wee scrote off the street who was paid to do it.'

Darren's eyes widened with terror. 'Okay, that doesn't help. And by the way, I'm coming with you.'

Teigan shook her head. 'No, you're not. No offence Darren, but you're not from this world. You're just a normal guy, a car salesman who's marrying the daughter of a gangster. You're not used to this kind of thing and Frank would eat you for breakfast in one bite.'

'Thanks,' he said.

'Look, I deal with high pressure situations all the time. Think about when I dealt with our factory fire. Did anything bad happen to me then? No, because I stay calm. My dad, on the other hand, doesn't deal well with tense scenarios. So, that's probably why Frank has called me. And most likely why my dad himself suggested I deal with him too.'

Darren shook his head. 'I don't like this life for you, Teegs. You could be so much more.'

She bit her lip again. She'd meant it when she told Ricky she wanted out last night. In the cold light of day, she knew that wasn't a possibility. Teigan would never be free from this life. 'But I'm not,' she said bluntly, partly to remind herself of the truth. 'And this is where we are.'

He blinked and opened his mouth to speak but closed it again as though he thought his response might not be the right one.

'I need to get ready,' Teigan said, grabbing a fresh towel from the linen cupboard and heading to the bathroom.

She stood under the stream of hot water and wished that she could do what Darren had said. Leave and be something other than the daughter of a gangster. One day, it would have all been hers. Now that Danica was on the scene, that notion seemed further away than ever. But the real question was, did Teigan even want it anymore?

Chapter Fifty-Three

It was the second morning that Elle had stood outside Teigan's building and watched as she left and headed down the street. She walked with an urgency that in Elle's world meant she was scared, although she had to remind herself that not all people were the same as Elle.

Why couldn't she just go up and introduce herself to her daughter? Why couldn't it be that simple? Going down a rabbit hole of her own thoughts, Elle almost lost sight of Teigan and had to quickly, but discreetly, rush down the street and around the corner onto Great Western Road.

Teigan was already a good fifty feet ahead of her, falling into the crowd as she headed in the direction of Crow Road. Elle fell into step with the people in front of her, keeping her head low but her eyes on Teigan as she pressed the button on the pedestrian crossing. A small crowd gathered, and Elle stood at the back, waiting for the signal to cross over the busy road. She took in the back of her daughter's head. Hair flowing beautifully, shining healthily in the sun. From the outside, it looked as if Teigan was happy with her life. She didn't appear stressed, or anxious. But then, Elle knew all about living a lie and pretending she was fine on the outside.

As the crowd moved to the other side of the busy street, Teigan headed down towards Jordanhill.

Elle glanced across to the grounds of the High School of Glasgow. A place that Ricky had once mentioned Teigan would be going to when the time came. He would have had the money to pay the fees, there was no doubt about that. Elle wondered if that was the school Teigan had gone to in the end. Thoughts of her daughter's schooling moved on to how she'd been brought up by Ricky. The fact that Teigan was working with him and had stuck around as an adult spoke volumes. She'd have wanted for nothing growing up. Money would never have been an issue.

But would all that money have stopped Teigan from finding it hard going through life without a mother? She'd missed all of her daughter's first moments. From crawling, to starting school, to finishing school. She hadn't been around for moments that might have been difficult, like exams, the politics around friendships and relationships. Elle puffed out her cheeks and sighed. She hoped that her absence hadn't damaged her daughter too much.

Passing by the cottages on the left-hand side, Elle made sure to keep the space between them as far as possible without losing sight of Teigan. Elle wasn't sure what she was expecting to find or why she was keeping a close eye on Teigan. Worry, concern that her daughter was in so deep that she might not be able to get out, much like Elle had been but on a different level. Teigan would have an unconditional loyalty to Ricky because to her, he was her dad. The man who was there when Elle wasn't.

The railway bridge came into view and Teigan suddenly disappeared into the little Italian eatery on the other side.

Shit. It was going to be harder to watch her in there without raising suspicion. And there was the possibility that Teigan would recognise her from Frank's club when she was doing the deal on Ricky's behalf.

Elle decided to cross the road and watch from afar, although what she was watching for she wasn't sure. Glancing from left to right, Elle jogged across the road and moved up a little, so she wasn't standing directly opposite the windows, which looked out onto the street. It frustrated her that all that was on the opposite side of the road from the restaurant was a wall. A plain, boring wall that meant Elle couldn't make herself look as though she was doing something like window shopping. There wasn't even a bus stop she could pretend to wait at. There was a petrol garage just up the road, but that was too far for Elle to be able to see Teigan properly.

So, she stood with her back against the wall, head down in her phone and every so often she glanced up at the window. Not much happened in the first five minutes and Elle thought that Teigan could simply be meeting someone for lunch. Just as she was about to leave and head back to her rental, she saw a man coming round the corner of the street that led up to the train station.

She froze, disbelief setting in quickly, rendering her unable to move. *What the fuck* was Frank doing here? Of course, she knew that the Fyfes were in business with him. But why was he up here in Glasgow? Why now?

She turned herself slightly away from his direction, hoping that he wouldn't see her. She wasn't about to explain her entire life's secrets to him in the middle of the street. Then he went inside the restaurant where Teigan was sitting at the window and joined her.

Chapter Fifty-Four

Teigan made sure to sit facing the door, so that she would be able to see Frank enter the restaurant. She needed to show strength, that she was powerful and that she wasn't to be messed with. Frank would be angry, but Teigan needed to make sure that she would not be intimidated by that anger.

The sound of the door opening made her sit up and she raised her eyes. Frank was walking towards her with a polite smile on his face. Was it genuine, or was he hiding his seething anger at the whole situation? She couldn't tell which.

'Mr Cranwell,' Teigan greeted him. 'Can I get you anything? A drink? Whisky? I'm sure we could persuade the staff to get you one even though it's not yet lunch time.'

Frank gave a wave of the hand. 'I think I'll take a leaf out of your book, Teigan, and keep a clear head for this one. Should have done that myself on our first meeting, if I'm honest.'

Fuck, she thought. He was quietly livid, the worst kind of angry.

'Coffee then?'

'Black. No sugar.'

Teigan waved the waitress over, ordered Frank's coffee and a latte for herself. She felt his eyes burning into her as she checked to make sure her phone was on silent. She hadn't bothered to tell her dad that she'd followed through on his command to meet Frank. She'd let him stew a little longer. He deserved nothing less.

'Right,' she said.

'What's going on with my product, Teigan?' Frank said, his voice low. He didn't sound angry, more disappointed, like her dad had been when she was only fourteen and got drunk down the woods with her friends from school. She'd genuinely thought he would be cool about her having a drink given that his work didn't exactly stay on the right side of the law. She'd been very wrong. Grounded for six weeks, mobile phone confiscated. It had been hell. She'd give anything to be back in that moment now, instead of dealing with Frank.

'In all honesty, Frank,' Teigan said, sitting back and trying to be as casual as she possibly could without coming across as arrogant. 'I don't know. It's been a shock to us too.'

Frank's brows knitted together, and he passed his tongue over his teeth. 'So much of a shock that I wasn't informed?'

'It all happened so quickly. Five across a weekend. It's awful.'

Frank nodded silently, as if waiting for her to continue.

'However, I can assure you that whatever has happened to the product was not a fault on our part.'

Frank stared at her for what felt like a million years. Silent. Unblinking. Then he said, 'Can you, though? Assure me, I mean?'

Teigan nodded. 'Yes. I can assure you. For want of a nicer expression, Frank, we do not shit on our own doorstep. And we certainly wouldn't want to ruin a perfectly good business relationship, for any reason.'

Frank settled back on his seat as the waitress appeared at the table, placing a mug of coffee in front of him, and a latte in front of Teigan. Frank smiled up at her, gave a nod of appreciation and lifted his mug as the waitress disappeared again.

'So, if it's nothing directly to do with you and your father, then who is it? Because my product has never, and I mean *never*, been called into question like this. Like I said, if not you, then I need you to tell me who you think has sabotaged it.'

Teigan puffed out her cheeks. 'Again, I don't know. Either it's someone on the front line, or...' She trailed off. Or what? She'd been about to suggest bad luck. But that was far from the truth. Five people didn't die in the same weekend by coincidence.

'Or?' Frank probed.

'Or nothing,' Teigan said. 'It must be someone on the front line. But my dad's used the same employees for years. We've never had a problem.'

'Well, you do now,' Frank snapped, before composing himself and drinking from the mug.

Teigan nodded, feeling the tension jump up a notch. 'I understand how frustrating this is for you, I really do. It's not a great situation for any of us to be dealing with. But please, rest assured, we'll sort this out.'

Frank shrugged. 'And where is Ricky in all of this?'

Teigan stared at him, narrowing her eyes. 'What do you mean?'

'*Where* is he? He hasn't answered any of my calls since I got wind of this. That's why I contacted you.'

Teigan closed her eyes and tried to force the anger back down. That was why he'd pushed for Teigan to meet with Frank. He'd been ignoring his fucking calls ever since this all started. He'd thrown her under the bus completely. For all Ricky knew, Frank could get violent with Teigan. But so long as he was okay, nothing else mattered. She was beginning to understand that there was a side to this business that made people very, very selfish, even to the point of using your own daughter as a fucking shield.

'He's busy planning his wedding,' Teigan replied, knowing how ridiculous it sounded.

Frank leaned in, smiled menacingly and said, 'Well, you can tell him from me that there won't be a fucking wedding if he doesn't fucking sort this. Got it?'

Teigan nodded. 'Understood, Mr Cranwell. We'll do our utmost to make sure we get to the bottom of this. We want to isolate these incidents and make sure we can fulfil the contract.'

He was staring out of the window as she spoke and she understood why, but his attitude stank. Surely, he didn't think that the Fyfes were stupid enough to fuck up his drugs. And for what reason? There was *no* logical reason. At all. Not that Teigan could come up with at least.

Frank got to his feet, took another gulp from his mug and placed it down. 'I'll be in touch.'

Teigan stood up too, but before she could reach out for a handshake, Frank had already left the table and was out of the restaurant before she'd had a chance to blink.

Chapter Fifty-Five

Shit. *Shit, shit, shit.* Frank had been staring at her before she'd realised and he was now out of his seat, heading for the restaurant door.

Turning, Elle decided to head towards the Arnold Clark garage not far up the street. If she could weave her way in and out of the cars on the forecourt, she might lose him. And maybe he'd take a second look at her and realise that her hair was totally different and change his mind. All the while, she was thinking about what she was going to say to him if he did eventually catch up with her.

Taking a sharp right into the forecourt, Elle weaved her way in and out of the Volkswagens, all of which were not high enough to properly conceal her.

This was Frank. The man who'd been like a dad to her for most of her life. Why was she running from him? A voice in the back of her mind told her the reason. That she wasn't ready to tell him the truth she'd kept hidden away for so many years.

She spotted a car on display, sitting on top of some kind of platform, and moved towards it. As she took position behind the brand-new vehicle, Elle wondered how long she would have to stand there until she could be sure Frank was gone.

'Why were you watching me from across the road?'

Not long, it would seem. The sound of Frank's voice so close to her ear made her jump high enough that she could almost see into the car.

'Jesus, *fuck!*' Elle gasped, clutching at her chest. She turned to see him, staring at her expectantly.

'Nope,' he said. 'Just me. Just Frank.'

Catching her breath, Elle composed herself and smiled at him and said, '*Watching* you?'

'Yes. You were watching me while I was having a meeting back at that Italian place. You were standing outside when I went in, although I didn't recognise it was you until I was about to leave.'

Elle parted her lips to reply but there was no lie she could tell that wouldn't make her sound like an idiot.

'You left Essex to come back to Glasgow?' Frank pushed and his tone was off. 'Why didn't you just tell me that?'

Elle frowned. 'There was nothing to tell.'

'Then tell me why you ran like a bolt of lightning when you saw me come out of that restaurant?'

Elle sighed loudly and shook her head. 'I have things to say that I don't want to say.'

'Like what? Elle? Because I can't think of a reason that would be a coincidence that you're up here at the same fucking time that my business with the Fyfes has gone to shit.'

The sound of that name made her stomach roll. 'Excuse me?'

'Are you working for them or something? Are you the one who's fucked up my supply?'

Elle's jaw dropped. 'What the hell are you on about?'

Frank's shoulders were up round his ears and just as Elle thought he was about to explode, a chirpy salesman rounded the corner and said very loudly, 'Is there anything I can help you with today?'

Elle smiled at him and shook her head. 'Just looking thanks.'

'Okay. If you need anything, my name is Paul, just give me a shout. We've got a great sale on just now and...'

'She said we're just looking,' Frank snapped, without turning to look at the man.

He held up his hands in defeat and said, 'I'll leave you both to it.'

Elle straightened her back and stared at Frank, who seemed angrier with her than she could ever have imagined.

'What on earth would make you think I'd deliberately try to sabotage your business?'

'Then why were you standing outside the restaurant, watching me?'

Elle closed her eyes and took a steadying breath. 'I wasn't watching you.'

'Then what the hell were you doing?'

Opening her eyes, she stared at Frank and knew that this was it. The moment she had to come clean and tell him everything.

'I was watching her,' she said quietly.

'Teigan? You were watching Teigan? Why?' His tone was demanding, and Elle was beginning to get frustrated that he thought she was the bad guy.

'Because...' She swallowed, gritting her teeth and reminding herself that none of this was her fault. None of it. 'Teigan Fyfe is my daughter.'

Frank's expression softened, his forehead slowly becoming less creased. 'She's your *daughter*?'

'Yes. She is. And Ricky is my ex-husband. Well, by law we're probably still married. I gave him divorce papers and he did sign them, but I never handed them back to my solicitor.'

Frank stared at her, disbelief etched in his expression.

'It's a long story. But he's a bad person. The worst. He's the reason I ended up in Essex. I had to leave everything because of him, even my baby. My brother-in-law was supposed to bring Teigan to me soon after I arrived, but he never showed up. I've been in hiding ever since.'

Frank looked down at the ground, as though trying to make sense of it all. Something Elle had been trying to do for almost three decades.

'Hold on a minute. You're trying to tell me, that you are *married* to Ricky Fyfe?'

Elle exhaled loudly and nodded. 'Biggest secret I've ever kept. Well that's not true.'

'What do you mean?'

'Well, you're probably not going to believe this. But Ricky thinks I'm dead.'

'Why would he think that?' Frank asked warily.

She looked up at the grey sky and realised that clouds had been following her around for most of her life.

'Because he thinks he killed me.'

Frank's face was awash with concern.

'Have you been living in Essex all this time, with Ricky thinking he killed you while he's been raising your daughter?'

'I wouldn't call it living – more surviving.'

As they stood in the middle of the forecourt, surrounded by cars that were way beyond anything Elle could ever dream of affording, she started to laugh.

'I fail to see what's funny about all this, Elle,' Frank said.

'It's not. I just never thought the moment I'd reveal my biggest secrets to you, I'd be standing in the middle of Arnold Clark.'

An awkward silence grew between them and Elle wondered if he believed her. She wouldn't blame him if he didn't. It all sounded like a drama series you'd watch on TV.

'Let's go get a drink,' Frank finally said. 'You can tell me everything.'

—

They sat in the pub next to the car showroom and Elle glanced down at her glass of wine.

'Not to your taste?' Frank asked.

'No, the wine is good. If anything, it's too good. I've used alcohol to numb everything out over the years. Not sure if you can tell but it's not really worked.'

'I've always known you're a drinker, Elle. It's not hard to miss.'

She thought about how she looked. The wear and tear of alcohol had tarnished her appearance over the years, on top of the tremendous amount of trauma she carried.

'So this is why,' he said, interrupting her thoughts. 'You've been blocking it all out?'

'The only other way to do that was to top myself. But that would mean never having the chance to see Teigan again. Not that I ever thought it possible until she walked through the doors of your club just a couple weeks ago.'

'That was the first time you'd seen her since she was a baby?' Frank asked, a sadness to his voice.

Elle sucked in a huge lungful of air and said, 'Yes. She was just weeks old. I was still...' She had been about to say breastfeeding, but then realised that wasn't a detail Frank needed to hear.

'Still what?'

'Still recovering from birth. Ricky was just utterly horrid towards me. Just cruel, all the time.'

'Is that why you left?'

Elle glanced down into the wine glass again and decided not to do her usual and take a large gulp to help her cope with her thoughts. 'No, I ran to save my life. If he knew I wasn't dead, he'd have tried to kill me again.'

Frank frowned. 'I'm so sorry, Elle.'

She glanced up at the dimly lit bulb above as it shone down on her like a spotlight. 'Ricky had something over me. Something that would have sent me to prison if he had his way.'

Frank frowned so deeply a line formed between his brows. 'What was it?'

'He murdered someone. A friend of mine who he believed I was having an affair with and who he thought was Teigan's biological father. He told me he dipped my dress in his blood and put it away for safe keeping. He said that if I ever tried to take Teigan away from him, he'd tip off the police about who was responsible for the murder. Then, when I said I was leaving with Teigan anyway, he hit me over the head with a bottle. I went down. And was out like a light. I woke up in the back of Chris Fyfe's car. Ricky had told him to get rid of me, just like that. The mother of his daughter.'

Frank took a small sip from his whisky glass and stared at her with dark eyes. 'And is she his daughter?'

Elle shook her head. 'No.'

'Was it the man he killed?'

She shook her head again, tears pooling in her eyes, this time in sadness for Jordan. 'No. It wasn't Jordan. Teigan is a Fyfe by blood. Just not Ricky's.'

'Chris? The brother?' Frank guessed. 'The brother, may I add, that Ricky has never mentioned in the fifteen years I've known him.'

'All the more reason for me to believe that Chris is dead,' Elle replied with a shake of her head. 'It was a one-night thing. I swear. After a night of being verbally and physically abused by Ricky, Chris told him to back off and sleep off the bevy. It just sort of happened. And never happened again.'

Frank held his hands up. 'There's no judgement from me, Elle. I couldn't give a shit who Teigan's father is. All I care about is you and that you're okay.'

Elle sniffed and wrapped her fingers around the stem of the glass. Still, she didn't drink. 'I'm not okay. Very far from okay. Since seeing Teigan down in Essex, I've not been able to get her out of my head. I left her with a monster who isn't even her father. I allowed him to back me into a corner with his bullshit and I left. Chris promised to bring Teigan to me within days. But he never did. Ricky has told people that

Chris and I left together. But I think he found out about us and killed him.'

Frank leaned back in his seat and expelled air from his lungs loudly. 'You think he's that bad that he'd kill his own brother?'

'If Ricky didn't kill him, then where is he? Why didn't he bring Teigan to me? And why did I never hear from him ever again?'

The questions hung heavily between them and Elle looked at Frank for some real answers.

'So, now that you're here, what are you planning to do?' Frank asked.

'I've already met with Danica. Ricky's fiancée.'

With wide eyes and a look of bewilderment, Frank sat forward, blinked and said, 'What the hell did you do that for?'

'Because she is the daughter of Jordan Burns, the man who Ricky murdered and set up fake evidence to put me in the frame as the killer. And she is planning on taking him down as revenge. She is the same age as Teigan and I'm worried that she is going to end up getting herself killed.'

Frank rested his forehead in his hands and said, 'I feel like I'm watching a fucking reality TV show.'

'Yeah, well it's not,' Elle said, her tone a little snappier than intended. 'Honestly, Frank, now that I'm here, I don't know what to do. I was in contact with Teigan under a false name and we'd arranged to meet but I couldn't go through with it. I just froze. What if I tell her the truth and she doesn't believe me? What if she rejects me?'

Frank raised his head, and his brow crept up a little. 'You're worried about your daughter rejecting you more than Ricky finding out you're alive and well? The man sounds unhinged.'

'And you never picked up on that in the years you've known him?'

Frank smirked. 'I don't know him, Elle. We're business acquaintances. We talk, agree a deal, sign the contract, move on. Although in this situation, I doubt I'll be moving on until I find out who the fuck has laced my drugs to kill five people in Glasgow in one weekend.'

Elle felt sick. Teigan was involved in all this mess. And it was Elle's fault.

'Whatever I decide to do, it's not going to be all rainbows and sunshine at the end. Someone is going to get hurt.'

Frank was quiet, as though he was deep in thought. After a few moments, he nodded and said, 'You're right, someone is going to get hurt. You need to back off.'

'What? What do you mean, back off? I can't walk away now. Teigan is my daughter. She's been living with a man who thinks he killed her mother and she deserves to know the truth. She deserves to be safe, to have a better life away from all this crap.'

Frank was nodding, his head bobbing up and down quickly in agreement. 'Yes. You're right. But it can't come from you. The only person you've met with is his fiancée, is that right?'

'Danica, yes.'

'And you're certain she isn't going to slip up and reveal that you're back? Or even tell him intentionally?'

'No. She hates him. She wants to make sure he ends up with nothing. I don't know how she is able to keep up the pretence.'

Elle thought about Danica and her relationship with Ricky. How had she managed to even initiate that? What had she done to turn his head? Likely not a lot. All she'd have had to do was flutter her eyelashes in his direction and he'd have proposed straight away. How was she coping with playing the role of a doting fiancée when she hated him with every fibre of her being?

'I have an idea,' Frank said. 'This should have been dealt with a long time ago. I always said I'd be there for you. And I have stuck by that in the time we've known each other. I want to help you, Elle.'

She felt her chest ache and her throat began to close up as a lump of emotion pushed its way up. Frank reached over and took her hand.

'Like I said, you've been like a daughter to me. I don't want to see you come to any harm, especially not from someone like Ricky Fyfe. He's fucked up our contract. I can use that as my way in. Of course, that's only if you're comfortable with that? If you'd prefer me not to?'

Elle thought about it briefly. Maybe Ricky coming up against someone of Frank's calibre wouldn't be such a bad thing.

'No,' she replied. 'I'd like your help. I should have come to you years ago. I just couldn't face everything that had happened. Sometimes, I believed that she was better off without me. I think it was easier for me to believe that.'

Frank gave her hand another gentle squeeze. 'It'll be alright, you know. I can promise you that.'

Elle wanted to believe Frank. She truly did. But with Ricky, nothing was ever all right. And anything was possible.

Chapter Fifty-Six

Ricky stared blankly at the images on his screen as Danica talked passionately about centrepieces and chair covers. Wedding chat was the last thing on his mind right now, but he couldn't very well dismiss her, not after he had almost taken her eye out when he'd thrown that glass in a rage.

'So, you're happy with them?' Danica asked, her voice filtering through the million thoughts running through his head.

'Happy with them?' he queried, having lost where they were at on the topic.

Danica rolled her eyes in that 'I love you but you're doing my head in' way that she often did when it came to the wedding plans. 'The centrepieces. I think the hurricane candle holders with the white lilies around the base are utterly stunning. A tad pricey, yes. But worth it, don't you think?'

Ricky forced a smile and said, 'Whatever makes you happy, Danica. All I care about is you being my wife, not about what's on the tables on the day.'

She raised a brow. 'And what if it was me on the table on the day?'

He felt a stir of excitement and laughed. 'Then I wouldn't have to worry about buying matches. You'd already be on fire.'

Danica laughed loudly and threw her head back. 'That was fucking cheesy, Fyfe, but I'll give you that one.'

He leaned up and kissed her exposed throat, running his finger along her collar bone. 'Like I said, whatever makes you happy. And if hurricane candle holders and lilies do that, then that's what you should spend the money on.'

He wanted her in that moment, but as he was about to take things further, his phone alerted him to a message. He glanced down and saw a text from Teigan.

'Shhhhiiit!' he said, gripping the phone in his hand.

Danica glanced down at his hand and then back to his face. 'What's wrong?'

'Frank's in Glasgow. Teigan's just out of a meeting with him. *Fuck.* Why didn't she tell me she was going?'

'Firstly, because you two fell out and she probably didn't want to speak to you. And secondly, you told her to deal with Frank herself. By the sounds of it, it didn't go well?'

Ricky pulled up Teigan's number to phone her, but as he opened up his contacts, his phone began to ring, and Frank's number flashed in front of his eyes.

'Jesus,' Ricky whispered.

'Nope. Frank,' Danica replied, glancing down at the screen. Before he could say anything in response to her sarcasm, she added, 'I'll leave you to it. Take a deep breath. Be calm and make sure you tell him that whatever is going on with his drugs is nothing to do with you.'

Ricky nodded, his thumb hovering over the green 'accept call' icon.

'Oh, and you'd better make sure you tell him that if he's going to kill you, to do it after our wedding. I didn't spend all that money on a dress not to be able to wear it,' she said in a sing-song voice.

Of course, he knew she was joking, but now was not the time. He glared at her as she gave him a cheeky wink and sauntered out of the office and downstairs.

'Frank? How's it all going?' Ricky answered.

'Things have been better. You know, five drug-related deaths in any city are never good. But when it's the city you've just started supplying, well, that's even worse. We need to discuss what's going on, Ricky,' Frank replied.

'I'm a bit tied up at the moment,' Ricky said, glancing down at the computer screen. 'Missus has me doing wedding stuff. Can we meet later?'

'I'm outside your front door, Ricky. And I know you're home because your car is outside. So, we can do this now. And I'll have a coffee.'

Ricky stuck out his jaw and closed his eyes. 'Of course. I'll be down in a minute.'

Ending the call, Ricky stood in the middle of his office and wondered how this was going to pan out.

He took a breath, straightened out his shirt and made his way down to the front door. If he was honest with himself, Ricky was a little angry that Frank had shown up to his house, unannounced, demanding to see him regardless of what was on Ricky's schedule. Not to mention the fact that he'd done nothing wrong at his end.

Ricky reached the front door, opened it wide and welcomed Frank in. As Frank Cranwell stepped into Ricky's home, he seemed to be scanning the place.

'Nice home you have here, Ricky,' Frank said. 'Just you and the wife to be living here?'

Ricky pulled his lips tightly across his teeth and nodded. He wasn't exactly going to tell Frank that he hoped his infertility issues would have ironed themselves out over the years. Hope being the key word. He knew it was never going to be the case, but the idea of giving up on having a child of his own wasn't an option. 'For now. We'll just see how things go.'

Frank raised a brow. 'Ooft, starting again at your age, Ricky?'

Ricky stared at him. 'My age? I'm not exactly a pensioner.'

'Ah, but you will be next year, will you not?'

Ricky but his tongue. He knew Frank was trying to get a rise out of him, the cheeky bastard. He wasn't in his youth either. Yes, he'd be classed as a pensioner by the government on his next birthday, but with his upcoming wedding to Danica, she certainly didn't make him feel like one.

'Very funny,' Ricky said.

'But do you really see yourself changing nappies, doing night feeds and wiping up baby sick in your sixties? You've got it all here. A good big house, all the money you could want, a fiancée most guys would kill for. Why would you want to swap all that for...' His words trailed off.

'Get to the point of why you're here, Frank,' Ricky said, unwilling to enter into a discussion about his private life.

'Ah, yes. My drugs. What the fuck has happened to my product?'

Ricky shook his head. 'To my knowledge, absolutely nothing. But I'm sure Teigan will have filled you in, given you've just come from a meeting with her?'

Frank gave a cold smile. 'You didn't answer any of my calls. I had to go to the next in charge.'

Ricky couldn't very well be annoyed with either of them. It's what Ricky had wanted from the start, for Teigan to deal with it. He wanted her to take the fall, to deal with Frank's wrath and leave Ricky out. Now, that wasn't the case.

'So, I'm assuming she told you the same thing I have? That as far as we're aware, your drugs haven't been tampered with?'

Frank nodded. 'She said that you'd do your utmost to find out what has happened. The Fyfes don't want to ruin a good business relationship.'

Nodding, Ricky said, 'That's right. Although, I can't help but wonder – and please don't take offence at this, Frank – but perhaps the drugs were already contaminated? Or merely just a substandard batch? I mean, it's a little bit of a coincidence that the second your drugs show up in Glasgow, there are multiple cocaine-related deaths. I've never had an issue with my product until now.'

Frank's eyes darkened. 'You're suggesting this is my fault?'

Silence hung in the air between them and Ricky's tongue froze. He'd crossed a line. What he'd said was like poking a bear.

'Because that would be a very serious accusation, Ricky. Very serious. I don't take kindly to my reputation being tarnished in that way.'

Ricky took a deep breath. He needed to fix this and quickly. 'Sorry, Frank. I didn't mean that. It's just, there's so much pressure on both of us, you know. And I just can't work out who the fuck would want to screw me over because no one who works for me has ever given me cause not to trust them.'

Frank regarded Ricky, eyes boring into his, unblinking. The silence was killing Ricky. Then Frank began rubbing his hands together quickly and the sudden movement made Ricky jump a little.

'So, how about that coffee, then?'

Ricky kept his cool and moved through to the kitchen, where he switched on the coffee machine and tried not to allow his anger to bubble to the surface.

He watched as Frank paced the kitchen floor, very, very slowly. He kept his eyes on the tiles, and circled around like a bird of prey. What the hell was he doing.

'So, your brother?'

Frowning as he placed a pod into the machine and a mug underneath, Ricky wondered why his brother was suddenly the topic of conversation. The brother who Frank knew nothing about; he never knew Chris even existed. 'How did you know I have a brother?'

'Teigan mentioned him briefly,' Frank replied.

Ricky narrowed his eyes. 'What about him?'

'He's no longer around?'

Ricky wondered where the hell this was all going. But he needed to be as cool about it as possible. 'Nope. Ran off with my wife – ex-wife. Haven't seen either of them in almost thirty years. And good fucking riddance is all I can say.'

'Ex-wife? You guys got divorced?'

'Aye, signed the papers right before she fucked off. She probably married the bastard. They're welcome to each other,' Ricky replied coolly. He had to hand it to himself, he had lying down to an art.

Frank was nodding. 'Who needs enemies when you have family like that, eh?'

Ricky handed the mug to Frank and shrugged. Hoping to change the subject quickly, he said, 'It was a long time ago. I'm over it now.'

'And Teigan, she's yours?'

That stopped him in his tracks, like he'd walked straight into a concrete wall. No one had ever asked him that before. Frank knew nothing about his past. Nothing. So why?

'Why would you ask me that?'

'I'm just wondering. You say she probably married him, so they must have been having an affair if they left together, never to be seen again. Unless you killed them both in a fit of rage?' Frank suggested, but he was laughing. Ricky felt his heart rate begin to quicken. This was getting too close to the bone.

Ricky swallowed hard, raised his hands and smiled. 'You got me. Gangster minds think alike.'

Frank laughed again and Ricky noticed where he was standing. Right in the exact spot Elle took her last breath.

'So,' Ricky said, needing to change the course of the conversation. 'You're worried about your drugs. I get that. I am too. But to reassure you, I can take you to where I'm storing the remainder of the stock until we find out how the last batch was sabotaged. I want you to see with your own eyes that it hasn't been tampered with.'

Frank's brows crept up. 'And how do I know that you're not keeping some set aside that hasn't yet been tampered with just to appease me?'

Ricky felt an eye roll coming on but suppressed it. 'Well, in all honesty, you don't. But I've never given you cause not to trust me prior to this problem. A problem that I did not create.'

He could almost see the cogs turning in Frank's head. Ricky had given him something to think about.

'As much as your arrogance has annoyed me, I have to say I suppose you're right. Although, I also have to say that right now, I'm not sure I do trust you.'

Ricky shrugged. 'And if I was in the wrong, I'd be trying to earn your trust. But again, I haven't caused this. All I can do is show you where I'm storing your product, and if you'd like to meet my street team, then I can arrange that too. Maybe you'll see something in my men that I haven't. Although, I doubt that very much. I have a strict screening process.'

'Is that right?' Frank asked, staring at Ricky through narrowing eyes. 'Well then, you might want to review that, because clearly someone has fucked about with my cocaine and if it wasn't you, then it had to be one of your men. And I'll tell you something, if you don't find out who it is within the next forty-eight hours, I'll make sure no one supplies you ever again. And don't think I'm kidding. I don't do empty threats, Ricky.'

Ricky glared at him and knew he wasn't lying. Frank Cranwell was ruthless; Ricky knew that. And if he made a threat like that, he meant it.

Swallowing down the hard lump of anger in his throat, Ricky gave a nod and said, 'Shall we?' leading the way to the front door. Frank followed closely behind in silence and a chill ran down Ricky's spine.

As much as Frank said it was Teigan who mentioned Chris and that was how he knew Ricky had a brother, something about that was off. Why would Teigan randomly talk about the uncle she'd never met? She wouldn't, would she? And if she hadn't, then how the hell did Frank know about him?

Chapter Fifty-Seven

Holy. Fuck.

Danica had listened to their confrontation from the sitting room next door to the kitchen. Frank Cranwell was utterly livid. The prospect made her nervous. If Ricky was going to be forced to introduce Frank to his street team, that could mean trouble for her.

Pulling her phone out, she called Aidan Doyle who, as instructed, answered immediately.

'Your boy better know how to keep his fucking mouth shut,' Danica said sharply into the speaker.

'What are you on about?'

'Frank Cranwell is in Glasgow, and he wants to meet all of Ricky's team. You better hope to god, or whoever the fuck you believe in, that he has a good poker face and the ability to keep his mouth shut.'

Aidan Doyle was silent, aside from short, raspy breaths on the other end of the line.

'Doyle, you there?'

'He won't say a word.'

'You sure about that? Even under pressure from his boss and the boss's boss? Because he could have them both breathing down his neck any minute now. You sure he isn't going to buckle and give us all up?'

'Us? There is no *us*, Danica. Your name was never mentioned. He has no idea who I'm working for, only that I'm paying him. And he's easily paid. He'd have to be, given the shitty wages you're throwing at me.'

Danica closed her eyes, irritated that she was even having to have this conversation.

'You could have said no if the wages didn't suit. I'd have found someone else,' she said bluntly.

'No, you wouldn't,' said Aidan. 'You don't know anyone as *desperate* as *me* for cash.'

Danica felt a very small pang of guilt hit her then. One she hadn't expected. Then she remembered why she was doing all this and allowed it to fizzle out.

'Worth giving him the heads up?' Danica asked.

'Nah,' Aidan replied. 'It'll only panic him. If it comes when he's not expecting it, he won't have time to think about it and he'll say what he's been told to say. That he's employed by Ricky and does as he's told by his boss. End of.'

Danica bit her bottom lip. 'I hope so. Let me know if you hear from him.'

Aidan ended the call without saying goodbye and Danica slipped the phone into her pocket. She hoped the faith Aidan had in his man would stand. She really did. If it didn't, and he grassed Aidan up, there would be nothing to stop Aidan telling Ricky everything. He'd have nothing more to lose if Ricky got hold of him.

She just had to hope that if that did happen, Ricky wouldn't believe any of it.

Chapter Fifty-Eight

Ricky pushed the door open and allowed Frank to go inside first. Tim looked up from the front desk and the smile on his face was reserved. He glanced between Ricky and Frank and then stood up, as he always did when anyone walked into the reception.

'Mr Fyfe,' Tim said, and he made the words sound like a question. A question Ricky understood.

'Tim, this is Mr Frank Cranwell, a business associate of mine. We're here to do some inventory.'

Ricky noticed how Frank looked around. He picked up a brochure, flicked through it uninterested.

'Absolutely,' Tim said, looking nervously at Frank. 'Anything I can do to help?'

Ricky gave a reassuring smile. 'No, we won't be long, then we'll be out of your hair.'

Tim lowered himself slowly back into his seat and Frank placed the brochure gently back down on top of the pile.

'Frank?' Ricky said, showing him through the door and down the stairs to the mortuary.

'You *own* a funeral home?' Frank asked as they moved down to the bottom.

Ricky shook his head and simply said, 'No.'

As they slipped deeper into the mortuary, he sensed Frank fall further behind. Turning, he saw that Frank had stopped walking.

'What's wrong?'

'Are you storing my drugs with dead bodies?'

Ricky laughed so loudly that his voice echoed off the metal drawers. 'It's not the dead you need to fear.'

Hesitantly, Frank took a step forward. 'I don't fear the dead. I just think it's... disrespectful.'

Ricky couldn't hide his surprise. 'Disrespectful? Seriously?'

Frank stared at him, unblinking, and seemingly unhappy with being questioned.

'Look, I'm not storing them beside the dead if that's what you're worried about. We have a few refrigerators down here that aren't switched on. They're just drawers. We store the drugs in there until they are ready to be distributed via my taxi firm, which of course you already know about.'

Frank raised a brow and Ricky proceeded to open the first drawer. He stood back, and gestured for Frank to look inside.

'As you can see, the packaging from your end hasn't been opened or tampered with in any way.'

'Yes, I can see that. But that doesn't mean it won't be tampered with once opened, does it?'

Ricky felt a rush of frustration but kept it in. 'I can understand why you would think that, Frank. But I really don't want any of this as much as you don't. So please believe me when I say, we're on the same side here.'

Frank began his inspections and Ricky decided to leave him to it.

Stepping away, Ricky pulled his key from his pocket and headed down towards the end of the mortuary, where the lockers stood in the corner. He opened number nine and peered inside.

As he inspected the contents, he thought about how far he'd come since the night he'd murdered Elle. And Chris. He'd vowed that night that he'd change his ways. He'd promised himself he'd never get that angry ever again. It hadn't been easy, but he'd worked bloody hard. Losing his temper with Teigan and throwing that glass was a low point. It wasn't even that bad compared to what he'd done before, yet he still felt like shit about it. Danica had borne the worst of it. He just hoped the cut wouldn't be visible on their wedding day or people might start asking questions.

Reaching into the back of the locker, he wrapped his fingers around the sealed plastic bag that contained Elle's dress. He closed his eyes and exhaled slowly. He never, ever wanted to get to that stage with Danica. She was different. She was special. Danica had shown him that love truly existed. Yes, at times she pushed his buttons and yes, there had been moments when he could have flown off the handle and slapped her for her cheek. But he had chosen not to. He didn't want to be that person. He remembered what it was like for his mother. She had often suffered at the hands of their father and unlike Chris, Ricky had turned a blind eye to it all. He'd idolised his dad, always wanted to be like him. Always wanted to be successful like him.

It wasn't until after killing Elle and Chris that he realised his dad hadn't lived a good life at all. He'd been powerful, successful, yes. But not one member of his family, other than Ricky, had loved him or cared about him. He'd been hated. Truly hated. Ricky didn't want that for himself as a husband or a dad. He wanted to be loved. Or was it more than that? Worshipped? And Danica did worship him. Or at least, that's how she made him feel. It was something he'd never experienced before, and he truly believed it was because he'd been different with her. Kind. Loving. Gentle.

Teigan, on the other hand, was a different kind of love entirely. He'd done everything in his power to be a good dad to her even though in the back of his head every single day, a little voice taunted him. *She's not yours. She's not yours. She's your niece, not your daughter.*

As he stared at Elle's dress inside the bag, a feeling he'd never experienced before washed over him. Guilt. But why now? Was it because Teigan had been speaking about her? Asking questions about why she'd left? He could hardly explain it all, could he?

He pulled the bag out from the locker and stared down at it. Things could have been so very different if she'd just behaved herself. If she'd just… Ricky closed his eyes and pictured her face. She'd loved him too. Maybe if he'd been better, she'd have come to worship him. He'd tried to achieve that in a way that he now understood to be impossible. Elle didn't worship him. She'd only obeyed him, and even then she wasn't very good at that.

'Ricky?'

The voice made him jump and he almost dropped the bag. Shoving it back into the locker and closing the door, Ricky turned to see Frank standing just two feet from him.

'I've checked the packages, and I can't believe I'm saying this, but you're right. They appear to be untouched,' Frank said. It struck Ricky as odd that he didn't react to the fright Frank had given him.

'As I thought,' Ricky replied, trying to keep his voice as steady as possible.

Frank regarded him, his eyes rolling across Ricky's face as though he was waiting for more.

'So,' Ricky continued. 'What's your plan now?'

'I want to speak to your men. I want to see their faces when asked if they have any idea how the drugs could have been tampered with. Because I don't see any other explanation, Ricky, as to how this could have happened.'

'I trust my team.'

Frank nodded. 'I can see that. But *I* don't know them. And if I'm being honest, I don't have any reason to trust them. So, make arrangements to meet with them. Now, please.'

Ricky locked the locker door and slipped the key into his pocket, before pulling out his phone and making the call.

—

'Okay,' Ricky started, with his men standing in front of him. He glanced at each of their faces. Some looked entirely normal, unfazed by Frank Cranwell's presence. Others looked nervous. 'You all know what's been going on. We have had five drug deaths. The police are launching an inquiry, and we've had to stop distribution until we can locate the source of the problem.'

Everyone was silent. Even Frank, which made Ricky a little tense. If that's how he was feeling, the boys who looked nervous must have been shitting themselves.

'Aye, and in the meantime,' one of the men piped up, 'we're no' gettin' paid.'

Ricky raised a brow. 'Dylan, isn't it?'

Dylan nodded. 'Aye. And I've got three weans in the hoose who're havin' tae live aff beans and toast fur the foreseeable.'

Ricky took a steadying breath. Dylan was relatively new to the team. A few months. Maybe six at the most. He'd always been quiet, had got on with the jobs assigned to him. But today, he seemed different. Agitated, somehow.

'Sorry to hear that,' Ricky said. 'I understand it's difficult when money is tight. However, myself and Mr Cranwell here, have a repu-tation to uphold as well as a business agreement. And until we can sort this problem out, distribution has ceased and will remain that way until we both see fit.'

Dylan rolled his eyes and gave a tut, and Ricky felt Frank nudge him. He understood the meaning behind it. This lad was protesting a little too hard. Something was off and he didn't need Frank to point it out.

Ricky straightened his shoulders and took a step forward. 'Does anyone else have anything to say about our decision?'

Everyone shook their heads and Ricky kept his eye on Dylan. 'Okay. Everyone, back to your cabs. You—' He glared at Dylan. 'My office. I want a word.'

If he'd had a measuring tape, Ricky could have sworn Dylan's stature had shrunk by a few inches. His face dropped and the colour left his cheeks immediately.

'I've got a taxi to get back on the road,' he protested, although a little less fiercely this time. 'If I'm only earning from that, I need to be out as much as possible.'

'This won't take long,' Ricky said, placing a hand on Dylan's back and gently yet firmly guiding him into the office.

Frank was at Ricky's back, still menacingly silent. Although now, Ricky didn't feel the tension was quite as thick around him. Dylan had shifted Frank's focus.

'Take a seat,' Ricky said, as he closed the door.

'Look, Mr Fyfe. I'm sorry if I came across as cheeky back there. I'm just struggling at the minute.'

Ricky nodded, slipping his hands into his coat pocket and keeping his gaze fixed firmly on the cheeky fucker in the seat in front of him.

'Tell us how you did it,' Frank said. Even Ricky felt a shiver run up his spine from the iciness in his tone.

'Did what?' Dylan replied.

'More to the point, *when* did you do it? And what did you use?'

Dylan's neck began to break out in hives and Ricky felt a wave of disappointment wash over him. Fuck. This lad had fucked up and now, he was going to have to suffer the consequences.

'I dunno wit yer talking aboot,' Dylan replied, although his voice was quieter now and he'd shrunk back in his chair.

Frank leaned in, placed both gloved hands on the lad's knees and said, 'Don't. Fuck. With. Me. Tell us everything now, and I might spare you.'

Ricky closed his eyes briefly. This wasn't going to end well. Regardless of whether Frank got information or not, there was going to be a clean-up job today.

Dylan was silent, staring up at Frank with fear in his eyes. The lump in his throat bobbed up and down as though he was trying not to cry.

'Please,' Dylan finally responded. 'Ave got three weans at hame. Am all they've got.'

'Then you'd better start fucking talking,' Frank replied. 'You've got one minute.'

Dylan's eyes met Ricky's, and he gave the lad a nod, indicating to tell the truth. Giving him hope that if he spoke up, then he'd be spared. Ricky knew that wasn't going to happen.

'I wis paid tae dae it,' he spat the words out. 'I didnae want tae. But I didnae huv a choice.'

Frank stood up, took his hands off Dylan's knees and stepped back. He was shoulder to shoulder with Ricky now. Two large men, dressed in suits and long coats, with guns in their pockets. Dylan knew who he was working for. Of course he did. How could he have been so fucking stupid?

'Go on,' Ricky said. 'Who paid you?'

Dylan hesitated.

'Forty seconds,' Frank said, slipping his hand into his pocket.

Dylan saw it and he swallowed hard. 'It wis Aidan Doyle. He paid me.'

Ricky frowned. 'Aidan Doyle? But he's on the run after the factory fire. Why would he pay you to lace the drugs?'

He could feel Frank's eyes on him, but he kept his gaze on Dylan.

'He *is* still on the run. Well, kinda. He's hiding oot.'

'Where?' Ricky pressed.

'I dunno. He never said.'

'Where did you meet him to get paid?' Ricky asked.

'Roon the back ae the Morrison's in Anniesland.'

'And how much were you paid for the job?' Frank interjected, his tone much darker than Ricky's.

Dylan bowed his head. Fuck. It wouldn't even have been worth it, Ricky thought.

'How much?' Frank said, a little louder this time.

'Two hundred,' Dylan said, his voice cracking.

Ricky shook his head. 'Fuck sake, Dylan. You can make more in a weekend driving the fucking taxi. Jesus, what the fuck were you thinking?'

'Aidan wouldnae let up aboot it, Mr Fyfe. He wis adamant I dae it. I didnae wantae but he said if I didnae then his boss would kill him.'

Ricky and Frank stole a glance and Frank said, 'Oh? And who is this Aidan's boss?'

Dylan shifted in his seat. 'I cannae tell ye.'

Before Ricky could say a word, Frank had pulled out a gun and pressed it into Dylan's forehead.

'Frank, wait.' Ricky held his hand up to the gun but didn't touch it. 'We need to know who Aidan Doyle is working for.'

'Yes, and this little shit is going to tell me before I blow his fucking head off.'

Dylan began to cry; all his bravado from earlier completely gone.

'I cannae tell ye cos I don't know. Aidan didnae geeus a name.'

'Bullshit!' Frank roared. 'You've got ten seconds.'

Dylan went on sobbing, pleading for his life. Ricky stood there, his eyes shifting between the two. He didn't need a dead body on his hands. He had to talk Frank down. But with less than ten seconds, it seemed impossible.

'Frank, wait,' Ricky said.

'Where does Aidan Doyle live?' Frank said, the gun still pressed into Dylan's head.

'I dunno.'

'If you're lying, now is the time to cut it out and tell us the truth,' Frank pushed.

'A'right, fine. He's dossin' in the basement ae the drug den where I met him to get the cash. But he's probably no there noo. He's mebbe...'

BANG!

The shot rang out so loudly that Ricky flew back and landed in the seat behind him, his eyes wide with shock at what had just happened.

Dylan, still in the chair, his head slumped to the side, stared blankly into the wall of death he'd just been driven into as blood trickled down the side of his face onto the carpet.

Frank tucked the gun back into his coat and cricked his neck.

'Jesus, Frank, was that really fucking necessary in my place of business?'

Frank turned and gave him an icy stare. 'Like you've never dealt with this situation before. I'd suggest a clean-up job immediately. I'm going to speak to this Aidan Doyle character. Stick with the freeze in distribution until I say so. Understood?'

Ricky got to his feet and nodded. 'Aye. Fine.'

'Your boys trustworthy on this?' Frank asked, eyeing Dylan's body.

'I've got a clean-up team at the ready if need be.'

Frank fixed the lapel of his coat and gave a nod. He moved around to the back of the chair holding Dylan's lifeless body, bent down and picked something up from the floor. When he got back up, Ricky noticed a bullet between his fingers. He pulled a tissue out from his coat pocket, wrapped the bullet up and slipped it back inside.

'Where will he be disposed of?' Frank asked.

'He'll be cremated.'

'Discreetly, I'd hope?'

'Of course.' Ricky closed his eyes. It annoyed him how little Frank thought of him and his team. 'It'll all look above board. There will be no come back.'

'I know. But just in case, I used your gun. Sorry about that. Can't be too careful these days.'

Ricky's eyes were wide. How the fuck had Frank managed to get hold of Ricky's gun. He reached into the pocket where he usually kept it and found it was missing.

'You can have it back when I can be assured this has been dealt with properly.'

Before Ricky could say anything, Frank was out the door and Ricky was left in his office, staring down at Dylan and the gaping hole in his head.

Chapter Fifty-Nine

Elle opened the door cautiously, even though she knew it was Frank on the other side. As she let him in, she waited for him to speak. He walked through to the living room and sat down on the sofa.

'Did you know Ricky was involved in the funeral business?' Frank asked.

Staring down at him, she nodded. 'Yes. Crawford Funeral Care. I think he said something about having shares in the business. But that was years ago, obviously. Why?'

Frank clasped his hands together and shook his head. 'Because that's where he's storing my drugs. And he doesn't own it, or have shares in it. He's using it to launder his money.'

'Did he tell you that?'

'No. But I'm in the same line of work, Elle. I know these things.'

Elle glanced up at the ceiling. 'Is it still Tim Crawford?'

'The man at the front desk was called Tim. You know who he is?'

'He was the loveliest man I've ever met in my life. He and I had a few conversations about his family. He's probably got grandkids by now. He always seemed utterly terrified of Ricky.'

Frank gave a nod. 'He did look scared out of his wits, to be honest.'

Elle sighed and sat down beside Frank. 'How did things go between you two?'

'Yeah, fine,' Frank replied, and then Elle realised that if things weren't fine, Frank wasn't going to tell her. Adding more pressure to her situation wasn't something he'd want.

'I didn't think he'd still be involved with the funeral place after all these years.'

'It's the perfect place to clean money, Elle. Especially if he doesn't own it. Rather than have his name on the books, which could lead police right to his door one day, he probably just pays that guy a handsome fee for his troubles and to keep his mouth shut,' Frank replied.

'But for thirty years? I mean, that's loyalty,' Elle said, staring at the blank television screen. 'Actually, it's probably more fear than loyalty. That man is in so much deeper than anyone else. He'll know Ricky's secrets, even the darkest ones.'

Frank nodded. 'Do *you* know his darkest secrets?'

'Pfft,' Elle scoffed. 'I *am* his darkest secret. And whatever happened to Chris. Then there's Jordan Burns and anything after that for almost three decades. Tim will know it all. And I'll bet my life on it that with access to a crematorium, Ricky has got rid of a few bodies in there.'

'But he didn't cremate you. So, how can you be sure he knows you're dead?'

Elle shrugged. 'I don't know. Maybe he doesn't know for certain.'

Elle watched as Frank shook his head. 'Why are you looking at me like that?' she asked.

'He said that he signed your divorce papers.'

'Yeah, he did. I watched him do it before he attacked me.'

'Could he have sent them to the solicitor after you'd gone? I mean, it would be the perfect cover up for your disappearance, wouldn't it? You were divorced, so why would he know where you were?'

Elle bit her lip. It did make sense. Ricky was many things, but stupid wasn't one of them. If he was getting married to Danica, then it would be legit.

'Maybe I really am his *ex*-wife then.'

Frank turned, scratched his chin. 'Why don't we go and have a chat with Tim?'

Elle raised a brow. 'Frank, the man probably thinks I'm dead. If I show up, he'll end up dead on his own mortuary slab after a heart attack.'

She thought about what her presence could do to other people. It could harm others involved with Ricky. Tim could tell Ricky for a start. Not to mention Teigan.

'If Tim has kept his mouth shut this long, then who's to say he'll blab now? Maybe you could get some information from him about Ricky's brother? Or about what he's having Tim do for him? The more information you're armed with, the easier it will be for Teigan to see what kind of monster he really is. That coupled with the fact that he isn't her biological father might be enough for her to walk away.'

Elle hadn't thought about how she was going to tell Teigan that not only was Ricky not her dad, but Chris was. 'I think that in Ricky's world, fear and loyalty go hand in hand. I think it's a risk if I go to Tim. And I doubt he'll betray Ricky that easily.'

'And I truly believe that it's a risk if you don't. He had something he didn't want me to see today.'

She glanced at him, narrowing her eyes. 'What do you mean?'

'He was holding something in his hand as he was standing in front of some lockers down in the basement of the funeral home. He thought I was busy doing something else, but when I said his name to get his attention, he shoved something into the locker and slammed the door shut. He looked proper jarred by it.'

Elle scoffed. 'Could have been anything.'

'The point is, he has something no one else is supposed to see. You could use it against him,' Frank replied.

She laughed, this time harder than she'd intended. 'No offence, Frank, but don't be so utterly ridiculous. I have nothing on Ricky.'

Frank tilted his head and stared at her. 'So, what are you going to do? Sit here until your rental runs out and do nothing? Then what?'

Sighing, Elle felt at a loss. She had no real clue what she was going to do.

'Maybe you could crash his wedding,' Frank laughed. 'The dead ex-wife shows up to stop the wedding. Imagine his face when he saw you.'

She blinked, the very image flashing into her mind's eye. What would happen if she did that? The wedding venue, packed with guests. He's just signed the register. Had his first kiss with his new wife. And then as he's walking back up the aisle, Elle is walking down it towards him, staring him straight in the eye, knowing what he was thinking: that everyone will believe she's come to crash the party and he would be the only one in the room who thought she'd risen from the dead.

'Elle?'

She laughed. 'That's ridiculous. Utterly ridiculous.'

'Is it?' Frank raised a brow.

'Yes, it is. And no, I'm definitely not doing that. If I'm going to have anything to do with that wedding, it's to stop it from going ahead at all.'

Chapter Sixty

She stood in her wedding dress and stared at herself in the mirror. The stunning gown flowed over her body, but she just felt numb. Getting married should be the single most exciting moment in her life, a day she should be sharing with her parents. Her dad should be walking her down the aisle. Her mum should be buying a mother-of-the-bride outfit and sharing a loving moment with Danica before she became a wife.

Instead, Danica was marrying the man who murdered her dad, and her plans for revenge were beginning to wear her down. Piece by piece, Danica felt like she was beginning to forget who she really was.

'What do you think?' the dress fitter called through the curtain chirpily.

Danica opened her mouth to speak, then shut it again. She was speechless and not for good reason. Could she truly go through with the wedding? Could she *actually* marry Ricky Fyfe? What if she bottled it on the day and left him at the altar? It would all have been for nothing. There would be no justice for Jordan and Georgia. Nor herself. Ricky would go on making people fucking miserable and continue to get away with it.

'Ms Campbell? Are you okay in there?'

Danica watched as the tears fell from her eyes and she instinctively wiped them away, stood up straight and said, 'Yes, just admiring it. I'll be out in a moment.'

'Do let me know if any of the alterations aren't right. Once you take the dress away today, you'll need to sign to say the process is complete so you need to be happy with everything.'

Happy? With everything? Was that even possible? Not just for Danica but for anyone? Being with Ricky for the last four years had shown her how easy it was to be unhappy. Had she done that to herself for being with him? Had she gone too far?

She ran her hands over the dress, turning slightly to get a look at the back. 'The alterations all seem fine,' Danica called back. 'No problems.'

'Oh, that's good to hear. I'll be back in a minute,' the dress fitter called back, and Danica listened as her footsteps moved away from the dressing room.

Danica imagined herself walking down the aisle towards him, Teigan having gone down first. She heard herself take her vows. And there was no reason for him to doubt her – she'd put the work in to make him fall in love with her and make him believe she felt the same.

It was all because of a decision he'd made when she was just weeks old. If she'd been a deep believer in the universe having a plan for you, she'd have thought she was put on the planet for the very task of bringing Ricky to his knees. But the more she imagined him losing everything and going to prison, the less satisfied she felt. Watching him lose everything he'd built wasn't going to be enough.

But she wasn't a killer. She didn't know anyone who was, other than Ricky himself.

Stepping out of the dress, Danica hung it back on its hanger and stared at it as she got dressed. Maybe if she took some more money out the wedding fund, she could pay someone to have him killed. But who?

The idea of having Ricky killed with his own money was a dream but equally a nightmare. Maybe she could ask Aidan to do it? It would be beneficial to them both. She shook her head. Aidan would never agree to anything like that.

She just had to hope that Frank Cranwell was so angry with the contaminated drugs on Ricky's watch that he did the deed for free after she'd married him. That way, she wouldn't have to get her hands dirty.

Chapter Sixty-One

The alley was quiet as Aidan Doyle sat with his back against the wall smoking a cigarette, when he heard footsteps approaching.

Turning, he saw a tall man in a black coat towering over him.

'Plenty space to get by, mate,' Aidan said, taking a draw on his cigarette.

'You're Aidan Doyle, yes?'

His heart froze. The accent. It was an Essex accent. *Shit.*

Stubbing out the cigarette on the ground next to him, Aidan noticed he was considerably shorter than the man in front of him.

'Depends on who wants to know?' But Aidan already knew who he was. It didn't take a genius to work it out.

'Dylan said you live here,' the man replied. Aidan knew the game was up.

'Dylan who?' Aidan said, playing it as coolly as he could, but even he had to admit that his voice gave him away. He was rattled.

'The same Dylan you paid to lace my drugs,' the man replied.

'Look,' he said, his breath catching in his throat. 'I don't know what that little bastard told you, but whatever it was, it's bullshit.'

'Okay then. If he was lying, then give it to me in your own words.'

'You're Frank Cranwell, aren't you?'

Aidan stared into his eyes and already knew the answer before it came. Of course this was Frank. They'd been expecting him. Well, Danica had been expecting him to show up in the city, but Aidan certainly hadn't expected to come face to face with him.

'I'm the man whose drugs you fucked with.'

'It wasn't me.'

'Then who?' Frank growled. The sound seemed to come from the pit of his stomach, making Aidan shiver.

'I... I don't know.'

'Let me tell you what I think. Dylan said you paid him, and he had no choice because he had three kids at home.'

Aidan noticed the past tense with the word 'had' but didn't want to question Frank and anger him any further.

'He then said that *your* boss would kill you if he didn't lace my drugs. So, if he's bullshitting, then where did he pluck that from?'

Aidan thought his stomach was going to fall out of his backside. Think, think, think. But he couldn't. He couldn't produce a lie. Not one that would stop his death. Even the truth wouldn't do that.

'Or he's not lying at all, and your boss did threaten death.'

Aidan sighed loudly and held his hands up. 'Right. Fine.' He composed himself and opened his mouth. 'She didn't say she'd kill me. But I had to say something to talk him round otherwise I wouldn't get paid.'

Frank frowned. 'She?'

'Aye. She.'

Frank raised a brow. 'Stop fucking about and give me a name.'

Should he just do it? Should he just grass her up and be done with the whole thing? It had got him into so much trouble already and it wasn't as if he or Danica shared a loyalty to one another. But if he gave her name, then he wouldn't get the passport or the twenty grand. He desperately needed both. But then, he knew he wasn't going to make it out of this situation alive. Not now. If he was going down, he was taking Danica with him.

'Would this woman protect your name if she was backed into a corner?' Frank asked and like a switch, Aidan knew what needed to be done.

'Danica Campbell. That's who paid me to do it.'

Frank's expression changed. His frown lines now softened; his eyes widened just a little. 'You're telling me that Ricky Fyfe's *fiancée* paid you to lace the drugs he was distributing for me?'

Aidan nodded and felt a sense of relief and dread wash over him at the exact same time. Shit. What had he done? She would be killed because of this. And then he reminded himself that it wasn't his fault. She'd decided to fuck over her husband-to-be. Aidan was just the dogsbody in all of this.

'Well… yes,' Aidan replied, his voice cracking with fear.

'Why?'

Aidan shrugged. 'I don't know. She never actually told me why. She put so much pressure on me, saying that she would give me up to Ricky if I didn't do what she said.'

'Give you up? You were in charge of the factory when it went up?'

Aidan glanced down at the ground and he knew that his time was limited. Either Frank would kill him. Or Ricky would.

'Aaaah,' Frank drew the word out. '*You* were the one who set the factory on fire.'

'Only because she told me to do it,' Aidan said quickly. 'She said it was an insurance job, and that Ricky wanted it to happen. I should never have believed her.'

Frank was quiet and his jaw was set in a tight grimace. Aidan wanted to run. But he knew the second he moved he'd have a bullet in his back.

'I'm sorry Aidan, but you carried out an instruction that has been detrimental to my income and reputation. I can't just let that slide,' Frank said.

'What about Danica?' Aidan said, but just as he uttered the last sound in her name, he saw the barrel of the gun pointing in his direction. There was no sound before the bullet entered his body. And strangely, no pain. Not at first.

He fell to his knees and just as his face hit the ground, everything went a deep black.

Chapter Sixty-Two

Hanging the dress up in the wardrobe in the spare room, Danica closed the door and glanced at herself in the mirror. She'd already fixed her make-up and she wanted to be ready for her fiancé coming through the door.

Right on cue, the front door slammed shut and Danica jumped, before running out to the landing. Peering down to the entrance hallway, she saw Ricky pacing the floor.

'What's wrong?' she asked, sounding genuinely concerned. So much so that she almost convinced herself that she cared.

'It was one of my own,' Ricky said.

'What are you talking about?' she asked, almost forgetting why he'd gone out with Frank earlier.

'The lad I employed six months ago. Dylan. It was him. He was the one who laced Frank's drugs. He was paid off by Aidan fucking Doyle.'

Danica felt her stomach lurch. Dylan had given Aidan up. Which could mean Aidan giving her up to save his own skin if he was ever found.

Shitshitshit.

'Seriously? That's wild,' Danica replied. 'How are you going to deal with it?'

Ricky threw his hands up in the air and let them fall, his hands smacking off his thighs so loudly it echoed off the walls. 'Oh, Frank took care of that himself. Shot Dylan right in front of me in the taxi office.'

A wave of nausea washed over her then and she felt a tremor in her legs. This was always a risk, but one she didn't think would play out.

'There's a dead man in your taxi office?'

Ricky shook his head and headed into the kitchen. She took the stairs quickly, two at a time and joined him as he poured himself a large whisky.

'Clean-up team are on it,' he said, throwing the whisky into the back of his throat and swallowing hard. He gasped and said, 'Now he's away to find Aidan Doyle. I wanted to go with him but he told me not to.'

Danica frowned. 'He won't find Aidan Doyle. He's been on the run since the factory went up.'

'Aye, well according to Dylan, before his brains ended up all over the walls, Aidan's staying in some drug den in the city centre. Frank will find him. He's like a fucking bloodhound when he gets going.'

Danica prayed that if Frank did find Aidan, that he took her secret to the grave.

She watched as Ricky threw back another whisky and then a third. The silence was deafening.

'I picked up my wedding dress today,' she said, chirpily, hoping it would deflect his thoughts from the events of the day with Frank.

He fixed her with a gaze and then smiled and she was flooded with relief. 'You happy with it?'

She nodded, forcing a smile. 'Yes, it's beautiful. I think you'll love it.'

'Well, not long to go now until the wedding and I'll get to see it,' he said, but he'd averted his eyes towards the whisky bottle again and Danica felt helpless. All she could think about was Aidan Doyle giving her up to Frank. Of course he would. And she wouldn't blame him. He'd do whatever he could to save himself. In his situation, she supposed she would too.

As Danica was about to open her mouth and chat about the wedding, Ricky's phone rang and her heart almost came up and out of her mouth.

'Frank?' Ricky said as he answered. She watched his expression, trying to gauge what was being said as his brows twitched and the corner of his mouth curled into a snarl. 'He said *nothing*? Not *one* word about who his boss was?'

Her legs almost gave way with relief, but she had to compose herself. If she didn't, he'd know something was wrong.

'Right,' he strung the word out painfully slowly. 'So, we're no further forward on who's causing the problem?'

Another moment of silence and Danica had to fight with everything she had not to grab the whisky bottle and drown herself in it.

'Fucking hell, Frank... Right, right fine... You've done it your way, so it doesn't matter.'

Ricky jabbed at the screen with his finger and sighed in frustration.

'What did he say?' Danica asked, trying to keep her voice as steady as possible.

'He's killed Aidan Doyle. Wee fucker wouldn't give a name. So, I know who was tampering with the product, but I don't know who told them to do it. Danica, there's someone out there who wants to fuck with me, and I genuinely haven't a clue who it could be.'

The words settled heavily in her stomach. Frank had murdered Aidan. He was dead and it was her fault. More blood on her hands. Her throat felt like it was beginning to close up, the guilt of these deaths clawing at her skin.

Taking as silent a deep breath as she could, Danica fixed her face with a solemn yet empathic expression. 'You don't think the rest of us are in danger, do you? Should we cancel the wedding until you find out who's doing this?'

Ricky scrunched up his face. 'Aye, that'll be right. I'm not putting our marriage on hold for some bastard who doesn't have the balls to face me themselves. No way. We get married as planned. And if the fucker has a brain cell in their head, they'll stay the hell away from me and my businesses from now on.'

Danica was nodding and slipped her arms around his waist. 'Maybe now that the two people involved with them are dead, they'll back off?'

'Aye,' he kissed her on the top of her forehead. 'You'd think. But I need to get in touch with Teigan. She needs to know about this. Fuck me. Frank's only been here about twenty-four hours, and he's already dealt with this. It makes me look like a fucking fool.'

Danica squeezed him tightly and breathed him in, although of course it was all for show. She was getting closer and closer to her dream of watching him unravel. She couldn't believe that Aidan hadn't dobbed her in. More than surprised. Maybe Frank hadn't given him a proper chance. There was no other reasonable explanation as to why he wouldn't have.

'What will happen to the bodies?' Danica asked.

'Not your concern, sweetheart. All you need to worry about is that your husband-to-be is still alive, still standing and very much the stronger for it. I will have my eyes wide open and on the back of my head now. Anything, or anyone, suspicious, I'll spot them a mile off now.'

Danica knew he couldn't see her face, and if she wasn't so terrified that her true persona was about to be revealed, she'd be smiling. He had his arms wrapped around the one person who was at the heart of this, and he did not have a single clue. He was a fool.

A *big* fucking fool.

Chapter Sixty-Three

Teigan stood outside the front door of her dad's house and instinctively reached for the handle, then remembered they weren't on the best of terms. Things had become so messy so quickly, and Teigan's head was all over the place with it all.

'Why are we just standing here?' Darren asked.

'I don't feel like I can just walk in. Not after everything that's happened,' Teigan replied.

Instead, she raised her finger to the doorbell and pressed it. Then she waited. It was Danica who opened the door with a solemn look on her face.

'Come in,' Danica said, taking a step back and pulling the door wide open for Teigan and Darren.

'Alright, Danica?' Darren said awkwardly.

She didn't respond with words, just gave an insincere smile.

'Your dad's in a bit of a mess,' Danica said to Teigan in a mumsy voice she'd never used before. 'He's had a few drinks.'

Teigan rolled her eyes. Not because Ricky had been drinking, but because of the way Danica had said it.

'Dad?' Teigan called out as she stood in the hallway.

Ricky appeared from the sitting room, and he'd never looked so scruffy. She'd barely seen her dad in anything other than a suit that was pressed to within an inch of its life and now, his shirt was crumpled, the buttons undone at the top and his tie was missing.

'Aidan Doyle fucked us,' he said, although he didn't slur his words. She glanced at Danica, wondering why she'd exaggerated his state.

'What do you mean, he's *fucked* us?' Teigan asked, a deep frown line forming between her brow. 'Other than the fire, what else?'

'He was the one who was responsible for the bad drugs. He paid one of the lads at the taxi firm to tamper with them. Seems as though Aidan has been out to get us the entire time.'

'Jesus,' Teigan said, wondering how they could have missed all this. Teigan stared at Ricky wide eyed and stole a glance at Darren, who'd learned to say nothing and just be present for Teigan.

'So, what's going to happen?' Teigan asked.

Ricky looked at Darren and then raised a brow.

'Oh, come on Dad, he's not going to say anything.'

'They're both dead,' Danica said bluntly. 'Frank shot Aidan and Dylan.'

'Erm, that wasn't your information to give,' Ricky snapped.

Teigan glanced at Darren, who's expression didn't fall. Not one bit. They'd been together long enough now for Darren to feel as normal about pieces of information like this as she did. On one hand, she felt pleased that he could handle it, on the other, it saddened her that he'd become desensitised to the violence and destruction her world brought. He'd been such an innocent soul when they'd met. Now, he was just like the rest of them.

'What? You weren't going to tell her because Darren is standing there? He's as much a part of this family as I am, Ricky. The more you trust those closest to you, the better.'

Teigan frowned. Then she turned her gaze back to her dad. 'So, Aidan Doyle is dead? Is that such a bad thing? He was responsible for the factory fire, wasn't he?'

'I wanted a name, though,' Ricky whined like a child, and Teigan couldn't help but raise a brow. 'He said his boss would kill him if Dylan didn't follow through. So, who was Aidan working for? Because that person wants to go against me, wants to bring me down.'

Teigan let out a long breath. 'Could he have just made it up in the hope that he would deflect attention away from himself?'

'That's possible,' Danica replied.

'But why would Aidan himself want me at loggerheads with Frank Cranwell?'

Frustrated and out of answers, Teigan shrugged and said, 'I don't know, Dad. But if I'm honest, Frank did you a favour killing them. They were trying to fuck us over. Now they're gone. You can get back to it and...' Teigan swallowed, unable to believe she was going to say this out loud. 'And focus on the wedding.'

Ricky stared into the empty glass in his hand and gave a pitiful nod of agreement.

'Oh, speaking of the wedding,' Danica chirped excitedly. 'I picked up my wedding dress today.'

Forcing a smile, Teigan looked at the cut on Danica's eyebrow. The glaring reminder that Ricky had lost his temper, because Teigan had been talking about her mother.

'That's exciting,' Darren said, filling in for Teigan's lack of response. 'Are you happy with it?'

Danica nodded quickly. 'Oh I love it. It's perfect. You two must be getting close to booking your own wedding, surely?'

Teigan wanted to punch her in the face. And Darren for entertaining her. 'Let's get this wedding out the way first,' she replied, although what she'd wanted to say was, 'let's get this shit-show sham of a wedding out the way first so you can start taking money that doesn't fucking belong to you', but she didn't. Instead, she smiled and said, 'Go on then, let's see the finished product.'

Danica blinked and shook her head. 'Nope. I'm not letting anyone see it until the day. I know you've seen me at the fitting, Teigan, but I want it to be special on the day. The final piece, you know?'

The final piece? Teigan thought. It's a dress, not a fucking Van Gogh. 'Fair enough,' she replied.

'I have your dress too. But I'll bring that on the day. You've had your final fitting so I'm not going to get it out of the bag. Plus, I want Ricky to see you in your dress for the first time on the day too.'

Teigan bit the inside of her mouth to stop herself from screaming. 'Yep, makes sense,' she said through gritted teeth. And then she glanced at Ricky. 'Can I have a word in private?'

Nodding, Ricky led her up to the office and once inside, Teigan got straight to the point.

'Look, I'm not going to apologise for asking questions about my mum. But what I will say is that I'm willing to move on from our argument and make peace with it. If you can too?'

Ricky nodded and she watched as his shoulders slumped a little. 'I shouldn't have reacted the way I did. I'm sorry.'

So taken aback with the apology, Teigan sat down on the edge of the desk and shook her head. 'You're sorry?'

'Yeah. Sorry that you had to grow up without a mum because she decided to leave with my brother. I still can't get my head around it after all these years.'

242

Teigan watched as his eyes turned glassy against the light. 'You didn't see it coming at all?'

He shook his head. 'Well, I knew she was leaving me. She did present me with divorce papers, which I willingly signed. I didn't want to make her feel like I was holding her against her will, you know. But I had no idea that she wasn't planning on taking you with her. I just thought we'd do what they call co-parenting these days. Instead, she abandoned you. I suppose she abandoned both of us.'

Teigan bowed her head. 'And they definitely left? Nothing else could have happened to them?'

'What's that supposed to mean?' he snapped.

'Well, they just upped and left, never to be heard from again. All I'm asking is that there isn't more to it?'

'I don't know, Teigan. Other than the finalised divorce papers coming through, I never heard from either of them ever again.'

Teigan took a steadying breath. 'I think I have.'

'You think you have what?' Ricky frowned.

'Heard from them. Well, one of them, anyway.'

He was quiet for a few moments, staring at the floor. Then he slowly began pacing. 'You can't have.'

'Why not? If they're out there somewhere, then *why not?*'

Ricky didn't answer the question. He remained silent and Teigan decided to keep talking.

'I got a message from someone called Sarah Parks on Facebook. No profile picture. No profile information. Just a simple message that said, "I'm sorry I left you."'

She watched as the colour slowly drained from her dad's face. Then he shook his head. 'It's clearly not her, Teigan. It's the wrong name for a start.'

'I *know* that. But she could have messaged under a false name so I wouldn't know for sure it was her. And, no offence when I say this, but she might not have wanted you to find out.'

He began to pace a little quicker, his breath matching each step. She watched his movements, saw how he seemed to be spiralling into an emotion she couldn't quite place. Panic? Anger?

'Dad, it's okay. It's not like this person is going to come and snatch me away. And it might not even be her.'

But he wasn't listening, or at least he didn't seem to be listening.

'Dad, what's wrong?' Teigan asked as she watched him raise a hand to his chest.

'Nothing, I'm fine. Look, it wouldn't have been your mother. Or your uncle. They're both...' He cleared his throat. 'They're both long gone. They left for a reason. To get away from me, clearly. And I'm sorry to say it, Teegs, but she left to get away from you too. Don't dwell on it. Please.'

Teigan felt her mouth drop open at the blunt force of his words. How could he say something like that out loud to her? 'How could you even say that? She divorced you, Dad, not me. It could have been severe post-natal depression that was never treated which made her leave me behind. Maybe now, after all these years, she finally wants to make amends for that?'

Teigan watched as Ricky tried to hold it together but she could tell he was about to have a panic attack. She decided to leave out the fact that she'd questioned the person and asked to meet, and had even arranged a meeting time but they'd not shown up. That could push him over the edge.

'And even if she does want to build a relationship with me, that doesn't make what we have any less important. You've moved on from her, Dad. It's fine. You're getting married in a few days. It's all good. Take some deep breaths.'

He stopped moving around, took a deep breath and then forced a smile. 'You're right. It's not a big deal.'

Cautiously, Teigan moved closer and gave her dad a hug. 'We good?'

'We're good, Teegs. We're always good. *My* girl. You'll always be *my* little girl.'

'Ha,' she laughed, trying to lighten the mood. 'Not so little if I keep packing away the chocolates with a cuppa.'

Silence fell between them and Teigan couldn't help but find his reaction odd. Maybe he'd *never* got over her leaving? Maybe marrying Danica on her mum's birthday was his way of trying to change how he felt about it, every year from now on? On some level, she understood.

He let go of her and disappeared out of the room for a few moments without saying a word. Emotion caught in her throat then. Was he trying to conceal his sadness about the whole situation?

'I have something you might want to see,' he said, returning to the room with a brown envelope in his hand.

'What is it?' Teigan asked, staring at it.

'It's not much, but I kept them because...' Ricky cleared his throat. 'I thought at some point in life you'd want to see them.'

He held the envelope out to her and Teigan stared at his outstretched hand with a feeling of unease. 'What is it?'

'It's a few photographs of you and your mum.'

Teigan had to hold in the emotional gasp that threatened to escape her throat. She had never seen a picture of Elle – had no clue what she looked like.

'Do you want it?' Ricky said, his hand still outstretched as Teigan continued to stare at it.

'You told me you didn't have any pictures,' Teigan said, the memory suddenly coming to her.

'Did I?' he replied, his brow furrowing. Then his face softened and he continued, 'Och, I know I did. When you asked me when you were sixteen, I just couldn't bring myself to show them to you. I didn't want to see you upset. You'd managed to go through life without her so well and I worried that if you saw her, it might trigger something in you. I didn't want to see you struggle with all the questions that you'd probably ask yourself about her that I couldn't answer.'

Teigan blinked and tears fell from her eyes as she took the envelope. 'So, why now?'

Ricky sighed and dropped his hand to his side. 'Well, you're an adult now, with your own life. You're able to decide what's best for you. I have no say in whether you decide to look for your mother or not.'

Teigan shot him a look. 'Look for her?'

'Well, yeah. Isn't that what you want to do?' Ricky asked.

Teigan shrugged. 'I don't know. I never thought about it before,' she lied. Teigan knew she wanted to actively look for her mum, but she wasn't going to admit that to Ricky. Not now. 'I always just wondered why she left me. I never stopped to think about finding her to ask why. And now I have a message from a random person and you've given me this. It's a lot to take in.'

Ricky nodded, his face still pale from when she first mentioned the message. 'It's all up to you, Teigan. There's no right or wrong decision.'

Nodding, Teigan glanced down at the envelope and exhaled sharply. She didn't know if she wanted to open it – if she'd ever be ready to see what Elle looked like. Would she see herself in the face of her mother?

Or would Teigan look at the images and see the woman who abandoned her? She wasn't sure she was ready to feel that rage flare up.

'Yeah, you're right. I'll take my time to think about it.'

Chapter Sixty-Four

Someone knew what he'd done. The only people who definitely did were Chris and Tim Crawford. Chris was dead. Tim wouldn't have a clue what Facebook was and even if he did, he wouldn't risk losing the massive cash injection every month, or his life. He would never involve himself in Ricky's business like that. Not now. Not when there was so much at stake.

So, who the *hell* was it?

He should never have given Teigan those pictures. But he didn't have a choice if he wanted to get Teigan back on side. He had to protect himself, protect his character. Jesus, he hadn't looked at those pictures in years. He didn't want to see *her* face ever again. The liar. The cheat. The last time he'd seen her, she was dead on his kitchen floor with Chris dragging her out to his car to get rid of the body. So, who the fuck had messaged his daughter, saying they were sorry for leaving? It had to be someone close.

He replayed the last time he laid eyes on Elle. Chris dragging her body out to the car. The next time he saw her was as he and Chris placed her body in the cremation chamber before getting rid of her. Her body was in a bag.

No. His eyes widened at the thought. He never actually saw that the body in the bag was in fact Elle. Ricky shook his head. No. No way. If Elle was still alive, Ricky would know by now. He'd seen her on the kitchen floor. He'd been the one to deliver the fatal blow. She was dead that night.

Balling up his fist, Ricky punched the wall next to the door, leaving blood smeared on the wallpaper. Turning, he moved through to that very spot in the kitchen and stood on top of where she'd died.

'You fucking ruined me, you *bitch*,' he whispered. 'You turned me into a fucking monster. Now I'm questioning what I saw with my own eyes, what I did with my own hands. Damn it.'

He'd managed to be Teigan's father for all these years without so much as Elle coming into his dreams at night. Once someone crossed him, he never looked back. Not until recently. And now, someone was fucking with his family. Pretending to be Elle and using a fake name so that he wouldn't find out who they were. But he would. He'd make it his mission. And *when* he found out who the bastard was that had messaged Teigan, just like Elle and Chris, he would turn them to ash too.

Chapter Sixty-Five

There were eight photographs in total and Teigan had spread them out on the coffee table in front of her. As she stared down at them, she felt the way her mother looked. Tense. Sad. Anxious.

'Do you think you look like her?' Darren asked, sipping on his coffee.

'Hmm,' Teigan said as she studied the pictures. Elle had the same turned-up nose as Teigan did. 'There,' she pointed it out to Darren. He glanced at her and nodded.

'Yeah, a little.'

'Sometimes I wonder if I'd have been better off adopted. I wouldn't have all this shit to deal with in my head if that was the case.'

Darren rubbed at her back as she leaned forward, studying the pictures. She picked up the one furthest to her left and stared at it.

'That's a nice one,' Darren said, referring to the image of Elle feeding her newborn.

'Strange,' Teigan replied. 'Strange that she was breastfeeding me and then just left. I mean, how did my dad cope with that? I was being fed by my mother, and then suddenly my source of survival was gone, and he had to work it out on his own.'

Darren sighed. 'Well, I mean, he did it, though. You're still here, alive and well. So, he couldn't have done too badly, eh?'

'I suppose not. And he ended up getting a nanny in. Several, actually,' Teigan said, putting the photograph down on the floor.

She stared down at the second one and the first thing she noticed was how small she was as a baby. Lying in her mother's arms on the sofa, her dad sitting next to them with his arm draped over Elle's shoulder. Every time she tried to justify what happened, Teigan hit a brick wall.

'That's some shiner on your mum's cheek,' Darren said, pointing to the bruising on the left side of Elle's face.

Teigan studied it, narrowing her eyes as if that was going to help.

'God, that does look sore,' Teigan replied. Then she looked down at the others, studying each area of her mother's exposed skin in every picture. Arms, legs, neck, face.

'Darren, she has bruising in each one.'

She turned round to look at him and as he stared down at the images, his lips were parted as though he was going to say something but couldn't think of the right words.

'Do you think she could have left because he was hitting her?' she said bluntly. 'Look at her face in this one.' She handed a picture to Darren and pointed to Elle's face.

'What about it?'

'He has his hand around her wrist. Look at her face. Look at her eyes. They're bloodshot, like she's been crying.'

'She'd just given birth to you. She was probably hormonal.' Darren looked incredulous. 'Come on, Teegs. Why would your dad give you a bunch of photographs of your mum all bruised like that if he was the one who'd given them to her? It must be something else.'

But what? she thought.

'Teegs?' Darren said again.

'What?'

'You're not going to say anything, are you?'

Her head felt like it was going to explode. First the message from Sarah Parks. Then the fall out with her dad because she'd asked questions about her mum. Now this? She shook her head and said quietly, 'No, I'm not.'

'I mean, I don't know how your dad would react if you did,' Darren continued. 'And it's not as if Danica is covered in bruises. If anything, I think Danica would knock your dad out if he tried anything like that.' He gave a laugh as if trying to inject some humour into the situation.

She remembered the broken glass on the office floor. Danica's bleeding eyebrow and how Ricky had turned so violent so quickly.

Teigan stared down at the photographs. Eight of them. And not one of them contained a picture of Elle where she wasn't bruised somewhere on her body.

'And you said it yourself,' Darren tried to fill the silence. 'Ricky changed when Danica came into his life. Your words were, *he seems nicer, less intense.*'

Teigan wanted to believe that what she was seeing in the pictures had a reasonable explanation. But the bruises and the look of terror in her eyes, along with the fact that she left, drove her mind to the conclusion that their relationship was abusive.

'I know I did,' Teigan replied. She wanted to say more. But she couldn't find the words.

Chapter Sixty-Six

The wedding venue was utterly stunning and Danica couldn't believe that she was getting married in this beautiful place to someone she hated more than she ever thought possible. 'What a fucking waste,' she muttered under her breath as she walked through the double doors of The Art House in the city centre.

'Ms Campbell?' the wedding co-ordinator greeted her with a smile. 'I'm just running a few minutes behind schedule. The bridal party prior to our meeting ran on later than expected and I haven't had a chance to get your file together. I do apologise.'

Danica waved a dismissive hand. 'Not a bother. I'm happy to wait. I don't have anything else going on today.'

'Sorry if I seem flustered, I don't usually have a run-through meeting this soon before a wedding. You're getting married in two days?' the woman said, sounding as flustered as she looked as she peered down at her diary.

'That's right.'

'Ooh, exciting stuff. I'll be right with you.'

Smiling and thanking her several times, the woman disappeared through one of the side doors in the main lobby and Danica took in the grandeur of the place once more. There had been three suites to choose from to get married in and have the wedding breakfast. Danica had chosen the most expensive. Might as well spend his money on a bit of luxury before he loses it all, she'd thought when she'd booked it. Ricky had told her to go ahead and do everything – he trusted her. Mistake number one.

Taking a seat on one of the high-backed leather chairs, Danica was scrolling through her phone when she sensed someone sit down on the seat next to her. When she looked up, Frank Cranwell was sitting beside her, his finger over his lips in a shooshing gesture. His eyes were darker than she'd ever seen in anyone, even Ricky when he got angry about something.

Danica pulled her eyes away from him and remained silent. She knew why he was here.

'Was he telling the truth?' Frank said, his voice like a low growl, which vibrated in his throat.

She took a breath and kept her eyes on the reception desk. The man behind it hadn't seemed to notice the distinct change in atmosphere.

'What are you talking about?' Danica replied, without turning to look at him.

'Aidan Doyle. Was he telling the truth when he said you were his boss?'

Feeling like she'd just been punched in the stomach, Danica tried her best to keep her composure. Swallowing the lump of fear that had crept into her throat, she parted her lips and said, 'Who?'

'Oh, fuck off.' Frank gave a breathy laugh. 'I know you're a good liar; you'd have to be, to be marrying the man who murdered your father in the name of revenge.'

She turned sharply, almost getting up from the chair but thinking better of it. 'Mr Cranwell, I don't doubt you've seen some elaborate shit over the years in your line of work, but that sounds more like a plot for a shite film or TV show than anything else.'

Frank leaned across a little, clasped his hands and replied, 'Don't treat me like I'm a fucking idiot, Danica. I know who you are. I know what your game is *and* your end goal. You thought you'd fuck up the deal between me and your husband-to-be and it's backfired.'

'What do you think you know?' she asked calmly, although deep down she was in major panic mode. If Frank knew, he could tell Ricky, couldn't he?

'Let's just say, I know someone who knew your father.'

Danica shook her head and then decided that there was no point in lying anymore. He knew and that was the end of it. Elle. It had to be Elle. Who else? 'Are you going to tell me who this person is?'

Frank shook his head.

She cleared her throat, sat up straight and said, 'It did *not* backfire. He's no longer bringing in the money from those...' She stopped, thought better of the words she had been about to say. 'From that contract.'

'And that money is also *my* money.' Frank gritted his teeth.

'I'm sorry, Mr Cranwell. But if, like you say, you know my game and my end goal, then you'll know why I'm doing what I'm doing.'

She kept her eyes on the reception desk, then on the entrance. Anywhere that wasn't Frank, but she could feel his eyes burning into the side of her face. Danica had become an incredible actress over the last four years of her relationship with Ricky, but she could tell that the terror she felt inside was written all over her face.

'Look,' she said calmly, 'if you're going to kill me, could you at least wait until after the wedding?'

'Why?'

She shook her head. 'I want to go through with the marriage. And if I'm going to die, then I need him to know that I never loved him. That I hated him with everything I have. If I can't bring him to his knees, if I can't destroy his business, at least let me break his fucking heart. It's the least he deserves after he destroyed my family.'

Frank was quiet then and Danica wanted the floor beneath her feet to swallow her whole. Frank sat up in his seat and cracked his knuckles; the sound made her shudder.

'I'm not going to kill you,' he said very quietly. 'Ricky Fyfe broke the heart of someone dear to me too and looking at you now, knowing what I know, I understand.'

'It's Elle, isn't it?' Danica looked at him, narrowing her eyes. 'You don't have to confirm it. I already know.'

'She came to me, a very long time ago, in a terrible state. I took her in. Looked after her. Gave her a job. You're going to end up like she did if you're not careful.'

'Careful, Frank. Remember who you are — you don't want folk thinking you care about people,' Danica said.

Frank laughed and Danica jumped.

'I think you and Elle should chat.'

'We already have. She's said all she needed to and so did I. She won't change my mind.'

'No, I'm sure no one could,' Frank said. 'And if I didn't see a little of Elle in you right now, believe me, you wouldn't be breathing. But I do believe that you are both one and the same. Just come with me, chat with her.'

It was Danica's turn to laugh. 'You really think I'm going to get in a car with you?'

Frank shrugged. 'Fine, you don't have to travel with me. Go to see Elle on your own.'

Danica stared at him with suspicion. 'Sorry, Frank. But your switch from the gangster who wanted to kill me just seconds ago to a nice guy who wants to help is either suspicious, or downright bipolar.'

He laughed again and got to his feet. 'Look, I saw what he did to Elle and the state he'd left her in. If you go through with the wedding, you'll end up like her. Trust me, I've met many men like him in my years and it's rare for the partners to get out alive.'

Danica dug her thumbnail into her palm as hard as she could to deflect her attention away from the truth of what he was saying. She knew that there was a massive risk to her life in marrying Ricky, especially if he discovered the truth before she intended. But there was no other way. None at all. The legal system had let her and her mother down in the worst way. Ricky had walked free and had been able to live a normal life.

'It's a risk I'm willing to take,' she replied ruefully.

'You're willing to die?' Frank asked, his words so sharp she felt them in her chest.

Swallowing hard, Danica dug her nail in so sharply she winced. 'If that's what it takes.'

Frank shook his head. 'It doesn't have to come to that, Danica. Trust me. If you go to Elle, talk to her, you'll see that for yourself.'

–

Switching off the engine, Danica got out of the car and headed across the road to the address that Elle had texted to her phone.

Before she could even knock on the door, Elle opened up and stood to the side to let her in. She could already see Frank sitting in the lounge as she stepped inside.

'Why do I feel like this is a setup?' Danica asked as Elle closed the door behind her.

'Because you're already on edge, that's why,' Elle replied. 'I know what you did. Frank told me. Do you have any idea how much danger you're putting yourself in?'

Danica frowned. 'This coming from the woman who abandoned her child?'

Elle bowed her head and Frank stood up. 'Oi, that's bang out of order,' he raised his voice.

'It's fine,' Elle replied, moving past Danica into the lounge to join Frank. 'Just come through. I want to talk to you about what you're doing.'

'Urgh.' Danica threw her hands up in the air. 'If you're going to try to talk me round again…'

'Frank saw something that you might need to help us with,' Elle said.

'What kind of something?' Danica was still standing in the hallway, peering through to the lounge. The unease in her stomach made her feel sick.

'Something that Ricky did not want me to see. He was hiding something, and we want you to go in and get it,' Frank replied. His eyes were fixed on hers and she noticed he wasn't blinking.

Danica raised both brows and glanced at Elle. 'What was it?'

'We don't know. But we wondered if it could have something to do with me, or even your dad?'

'Nah, that's too easy,' Danica said and then she laughed. 'Ricky is a clever bastard. How else do you think he walked free of my dad's murder?'

'All the more reason to find out what he got so spooked about. You said they never found your dad's body, but maybe he has some evidence that could…' Elle's voice trailed off.

'Exactly. You're clutching at straws here,' Danica replied. 'Look, I really don't have time for this. My wedding is in two days.'

Danica turned and as she reached the door, she held the handle but didn't open it. Something screamed inside her to run as far away as she could. She knew she was in deeper than she could have ever imagined. The depths of Ricky's black soul gripped at her throat, and she wanted to break free. But she just refused to allow herself to be one of his victims.

'Where?' she finally said, without turning to look at either Elle or Frank.

'At the funeral home,' Elle said.

Danica let go of the door handle and spun around. 'What funeral home?'

'The one Ricky injects his money into every month to be cleaned,' Frank said.

'What are you talking about?'

Elle closed her eyes briefly. 'You don't know about Crawford Funeral Care?'

Danica shook her head. 'He doesn't own a funeral business.'

'No, he doesn't,' Frank replied. 'He pays the owner off to put money through the books.'

'He's been doing it for years,' Elle said. 'How long have you two been together that you wouldn't know about it?'

'Four years,' Danica replied. *Four years longer than I can handle*, she thought to herself.

How could she not have known about this place? How could Ricky not have told her about it? She knew why, though. She'd only been part of his life for four years. He wasn't going to give away his trade secrets. Not to an outsider. And that's what she was. Which is why she had to marry him. She could only ruin him from the inside.

Elle and Frank were silent as Danica walked slowly through to the lounge and sat down on the sofa.

'Okay,' she took a breath. 'What exactly am I looking for?'

'There was a set of lockers on the back wall of the mortuary,' Frank began. 'You need to get the key for locker number nine and look inside. Don't remove anything. Just take photos of what you find. Then bring them to us.'

Danica was staring at the floor, listening to Frank's instructions. But the entire time, all she heard over and over was the number nine.

'I already have a key for it,' she said. 'I found it in his safe the other day. There were two. I took one.'

Frank pursed his lips and then looked at Elle.

'Are you sure?'

'Well, it has the number nine on it. So, what else would it be for?'

The only thing she had to ask herself was how she was going to get into the mortuary without arousing suspicion. If Ricky had never told her about the funeral place, then the people in charge there could question her presence.

'What's your plan then?' Frank asked.

She didn't know. But she'd come up with something. She always did.

Chapter Sixty-Seven

Danica stood outside the bathroom door, listening for the sounds of Ricky preparing for a shower. They were always the same. His Spotify playlist would come on via the inbuilt sound system in the house, usually ACDC first. She'd hear the bathroom window being opened then the sound of the running water changing as he stepped beneath it.

That was it. Her moment. His phone sat on the chaise longue alongside his clothes, and she picked it up quickly before the screensaver kicked in. She opened the contacts, found Tim Crawford's number and took a picture of it with her own phone before placing the phone quickly back where she'd found it.

Breathing a sigh of relief, Danica thought about how to start the message. She briefly read over some messages from Ricky to gauge how he composed one himself and then she began to type a message from her own phone.

> Tim, it's Ricky. My phone is out of battery so I'm sending this from Danica's phone. I'm out this afternoon for a kilt fitting. I'm sending Danica in with some funds today. I've told her what to do. Just show her where to deposit the cash and leave her to it so she will be out of your way quickly. Cheers. Ricky.

Hitting send, she chewed on her thumbnail as she waited for a reply. Damn it, she should have told Tim to reply when he got the message. What if he suspected? What if he tried to call Ricky to check?

As quickly as her thoughts came to her, the phone beeped and she looked down at the screen.

She exhaled sharply and slipped her phone into her bag. Then she tapped on the bathroom door and peered her head around into the bathroom.

'Hope the kilt fitting goes well,' she said, echoing Tim's text. 'I'll see you for dinner?'

Ricky had a headful of shampoo lather and with his eyes shut he said, 'Aye, I'll see you later. I'll text you a picture when I'm in the kilt.'

'No boxers please,' Danica quipped before closing the door. Securing her handbag over her shoulder and patting it, feeling the envelope of cash inside, she walked out of the bedroom and down to the drive.

The journey to Crawford Funeral Care felt long and intense. She continually checked her mirrors, expecting Ricky to be following her. In the back of her head, she often wondered if he was playing her at her own game. But she knew that could never be the case because he'd never be able to keep under wraps that he knew who she was and what she was doing. He was too hot headed, too violent under the right circumstances to be able to keep his cool. If he knew she was trying to mess with his source of income, trying to mess with his life, he'd end her immediately without so much as blinking.

Heart thumping as she parked the car just along the road from the main entrance, Danica got out and walked towards Crawford Funeral Care. Before she opened the door, she painted on her best smile, took a deep breath and got rid of the jitters.

'Tim?' she said, smiling widely. 'It's so good to *finally* meet you. I'm Danica – soon to be Danica Fyfe.'

The man behind the reception desk, who looked old enough to be dead, got to his feet and smiled while holding out a hand.

'And you, Mrs Fyfe-to-be.' He smiled back at her. 'Mr Fyfe sent instructions, so please follow me.'

Good, she thought. Straight to it.

Tim led her down a set of stairs and the lights at the bottom illuminated the concrete floor. The temperature suddenly dropped and the hairs on Danica's arms stood on end.

'The drawer at the end is where Mr Fyfe stores the cash. All you have to do is put in there what you have with you. It doesn't usually take him more than a few minutes. I do all the counting and recording on his instruction, if Teigan can't.'

Danica was smiling and nodding like one of those lucky Chinese cats often on display in the Chinese takeaway at the bottom of the road.

'I'll leave you to get on with it,' Tim said. He turned and headed back up the stairs. And suddenly, she was very aware that she was in a mortuary. Were there any dead bodies in with her? The thought made her blood run cold. Scanning the room, she spotted the cremation chamber at the very back of the room and it made her shiver.

Get on with it, she told herself, turning her attention back to the task in hand. She slid open the drawer at the end and placed the envelope of cash inside, before closing it again. There wasn't much in it. A grand from the wedding fund, give or take a few pounds. Danica couldn't very well leave nothing behind. That would make Tim worry and he might contact Ricky about it.

She spotted the set of storage lockers on the opposite wall and her stomach lurched. Moving across to them, locker number nine came into view immediately and she pulled the key from her bag. Taking a deep breath, she slipped the key into the lock, turned it and the door sprang open from the mechanism.

There was no time for hesitating, so Danica pulled the door open and inside she saw a few clear, zip lock bags. Frowning, she pulled the ones closest to the front out and peered at the items inside.

What lay in her hands made her freeze with abject fear. An item of clothing with dried blood stains all over it.

'Is this a joke?' she found herself saying out loud as she stared at it. Then she pulled out her phone and took some pictures of it, before pulling out the next bag.

As Danica processed what was in her hand, a wave of nausea and fear washed over her so quickly that she had to put her hand up on the wall to steady herself. This couldn't be happening. This wasn't real, surely? After all these years, after all the heartache and the wondering, it all came down to this.

Breathing through the nausea and the tears, Danica tried to steady her shaking hand to be able to take a picture of the bagged item in her grip.

Closing her eyes she tried to breathe but her throat was closing up and she couldn't get the air in. Sucking as hard as she could but failing, Danica fell to the floor and tried to focus.

Five things you can see. A locker. A key. The floor. My shoes. The bag in my hand.

Four things you can smell. My perfume. The perspiration coming from my hands. The coldness of the air, strangely. Death.

Three things you can hear. My heart thumping in my chest. The blood rushing in my ears. The hum of the refrigerators keeping the dead bodies from decaying too quickly.

Two things you can touch. The floor. My dead dad's wedding ring in my hand.

One thing you can taste. The blood in my mouth.

She winced at the pain of chewing the inside of her cheek and felt herself begin to come back around. Breathing slowly, Danica got to her feet and clasped her fingers around the ring in her hand. The ring matched the one she had that had belonged to her mum before she'd died. The only difference was the inscription. It was reversed.

Frank's words echoed in her mind. *Take pictures and bring them back.*

No way. No *fucking way* on this planet was Danica going to put her dad's ring back in that locker. But she had to, because if she removed it from Ricky's lockers, then there was no way to prove it was ever there in the first place.

As her thoughts spiralled quicker than she ever thought possible, a realisation hit her right between the eyes. The pain and wondering of what had happened to her dad's body after Ricky had killed him; the reason no one had ever found Jordan's remains. Ricky had access to body disposal. He'd committed the perfect crime. No body. No evidence. Simple. But it wasn't so simple because he'd kept Jordan's wedding ring. The inscription was there, blood stained and all.

Danica raised her eyes from the bag in her hand and placed it back into the locker before closing it and pulling the key out. She slowly turned towards the cremation chamber, and she had to suppress the scream that rushed up from her throat and tried to escape.

Chapter Sixty-Eight

Elle opened the door of her rental home and Danica practically fell into her arms. Once she had managed to settle her down, Elle stared down at the pictures Danica had sent to her and felt the biggest urge to sink a bottle of gin. She'd always known about the falsified evidence Ricky had claimed to have on her. But to see it with her own eyes made her feel sick.

'He's a fucking monster,' Danica sobbed as she held onto a glass of water with a trembling hand. 'I don't know if I can go through with this. I don't know if I can stand there and marry him now that I have the proof he killed my dad.'

Frank was slowly pacing the floor, deep in thought.

Elle sat down on the floor in front of Danica and cupped her face. 'You don't have to do anything of the sort, Danica. You should never have put yourself in this situation in the first place.'

The violent sobs coming from Danica hit Elle hard and she felt a lump growing in her throat.

'But he'll get away with it if I walk away,' she said, her voice turning to a whisper. She stared at Elle, Danica's eyes bloodshot and exhausted as the tears continued to stream.

Elle parted her lips to speak, but she didn't know what to say. As much as she hated to admit it, Danica was right. A not proven verdict meant no retrial. Ever. Unless compelling new evidence was found. One ring in his possession didn't seem like it would be enough. And then there was Elle's dress.

Danica moaned in anger laced with sadness. 'There's no other way. I have to do this.'

Elle lowered her hands and Danica put down the glass, wiped away her tears and exhaled slowly. Then, she got to her feet and stared out of the window.

Frank said, 'Look, I think the obvious solution here is if I take him out. But in doing that, I am potentially starting a gang war between Essex and Glasgow and that is something I don't want hanging over me. It's bad for business and quite honestly, I don't need the headache. I think you need to marry him. Once he's legally bound to you, you could *hire* someone to kill him.'

Elle shot Frank a look and gasped. 'You can't be fucking serious, Frank. She's just a young woman with her whole life ahead of her. You can't expect her to do that.'

Frank raised a brow but Danica was already nodding.

'Yeah,' she said. 'I will.'

Closing her eyes, Elle took a few deep breaths and said, 'Danica, think about this. If you marry him and then he ends up dead, the police are going to suspect you immediately. He's a millionaire.'

Danica chewed obsessively on the inside of her cheek. 'You know what, Elle. I don't give a fuck about his money anymore. I just want him dead. Cremated in the same fucking chamber that he burned my dad's body in.' Then she turned to Frank and said, 'You know someone who can do it?'

Frank was quiet for a moment and then nodded. 'I know a few. I'll speak to them. But you have to be *absolutely* sure about this.'

'If I knew I wouldn't miss, I'd shoot the bastard in the head myself,' Danica said, wiping angrily at a stray tear.

Elle was staring at Danica in disbelief. 'There must be another way, Danica. Your parents wouldn't want this for you.'

Turning sharply, Danica gave Elle a look that pierced through her. 'This is exactly what they'd have wanted. I'm doing what the police and the courts couldn't. And I'm only taking what he took from my mum and dad. What's that saying from the bible? An eye for an eye? Fuck him. I don't give a shit what happens to me afterwards.'

She turned to Frank and a look of certainty crossed her face. 'Make the calls. Tell me how much and I'll pay.'

'When?' Frank asked.

'Any point after we've signed the fucking register. On the day or a week later. But I don't want to know about it. I want to be as surprised as possible. I need to look innocent.'

Elle couldn't believe what was being discussed in front of her. She turned and pleaded with Frank. 'Please don't do this.'

'Elle, love. This is you standing here again, just a few decades later. This man needs to be stopped. And I'm more than willing.'

'But...' She searched for any excuse to make him rethink his decision. 'What about your deal with the Fyfes?'

He gave a smile. 'That's done, Elle. After Danica's little stunt, I don't want my product anywhere near this city. And don't think I've forgotten about that,' he said, eyeing Danica. Although his words didn't sound threatening.

Danica, however, didn't seem to care. She looked far away in her own thoughts.

'What about Teigan? This will kill her,' Elle said and then she heard her words.

'He's *not* even her fucking dad, Elle,' said Frank.

Danica spun around and her face was contorted. 'He's not her *what*?'

Elle closed her eyes. She hadn't wanted anyone else to know about it until she'd told Teigan herself.

'*Frank!* For *fuck's* sake!' Elle gritted her teeth.

'He's not Teigan's real dad? Then who the hell is?' Danica barked.

Elle shook her head. 'I'm not saying a thing until I've spoken to Teigan. And you *did not* hear that.' She shot another look of contempt at Frank, who held his hands up in mock defeat.

'Sorry, Elle.'

Ricky *deserved* to die. Of course he did. Elle of all people knew that. But it didn't have to be Danica who planned it. Drawing her eyes away from Frank, Elle sighed loudly. 'There's nothing I can do to stop this, is there?'

Silence filled the room. A long, heavy silence that told Elle everything she needed to know.

Chapter Sixty-Nine

'Are you alright? You've been quiet for a couple of days now,' Ricky asked as Danica applied her make-up.

'I'm okay.' She smiled sweetly. 'Just have a bit of a headache. Think the wedding planning has become a bit overwhelming considering I only had a few weeks to bring it all together.'

'We could cancel our rehearsal today, if you wanted?' Ricky offered, noticing the tension in his fiancée's shoulders. 'I mean, how can you really rehearse a wedding that's happening the next day?'

Danica blinked and then hesitated, as if she was going to agree with him. Then she shook her head. 'No. I think the rehearsal will be good for me. Means I know where everyone is going to be on the day. And I can practise walking down the aisle without decking it in my heels in front of all your business associates and friends.'

Ricky laughed. 'Fair enough. Well, we need to leave in five minutes. I'll wait for you in the car.'

As he walked down the stairs, a memory popped into his head. One that he didn't want to see, but it was there regardless. Elle, walking down the stairs of the house on the day he married her at the registry office. She'd been wearing a plain white dress that he'd picked for her.

Closing his eyes against the images, Ricky got to the bottom of the stairs and tried to push Elle out of his head. Why was she there, after all this time? Was it because he was getting married again?

'Right,' he heard Danica's voice. He turned to see her coming down the stairs and Elle's face was there, staring back at him. 'I'm ready.'

He opened the door and moved out to the car, unable to get himself together.

'What's wrong?' Danica asked.

'Nothing. Let's just go,' Ricky replied bluntly. His harsh reply silenced Danica for the journey.

Taking the glass of champagne from the silver tray balancing on the tips of a waiter's fingers, Ricky handed it to Danica and then took one for himself.

'So,' she asked excitedly. 'What do you think of the venue?'

Nodding as he took in the surroundings and the décor, Ricky smiled. 'It's great.'

Rolling her eyes, Danica took a sip from the glass and said, 'It's very elegant, yet extravagant. Thought it would match us as a couple.'

Narrowing his eyes, he pulled Danica in at the waist and whispered in her ear, 'It looks expensive. You did stick to the budget, didn't you?'

He felt her flinch and then she pulled away a little. 'Well, I went over a teeny, little bit. But you're marrying someone more than half your age who you can't keep up with in the bedroom, so I thought you wouldn't mind.'

A bubble of laughter burst out of him just as Teigan stepped into the room.

'What's so funny?' Teigan asked, as she approached them with a glass in her hand. Darren was by her side and smiling like the goon he always had been. She could do so much better than that guy, he thought.

'Nothing,' Ricky replied and then Danica took Teigan by the crook of her elbow and led her away, chatting about walking down the aisle and hoping the dresses fit properly. He turned to Darren awkwardly and said, 'How has Teigan been?'

Darren took a breath and then looked down at the floor before meeting Ricky's eye. 'Honestly? Not great.'

Ricky raised a brow. 'Why not?'

'Well, you know she's been talking a lot about her mum. And you gave her those photos. So, her head's a bit all over the place.'

Staring at Darren through narrowing eyes, Ricky felt a wave of frustration wash over him.

'I know she told you that someone messaged her that sounded as if it was her mum,' Darren continued, as though he was trying to fill the awkward silence. 'Well, now she's wondering if her mum really *is* trying to get in touch with her. Like, maybe she's feeling guilty for leaving all those years ago and wants to make up for it.'

Ricky sipped on the champagne, which quite frankly tasted like piss, and tried to ease his growing anger. Getting angry wasn't the way to go about things now. He'd learned his lesson on that a long time ago.

'Oh, it definitely *won't* be Elle,' he said, very matter of fact.

'How can you be so sure?' Darren asked, his expression one of puzzlement.

'Probably because I killed her,' Ricky replied. He kept his gaze on Darren, whose eyes began to widen to the point where Ricky wondered if they'd pop right out of their sockets.

A long bout of silence followed before Ricky laughed loudly in Darren's face, slapped him on the back and took a large gulp of champagne.

Darren's expression softened, and the corners of his mouth threatened to raise into a smile, but he never quite got there.

'Fuck's *sake*, Darren. I'm kidding,' Ricky said, but he made sure that his tone was laced with warning. 'Elle isn't going to randomly message Teigan after all this time. She fucking abandoned our daughter when she was a baby, just weeks old. Tell you what though, I could've killed her for that very act. I mean, what kind of mother does that, eh?'

He gave Darren another slap on the back before walking in Danica and Teigan's direction. But just as he did, Darren spoke.

'So, if it wasn't Elle, who messaged to say "sorry for leaving you", then who was it? Because if you ask me, that's weird.'

Ricky spun around, gave Darren an icy stare and said, 'I didn't ask you though, did I? Because really, Darren, why would I? I gave Teigan those photos to ease her thoughts and stop her imagination running wild on the whole shit-show that was her mother. And honestly, I don't know why I'm even discussing this with you because it's none of your business. Elle was part of our life for a short time, a very, *very* long time ago. So long that Teigan genuinely wouldn't know Elle if she fell over her in the street. So, keep it buttoned, eh? I don't want you upsetting my daughter by keeping these conversations going, alright?'

The look on Darren's face was one of shock, like he couldn't comprehend what was just said. Not that it was surprising, Ricky didn't think the boy had two brain cells to rub together. How he'd managed to woo Teigan was a mystery.

'*Capiche?*'

Darren nodded, then turned his eye from Ricky with an awkward look of fear that filled Ricky with a feeling of euphoria.

'Good lad,' Ricky said, moving towards Teigan and Danica.

'Okay,' Danica said, her excitement clearly still as high as it was when they'd first arrived. 'So, this is where we'll *actually* get married.'

He smiled and nodded along as Danica manoeuvred him around the aisle setup. But his mind was far away from the wedding. Very, very far away.

Chapter Seventy

'This champagne tastes like shit,' Teigan said as Darren came walking towards her, his own glass barely touched by the looks of it.

Darren didn't respond, just stood next to her as Danica pulled Ricky around the room, showing him where the ceremony would be, where they'd sign the register, where they'd have their first dance. But something about Darren's mood felt off.

'I take it you thought so too, since you've not touched yours?' Teigan pressed, attempting to see if he was even listening to her. When he didn't respond, something inside her stomach curled.

'What's wrong?' she asked, lowering her tone.

Darren's grave expression didn't match his response. 'Nothing,' he said, before taking a sip and wincing at the taste.

'You were talking to my dad before you came over here. Did you two have words or something?'

Darren pulled his lips into a thin line and kept his gaze set on the bride and groom. That unsettled her even more. Darren was the most relaxed man she'd ever met, always jovial. But something was wrong.

'Nope,' he said, sucking air in through his teeth.

'Oh shit, you said something to him about the pictures, didn't you? Fucking hell, Darren,' she hissed.

Darren glanced down at her and shook his head. 'He asked if you were okay, and I said that you weren't. He asked why and I told him your head was all over the place with thoughts about your mum and the fact that someone messaged you sounding as if they could be her. He got really arsey with me. Told me that Elle was none of my business and that I should keep my mouth shut so I don't upset you.'

Teigan frowned. 'Cheeky git. He shouldn't have spoken to you like that.'

'That's not the worst bit,' Darren continued. When he pulled his eyes away from her dad to look at her, she saw something in his face that worried her. Scared her, in fact.

'What is it?' Teigan whispered, turning her back on the room so she could only see him.

'He said he was kidding, but when I questioned who else could have sent you those messages, he said it definitely couldn't have been your mum because...' His voice trailed off and he licked his lips before taking a long gulp of champagne.

'Fuck's sake, Darren. Spit it out.' Teigan laughed nervously.

'He said it couldn't have been her because she's dead and that he killed her. Then he laughed and said he was joking.'

Teigan's stomach rolled and her entire body felt like it had been given an electric shock.

'He said *what*?'

Nodding sharply, Darren took a huge breath. 'I know, I can't believe I'm even repeating it. The look in his eyes, Teigan. It was fucking weird.'

Teigan jumped as the speakers started to play the music for the first dance rehearsal. She didn't turn to watch, instead kept her eyes on Darren.

'He *actually* said those words? Those exact words? You didn't mishear him?'

Darren's unsettled expression turned to one of empathy. 'I'm sorry, Teegs. But that's not something you joke about. Not in this situation. It might be different if they'd been married for years, and had one of those relationships where you make shit jokes about getting less for murder. But your mum hasn't been around for your entire life. It was...'

'Bang out of order,' she finished for him.

Their eyes met, and Teigan felt sick.

Eric Clapton stopped singing about his wife looking *wonderful tonight* and Teigan walked towards Ricky.

'I need a word,' she said sternly.

Ricky looked down at her and she felt Darren place his hand on her back.

'You look like you've seen a ghost,' he laughed.

'Why did you joke about killing my mum?' she spat the words out and saw his eyes flicker towards Darren.

'Fuck,' he said quietly, looking up at the ceiling. 'It was tasteless. As soon as the words were out of my mouth, I immediately knew it. If I was a comedian I'd be cancelled by now.'

She stood deathly still, unsure how to react. Her own silence deafened her and the answer to the one question she wanted to ask was on the very edge of her lips, but asking it could change everything. Why did her mum have bruises in those pictures?

'You don't really think he was being serious, do you, Teigan?' Danica scoffed. Then she touched Ricky on the arm, laughed and said, 'Oh, should I be worried? Will you kill me off next?'

The fury Teigan felt in her veins, in her bones, scared her. Her eyes shifted to Danica and then back to her dad.

'*Is* my mum dead?' The words left her mouth so quickly she barely heard them herself.

The atmosphere changed in that very moment. Everyone fell silent and Teigan's urge to cry was almost crippling.

'I mean, she could be. She left you twenty-seven years ago, Teegs. So, I truly don't know,' he replied. His tone carried less humour now.

Teigan felt Darren's hand slip into her own and he gently pulled her back. 'Come on,' he whispered. 'Let's find somewhere to cool off for a bit.'

Ricky shot him a glance and said, 'This is your fault. I told you I was joking but you went and blew this up to be something it's not.'

Teigan pulled her hand from Darren's gentle grip and, in what felt like an out-of-body experience, she watched herself slap her dad in the face so hard that pain shot up her arm and into her shoulder.

Danica gasped so loudly alongside the echo of the slap that Teigan barely noticed the sheer rage on her dad's face.

'No! You've made this into something big. Not Darren. Who the *fuck* makes a joke like that? And here of all places.' Teigan threw her arms up, gesturing to the wedding venue. 'When you're getting ready to marry this *bint* on my mum's birthday. Did you kill her on her birthday too? Because that's what you said, isn't it? That you killed her.'

Ricky's cheek glowed a deep crimson and he glared at her. She noticed how his fists curled into a ball and for a moment she wondered if he was going to hit her back.

He raised a hand and ran it across his cheek, glancing at it as though he was expecting to see blood, then said through gritted teeth, 'It was a tasteless joke. I know that now. I said I was sorry.'

'Actually, you didn't. You fucking laughed it off,' Teigan said, trying with every fibre of her being not to scream at him and slap him again. She didn't give a shit who was watching, or how utterly disrespected he would have felt. Right now, Teigan was close to telling him she never wanted to see him again.

Danica stood in front of Ricky and stared silently at Teigan. Her expression was strange. She didn't look angry that she'd just been called a bint, nor did she look annoyed that she'd just witnessed her fiancé being assaulted. It was something else. Was it empathy? Concern?

'Not here,' she mouthed silently, and Teigan frowned. Then, Danica took a breath, turned and stroked Ricky's cheek. 'I think we all need to cool off a little. Then we can come back together and talk this through.'

'This is between me and my daughter,' Ricky growled, pulling away from Danica's touch. 'You do not ever raise your hand to me, especially not on a night like this. Do you hear me, Teigan?'

'I can't do this,' Teigan said, a wave of emotion washing over her suddenly before turning and running towards the exit. Darren followed her, her hand enveloped in his.

Once outside, Teigan sucked in as much air as she could and let out a sob. She was in Darren's arms just before her legs gave way.

–

'I think I overreacted,' Teigan said, staring up at the ceiling in the living room.

'I don't think so,' Darren replied. 'I think you were well within your rights to question him. The way he said it, Teegs, it made my blood run cold. It was like he was hiding in plain sight or something.'

She couldn't stop the words from running around in her head. But it didn't make sense. Not one bit. The woman who'd sent that message; it *had* to be Elle. *Had* to be.

'I need to know for sure if this Sarah Parks person is my mum. Because if she is, then I'll know for certain that my dad really was just making a sick, quite frankly sadistic, joke and I can try to move on from it,' Teigan said.

Darren was quiet as she pulled out her phone and sent a message. She hit send, and stared at her phone screen, hoping that she would get a message back that would keep her life as it was. Any other response could collapse her entire world.

Chapter Seventy-One

What. The. Fuck?

That was the first thought that came to mind as Elle read over the message.

> Are you Elle Fyfe? If you're my mother, I need to see your face, just once. I need to know my dad didn't kill you.

She placed the phone down next to her on the sofa with trembling hands and closed her eyes.

Why was Teigan asking this? Why would she think that Ricky had killed her? The only people who knew about that was Ricky himself, and he wasn't very well going to tell her that. Chris was probably dead since he hadn't been seen in decades. And now, Frank and Danica.

Had Danica told her? Had Frank?

There was only one way to find out.

She picked up the phone, the message thread still open, and hit the telephone icon next to Teigan's name, trembling uncontrollably as she heard the first ring.

Chapter Seventy-Two

Thrusting the phone at Darren, Teigan said, 'Answer that, I can't.'

He took the phone from her and answered. 'Hello?'

Teigan watched him through wide eyes as he listened, and then his eyes met hers.

'She's here,' he said.

'Put it on loudspeaker,' Teigan whispered and Darren did as requested. Then, taking a deep breath, she opened her mouth to speak but the woman on the other end spoke first.

'I'm here,' she said. 'It's me. Your mum.'

Tears pooled instantly and her throat ached with emotion.

'Elle?' Teigan said, her voice cracking.

'Yeah, it's me.'

Teigan glanced at Darren, whose mouth was agape. He nodded at her, as if gesturing for her to speak.

'I'm not dead,' Elle continued, filling the silence. Her voice was low as if she was trying not to cry herself.

'Okay,' Teigan replied, unsure of what else to say. 'Where are you?'

There was a short silence and for a moment, Teigan thought the call had been disconnected. She looked down at the screen and saw the line was still open.

'Mum?' the word left her mouth before she could stop it. It felt strange. She'd never called anyone that name before. 'Are you there?'

'Yes, love. I'm here.'

Teigan's heart was thumping in her chest. 'I want to see you.'

'Oh, Teigan. I would love to see you. But I'm not sure it's a good idea for us to meet just yet.'

Darren took her hand in his and gave it a squeeze.

'It's not because I don't want to see you. Believe me, I want nothing more. I just don't think it's safe for you.'

'I don't care. You have the answers to my questions. I've already asked my dad. He doesn't want to discuss you. Now I'm beginning to wonder what the hell he's been hiding from me all these years.'

The pictures of Elle flashed into her mind then. The bruises. Then what he'd said to Darren. There was something more to this.

'You owe me one meeting, at least.'

The sound of blood rushing in Teigan's ears almost drowned out the sound of Elle's voice. She turned up the volume on the phone and listened.

'Yes, alright,' Elle sighed. 'But you can't tell him. You cannot tell your dad that you're meeting with me. Promise me, Teigan. For your own safety as well as mine.'

The urgency laced with fear already had Teigan nodding. 'I won't say a word. We can meet in public, if that sets your mind at ease?'

They made arrangements and when the call ended, Teigan let out twenty-seven years' worth of tears.

Chapter Seventy-Three

Elle sat in Frank's car around the corner from the coffee shop and felt her legs weaken, but there was no way she was going to walk away from Teigan now. This had gone on for too long. She needed to know the truth. All of it.

'You'll be just fine,' Frank said, giving her hand a squeeze. She looked across at him as he sat in the driver's seat and smiled.

'You think so?' she replied.

'You've been through far worse, Elle. I know you can do this. She's opened up a door for you. All you have to do is tell her the truth. Whether she believes it or not is up to her. The fact she has mentioned she needs to know her dad didn't try to kill you, shows that an element of trust in him has gone. This is your chance to put things right on your end.'

Nodding and trying not to allow her emotions to bubble up to the surface, Elle slipped her hand out from Frank's grip and took a steadying breath.

'I'll be here the entire time, keeping an eye on you. If I see Ricky, his feet won't touch the fucking ground,' Frank said in a poisonous tone.

'Your hit man won't be too happy with that,' she laughed, although it wasn't funny. She still hoped that she could talk Frank and Danica out of that whole idea.

Frank smiled, nodded and said, 'On you go. I'll be here until you're done.'

Stepping out of the car and walking the short distance around the corner, Elle went inside. She took a seat near the window so she could keep an eye out for Teigan arriving. It wasn't long before Elle could see her daughter walking towards her. Elle got to her feet and watched as Teigan pushed the door open. She wasn't alone. She had a man with her. Their eyes met and Elle couldn't help the smile creeping onto her face at the sight of her daughter in the flesh. Not like the last time, when Elle had been too scared to go in and had left Teigan waiting for her.

'Teigan?' Elle said as she walked towards her.

'Mum?' Teigan replied, and the sound of that word coming from her mouth made Elle want to cry. 'This is my fiancé, Darren.'

The man, Darren, held his hand out. 'Nice to meet you,' he said. Elle smiled, shook his hand and then gestured for them to sit down.

Elle stared at her daughter and took a sudden, deep breath. 'And you.'

All three of them sat silently. The moment was surreal. As the years had gone on, spending decades without her daughter, seeing Teigan again was something Elle could never have imagined. And now, the moment was here.

'Right, I'll get the drinks in, you two get acquainted,' Darren said, before taking a note of their order and heading up to the counter.

Elle couldn't believe the risk she was taking, meeting Teigan in public on Ricky's patch, but it was worth it to look into the eyes of her daughter and put everything straight, especially given that she'd asked Elle to confirm Ricky hadn't killed her.

Teigan was sitting on the cushioned bench opposite Elle. Surrounded by wooden panels, Elle felt like they were sat on the lower deck of an old boat. The sensation in her stomach matched that feeling. They sat silently, just looking at one another. Elle studied Teigan's face and it seemed Teigan was studying Elle's. Taking in every detail about her daughter, looking for herself in her features. All she kept thinking to herself was how amazing it felt that the moment was real and not a dream, like it had been for so long.

Darren appeared at the table and placed the drinks down in front of them. 'Shall I leave you both to it?'

Teigan shook her head and glanced at Elle. 'Would you mind if Darren stayed?'

'Not at all.' Elle smiled, wringing her hands together. She stared down at the coffee in front of her and wished it was something stronger.

Darren slid in beside Teigan and awkwardly sipped from his coffee cup.

'So...' Teigan said, clutching her own mug and staring down at the table.

'This must be strange for you,' Elle said.

'Hard is the word I'd use,' Teigan replied.

Elle nodded and raised the coffee mug to her mouth. 'Your message last night, it was very specific. What made you think that your dad killed me?'

Teigan glanced at Darren; he put his cup on the table and straightened his back. 'Because he said that he did.'

Elle frowned. 'He said what?'

Elle listened as Darren explained what Ricky had said to him, and she couldn't stop her jaw from dropping. The utter audacity of Ricky to make a joke about something so severe, and something he believed to be true, really did cast him in the worst light.

'So basically,' Teigan said, clearing her throat. 'I would like your version of events. If he didn't kill you, and was just making a horrible, tasteless joke, then why did you leave?'

It was Elle's turn to clear her throat, the answer to the question sticking to her tongue. 'It wasn't without difficulty.'

'Really?' Teigan asked incredulously.

'You weren't supposed to be left behind. You were supposed to be brought to me just a few days after I left,' Elle said, struggling with the memories in her mind. 'But it didn't turn out that way, and I couldn't come back to Glasgow to get you.'

A deep line furrowed on Teigan's brow. 'Why not?'

Elle sighed a long breath. This wasn't going to be easy. The girl had already been dealt a bad hand and now Elle was about to say just a few sentences that would change her life forever, and not necessarily for the better.

'Well, when Ricky joked with you,' she glanced at Darren, 'that I couldn't have been the one to message you because he killed me, there is some truth to that.'

Darren stared at her with a raised brow, and Teigan clutched her coffee mug, her knuckles white from the grip.

'What do you mean?'

Elle closed her eyes and transported herself back to that night in the kitchen. Telling Ricky she was going to leave. Him saying that he had orchestrated her incarceration if she did. Then the blow to the head. Waking up in the back of Chris's car.

'He hit me,' Elle said.

'Hit you?' Darren asked, as though he hadn't heard her correctly.

Elle nodded. 'He hit me so hard, I was out like a light.'

'What happened? What was his reason for attacking you?' Teigan asked as she leaned on the table, as though trying to get closer to hear better.

'We were arguing.'

'About what?' Teigan asked.

Elle puffed out her cheeks and fixed her eyes on her daughter. 'Are you sure you want the truth, Teigan. Because once I tell you everything, and I mean everything, there is no going back. I can't *take* it back. Not any of it. It's going to change your life as you know it, Teigan. And it's going to change the life you thought you had.'

Teigan glanced at Darren and then back at Elle. 'When you put it like that, how can I say I don't want to know.'

Elle nodded. 'It's a lot. But please, before I tell you the truth, I want you to know that none of what happened had anything to do with you. None of it is your fault, none of it was because I didn't love you. Because I did.'

Teigan closed her eyes and raised a hand. 'Just tell me, Elle. Just tell me what happened on the night you left.'

Clasping her hands together, Elle nodded and began with the day she gave birth. The music that was playing on the radio when Teigan was born. And then she told her everything. Every single detail, from the accusations of Jordan Burns being Teigan's real dad, to Ricky killing him and framing Elle in case she left. How Ricky attacked her with the beer bottle, and how he made Chris get rid of her body. The only detail she left out was Danica's true identity. She had considered telling her what was going to happen, and why Danica was marrying Ricky. But that would mean implicating Teigan and Elle didn't want that for her. She'd been through enough.

When she'd finished, the tears that streamed down Teigan's face broke Elle's heart.

'I'm so sorry, Teigan. I should never have left you. I should never have allowed any of this to go on for as long as it has. I should have come for you and taken you away.'

Teigan sucked air in through her nostrils and dabbed at her eyes with a napkin. 'He gave me an envelope of pictures of you before he said you

left. You're covered in bruises in all of them. Did he do that to you?'
Then she scoffed. 'Of course he did, why am I even asking?'

'Yeah, he did,' Elle replied sadly. 'There's one more thing,' she said.

Darren wrapped an arm around Teigan's shoulder and pulled her close.

'There is no easy way to say this. Ricky isn't your real dad.'

Teigan was silent, staring at Elle through bloodshot eyes.

'If Ricky isn't Teigan's dad, then who the fuck is?' Darren asked, sounding a little irritated.

'Chris Fyfe. He's your biological father. And I believe he's dead, Teigan. Because I did not leave with him. He was supposed to bring you to me, and he never did. I never heard from him again. I never told Ricky to spare him. But he knew you weren't his. I think somehow, Ricky found out the truth and killed him out of rage.'

Teigan got to her feet and clambered over Darren before running to the bathroom at the back of the coffee shop.

—

She barely made it into the toilet cubicle before she threw up her half-drunk coffee.

Head swimming with everything she'd just been told, Teigan placed her hands on the plastic toilet seat and tried to steady herself.

Why? Why? Why? Why did this have to happen? Why was this her life? She'd been lied to for her entire twenty-seven years. Had been brought up by a man who wasn't even her dad, a man who *knew* he wasn't her dad.

Wiping aggressively at her mouth with some toilet paper, Teigan flushed the toilet and pulled herself up to sit on it, resting her elbows on her knees and clasping her hands together. Slowing her breathing, Teigan tried to process what she'd just heard.

At the sound of the door opening and footsteps approaching, Teigan sat up straight.

'Teegs,' Darren's voice came. 'Are you okay?'

Getting to her feet, she opened the door and stared at him. 'No. Not at all.'

'What are you going to do?'

Shrugging, she stood there, feeling somewhat numb. 'I don't know.'

'Are you going to talk to him?'
She didn't have the answers. She didn't want any of it to be true.

Chapter Seventy-Four

Teigan hadn't slept all night. The unravelling of the truth had rendered her the most awake she'd ever been. She was wired. But she knew that the wedding day had to go ahead. She had to be there. There was no other way.

'I'm sorry I slapped you,' Teigan said as Ricky opened the door. He stood to the side and let her through to the hallway. Darren followed her. He was silent.

'I'm sorry for saying what I did about your mum. It was out of order,' he replied.

Teigan merely nodded, gave a smile and said, 'I just wanted to clear the air before the wedding.'

Ricky looked solemn, but he gave a nod and said, 'I appreciate that. I'd hate to be fighting with my daughter on the day I'm getting married.'

Daughter. The word that meant nothing now.

'Yeah,' she said. 'Same. So, shall we start to get ready?'

Ricky sighed loudly and then smiled. 'I'll get us a drink.'

She turned to Darren, who's eyes were ablaze with concern.

'Are you sure about this, Teigan?'

She bit her lip so hard she almost drew blood. 'I don't have any other choice. He can't get away with all this, Darren. He needs to pay for what he's done.'

Chapter Seventy-Five

Today was the day. Her wedding day. There had been nothing she wanted – and dreaded – more.

As she was helped out of the wedding car by the driver, Danica looked up at the venue and saw the beautiful glass sign. *Welcome to the wedding of Danica and Ricky.* Soon to be a widow, she thought to herself. Frank had made his arrangements; Danica had made the payment. She wondered why Frank didn't just kill Ricky himself? Either way, all she wanted was for Ricky to no longer exist. All she had to do now was marry him and wait.

'Ready?' Teigan asked. Danica glanced down at the door and smiled.

'I didn't even see you come out,' Danica replied. 'Are you alright? You look ill.'

'I'm fine, just don't feel too great.'

'What about your dad?'

Teigan slowly nodded. 'He's… fine. Sank a couple of whiskies when we got here to settle the nerves I think.'

Danica nodded. 'Does he look as nervous as you do?'

Teigan didn't reply; she simply turned her back and the red dress flowed behind her as she walked back into the venue.

Frowning, Danica followed her inside and they both stopped at the door. A photographer was taking pictures of the flowers, the dresses, the shoes, the hairstyles. All Danica could think about was how much she was supposed to smile but how much she wanted to scream.

The wedding co-ordinator moved towards her with a beaming smile and said, 'Right, Danica. It's time. So, the plan is that when the music starts, Teigan will walk down the aisle first and take her place next to Ricky. Then you will follow on my command. Walk slowly, smile and you will be just fine. If you feel overwhelmed, just try to block out the other guests and focus on your groom.'

Danica closed her eyes, pushing out thoughts of a last-minute getaway. Then, she opened them, smiled and nodded. 'Got it.'

The woman ushered Danica back from the door and moved Teigan into position. She turned and gave Danica a look that was laced with sadness. Something was off.

'Teigan, is there something you're not telling me?' Danica asked. But before anything else could be said, the double doors opened, and Teigan turned to face the room.

The music started and Teigan stepped into the aisle. Danica frowned. This wasn't the right song. She hadn't picked this.

'Wait,' Danica said as Marti Pellow began singing 'Love Is All Around'. But it was too late. Teigan was already out of sight, and the wedding co-ordinator was guiding Danica towards the open doors.

Chapter Seventy-Six

'If you could all rise for the wedding party,' the humanist celebrant said and Ricky listened to the rustling of people getting to their feet. He was nervous, but the whisky had helped take the edge off. Even though Teigan had apologised for her behaviour at the wedding rehearsal the previous evening, she had been quiet that morning as they'd got ready. They'd barely spoken about anything outside of getting him into his kilt properly and making sure he didn't forget to put on the button hole. That was good enough for him and Ricky had decided to put the incident behind them. It was his wedding day after all. He didn't want any issues on the biggest day of his life.

The last few months had been a complete nightmare. The factory fire. Aidan fleeing. Production and distribution coming to a halt. Then the deal going wrong with Frank. It was all such a headache. But now, he was about to put all that behind him. Start afresh with Danica. From now on, life was going to be good.

The double doors at the top of the room opened and as they did, he saw Teigan standing there in her beautiful red dress and he'd never felt prouder. It was as if the last twenty-four hours hadn't taken place once he'd set eyes on her.

But then the music started and his blood ran cold. No, no, no. Had he gone back in fucking time? This was the song that was playing when Elle gave birth to the daughter that wasn't his. This wasn't right.

Teigan reached him and he took her hand. 'You look beautiful.'

She gave a slight smile but seemed tense in his grip. He stared at her through narrowed eyes but before he could overthink it, Danica made her entrance.

Holding his daughter's hand as he watched his fiancée walk down the aisle was a moment he never thought he'd experience. And yet, it was tainted by the bloody song choice. It was a reminder of a bittersweet moment for him. There must have been a mistake made by the events team. Danica wouldn't have known this was the song that was playing in the hospital when Teigan was born. The daughter that wasn't his daughter at all. The moment that should have been the best in his life was tainted with Elle's lies, and he'd had to go along with it because his heart had already fallen in love with being a dad to the tiny baby being born. But he couldn't think about that now. All he wanted to do was get married and forget about that fucking witch from his past.

Danica looked stunning in white. She'd look even more stunning if she smiled. Ricky frowned. Fucking hell, she didn't exactly look like a woman ecstatic to be getting married. And then he saw it. Her bottom lip trembled and not in a way that screamed happiness.

Something was wrong.

Chapter Seventy-Seven

Danica looked at the back of Teigan's head as she stood next to Ricky at the end of the aisle. The sight of him made her feel sick. She was about to marry a monster. A murderer. The man who made her an orphan. But she'd come this far. She couldn't back out now as she walked down the aisle – on her own. No dad to give her away. No mum standing there, crying with pride. Both of them were dead because of the man Danica was about to marry.

The faces of all Ricky's business associates, past and present, staring at her. Not one single family member from either of them other than Teigan. That said it all.

Then her eyes met his. His face darkened. He knew something was wrong. Her bottom lip quivered, not in emotion but in sheer terror. Could she do this? *Really* do this?

Before she could answer her own question, she was there, standing next to Ricky Fyfe and about to become Mrs Danica Fyfe.

There weren't many words for how she felt. *Fuck* was enough.

She reached Ricky and smiled up at him, noticing how irritated he looked.

'What's wrong?' he asked.

'Nothing. I'm nervous,' she whispered as the song faded out and the celebrant asked everyone to be seated.

Both she and Ricky turned to face the celebrant and Danica handed her bouquet to Teigan. She reached out for it with a trembling hand and Danica frowned. Teigan looked like she was about to keel over.

'We're gathered here today,' the celebrant began, as gentle piano versions of love songs played in the background.

Danica wasn't listening, not to the bits that weren't important at least. She'd get right the 'I do' and 'I will' but all she could think about was her parents.

The wedding guests laughed and 'awed' in moments that made Danica force a smile. And then, the celebrant said, laughing, 'This is the legal bit that everyone gets nervous about. If anyone here has any reason why Danica and Ricky should not unite in marriage, please speak up now.'

There was a silence and everyone laughed nervously. Danica didn't know whether to be relieved or disappointed.

Then, she heard the scraping of a chair and the rustling of a dress before a gentle gasp from the congregation.

'I have one.'

It was Teigan. Danica had to refrain from rolling her eyes.

'Teigan, not now,' Ricky said through gritted teeth. 'I know you have had a hard time accepting my relationship with Danica, but really, now?'

'It's not about her,' Teigan said flatly. 'It's nothing to do with Danica.'

Danica leaned across and grabbed Teigan's arm before she hissed, 'What the fuck are you doing?'

Ricky simply placed his hand on Danica's wrist and pushed it down, forcing her to let go.

'It's not about you,' Teigan said to Danica, her voice softer now. 'I swear.'

Ricky threw his arms up in the air and raised his voice. 'Then what the hell is it about?'

The celebrant cleared her throat and stepped closer, closing the book in her hand. 'Should we take this somewhere more private?'

Ricky gritted his teeth and stormed up the aisle towards the open doors. Once out in the empty foyer he heard the celebrant declare that the bridal party 'just needed a moment to gather themselves', before she followed him out, with Danica and Teigan close behind.

The celebrant closed the doors and excused herself.

'Right, what the fuck is going on, Teigan? Are you really going to be a brat about this? I know you've had issues with Danica since we got together. I get that she is the same age as you and you think she's after my money, but to do this to me on my wedding day? Seriously? You've been quiet all morning. You couldn't have said anything before now?'

He stared at her, waiting for an answer. Then, the sound of a door opening just a few feet away made him turn. His jaw dropped.

'Hello Ricky. Long time no see,' Elle said.

Time seemed to stop as Danica absorbed the looks on the faces around her. Ricky. Teigan. Elle. What was she doing here?

He was about to open his mouth to speak when Frank Cranwell appeared at Elle's back, and Darren came through from the ceremony room and took his place beside Teigan. Danica began to panic.

'Aren't you going to wish me a happy birthday?' Elle pressed, although she didn't sound smug. There was fear in her voice and Danica felt that same fear in her own stomach.

Ricky didn't utter a word, as if he'd been rendered speechless.

'When she tried to leave you and take me with her, did you threaten to kill her?' Teigan asked, placing herself in front of him.

He swallowed hard, as if trying to gather his thoughts. 'What has she told you?'

'Everything. She's told me everything. You know, when you gave me those pictures, did you realise she was covered in bruises in every single one? Looked *terrified* in every single one?'

There was a fire in her eyes as she pummelled him with questions. Danica felt like she couldn't breathe.

'When you made that comment to Darren at the wedding rehearsal, it just didn't sit right with me. You joked about killing her after I saw those pictures and something inside me just went off like a bomb. So, I contacted her and when we met, she told me the truth.'

Ricky stared at her with wide eyes and then spun to face Danica. 'Did *you* know about any of this?'

Danica shook her head, but he glared at her with fury and suspicion.

'You're lying,' he said quietly.

'I'm not,' she replied, and then, glancing down at her dress, Danica took a long breath and raised her eyes. 'Can we please get on with the ceremony? We have guests waiting.'

His face contorted and she watched as he flexed his fingers not so subtly. The look on his face was strange, the colour drained a little, but his eyes remained dark as his tongue slithered across his teeth.

'She knew I was still alive,' Elle interjected.

Ricky's eyes were wide as they darted between Elle and Danica.

'What the fuck are you on about?' he growled at Elle.

'You do remember why you tried to kill me, don't you?' Elle's voice floated across the room. 'Do you remember why you cracked that bottle over my head and made your brother dispose of my body?'

Danica watched as Ricky's chest movements became rapid. He was panicking as all eyes laid upon him. He was backed into a corner and there was no way out. All she could think about was how they weren't married yet.

'Well, someone cracked you over the head, that's for sure. But if you haven't noticed, Elle, you're not dead. And if Chris was supposed to have got rid of you, he didn't do a very good job of it, did he?' Ricky said, although Danica could almost see the cogs turning in his head. He was trying to work out exactly how she was standing in front of him.

'Go on, tell Teigan why you tried to kill me,' Elle said, her voice even.

'You're a fucking loony,' Ricky replied. Then he turned to Teigan. 'This is insane, Teegs. You have to believe that. This is who I was married too. She did us a favour by leaving.'

It was in that moment, as Danica watched her fiancé trying to lie his way out of what he'd done, that she decided this was it. The moment she'd wanted for so long. She didn't have to marry him for his life to crumble beneath him. She could execute her plan right now, in front of everyone.

'I'll say it then, since you don't have the balls,' Danica replied, lifting her gown and taking a step forward. 'The reason you tried to kill Elle was because you found out that Teigan isn't yours.'

Ricky shot Teigan a concerned look, then set his blazing eyes on Danica. 'That's utter bullshit. Of course she's mine. And why the hell would you, of all people, say something like that, Danica?'

With tears in her eyes, Teigan stared through Ricky in silence. Danica felt sorry for her. She knew what was coming for her. Years of heartache and a million questions.

'But you were *utterly* convinced that Jordan Burns was her father. Which would make Teigan my half-sister.' Danica looked across at Teigan and softened her gaze. 'We're not, by the way.'

'I know,' Teigan whispered, her voice cracking.

'But we could have grown up to be best friends,' Danica continued. Then she turned, jabbed a finger in Ricky's direction and said, 'If *he* hadn't murdered my dad, Jordan Burns.'

She waited for the penny to drop and as it did, Ricky's eyes widened and his mouth fell open.

'No. *Fucking*. Way.' Ricky said.

'Oh, wait. It gets better,' Frank said, leaning back against the wall with a grin on his face.

Teigan moved closer to Ricky and stared up at him, tears rolling down her face as she cried quietly. 'You knew I wasn't yours all along and you forced my mum out of my life.'

Ricky stared down at Teigan and then glanced around the room. 'I have a hall full of wedding guests out there. This is fucking ludicrous.'

'No it's fucking not!' Teigan screamed and everyone, besides Frank, jumped. 'You let me live my *entire* life thinking that she'd fucked off with your brother when really you thought she was dead because you'd killed her. You let me go through some of the hardest years of my life without a mum to turn to.'

He was speechless – Danica could see that even if she had her eyes shut. But this wasn't how she'd wanted things to go. It all seemed too calm.

'Don't you want to know who her *real* dad is?' Danica asked, raising a brow as he threw her a dirty look.

'Are you fucking enjoying this or something?' Teigan spat. 'I suppose I can't say I'm surprised; this was always your plan, wasn't it? I knew there was something off about you.'

'Oi.' Danica knitted her brows together. 'I'm on the same fucking side as you here.'

'Enough,' Elle said, stepping between them. But just as she did, Ricky raised his arm to her. Danica stared in fear as Teigan launched herself in front of Elle.

Ricky didn't retract quickly enough, and the back of his hand connected with Teigan's face. He hit her so hard that she flew back and dropped to the ground.

Darren leapt on Ricky then, throwing wild punches, and the sound of knuckles beating against flesh and bone made Danica feel sick.

'Darren, lad, stop,' Frank said, getting between them. He spun around to face Ricky. The sound of a click made everyone stop. 'The game's up, Ricky. You're done.'

'Fuck off, Frank. This has nothing to do with you,' Ricky hissed, feeling the gun pressing into the side of his head. 'We've a fucking room full of guests. You think you're going to get away with shooting me in here?'

Frank sniggered and the air chilled as Elle's whispering voice sounded louder with each word she spoke.

'Teigan? Teigan, open your eyes. Teigan, sweetheart, can you look at me?'

Danica glanced down at the floor and noticed the blood smeared on the corner of the console table against the wall. Her eyes traced down the leg of the table to the floor, where a pool of blood saturated the carpet beneath Teigan's head.

She turned and glared at Ricky, while Frank still held the gun to his head. He was staring down at Teigan, his eyes wide and dazed.

Elle was sobbing now as she lifted Teigan's head and cradled her in her arms. 'Wake up, sweetheart. Wake up. Please, Teigan.'

Darren dropped to his knees next to Teigan, his hands hovering over her as Elle rocked back and forward. 'Teigan?' But his voice wasn't strong. It was broken.

Darren and Elle met each other's eyes and a sob escaped Danica's throat, which she hadn't expected. She, too, fell to the floor next to Elle and all three of them stared down at Teigan. Her eyes were closed. Her hair was soaked with blood.

Elle began to scream inaudible words between sobs. Darren bent his head low, his forehead gently pressed against Teigan's torso, he too was sobbing.

'Teigan,' Ricky said, as though he thought the whole thing was a joke. 'Teigan, open your eyes for fuck's sake.'

Danica stood up sharply and shoved him hard in the shoulders. 'This was you. This was *all* you. You killed your own fucking daughter.'

He blinked, shook his head. 'She's not...' He cleared his throat. 'She's not...' Ricky couldn't get his words out.

'What? She's not what? Your daughter?' Frank said. 'Does that make it alright?'

Danica turned her attention to Frank and her words came in a choked sob. 'Are you going to put an end to this?'

The sound of Elle's screams rang in her ears as she stared expectantly at Frank who kept his eye firmly on Ricky.

'I didn't do this. This wasn't my fault,' Ricky said quietly, still looking down at Teigan as blood poured from her head. Elle was screaming and Darren now visibly trembling.

'You fucking hit her,' Danica screamed. 'But this is who you are. A killer. You can't help it. It's in your blood.'

He reached up, grabbed at Danica's dress as he pulled her close and screamed in her face. A painful cry that scared her to the very depths of her soul.

'Why, Danica? Why did you do this?'

'You stole the life I should have had,' she sneered, their noses almost touching. 'You murdered my dad, took him from me before I could even remember who he was. Six years later, my mum died because it was all too much for her. You made me a fucking orphan. I wanted to see you lose *everything* the way I did. I orchestrated our relationship, and you know what, Ricky? You fucking fell for every single word I fed you because you were a pathetic, middle-aged man, who was easily flattered.'

Ricky stared into her eyes, his own glistening with fire and tears.

'Do you know who her dad was?' Danica whispered in his ear. 'It was your brother,' Danica said. 'Your own brother, Chris, was Teigan's dad.'

'You're a fucking bitch,' Ricky growled. Then he lowered his voice even more. 'Of course I fucking knew. Those were his last words to me right before I fucking killed him.'

She gritted her teeth, knowing that this man would go to any length to keep his secrets safe. He was as good as a serial killer. And she was face to face with him. 'I know why he was never found, my dad. You cremated him, didn't you? Probably cremated your brother too. Did you kill him in a fit of rage?'

'I didn't kill your precious daddy,' Ricky leaned in and whispered. 'It was my brother who pulled the trigger.'

Danica glared at him. She didn't know if he was lying or not. Not that it mattered now. Whether Ricky shot the gun or not, it was all his fault.

They stared at each other in silence for a brief moment before Danica decided to hit him where it would really hurt. 'Did your brother tell you with *pride* that Teigan was *his* daughter and not yours?'

He let go of her, pushed her away and as he did, he sunk his hand into the jacket of his hired kilt attire and pulled out his own gun. Frank threw himself at Ricky, knocking the gun from his hand. It fell to the floor and Danica grabbed for it. She stood tall, pointed it at Ricky and a sound escaped him that resembled an angry dog.

'You've not got the fucking…'

She pulled the trigger and the power behind the force of the bullet leaving the barrel threw her back. She landed on her back, staring up at the ceiling. Elle and Darren's sobs were ringing in her ears as Danica sat up.

'He's dead,' Frank said. His tone was calm.

'Good,' Danica said. She glanced down at the gun beside her on the floor. It must've fallen from her grip when she shot Ricky. Picking it up, she got to her feet and turned to look at Elle.

'I'm so sorry about Teigan,' Danica said. 'But I had to do this, Elle. You must understand that I had to take him down. I'm sorry Teigan was caught in the crossfire. I've done what I had to do.'

Elle's sobs were the last thing that Danica heard before she turned the gun on herself.

Chapter Seventy-Eight

One month later

Teigan stood next to her mum as Danica's coffin was lowered into the same grave as her own mother. An entire family gone because of Ricky Fyfe.

'Are you okay?' Teigan asked as Elle wiped away her tears.

'Not really,' Elle replied. 'I don't even know what to say right now.'

Teigan nodded. She felt the same. There were no words for what had happened at the wedding, nor what had happened in the last twenty-seven years to lead them to this point.

'I'm just so grateful that we're not burying you too,' Elle said.

'Ah, I'm made of tough stuff,' Teigan replied.

'We thought you were dead,' Darren said, as the minister invited them to throw earth into the grave.

They each took a handful and silently let the earth fall through their fingers. Teigan didn't allow herself to think about that day. The wedding. The man she thought was her dad had hit her so hard that she'd cracked her head open and fallen unconscious. She'd missed everything that happened between Danica and Ricky.

According to Darren and Elle, Danica had shot Ricky dead then turned the gun on herself.

'Well, I'm not dead,' Teigan replied. 'And as much as I hated Danica, I never wished her dead. She must have been truly traumatised to have gone to the lengths that she did.'

Elle nodded. 'All because of him.'

Him. Ricky Fyfe. Her dad. Teigan had never known him as anything but Dad. That was why she was struggling with her grief.

'How can you miss and hate someone all at once?' Teigan asked.

Elle sighed. 'You must be going through hell right now.'

Teigan had lost and gained a parent all at once. 'Yeah, it's not easy,' she replied. 'But I'm not sure what's worse; me finding out my entire life was a lie, or you having to pretend you were dead for twenty-seven years to keep yourself safe?'

Elle pulled her lips into a thin line and sighed. 'I've always known who I am, even if I don't like her much. I want you to know, if I could go back and change what happened, I would. If I could fill in the gaps from the time we spent apart, I would.'

'I know. The upside to that is we've got twenty-seven years of catching up to do.'

Elle smiled as they walked along the path towards the cemetery gates. 'We do.'

Glasgow Gazette (MAY 2024)

www.glasgowgazette.co.uk

Well-known Glasgow businessman Ricky Fyfe laid to rest.

Today, a Glasgow businessman was laid to rest at Glasgow's crematorium. There was a high level of police presence at the burial. Several criminal figures were in attendance, excluding Essex businessman Frank Cranwell, who is due to appear in court on a number of organised-crime charges.

Ricky's daughter, Teigan Fyfe, was not in attendance.

Ricky's fiancée, Danica Campbell's funeral was held earlier the same day in a private ceremony.

It is reported that during a search of Crawford Funeral Care, items belonging to that of missing man Jordan Burns were recovered, including a wedding ring. Tim Crawford, owner of the funeral home, has been arrested on suspicion of involvement in organised crime. He has been released on bail.

Back in 1998, Ricky Fyfe walked free from court following a not proven verdict in the case of the disappearance of Jordan Burns. Police Scotland have announced that due to new evidence, the Jordan Burns case has been reopened pending a new investigation.

Chapter Seventy-Nine

Elle stared down at the article on the *Glasgow Gazette* app on her phone and a sadness washed over her. Those who died because of Ricky deserved justice. Giving the new evidence to the police had been like a weight lifting from her shoulders. She finally felt free after all the years of hiding.

Elle slid the phone back into her pocket and turned to Teigan.

'Thank you for bringing me to my meeting today,' Elle said as she placed a hand on the door. 'You really didn't have to.'

'It's the least I can do,' Teigan replied.

Elle sighed. 'I've always wanted to get sober, Teigan. I've just never had the courage. AA meetings can be overwhelming. The counselling is better for me.'

'You owe it to yourself to get well, to be sober and to live your life happily. You never got that chance. I suppose I never did either.'

Elle closed her eyes. 'I'd like to think we can come out the other end of this.'

'I think we can,' Teigan replied. 'Would you like me to come in with you?'

'I've been using alcohol to cope for a lot longer than I'd care to admit. I've been to some dark places. I've tried to stop so many times. I just can't do it on my own. Do you really want to hear all that?'

Teigan nodded. 'Yeah, I do.'

They got out of the car and Teigan held out her hand. 'After everything you've been through, you deserve to have someone there to support you. I would like to help in whatever way I can because we missed out on so much.'

Tears pricked her eyes and Elle took a deep breath. 'I don't want to lose you again. I have my priorities back. It's hard. But I'll get there.'

'You won't lose me.' Teigan smiled, pulling Elle in and hugging her tightly. 'It's you and me now. Like it should have been from the start. Nothing will get between us ever again.'

Elle pulled away and looked at her daughter through the tears. 'You have no idea how much I've missed you.'

'I've missed you too, Mum.'

Together, they walked hand in hand to Elle's first counselling session. Elle turned to Teigan and said, 'Thanks for sticking with me.'

A letter from Alex

Hello everyone. So, book twelve. *The Second Wife*. And my first hard-back book. This is so exciting for me.

I have thoroughly enjoyed writing this story and creating these characters. Although, I think this one was hard to write. I wanted to get the trauma, the conflicts and the drama just right and I put a lot of planning into this one. If you're a regular reader of my work, or you follow me on social media, you'll know that I'm a pantser. So, to plan a book was quite difficult. But I still enjoyed the process.

The wedding scene… if you've read it, then I hope you felt the tension I did when I was creating that scene. If you've come straight to this letter first, then I hope you enjoy it.

I want to thank you. If you're a returning reader, welcome back. If you're a newbie, hi, and thank you for picking up this book. If you haven't already, you can follow me on all the socials. Or you can contact me via email, at alexkaneauthor@gmail.com.

I want to take a moment to mention my gran, Margaret, who sadly passed in August 24. And my dad, Alex, who passed away during the structural edit process of this one and just nine weeks after my gran, his mother. My family was hit hard this year, and I kind of threw myself at this book when my dad left us, and I know he wouldn't have wanted it any other way. I will miss him forever. He was a quiet man, and quietly proud of what I've achieved. I'll miss the pats on the back and the 'Well done, hen,' when a new book comes out.

So, in the way he'd sign off on a phone call, or a text, Cheers.

Acknowledgements

To all at Hera Books: Keshini, Dan and Jennie. You all work so hard and I'm eternally grateful. As always, special thanks to Keshini for being so flexible under such difficult circumstances.

Thank you to all the editors who have worked on the book with me through all the processes.

Thank you to my agent, Jo, and all at Bell Lomax Moreton. Thank you to my husband for being my rock as always and to family and friends for all your support over the last wee while. You know.

Special thanks to my dad, Alex. Just for being my dad. This is the last book he was around to hear me bang on about, and he never got to hold that first hardback in his hands. He'd have been so happy to see that.

Thank you to everyone. 2024 was rough for me, personally. Here's to a smoother 2025.